THE MARKED AND THE BROKEN

THE LOST SENTINEL BOOK 3

IVY ASHER

Copyright © 2019 Ivy Asher

All rights reserved. This book or parts thereof may not be reproduced in any form, stored in any retrieval system, or transmitted in any form by any means—electronic, mechanical, photocopy, recording, or otherwise—without prior written permission of the author, except in cases of a reviewer quoting brief passages in a review.

This is a work of fiction. Names, characters, places, and incidents either are the products of the author's imagination or are used fictitiously. Any resemblance to actual persons, living or dead, businesses, companies, events, or locales is entirely coincidental.

Edited by Polished Perfection

Cover Design by Story Wrappers

For the Badasses.

PROLOGUE

I rush to insert myself in front of Knox and Bastien as they're pulled back, and when I see the looks on their faces, it scares the shit out of me. I've never seen them so angry.

"You fucking shit bag liar, I'm going to kill you!" Knox bellows over me as he struggles to get out of Aydin and Sabin's hold.

It's a good fucking thing he has no idea how to use his Sentinel strength yet, or we would be in some serious trouble. I spin around, focusing on a swollen-eyed, bloody-lipped Enoch.

"What the fuck is happening here?"

"I swear on everything, Vinna, I have no idea how it happened. They just showed up."

I'm confused as fuck about what Enoch is rambling about. *They just showed up? Who showed up?* Enoch swipes at the blood on his lip, and everything inside of me plummets as I take in the black marks on his finger.

No. Fucking. Way.

I spring for him, my bloodlust demanding action. The betrayal I feel screaming through every part of me. I catch him with a right hook to the cheek, and he falls back, avoiding my follow up hit. I'm raging inside, but I say nothing as I pounce on him, ready to smash his face in. Kallan steps in front of me, and I move to go around him until I spot what's on his hands, too. My seething gaze find his, and the only thing that keeps me from killing him is the terror in his eyes.

"How the fuck do you have runes, too?!" I demand.

Arms wrap around me from behind, yanking me away from the people who need to give me answers right fucking now. My Chosen may not know what they're capable of yet, but I sure as fuck do, and I push magic into all of my limbs and fight to get away from whoever is holding me back. I writhe and flail and do everything short of hitting and stabbing my captor, but fuck they're strong. Lips press close to my ear.

"I can do this all day, Witch. But if you'd stop rubbing yourself all over me for just a second, I'd like to point something out."

Torrez's arms tighten around me, and the shock of his deep voice makes me pause. He pushes a hand out in front of my face and nuzzles my neck.

"They're not the same."

His words and silky tone reverberate through me, and it takes me a minute to figure out what he means. I stare at the dark-tan tone of his skin and the runes that mark his entire ring finger. The second rune, the one marking him as mine, sits black and prominent. Its presence pushes the other runes representing my Chosen down, the last rune resting on his knuckle. He moves his palm slightly, and I look through his large splayed fingers, honing in on Enoch's hand.

He's right... The runes on Enoch's finger aren't mine. So, whose the fuck are they?

1

My eyes run over the runes on Enoch's middle finger. I trace the details over and over again as if staring at them long enough will somehow unlock their secrets.

What the fuck is going on?

Torrez nips at the lobe of my ear, and the feel of it pulls me from the hundreds of questions surging inside of me. As much as my vagina is stoked that I'm wrapped up in Torrez's arms, I'm going to need her to keep her greedy hopes to herself so I can focus on the war that's trying to break out in the living room. I push to break Torrez's strong hold so he'll let me go, but his arms around me don't budge. All I really manage to do is grind my ass against his obvious erection, and unfortunately, the generous bulge in his pants is not what I need to be paying attention to right now. I feel Torrez's growl of approval rumble against my back, but I refuse to acknowledge what that sound is currently doing to my body.

Not the time or the place, Vinna.

I'm *very* aware that I need to address the fact that I have a new addition to my Chosen, but I don't fucking know where to start with that either. I have no answers, a shit ton of unknowns, and more questions than I can keep track of anymore. Maybe I should just focus on Torrez's hard-on; at least that's something I can handle...I think. I smack my libido across the face and get my head in the game. I need to deal with Enoch and his coven first, and then I can sort out my new Chosen.

The word *Chosen* echoes through my jumbled thoughts, and worry tumbles through me like a drunken gymnast. I see my mark, Torrez's mark, and my other Chosen marks on Torrez's ring finger, but his rune is nowhere to be seen on me. I turn to my guys and search for any new runes on their hands, but there's nothing. My stomach sinks. I press down the unease that crawls through me.

Did I mess up somehow and not complete the connection with Torrez?

"Vinna?" My name on Enoch's lips is both a question and a demand for answers, but I still don't have shit that I can say that explains any of this. I don't know how he has runes. Or why they're different or what the fuck any of it means for me or for them.

I scrub at my face, my hands cold against my fevered skin. I'm fucking tired and reeling from everything that's going on. I turn back to Enoch and the unfamiliar runes that he and his coven now have.

"I don't know," I admit unhelpfully, and the room explodes into a giant argument again.

Aggression and fury whip out from the guys, snapping toward Enoch, Kallan, Nash and Becket. It hits its mark, but Enoch and the others just ball it up and throw it back. Aydin and Evrin are trying—and failing—to get control of either side. Their calm words volley back and forth, only to fall to the ground and get trampled by rage and insults.

"Could they be from another Sentinel?" I toss out, but

I'm pretty sure no one besides Torrez—who is currently *way* too interested in sniffing my shoulder right now—can hear anything I'm saying over the yelling that's going on.

It's possible somehow that their runes aren't mine. I have suspected in the past that my *Last Sentinel* status might not be completely accurate, but there's no way of knowing if these mystery runes are proof that I'm right. Well, not unless the hypothetical mystery Sentinel knocks on the door right now with a "*my bad, let me just take these guys off your hands.*" That would be pretty definitive.

Or, my exhausted mind counters, maybe the mystery Sentinel *can't* come knocking on the door because they're not nearby? I don't know the ins and outs of selecting Chosen, but if I can mark Torrez or others simply because I want to, can other Sentinels send their magic out into the world and have it mark the best match for them?

Can selecting Chosen work like some kind of primitive Sentinel Bachelorette? Only instead of a rose and a sham engagement, the Chosen get a lifetime commitment—whether they want it or not—and a fuck ton of new magic and abilities? Did I somehow magically facilitate a match? An image of me holding a clipboard, wearing a Chris Harrison-esque suit, while women sing "Matchmaker, Matchmaker" to me, flashes through my mind. I shake away the weird ass picture and focus on the here and now.

I need caffeine or, better yet, sleep. I'm on the verge of going bat shit crazy.

Knox and Bastien are spitting out threats and struggling against Aydin, Evrin, and the rest of my Chosen, trying to get to Enoch and his coven. I take a deep breath and let the tension and fight leak out of my body. I relax in Torrez's arms, and on my second deep exhale, he lets me go, clearly trusting that I've now gained control of myself. I step into Bastien and Knox's line of sight, and Knox looks at me as I square off with him and the rest of my Chosen. Bastien doesn't seem to see anything other than Enoch, Nash, Kallan, and Becket, who he very clearly wants to rip apart. Indignation and hurt flash through Knox's eyes, and I want to punch my magic hard for making Knox feel that way.

I activate the runes that allow all of us to speak mentally, and shout, *"Stop!"* The guys cringe at the invasive volume of my command, but it has the desired effect, and they turn their attention to me. Frustration and anger radiate off each of them in thick waves, and before I can even open my mouth to say anything, Knox cuts me off.

"Don't you fucking say it, Vinna." He shakes his head vehemently. "I won't accept them."

His gray eyes have gone from stormy to solid stone, and I'm shocked by the venom in Knox's tone and the finality in his statement. I can't really blame him for feeling that way. I *did* just try to rip Enoch apart too. I probably would have if Torrez hadn't pointed out my shitty attention to detail. "You don't want me to tell you that they're not Chosen? Is that what you *don't* want me to say?"

Knox opens his mouth to argue but stops as my words register.

"Wait, what?" Bastien and Valen ask at the same time.

"The runes are on the wrong finger. They're not Chosen runes. They're not even my runes from what I can tell."

All of the guys drop their gazes to my hands, and then their eyes flit behind me to take in the marks on Enoch and the others.

"These aren't mate marks?" Enoch asks, confused, and Knox takes a step forward to go after him again. Sabin stops his advance, but Knox stares daggers at Enoch, and his whole body vibrates with anger.

I turn to face Enoch and step in front of Knox slightly. He'll have to go through me to get to them, but hopefully it won't come to that. Enoch's eye is swelling, and from the look of Kallan's bruising cheek and the cut on his eyebrow, he clearly took a couple of hits to the face, too. I suddenly feel like shit about the fuck-ton of *attack first, ask questions later* that's floating around the room.

"No," I answer.

I step toward Enoch and his coven, and I don't miss when Kallan tenses at my approach. I look at him and hope that my lapse in judgement hasn't fucked up our friendship beyond repair. I'm not sure what the standard time for friendship-recovery is when one person tries to kill the other, but I don't push him. I stop a few feet away and hold up my hand, my fingers splayed and my palm facing me.

"My Chosen runes all run down the lines of my *ring* finger. Your runes are on your *middle* fingers," I point out.

Kallan and Enoch aren't the only ones to look at their hands, and I try not to feel even more unsettled when I see that Becket and Nash are marked too. They all stare at their runes, and the room grows quiet for a couple of seconds.

"Wait, but these ones look the same," Enoch announces, and he twists his hand so that I can see the side of his middle finger and the small symbols etched there.

I step closer to him and grab his hand, moving it so I can see the symbols that run up one side of his finger and down the other side. Sure enough, I have the exact same runes there. *Well, that sure as fuck complicates things.* I guess there goes my *I didn't do this* theory. I look at the others' hands to double-check. The runes on each side of their middle fingers match the runes I have in the same place, symbol for symbol.

For whatever reason, I'm just missing the symbols that they have running up the center of their fingers. The first rune, the one that starts just below Enoch's nail, is a black circle. Inside the circle, it looks as if an eight-pointed star has been cut out. Below that mystery rune are four others that I've never seen before. My thoughts drift to Torrez and the same issue we seem to be having of missing runes.

Is this the same problem? Did I somehow mark them but do it wrong?

I'm not sure why I keep asking myself any questions; it's not like my magic has a habit of explaining anything that it does. I reach for Kallan's hand, and a surge of relief washes through me when he doesn't flinch away or stop me. I run my eyes over the same marks on his hand. Oddly, he has an extra mark on the side of his palm. It's a twin to the mark that showed up on me when I magicjacked Elder Kowka the day the elders took me away from Lachlan. I hold up his hand and then look at his coven.

"Anyone else get this rune?" I ask, pointing at it, and they all double-check before answering no.

"We all have more marks on us, but each of them is different," Enoch informs me, and a new wave of frustrated confusion flashes through me, but I mask it. What the fuck does he mean that they have more marks, but they're all different?

Enoch turns around and pulls up the back of his shirt. He has two lines of runes that run down his spine. Runes that I would know anywhere because they're for my long sword and my staff. Nash pulls up the side of his shirt, revealing the runes for my short swords on each side of his ribs. I look at Becket expectantly, and that's when reality slams into me like a fucking freight train.

Shit. Does he know what just went down with his dad?

I give him a small smile, and he offers me a tentative one back. I can't help the tinge of suspicion that seeps into my thoughts as I watch him, waiting for him to show me which of my runes he somehow ended up with. I think back to the day the elders were testing my magic. Becket and his dad seemed close, closer than I thought Enoch and his dad appeared to be. Could Becket have been in on what his dad was up to?

I look over to find Torrez leaning against the wall. When my eyes meet his, he immediately pushes off and strides over.

"Yes, Witch?" he asks me, his voice deliciously growly and momentarily distracting.

I shake away any reaction I have to his tone, and I lean into him, dropping my voice. "Can you do that whole *smell the truth* thing that you do?" He nods, and I sneak a deep comforting pull of his scent before turning back to Becket.

For a quick second, I wonder if he already knows about his dad and what happened tonight. It's been hours since everything went down, plenty of time for someone to fill him in, but looking at him now, I have a sinking feeling that I'm not that lucky. I just don't see him handling the *I killed your dad because he was a massive piece of shit* news this well.

Becket pulls the neck of his shirt to the side to reveal runes on the top of his shoulder. It looks like he now has some of my shields and my bow and arrows. "I have a rune that showed up on my toe too," Becket announces, and I nod absently, as I try to figure out how to say what I need to say to him.

"Becket," I pause. "Um...I had a run in with your dad tonight," I clear my throat unnecessarily. "Has, um, anyone told you anything about that?" I blurt awkwardly and then hold my breath and wait for his response.

I send out a silent plea to the universe, hoping that somehow he already knows what happened and really *is* just taking it all in stride. But that hope shrivels up into a nasty ass raisin as confusion stretches across Becket's face. Yup, looks like I'm about to be the one to tell him that I killed his dad.

Fuck.

"Did you...know anything about what he was planning or what he's been up to?" I ask vaguely, and Torrez steps into me, his body just barely skimming mine. I feel the rest of my Chosen step up behind me in support, and gratitude washes through me.

"What do you mean?" Becket asks, and he looks even more uncomfortable and confused by the wall of Chosen that just formed behind me.

"Did you know your dad was working with a lamia named Adriel?" I ask Becket, and I scour his reaction for any hint of deception or recognition.

Becket slowly starts to shake his head. "No, but what's the issue with that?"

"Adriel was the lamia responsible for at least one group of paladin—that we know of, anyway—going missing. He was also the lamia responsible for our abduction," I explain and gesture toward the rest of Becket's coven.

Understanding dawns on Becket's face, and then confusion takes over again.

"My dad wouldn't have worked with him if he knew that's what this Adriel guy was doing," Becket states. His tone is filled with such certainty and conviction that it squeezes at my heart for what I'm about to tell him.

I don't know what the runes on Becket or his coven mean, but I'm sure, in this moment, that however they connect Becket to me, he's going to want to cut those runes from his skin when he hears the rest of what I have to tell him. There is no part of *I killed your dad tonight* that's going to be okay for him, and I gear up for the shitstorm of a reaction I know is about to come my way. Sabin steps closer to my side and places a hand on the small of my back.

"Elder Albrecht and Elder Balfour hired a group of

shifters to kidnap Vinna. They attacked us tonight," Sabin tells Becket, who immediately bristles at the information.

"Why would my dad do that?" Becket challenges.

"They wanted Vinna to transfer her magic to them."

I suppress a shudder at Sabin's words and watch as Becket grows even more puzzled.

"I thought you had to fuck them in order to give them your magic?" Becket asks, tipping his chin toward my Chosen.

Sabin and I both stay quiet, and the bewilderment Becket's wearing quickly snaps into outrage.

"My dad is an elder. He's not a rapist, and he sure as hell isn't helping some leech kidnap and kill his own people. My dad loves this community! He would never jeopardize it!"

"Elder Cleary heard him confess everything before..." Sabin trails off. Silence fills up the space of what he's not saying, and it presses in on me and makes my heart start to race.

At hearing his dad was also somehow involved, Enoch's head snaps to Sabin.

"Before what?" Becket demands, but I can hear the sliver of hesitancy in his voice. I know that sliver. It screams *don't tell me, don't confirm my worst fear, let me stay ignorant just a little longer*.

Sabin takes a fortifying breath, ready to deliver the news and become the *bringer of pain*. I appreciate him so much for wanting to take that off my shoulders, but no matter how much I want to pass the buck right now, the reality is what I did will shatter Becket's world, and I have to own that. When I watched the life leak out of Elder Albrecht's face, I knew the world would be better off without him. But as I sit here and stare at the fear and anger in Becket's features, I see another side to this, one I hadn't given much thought to. I don't know if Becket will be better off without his dad.

Elder Albrecht was a power-hungry monster, but maybe not to his son. To Becket, he could have just been a good dad who loved his kid.

"Before what?" he insists again.

"Before I killed him," I say, meeting Becket's eyes, and everything else in the room fades away.

Becket and I watch each other for a moment, and it's as if I can see my words wrapping around him, sinking in, and changing who he is right in front of my eyes. Becket's face scrunches up in agony, and the desolation that pulses out of him feels like a vicious punch to the gut. I deserve it, and I stand strong to take it.

He starts to shake his head as if somehow the movement alone can keep it all from being true. He looks so fucking lost, and I hate it. I've been where he is right now, on the receiving end of devastating news. News that's impossible to recover from. I remember looking through a glass window at my little sister laid out on a stainless steel table. There was a stiff white sheet draped over her, black bruises marring her little neck, and an emptiness in her eyes, the room, and my soul. I'll never forget the sound of the police officer's voice as he recounted how she died. I know what it feels like when death robs you of something precious.

The officers showed me a picture of Laiken's murderer. They asked me if I knew him, before they delivered the blow of what he did to her. I can never recall all the details of that man's face. Maybe if they had shown me his picture *after* I had been clued in to what he took from me, it would be seared into my brain. Becket stares at me, and I know there won't be a haze over the memory of his dad's killer. Whenever this moment haunts him in the future, it will always be a clear picture of *me* in his mind.

Tears pool in his brown eyes, and his pain practically

reaches out to hold hands with my own. I take a step toward him.

"Don't you fucking come near me," he warns, and his grief morphs into cold rage. "You stay the fuck away from me, do you hear me?" he yells as he steps back, demanding more distance between us.

Sorrow moves through me like an icy breeze, and I immediately retreat, my back meeting a wall of Chosen.

"Beck," Enoch consoles as he steps toward his friend. I can see the sorry that sits on Enoch's lips, but Becket rounds on him before Enoch can offer it.

"*Your* dad did this! He's the twisted one, not *my* dad!" Becket accuses, and the sympathy on Enoch's face is quickly replaced by indignation.

Nash and Kallan step between their coven mates, both of them offering consolation and trying to keep things from escalating as Becket and Enoch square off against each other. They both go quiet after a minute, and tension seeps from everyone in the room. Enoch pulls his phone from his pocket, and after a couple swipes and clicks of the screen, it starts ringing, the shrill sound slicing through the thick fog of anger that surrounds all of us.

"Hey, son," Elder Cleary answers. "Can I call you back a little later? Things are a bit crazy at the moment."

"Dad, I'm at Vinna's house. She just told us what happened."

"Oh," Elder Cleary responds surprised. "Is your coven there with you?" he asks.

"Yes," Enoch responds.

"Okay, I have her address. I'm going to send some paladin there. They'll escort Becket here; we need to ask him some questions and make sure he isn't somehow tangled up in this mess his dad created," Elder Cleary tells Enoch, his tone distracted.

"My dad wouldn't have done any of this! I don't care what you're trying to pin on him, I know him!" Becket shouts, and Elder Cleary swears.

"Am I on speakerphone, Enoch?" Elder Cleary demands. "You should know better than that," he chastises his son, and Enoch hurries to take his dad off speaker and quickly steps away from us to continue the rest of the conversation more privately.

Becket runs his hands through his golden brown hair, and every inch of him is pulsing with frustration and disbelief. Kallan and Nash watch him, and they look unsure of what to do or what to say. I wish someone would just hug him, but he doesn't want to hear from me, so I continue to just shut the fuck up.

"I'm out of here," Becket announces suddenly. "I need to get to the bottom of this, and there's no way in hell I'm going to trust *his* dad to do it." Becket points at Enoch and then gives the rest of us a scathing look before he turns toward the door.

Enoch shoves his phone back into his pocket and steps into Becket's path, and Becket's features become murderous.

"Oh it's like that, Cleary? One word from *daddy*, and you're ready to betray your own coven...again?" Becket's chest heaves as he pulls in angry breaths. "The fact that anyone thinks they can pin this on my dad, after the shit you and your dad pull on the regular, is a fucking joke. *Move.*"

Becket takes another step toward Enoch, and a red mist forms just above Enoch's upturned palm. I'm shocked that Enoch's just threatened Becket, and I don't miss the hurt that courses through Becket's brown eyes and is gone in a flash. A bright yellow barrier pops into place around Becket, but the violet hues that appear to slither in and out of his barrier give all of us pause. My eyes snap from Becket's dual colored magic to Enoch's. I spot purple flashes sparking in and out of the red mist still hovering over Enoch's hand.

I've trained with this coven a lot, so I know that Enoch's Offensive magic is fire engine red, his Elemental magic is an olive green, and Becket's Defensive magic is always bright, lemon yellow. I watch the violet flickers that invade both of their magic, and I could fucking scream in frustration. There is obviously a connection now, but what the fuck is it? And is it to Sentinel magic or to me? Am I wrong?

Are they Chosen? And if they are, then whose?

2

"Just let him go, E," Nash tells his coven mate. "He has a right to find out for himself what happened. He said he didn't know, and we should trust him. He's coven."

At Nash's words, I remember my lie detector with paws. I turn to Torrez, but I don't even have to ask him before he nods his head once at me. "He didn't know about the connection between his dad and the leech, and he genuinely thinks his dad isn't capable of anything that you and Slytherin over there said."

I cock an eyebrow at Torrez. "Slytherin, really?"

"Yeah, it's not my best work. I'll google wizard nicknames later," he tells me with a straight face, and Ryker gives an amused snort behind me.

I turn my attention back to the standoff between Enoch and Becket. They're just staring at each other, and I can practically see the debate that's going on in Enoch's head. After a moment of pause, the red mist hovering above his palm disappears, and he steps away from the door. Becket doesn't release his hold on the barrier that's surrounding him as he walks past his coven mate without a word. We all stand there watching the door slam shut, none of us really sure what to do or say.

"Do you think my dad was involved?" Enoch asks, his uncertain pewter-blue eyes landing on mine.

"I don't have the built-in lie detector like he does," I say, pointing at Torrez, "but he seemed surprised when he walked in on what was happening, and he helped Sabin and me get out of there." *Which shocked the fuck out of me.* I decide to censor that last part.

"Why'd you break my dad's nose then?" he queries, and I can't tell if he's bothered by that fact or still just trying to put the pieces together. I can just picture Elder Cleary whining about it to his son over the phone.

I shrug. "Anger issues. I get especially ragey when I'm threatened."

"I thought you said he helped you?"

"Yeah, with this he did, but he also threatened me at the dinner from hell," I remind him.

My statement makes me think of Becket's mom and how she came for me between the third and nine-thousandth course. Pretty sure taking out one of her mates isn't going to cause her feelings to thaw for me anytime soon.

Enoch surprises me when he just nods and runs his fingers through his disheveled blond hair. "Fair enough," he tells me and holds up his hand. "So if these aren't mate marks, what are they?"

"No fucking clue," I answer honestly.

"So then they could be mate marks?" Nash counters. He tucks a black curly lock behind his ear, and his dark blue eyes meet mine, his gaze challenging. Someone behind me gives an irritated huff.

"Wishful thinking, asshole, but you'll never be one of us," Knox announces, and everyone in the room bristles.

"Fuck you, Howell. It's not your choice to make," Kallan spits back.

And now we've come full circle, because everyone is back to wanting to fuck each other up.

"*Enough!*" bellows throughout the room, and I turn to find Aydin's giant, pissed off ass stomping to get in the middle of things. "We don't have time for this shit. You all can decide who wins this fight later, but spoilers...it will be Vinna. She can kick all of your asses, probably at the same time."

I smile at Aydin, and he tilts his head at me in acknowledgement.

"We have to go, so this pissing match will need to be rescheduled for a later date," he announces.

"Where are you going?" Enoch asks, taking a step toward me, which earns him a warning growl from Torrez and I'm pretty sure Bastien and Knox, too.

"My dumbass uncle got himself taken by Adriel. We're off to save the day."

I turn to the guys to check that we're ready to load up and head out, when Nash's voice spins me back around.

"Wherever you're going, so are we."

I turn and fix him with a look that oozes *you've got to be kidding me*.

"Yeah, I don't think that's such a good idea," I counter.

"Until we know what the hell is going on with these"—he lifts his shirt reminding me of the runes that now run down his sides,—"it's probably best if we all stick together."

I open my mouth to argue but stop. It's not the worst idea I've ever heard. We're not exactly going to overwhelm Adriel and his nest with our current numbers, and we could use all the help we could get. My gaze wanders around the room in thought, and I catch Evrin's brown eyes.

"They are targets now," he tells me, clearly hopping on a similar train of thought to the one I'm currently riding on.

"They don't belong with us," Bastien argues, and Evrin throws up a hand that clearly states he doesn't want to hear it.

I turn to Bastien. "I may not know exactly why Enoch and the others are marked, but they're marked. You just saw what I saw; they somehow have pieces of my—or maybe someone else's—Sentinel magic. Not as much as you guys, but they'll need to train and learn how to protect themselves all the same."

Bastien looks away from me, his eyes hard and his lips pursed like he's trying to keep from swallowing something he finds disgusting. No one says anything, but it's clear they're fucking pissed.

"We need to leave. If you can grab your passports and pack a bag in twenty minutes, we'll wait, but we can't give you more time than that," Evrin announces, taking control of the decision. Nash and Enoch move for the door almost instantly. Kallan is just a beat behind them, his mouth open like he's going to say something. He seems to decide against it, and he turns around and leaves. Evrin turns to Torrez, his eyebrows raised in question.

"I have a passport and a go bag, but they're in my truck about five miles south of here," Torrez tells him.

"Well, let's go then," Evrin announces and heads for the door.

Torrez turns to me and gives me a wink. "I'll be right back, Witch. Try not to miss me too much while I'm gone."

I snort with amusement and shake my head. He throws a lopsided smile my way and then disappears out the door.

"Okay then," Aydin says to no one in particular and then claps his hands together once. "I'll be throwing the rest of our shit in the cars. We have a couple hours' drive to the airport, and we will not be stopping to piss or for any other reasons."

"Yes, mother," I joke and then laugh when Aydin blows an air kiss at me and then flips me off. Aydin walks out of the living room with a smile, and I turn to deal with the guys. I stop laughing when I meet each of their unamused faces.

"We don't need them," Knox insists, his words and movement agitated.

I let out a deep, tired breath. "We need all the fucking help we can get, and Evrin's right; they're targets now. We all know that Solace isn't exactly safe for Sentinels."

"They're not Sentinels," Bastien counters, and I rub at the back of my neck, frustrated that they're being so stubborn about this.

"I don't know what the fuck they are, but what would it hurt?" I ask. "More magic and skilled fighters in this situation is the opposite of a fucking bad thing. I get that you're pissed, but they have runes. They need to be trained just like you do," I tell them.

"So you would accept them as Chosen if that's what they turn out to be?" Knox asks, his steely gray eyes bouncing between each of mine, and I'm not sure what he's looking for.

"Knox, it doesn't feel like that with them. I don't know how to explain it. You just have to trust me when I tell you that whatever happened, it doesn't feel like it does with you guys."

"That doesn't answer my question," Knox presses, his gaze dropping away from mine.

I glare at him. "I know there's history between all of you guys and their coven. I know that makes all of this harder to deal with, but I'm not trying to collect more mates. I was never trying to collect any in the first place," I tell them exasperated. "Then you five were marked, and *we* happened," I say a little softer, gesturing to all of us. "I thought I was good to go, but then the whole Torrez thing happened. I don't know what you want me to say. I have no control over what my magic does sometimes, and I promise that's equally as frustrating for me as it is for you guys in this case."

"Answer the fucking question, Vinna," Knox grinds out. His tone is pure vitriol, and I'm shocked to hear it coming from Knox and even more stunned that it's directed toward me. I move to get in his face, and Ryker steps between us. "Fuck you, Knox. How the hell am I supposed to answer that? I don't know. They don't feel like Chosen to me, but if somehow they are, I'm—what? Just supposed to turn my back on that? I trust my magic. That's all I can fucking say."

Sabin and Ryker are the only two looking at me and not wearing expressions that make me feel like I just told them they can never eat bacon again. I take a couple deep breaths and try to exhale the indignation boiling inside of me.

"I get that this is hard, but I didn't do any of this on purpose. I mean, I did with Torrez, but that seems all fucked up as it is, so maybe it doesn't count. Anyway, my point is I get that you aren't happy about the situation with Enoch and his coven, but stop acting like I did this on purpose."

"Torrez isn't the problem here, and neither is your magic choosing another mate. The issue is *that* coven," Bastien tells me. At the same time, Ryker asks, "What do you mean the situation with Torrez is fucked up?"

I turn to Ryker. "I mean he has our runes on him, but none of us have his rune. I don't think the connection is there yet, and I can't tell you why."

"Maybe it's because he's a shifter; it's possible your magic works differently with him than it does with casters," Sabin hypothesizes.

I shrug my shoulders. "Maybe, who knows? We'll just

have to wait and see, I guess." I turn to Bastien, his hazel eyes still stony. "Like I said, I understand that you all have an issue with Enoch and his coven, but I'm not going to throw them aside and leave them to get picked off because you guys have bad blood. You can either trust me and the magic that brought us together, or not. That's your choice," I tell him, finality in my tone, and I hate that I can't say for sure which he'll actually choose.

I've been independent and on my own for so long, but I've just started to see what my life could be like if I had more. If I had them. Part of me wants to say, "Fuck it, I am who I am, my magic is what it is, take it or leave it." And the other side of me is terrified that this has pushed them too far, too out of reach, and nothing I can do or say is going to pull them back into me.

"And what about trusting us?" Bastien counters, pulling me from my worried thoughts. "We are telling you that we don't trust them, and yet here you are, going against that and defending them."

"Because my experiences aren't your experiences, Bas. You all grew up together, and you compete against each other, and you just don't like each other. I lived with them; I've trained and fought with them. I don't have the same hang-ups that you do. I don't trust Lachlan or Silva, but I accept that your experiences with them are different than mine. I have never, and will never, ask you to turn your back on them just because I don't like or trust them."

"Yeah, but that's family, that's not the same thing," Knox argues. "And you can say that you trust Enoch and his coven all you want, but you went after them just like we did when you first saw their markings. Doesn't that prove that deep down you don't trust them either?"

I rub my hands over my face and take a minute to collect my thoughts. "The word *family* doesn't mean the same thing to me that it does to you. However if I apply your logic, Knox, then Valen and Bastien are biologically connected to Silva and his coven, so there's an exception for them. But I might be *magically* connected to Enoch, Kallan, Nash and—yay for me—Becket. So wouldn't the same exception apply?"

"Why are you fighting so hard for them, Vinna? What's really going on here?" Knox asks, and I don't like the tinge of suspicion or accusation in his tone.

"I have no idea, Knox. I didn't intentionally mark them, so whatever it is you're accusing me of right now, shut it the fuck down. I haven't done anything to earn the betrayal that's leaking out of your eyes."

Knox runs a hand over his face, and my chest aches. How the hell is this all going so wrong? This is me he's talking to. I take a step toward Knox and reach for his hand, but he crosses his arms, physically shutting me out. I'm so surprised by his denial that I'm not sure what to say. It's like he's taken something fragile and beautiful that I've given him and smashed it on the ground, and now I'm staring at the pieces, desperate to put them back together but with no idea how. I just look at him, shocked and suddenly lost.

"I don't trust them," Knox tells me.

"I don't either," Bastien agrees, and his stance mirrors Knox's.

I step back and remind myself that, as much as I think they should cut me some fucking slack, I need to do the same for them too. A ton of shit has gone down in the last twenty-four hours, so I'll treat them how I want to be treated instead of junk punching them, which is what I want to do. I cross my arms over my chest since apparently it's the go-to move for stubborn assholes.

"Your mistrust is noted," I tell Knox and Bastien coldly. "I would also like it noted that I never know what the fuck my magic is going to do, but it always works out in the best possible way in the end."

No one says anything, and I ignore the ache in my chest when Bastien and then Knox walk out of the living room. I watch their backs as they disappear through the kitchen, and refuse to flinch when the door that leads out to the garage slams loudly behind them. I stare at the wall, not sure what to think or feel. Valen steps in front of me and waits patiently for my eyes to move from the wall to him.

"I'll talk to them," he reassures me. "It's been a long night, it'll blow over."

I nod at Valen's words, not trusting myself to say anything right now. He leans down, his lips skimming mine, and I can taste hesitancy. I hate that it's flavoring his lips, so I reach up and grab the back of his neck and pull his mouth firmly to mine. I fill my kiss with as much reassurance as I can, and Valen drinks it up and asks for more. I kiss him until the ground feels more solid under my feet and he doesn't feel so far away. We pull apart, and he rests his forehead against mine, grounding me in a way I desperately need.

"Can we just try to make the best of this? Do what we can to superhero it up, kill Adriel, save some ungrateful assholes who probably aren't worth it and definitely won't appreciate it?" I ask him as we stand there, breathing each other in.

He reaches up and caresses my cheek with his thumb, and gives me a small smile that doesn't resonate in his eyes. He kisses the tip of my nose and then pulls away from me. My questions trail after him, unanswered, and I watch hollowly as he disappears through the kitchen door.

"You alright?" Sabin asks me as he pulls on a strand of hair that's fallen out of my messy bun.

Everything inside of me screams *no* at his question, but I

know if I speak that truth, I'm going to fucking fall apart. I shrug instead and swallow down just how not alright I currently am. I get the sinking feeling it's going to become my go-to response with all of the shit that's going down, but I plaster a fake ass smile on my face and try not to cry when Sabin pulls me into a hug and kisses the top of my head.

"Let's get going before Aydin blows a gasket."

I nod and nuzzle into the comfort of Sabin's chest and the strong arms that he's wrapped around me. "Why are we doing this again?" I tease, trying to lighten the mood.

"Because it's the right thing to do."

I nod at the simple answer and ignore all the thoughts that tell me, if the roles were reversed, I'd probably be the property of Adriel for the rest of my days. I'm pretty sure Lachlan would continue on with his life and just pretend I never existed, rather than stick his neck out for me. Fuck. Sometimes being the bigger person sucks unwashed, hairy balls. Laughter vibrates in Sabin's chest, and I realize I must have said that last part out loud.

I look around the house that I've barely had enough time to call my own, and take a deep breath. Belarus, ready or not, here we fucking come.

3

I stare out the window of the plane into star kissed darkness. An occasional patch of clouds appears below the plane, and I like thinking we're surfing the night sky as we make our way from Solace to Belarus. In my earbuds, Nothing More's "Go to War" comes to an end, and Chevelle's "The Red" picks up. I tap my fingers to the beat on the cream leather of the oversized seat I'm leaning back in. I lose myself in the music, using it to work out the tension that's settled in my body since we climbed up the stairs onto this plane.

Enoch's face appears above me, and before I can so much as pluck an earbud out to hear what he has to say, his head snaps to the left. His face turns from hesitant and questioning to pissed in less than a second. I sit up a little to track who Enoch is now snarling at, and feel zero surprise at finding Bastien on the other side of whatever the fuck is going down. I debate for a second if I even want to know. I'm about two seconds away from just leaning back in the chair and letting them figure it the fuck out when Enoch goes from pissed to enraged and rounds on Bastien.

I rip the music from my ears and unbuckle myself, ready to intervene.

"We would never fucking do that!" Enoch shouts at Bastien, his hands slashing away from each other, his body language punctuating his point. His eyes are filled with fire.

"Bullshit! You fucking knew what your dad and the other elders were going to do. You were all too eager to welcome her into your home and start working with her so you could see what her magic could do. Do you think we're that fucking stupid? You think we didn't know that you and your daddy were trying to set her up with you?" Bastien accuses.

"Oh please, Fierro. Despite your delusional conspiracy theory, there wasn't some big evil plan to steal Vinna away. No one even knew your coven wanted to claim her until the fucking trial," Nash interjects.

"Somebody needed to do something," Enoch adds. "It's not like you guys were stopping her uncle from treating her like shit."

"You better shut the fuck up right now, Cleary," Knox shouts and rears up out of his seat on the plane. The rest of the guys on both sides of the argument stand up too, and the tension goes from thick and uncomfortable to suffocating. "You don't get to pretend that you're some fucking hero, not when we all know what you let happen to Ryker!"

Enoch throws his hands up in exasperation. "I was a fucking kid! I didn't know. I thought everyone's home life was like mine. I had no fucking clue what he was going through with his dad!"

"You were his best friend, and it was fucking obvious. I told my parents that something was wrong, and they went to the council that same day. *Your* dad tried to convince the elders not to look into it at all," Knox bellows, his face red and furious.

I'm shocked by Knox's revelation, and my gaze immediately jumps to Ryker. He's standing next to Knox with his hand on Knox's chest to keep him from advancing any further. His face is hard and unreadable, but his sky-blue eyes flash from torn to sad.

"Here we go again with the *your fucking dad* bullshit. My parents were friends with his parents; they didn't think Trevor was hurting Ryker. Either way though, that has nothing to do with me. You think my dad listens to shit I say when it comes to his decisions as an elder? I'm fucking sick and tired of you assholes blaming me and Becket every time the elders do something you don't like."

"Something we don't like? They set our parents up to get captured and then refused to lead a proper search for them," Valen counters. He brushes the loose strands of his dark brown hair out of his face and takes an angry step toward Enoch.

"Once again that's not our fault, and once again no one knew about Elder Albrecht and what he was doing before tonight!" Kallan throws out, his tone fed up and tired.

"Please. It's clear the apple doesn't fall far from the fucking tree, Cleary. You took Vinna from our protection, where she was attacked, spied on like a fucking criminal, and threatened by your piece of shit dad that he would fucking expose her if she didn't choose your coven over ours. You knew what she was the whole time, and you *lied* to her about it. And then when she wouldn't give you what you wanted, you took it without her permission," Bastien spits out venomously, and both sides press even closer together.

I scramble out of my seat and magic myself between them before the fists that both sides have clenched in anger start getting thrown. I pop up in front of Bastien out of nowhere. Which might not have been the smartest move on my part, because he slams into the back of me in an effort to get to Enoch, and I fly forward and slam into Nash hard. Pain slices through my stomach as I grab onto Nash's shoulders to keep from falling. His dark blue eyes widen in shock, and fear lights up his entire face. I gasp, stunned and hurting, and we both look down at the same time to see the blue tinged blade in his grip. The blade that's just been pushed through my stomach.

"Oh fuck!" he shouts out in panic. I reach down and wrap my hand around his, the one still holding the handle of the short sword he just stabbed me with, and I sag against him slightly. A whimper escapes me, and it's like somehow the small innocuous noise penetrates the yelling, and the plane goes quiet for a breath.

"What the fuck did you do?" roars around me, and I can picture how Knox looks as the words leave his anguished and rage-filled face.

"No one fucking touch her," Ryker commands, and I can feel the way his order lashes out at everyone, making them freeze.

"I'm sorry," Nash laments. "I don't know how it happened. Bastien came at us, and the next thing I know, I'm holding this, and then she was slamming into me," Nash blurts, hurried and in shock.

"It's okay," I offer Nash with a pained croak. "My magic always does weird shit when I felt threatened," I try to explain, but it's hard to get the air out to speak and then back in to breathe. If it didn't fucking hurt so bad, I might actually find this funny. I've been trying to get the guys to fight with me and deliver blows like this since they got their runes, but they refuse. At least Nash will be better equipped the next time he goes to stab someone on purpose. He'll know what it feels like and rebound better in a fight because of it.

My eyes bounce from Nash's dark blue terrified gaze to

Ryker's bright blue assessing stare as he moves over to us. His hand presses next to where the blue blade sticks out of my back, and I can feel his Healing magic as it moves through me.

"Don't let go of the magic or the blade yet," Ryker instructs Nash. "Let me deal with what internal damage I can first."

Nash nods, and I feel his grip tighten on the handle under mine. "I'm so sorry, Vinna. I swear by the stars, I didn't mean to hurt you," Nash tells me over and over again as Ryker continues to magically put me back together. I can't talk very well, so I just pat Nash's shoulder reassuringly and hope it communicates that I'm not mad.

"Okay, that should keep her from bleeding faster than we can fix once the sword is out. Alright, Nash, when you're ready, you can let go of the handle, and the sword should disappear. Then I'm going to need you to heal what you can from the front while I work on the back."

Nash seems to gain some composure with Ryker's instructions, and he looks at me for a second and then back at Ryker. He gives him a nod, and then he lets go of the handle and immediately presses his palms into my stomach.

Motherfucker! I shout internally, and externally I cry out hoarsely.

"Shit, the sword's still in her!" Nash announces, and he presses harder against the wound in my stomach.

"You have to let go of the magic," Valen tells Nash calmly, his cadence patient and his tone reassuring. He joins Ryker, Nash and me, and puts his hand on Nash's shoulder. "Take a deep breath and feel for the tether of new magic in your chest. It will feel familiar but different than the Healing magic you've always had." Nash does exactly what Valen's hypnotic voice instructs him to do, and in a blink, the short sword disappears from where it was sitting in my abdomen.

Healing magic slams into me, and Ryker and Nash sandwich me between them as they both work to fix my giant stab wound. I can feel subtle differences in their magic as it swells through me, knitting organs, muscle, and tissue together. The pain recedes, and I fill my lungs with a deep grateful breath. I give Valen a reassuring smile, and as soon as I do, he yanks Nash away from me.

"Fuck, Fierro, I wasn't finished," Nash objects, but the rest of my Chosen close ranks and move Nash, Enoch and Kallan farther away from me.

"We'll take care of *our* mate from here. You've done enough," Valen tells him.

I turn to tell him to knock it the fuck off, but Ryker pulls his palm away from my back. He's got an arm behind my knees in a blink, and he swings me up into a bridal carry before I can even find my voice to object. He hurries me away to the back of the plane and sits down, setting me in his lap. Ryker immediately shoves his hand up my shirt and pushes more Healing magic into me to get anything that Nash might have missed.

I grab his chin and turn his attention to my face. "It was an accident, Ryker," I tell him, urging him with my eyes not to look so completely and utterly pissed.

His magic surges into me for a couple seconds more, and then he pulls it back. He leaves his warm hand on my stomach and puts his other palm on the back of my neck. He pulls my head down and presses his forehead to mine. Ryker huffs out a worried breath, and I run my fingers soothingly through his shoulder-length blond hair.

"You could have been hurt so much worse," he tells me, his tone haunted.

"But I wasn't. They'll get control over their magic, and it

will be fine. This was a fluke, not an assassination attempt," I challenge and shoot a look over my shoulder at the rest of my guys who are standing guard to keep everyone else away from me. "Besides, I've never been stabbed before. Now I know what it feels like, and I'll be more prepared to deal with it next time," I reassure them, and Ryker shakes his head at me.

"Of course you would think somehow taking a sword to your gut is a good thing, you weirdo," Ryker chuckles, and he pulls my lips to his. I open for him, but Ryker doesn't deepen the kiss the way I'm encouraging him to. He kisses me slowly, savoring my lips, and I can taste the worry and the relief in it.

"You know you like my weird," I tease as I pull away.

"It's a good thing you're hot, Squeaks, with some of the shit you put us through," he teases, and I chuckle and play with the ends of his hair.

"I didn't know you and Enoch used to be friends," I tell him, curious about the history that spilled out with this fight.

Ryker gives me a peck and runs his thumb across my cheek. "Yeah, we were close when we were younger," he admits, but then his features shutter, and it's clear that he doesn't want to talk about this anymore. I want to ask him if he thinks Enoch knew about the neglect and what he was going through with his father, but I don't want to press him. He looked conflicted when Knox and Enoch were fighting about it, and I suspect maybe he doesn't really know what to think or how to feel. The tinge of sadness in his eyes makes me ache, and I want him to know it's okay if he tucks this piece of pain away again. He doesn't have to look at it just because I want him to.

"Think we can kick Evrin or Aydin out of one of the beds in the back and go make out?" I ask, my body warming as his fingers graze the skin of my abdomen, his lips mere inches from mine. A spark of relief and then heat fills his gaze, and I can practically see some of the weight and pain lift off of him. A flash of Ryker sucking on my nipple and pinching the other with his fingers, while Knox circled my clit with his tongue, pops into my head. I nuzzle the tip of his nose with mine, and Ryker laughs and then *tsks* reproachfully at me.

"You are recovering from a stab wound," he argues.

"No, I've recovered from a stab wound. There's a difference," I tease.

Ryker's beautiful blue eyes fill with heat, and his full lips turn up into a dazzling smile that takes my breath away. He's so incredibly beautiful both inside and out, and I don't know where I would be without him and the others. I hate that they're mad about this whole situation, and I desperately want to go back to all of us joking and having fun with each other. Maybe we can just run away from all of this drama and foreboding shit. Hole up on an island out in the middle of the ocean, where clothing is optional and our problems can't find us.

"Mmmm, Squeaks, you have no idea how much I'd love to disappear somewhere with you and discover how many times I can make you scream, but I want to take my time the next chance I get to play with you," he whispers against the shell of my ear, and goosebumps speckle my skin. "When all of this shit that's going on settles, you and I are locking ourselves in a room for a week. We'll live off of orgasms and granola bars and be so noisy that no one else will be able to get anything done in the rest of the house," he tells me, and I can feel the smile in his voice. "What do you think, Squeaks, are you in or out?"

A loud laugh escapes my lips, and I think back to the night Ryker and I were first together and I laid down that same challenge. I press a hand against Ryker's chest until we're face to face again, and I place a tender and worshipping kiss on his lips. I tap on my soul, and it unveils the words that Ryker deposited that night. I pull back and stare into his bright blue eyes, my gaze radiating everything he means to me.

"In. I'll always be in when it comes to you."

4

It's dark when we land in Vitebsk. I've never been out of the country, and I was looking forward to taking in the unfamiliar geography of Belarus from the plane and car, but all I see is twinkling lights and shadowed silhouettes. It seems like there are a lot of trees, but it's hard to identify details without the help of more light.

"Have your passports ready, everyone. We need to get through immigration and customs quickly," Aydin announces and then proceeds to hand me a passport.

It says something about all the crazy shit that's been running through my head this whole time, because up until right now, I hadn't given any thought to the fact that I didn't have a passport. I stare at the small blue booklet, confused for a moment, before I flip it open to find an unsmiling picture of myself staring back at me.

"Where the hell did this come from?" I ask Aydin, who seems to be taking a headcount of our group like the responsible chaperone of a field trip would.

"Lachlan had it made."

Someone pokes a head out of the cockpit, and Aydin

moves up to talk to him. I'm left staring at his bulky back as questions and a shit ton of suspicion surge through me. The door to the plane opens, and my concern over why and how Lachlan had a passport made is drowned out by my eagerness to get the hell off the plane and out onto land again.

The last third of the flight passed uneventfully, but there's so much tension and anger floating around this plane right now that it's stifling. I thought the cuddle party Ryker and I had going on would help the drama feel less stifling, but as the wheels of the plane touchdown on the runway, the grumbles, glares, and passive aggressive digs start up again. I blow out an irritated huff and rub my temples. The renewed bickering is bringing me dangerously close to losing it. I need air and time to figure out an effective way to deal with all of this shit, and as much as I'm trying to be empathetic and understanding, what I'm mostly feeling is fucking pissed.

Clean, fresh air brushes past me, and it blows back stray locks from the bird's nest I'm calling a messy bun. I pull the air deep into my lungs, and I can taste pine needles and birch bark on the breeze. The air is cool, and a hint of fog kisses the ground as we step off the plane and make our way to a small building.

We're through immigration and customs in no time, and the next thing I know, I'm being loaded into one of three black vans. I stare at the signs that look like they're written in Russian as they flash by my window, and I peer hard into the dark night, trying to get a feel for what's around me.

"How you holding up, Little Badass?" Aydin asks, and I follow the trail of his voice to find him sitting in the front seat, his denim blue eyes fixed on me from over his shoulder.

I didn't pay attention to who else got in the van, but I'm

surprised when I look over and only find Evrin and a driver. I let out a sigh of relief, and Aydin starts to chuckle.

"The boys and Teo are in one van, and Enoch and his group are in the other," he tells me.

My brow scrunches with confusion at the name Teo.

"Your wolf," Evrin clarifies, when he sees the puzzled look on my face. "Mateo Torrez, he told us to call him Teo."

Understanding dawns on me, and I nod as the pieces fit together. I've always called him Torrez or Wolf-man or whatever. I never asked if he had a preference. I rub tired hands over my tired face. "What the fuck am I doing? I've marked a dude whose first name I didn't even remember until you just told me, five other guys—two of which can barely even look at me—and I couldn't begin to tell you what the fuck is going on with Nash, Kallan and Enoch. How the hell are we going to take on the big bad Adriel with this crew?"

"We're not exactly driving over to his house tonight and challenging him to a duel, Little Badass. You have time to set your males straight and get everything sorted. We need to do some reconnaissance, get a plan together, and a ton of other shit before we can make a move."

I snort. "They're not goats, Aydin. I can't just herd these guys in whatever direction I want them to go in."

"Can't you?" Evrin chuckles.

I shake my head at him and try hard not to let his cheeky smile become contagious. "Neither me nor my vagina are that fucking magical, Evrin."

The driver of the van starts to cough and pound on his chest. Oops, looks like he speaks English. A smile breaks open on my face, and I'm surprised I'm even capable of the movement anymore. I've spent the whole flight over here being pissed at my magic and its inability to keep its pants on. Or pissed at the guys for being stubborn pricks.

"Just train them hard and get them all as ready as you

can. They'll work it out or take each other out. Either way, problem solved," Aydin says casually with a shrug.

I lean forward and punch him in the shoulder. He laughs and rubs his arm and then bleats like a goat at me. Evrin and I crack up, and I throw my hands up in exasperation.

"They're not goats!"

Aydin winks at me and then faces forward as we turn off the road we've been driving down for a while. We're surrounded by trees just like in Solace, but the terrain feels different. It's flat, and the air is heavy with moisture that carries the cold deep inside of me. We drive up to a large white concrete wall. There's a dark brown gate that smoothly opens as we get closer, allowing us through.

My skin tingles as we pass through a magical barrier, and I shake off the feel of someone else's magic on my skin. I look around as we drive forward. There are three buildings, all white with slanted dark brown roofs. The van drives toward the middle one, which also happens to be the largest. I don't know shit about architecture, but the homes look somewhat French to me, or maybe European-cottage is more accurate. They have evenly spaced windows on what looks to be two-story buildings, and an arched entryway encompassing the front door. They look simple, sturdy, and at home surrounded by patchy grass and huge trees that hug the perimeter of the property.

Silva appears at the front door of the middle house and bounds down a couple steps to greet the van. Wind picks up his curly black hair and forces it to dance around his head. I focus on his face and the frown line that appears between his dark eyebrows, and the way his caramel-colored eyes narrow as he counts the number of vehicles that gradually pull up in front of the houses. The brakes of our van squeak slightly as we pull to a stop, and Aydin opens the door and climbs out. Silva opens his arms in greeting, and they both close the distance until they pull each other into a tight hug.

Relief spills out from both of them, and I'm reminded that the last time Aydin probably saw Silva was just before he left the coven. Evrin slides the door of the van back and steps out to join in the greeting. I stay sitting exactly where I am, not ready to abandon the respite of the solitude just yet. Valen and Bastien step out of their van first and make a beeline for their uncle. They hug and joke with each other, but the lines around Silva's eyes are tight, and it's clear he's not as happy as he's pretending to be that they're here.

The rest of my Chosen join the twins, and Torrez slowly unfolds himself from what looks like the back seat. Immediately his eyes find mine. The windows on all of the vans are tinted almost black, and I doubt that he can actually see me, but it's weird how his gaze lands on mine like that. I run the tip of my finger over my Chosen runes, aware that Torrez's mark still isn't among them. The five other guys' heads snap in my direction, and I immediately pull my hand away from their markings, not meaning to have called them. Valen moves in my direction, but Silva steps into his path.

"Aydin, you shouldn't have brought them here, it's not safe, and they're not paladin yet," Silva chastises as he pats Valen on the back.

"I couldn't exactly stop them. So I figured best to have them here where we can keep an eye on them," Aydin defends, as Silva pulls Bastien into another hug.

Bastien's eyes flick back in my direction as he hugs his uncle, and I know my words about not trusting Silva are dancing around in his mind. The sudden need to reassure Bastien that he doesn't have to choose fills me, and I slide out from my hiding spot in the van. I don't care how mad I am at Silva, Bastien should know that he can love the uncle that raised him even if Silva hates me, even if I don't trust him, and I would never expect otherwise.

I haven't even stepped all the way out of the van into the chill night when I hear Silva demand, "What the hell are they doing here?" and his attention is locked onto Enoch and his coven. "I told you specifically not to involve the elders; what did you two do?" Silva accuses as he turns to Evrin and Aydin.

"We didn't tell the elders, asshole," Aydin informs Silva with an irritated glare. "They have a rune situation going on, and they're here to train with Vinna."

I don't miss the way Silva stiffens at the sound of my name or the way he looks over Enoch and his coven and then runs his eyes over the new runes that Bastien, Knox and Ryker now have. Silva turns to find me, and the disapproval and mistrust in his eyes lashes out at me like a whip. He says nothing as he stares at me, but I can feel the unspoken contempt he has for the fact that I've marked more casters and tainted them with what I am.

Silva never saw my marking *the boys* as a good thing. Even after Reader Tearson explained that I was a Sentinel and that being Chosen was, according to him, an honor. Aydin's words echo through my mind as he tells me about the lamia they tortured and the ominous warning he gave about me and what I am. I tell myself that this fear, *this misconception*, is what's fueling Silva's feelings and actions, but as I meet Silva's glare and feel the judgment pulsating from him, I decide I just don't give a fuck about the *why* behind his issues anymore.

Maybe I've been trying too hard to be understanding of Bastien and Knox and the shit that went down before we came here, but I'm tired of trying to walk in other people's shoes or giving them the benefit of the doubt if they aren't willing to do the same for me.

Fuck 'em.

I shore up my walls and refuse to absorb anymore of Silva's vitriol. I let my gaze fill up with my own disappointment. Whether he likes it or not, I'm with his nephews. It's time for him to grow the fuck up and let go of his bullshit assumptions about me and see me for who I really am. It's time he learns that he can't pull this shit with me anymore. In the beginning I kept quiet, not sure where I fit and not willing to put a stop to the hate aimed my way if it meant risking the answers I was so desperate for. But I'm fresh out of fucks these days.

"Word on the street is that two-thirds of your idiot brigade managed to get themselves caught and now need rescuing," I say to him, my tone casual, but my eyes are bleeding just as much disdain and judgment as his are. "Want to fill all of us in on how you ended up here in the first place?" I ask, pushing for answers to the questions that have been churning inside of me since the sisters mentioned that Lachlan, Keegan, and Silva were here following some mystery lead.

Silva's gaze narrows slightly before he looks away and turns his displeasure on Aydin. "What the hell, Aydin?" he asks, giving him a pointed look, like somehow his real question isn't obvious.

I step toward Aydin, refusing to be dismissed. "What do you mean, Silva, you don't need help? You've got things covered here?"

He doesn't say anything, and all I can do is shake my head at how ridiculous he's being. Looks like all this time spent with Lachlan has pushed Silva even further into his dislike for me, although why I feel surprised and frustrated by that, I don't know.

"It's cool, Silva," I tell him when it's clear he's not going to speak to me directly. I walk back to the van. "Let me know when you're ready to pull your head out of your ass and realize I'm probably your best bet at getting your coven back," I tell him over my shoulder as I pull my bag out and move toward the house on the left.

"Little Badass, where are you going?" Aydin calls at my back.

"To find somewhere to crash."

"Those houses haven't been opened up yet," Silva informs me, abandoning the silent treatment he seemed hell-bent on administering.

"I've stayed in worse places," I tell him nonchalantly. "I'm sure as fuck not staying with you or anyone else incapable of getting over themselves." With that, I shoot a look over my shoulder at Knox and Bastien.

They both meet my frustrated gaze head on, neither one of them ready to back down yet. I shake my head and walk out of the halo of light the center house is providing and out into the dark cold of the Belarusian night. If they want to stew in their anger, that's their choice, but they can stay with their uncle, who I'm sure would be all too happy to fan the flames of discord.

Pain flashes through my chest at the thought that maybe Knox and Bastien might never come around. That maybe they'll start looking at me the way Silva and Lachlan do. I let anger drop kick the hurt right out of my chest and steel myself. If this is all it takes to break their faith in me, then I probably never had it in the first place and I'm better off without them.

I twist the knob to the front door of the dark building I've claimed as mine. The wood of the door sticks to the frame, so I shove my shoulder into it and force it open. I'm not sure what I expected, maybe dust and cobwebs all over, but it looks pretty clean past the stale feel of the place and the cold air that greets me from the entryway. I flip a switch to my left, and the lights blink on. The scuffling of feet sounds just behind me, and I turn to find Torrez.

"So, Witch, or should I say Sentinel?" he queries, half his beautiful mouth turned up in a smile. I chuckle. "Yep, the guys filled me in on the car ride over. I always knew there was something different about you," he taps his nose, and I reach out to flick it. "Where's our room?" he asks with a sly grin as he dodges my assault.

"Our room?" I ask.

"Definitely our room. You need time to process, and I have no issue with that, but you're mine now, and I'm yours. I don't see any point pretending things are any other way."

I raise an eyebrow in question at his statement. He's right, and I did just say anyone staying here needed to get over themselves, and I have no trouble admitting that applies to me too. He is mine. Which is exactly the way that I wanted it when I marked him.

"Lead the way, Wolf," I tell him with a cheeky grin and a wave of my arm into the house.

Torrez's half smile morphs into a full-blown grin, and he swings a duffle over his shoulder and steps past me.

His shoulder brushes against mine, and it sends a dusting of goosebumps all over my body. "Torrez?"

He turns his deep brown eyes to mine.

"I'm glad you're here," I admit.

I raise my hand and brush the tips of my fingers against the black scruff on his cheek. His molten gaze takes me in for a moment before he leans into my palm. He turns his head and kisses the inside of my hand softly before moving down a hallway to our right.

"Ooh bunk beds," he shouts out from the room he just disappeared into. "You want the top or the bottom, Witch?"

I laugh and follow him further into the house. The smile I'm once again wearing tricks me into feeling soft for a moment, hopeful. Maybe this won't be the cluster fuck that I'm worried it will be. Maybe Valen's right, and with a little bit of time, it will all blow over. Then the faint sound of arguing permeates the walls of the house, and I release a deep exasperated breath. Who am I kidding? This is going to be a fucking bloodbath.

5

I wake up cold, my cloudy breath in the air, my body just on the verge of a shiver. I crack open my eyelids. The light in the room is muted. It looks like either the sun hasn't come up yet or just now dipped below the horizon. I'm disoriented and not quite sure if I've crashed for only a little while or if I've slept the day away. I'm alone, and I look around the room, taking in the piles of blankets strewn about the makeshift bed situation.

Apparently, king size beds are an American thing, because the biggest bed we could find in this house was a full. Not satisfied with that situation, Ryker and the others pulled all the mattresses they could find off the beds and Tetris-ed the shit out of them on the floor of the biggest bedroom in the house. So now this room is absent of all furniture and has been redecorated with a very minimalistic and modern mattress floor.

I sit up and stretch out my arms and my back. I feel run down as fuck, which really shouldn't surprise me after everything that's happened in the last few days. I wipe the sleep from my eyes and get up, bouncing from one mattress to another until I'm standing in the doorway that leads to the small attached bathroom. My bag has been left right next to the doorframe, and I silently thank whoever put it there as I dig out a clean set of clothes and my toiletries. I'm in and out of the—thankfully warm—shower in less than ten minutes, and then I'm brushed, magically dried, styled, and ready to go in under fifteen.

I step out of the room and head down the hall into the kitchen, where I find all of my Chosen leaning against the counters, whisper-growling back and forth.

"Don't be a fucking numpty, Knox, this is Vinna and Vinna's magic we're talking about," Sabin chastises.

"Oh that's rich coming from you. You did everything you could to keep all of us apart in the beginning because you didn't trust the situation either."

"Yeah, but that was in the beginning. After she marked us, it was like I could feel her intention and the purity in what her magic had done. Don't sit here and tell me that you didn't. You've always gone on and on about how you knew she was for you, right from the beginning."

"So it's official, you don't trust me now?" I ask, my calm voice like a cannon in the room amidst all the aggressive whispers.

Five heads snap in my direction. Torrez keeps his eyes on the floor as he shakes his head. He's probably been aware of my movements and exactly where I was in the house from the minute I woke up. I wonder how annoying it would be to have sensitive hearing like that and not be able to turn it off like I can. Although, if this is how it's going to be with my Chosen these days, maybe I should keep my extra hearing on all the time.

"It's not you that's the issue, it's the situation I don't trust. I don't trust them," Knox defends, his arm gesturing out the window in the direction of wherever Enoch and his coven are right now.

I throw my head back and release a frustrated yell. "Okay! I fucking get it. You've said it a million times! You don't trust them, which is why you're pissed at me and acting like an asshole! Can we move the fuck on already?" I ask as I scan the kitchen for food. I need something other than frustration and insecurity in my stomach if we're going to try and tackle this shit again. Valen tosses me an apple, and I snatch it from the air and practically bite it in half as I continue to scan for more.

"Bruiser, we're not pissed at you. We're pissed about whatever the fuck they did to get those runes," Bastien tells me.

"But what if they didn't do anything? What if this is another case of my magic highjacking others just because it can?" I ask him. "I mean fuck, Bas, it's not like we have any clue why half the shit that happens around me does, but I thought you all were cool with that." I swallow down the rest of the apple as we all stare at each other in awkward silence. "You don't trust them, fine, but if you trust me, then it's time to Sentinel up and get to fucking work."

Bastien shakes his head dismissively, and frustration burns through me.

"Okay, so you think somehow they stole my magic and marked themselves?"

"Yes," Bastien agrees.

His words send a shiver of unease through me. I know he said something similar on the plane when everyone was fighting, but then that whole getting stabbed thing happened, and I never circled back to what he was accusing. *Fuck, could they have forced this somehow?* I picture Enoch, Kallan, Becket, and Nash, and try to process if I think they'd be capable of this kind of fucked up violation. But what if it wasn't even them that did it?

I struggle to accept that Enoch and his coven could do

something so wrong, but I sure as fuck can't say the same about Elder Cleary or Elder Albrecht. They'd definitely have something to gain if their sons had my power. Then again, if Elder Albrecht knew how to force a marking, wouldn't he have done it when he had me and Sabin at his mercy? It's all just more questions I don't have the answers to, and I shove away the worry and the frustration.

"Okay, fine," I announce. "We put this shit aside for now and start to train. If we find out at some point that they somehow stole their markings, then you can kill them."

Ryker snorts out a chuckle.

"We can kill them? Just like that?" Bastien mocks.

"Yeah, why not?" I shrug. "I don't distrust them. I think I've seen sides to them that you haven't, but if they forced me to mark them, then it's a horrible violation. If somehow they've figured out how to do that, then it's on us to make sure it never happens again. Which means we *should* kill them."

"You're hot when you're ruthless," Knox teases, a cheeky smile on his face, and its appearance almost makes me want to cry. Knox has always been supportive no matter what, so to have him distance himself from me the way he and Bastien have, fucking hurts.

"She's hot all the time," Torrez corrects, and the others chuckle and bob their heads in agreement.

The tension in the room lessens infinitesimally, and I let out a relieved breath. "Okay now that the Enoch issue is on hold until further evidence one way or another surfaces, let's move on to the Torrez issue," I announce, and Torrez's eyebrows drop in confusion, and his body goes stiff.

"You going to off me too, Witch?" he asks, and even though he's wearing a smile and has a glint in his eye, I sense the layer of seriousness beneath it all.

"Of course not, Wolf, I'm talking about whatever the

glitch is that put all of our runes on you and none of your runes on us."

With that, he starts looking over the others' hands and then studies his own again. He looks up at me, and before he can put a voice to the question in his gaze, I cut him off.

"I have no idea what this means or why it happened, so don't even ask," I tell him, and he chuckles.

"Maybe it doesn't have anything to do with him being a shifter and more to do with the fact that you marked him on purpose. Maybe the process is different when that happens as opposed to what happened with us?" Ryker queries, and I run my gaze over the runes on all of their ring fingers.

"Maybe. Marking him was not the *fun times* I was experiencing when all of you got your runes," I admit, and everyone but Torrez laughs.

I bring my eyes to Valen's hazel gaze, and I like the heat that I find there.

"What do you mean?" Torrez asks, his dark brown stare jumping from one guy in the group to the next, looking for answers.

I laugh at his needy expression. "I was mid-orgasm when my magic did its thing with them. With you, it was mid-battle, and I thought you were dying."

"So you're saying I need to give you an orgasm in order to solidify the connection?" Torrez asks, his eyes banking with want as he licks his lips.

"Whoa, that's not what I meant," I squeak out as Torrez takes a step toward me.

"Well, hold on there, Squeaks, maybe he's onto something with that. You and Valen were intimate, and then we all got our runes. When you have sex with us now, it completes the bond and we inherit your full arsenal. Maybe he does need to be intimate with you in order to kickstart things," Ryker hypothesizes.

Torrez takes another step toward me, and I get the distinct feeling that he's hunting me right now, and I'm not sure how I feel about it. I look to the other guys with *help* in my eyes as Torrez stalks even closer, but they all seem to be either lost in thought or amused by this development.

"Um, well, this escalated to a place I did *not* see coming," I admit and take an involuntary step back from the prowling shifter that's closing in on me with his heated stare and the promises of orgasms in that blazing gaze.

Wait, why am I against this idea? I pause, taking another step back. A satisfied rumble starts in Torrez's chest.

"Oh please run, Witch. My wolf loves the chase, and it will take this to a whole other level of fun."

His words and gravelly tone shoot right between my thighs, and I squirm.

"So you guys are just okay with this?" I ask as I take another slow step back. "We're just going to go fuck in the other room, and you guys will just be here shooting the shit until we're done, and that's not weird at all?"

They all laugh and seem to be extremely amused over my obvious discomfort.

"We'll all watch each other have sex with you when we do our Bonding Ceremony, so no, this isn't really a big deal," Sabin waves off casually.

"Wait! What?" I shout out in panic.

I momentarily forget about the big bad wolf that's currently stalking me and take a step toward Sabin so I can shake him and demand he explain what the hell he's talking about.

Valen laughs even harder. "We told you about the Bonding Ceremony, didn't we?"

"No, you fucking didn't!"

"Huh, I could have sworn we did that day at the lake," he says absently.

"Squeaks, why do you look so panicked? It's not like group sex was an issue when Knox and I...you know, became Sentinels," Ryker tells me, and Knox barks out a laugh.

I glare at them. "Yeah, I'm not waving my prude flag here, but that's a big thing to just throw out at a girl without a little warning"—I look at Torrez who's about two steps away from me now—"and when *said* girl is potential prey."

I don't hear what Sabin says next, because I grab his shoulder and shove him toward Torrez as I turn around and run. I sprint for the front door, and Sabin's protest at being used as an obstacle is joined by whoops of encouragement and shouts to run. I fling the door open and bolt out of the house into the cool dark day, or maybe it's night; I still have no idea what time it is. I push magic into my legs and pump harder, not even bothering to look behind me, because I know Torrez is close. Excitement and adrenaline flash through me, and I can't tell if I want to best him or get caught.

I push harder to gain more of a lead and round the corner of the house. I slam into something hard, and it goes flying away from me as I stumble forward, moving too fast to get my feet underneath me. I'm plucked from the air like a dainty little feather and pulled back into a strong muscled chest.

"Gotchya," Torrez growls into my ear and then nips at the top of my left shoulder.

His teeth graze over the runes there, and it sends a heated flash throughout my entire body.

"No way, I was fouled," I argue as Torrez's strong arms wrap around me.

He steadies me as I struggle to catch my balance, and I simultaneously soak my underwear and try not to rub up against every inch of him that's currently pressed against me. I look around to see who or what ricocheted off of me and find Aydin getting up and dusting himself off. I point to the ginger giant. "See, I call interference."

"Where's the fire, Little Badass?"

"No fire, just a hungry wolf," I tell him as I step out of Torrez's hold and away from the vibrating laughter in his chest. "Where are you coming from?" I ask in an effort to distract myself from the pressing need of my magic-tainted libido. You'd think I'd be used to the magical pull to solidify the Chosen bond, but nope, I'm not.

"There's a barn just past the trees that Silva has set up as a war room with maps of the area and supplies. We were just going over where we need to stake out and the best places to try and get info about Lach and Kee."

I look past Aydin's massive arm. I don't see the building he's pointing to, but I do spot its dark brown roof peeking just above the trees. I close the door on my frowning hormones and immediately go into battle prep mode. There's quite a bit of open space and flat ground back here before the dense tree line begins, and I start working through training scenarios in my mind as Aydin and Torrez chat about something.

"Have any lamia been spotted nearby? How much do we know about Adriel's nest size and location?" I ask.

Aydin lets out a sigh and rubs at the back of his neck. "We don't know much, unfortunately. The closest lamia spotting was a couple towns over. It seems there are clusters that move in and out of some border towns, near Russia mostly. Lachlan and Keegan were trying to see if there was a pattern to their movements when they were taken."

"So how do we know that Adriel even has them?" I ask, as I quickly think through a training schedule and try to see if there's any other way to get Lachlan and Keegan without things turning into an all-out war we're not ready for.

"Because there were spelled signs saying so pinned all over town. When Silva went to look for them after they missed a check in, he found the signs but no hint of Lachlan and Keegan anywhere, and no lamia. Silva, Evrin and I are going to head out and see what we can find. As soon as we have more information, we can start strategizing," Aydin tells me like he can read exactly where my mind has gone.

I blow out an exasperated breath and take one more look around before locking eyes with Torrez.

"We need to train our asses off, and we need to start *now*."

6

Enoch, Kallan, and Nash walk out onto the patchy grass and hard packed dirt of the yard behind the houses we're all staying in. I can feel the tension around me rise as they do. I try to shrug it off from where it attempts to cling to my shoulders, but with no luck. Enoch looks around warily until his eyes land on mine, and his mouth tilts up in a smile. Bastien mumbles something as Kallan, Nash, and Enoch move closer, and I elbow him in the side. We haven't even started to try to train together, and despite my explanations of why we *need* to train, I'm still worried about what will happen if Bastien and the others refuse to play nice.

Nash, Kallan, and Enoch stop directly across from my Chosen, and they square off with each other. They're all puffed up chests, resentful eyes, and anger-clenched jaws, and I can't help but huff out a sigh. I stand at the head of it all, ignoring the symbolism in my place and theirs, and tap into my inner boss bitch. I can let them go at each other again, or I can take this shit by the short hairs and get all of us to a place that won't lead to our mass slaughter when things go down with Adriel.

"We're here to train," I shout out into the tension and death stares. "I don't fucking care how you feel about each other, your history, or any of your reasons for mistrust when we're out here. All I care about is that each and every one of you has runes, and that makes you an asset and a target." I look at each of them as I talk, my eyes hard and my words brokering no argument. "Like it or not, Adriel's coming for us, and it just might take each and every one of us to end him. If we can't figure out how to work together and watch each other's backs, then we might as well just hand ourselves over to him now."

No one says anything to that, and a few of them drop their eyes away from my steely gaze. Knox meets my stare head-on, and I can practically see the *never going to happen* in it. My eyes stay fixed on his for a couple of beats, and I communicate a very clear *get with the plan or get the fuck out*. I look around and quickly map out areas where I'm going to set up teams. Enoch and his coven had me train in a gladiator-like style, but this group needs to learn little things about their runes and what they can do first, so I'm starting with Sentinel baby steps.

"As much as I'm sure you're all hoping to magically beat the shit out of each other like you do in paladin training, that's not going to work for this situation. So instead, I'm going to pair you up based on your natural branch of magic. Enoch and Sabin, you're together." Sabin nods and then moves so that he's standing in front of Enoch. "Kallan, you're with Valen. Nash with Ryker. Knox and Torrez, and Bastien, you'll be with me."

All of them pair off somewhat reluctantly, but I treat the fact that they did it without arguing as the small victory that it is.

"Every day, we're going to work on activating the runes that you have. Once everyone is proficient at that, we'll start sparring. You will spar only with the weapons or magic that your partner has access to. When you're good enough with those, I will mix up the partners so that everyone gets a chance to work different skills and weapons against different opponents, including me."

Some of my Chosen begin to grumble their disagreement, and I shut it down with a slash of my hand through the air.

"I don't care if you have issues with fighting your mate or a girl or whatever the excuse is when it comes to facing off with me. This is not up for debate. I can teach you things that you'll need to know, and I imagine that I can learn plenty from you, too. If it's not a mortal blow, then deliver it. We have healers, and we don't have time to pull punches and take things at a leisurely pace. This shit is life and death, so Sentinel up and treat it that way."

I pat myself on the back for channeling my inner Braveheart just enough to put a hint of fire in everyone's eyes but not so much that I'm screaming *freedom* and looking for something to paint my face blue. I assign each pair to stand in a different area so that they're spread out but can still hear me call out instructions. Bastien stands to my left as I take in my marked army and try not to feel completely underqualified to lead them.

"Quickly think through the runes that you have and decide which of those runes you'll be working to activate first. Those with weapons, I would suggest focusing on one of them. Those of you without weapons yet, focus on an ability," I instruct before turning to Bastien.

He's smirking at me. "I find you very appealing when you're being bossy," he tells me, and I laugh.

"Don't think buttering me up means I'm going to take it easy on you," I warn.

Bastien's hazel eyes light up with mirth, making him

even more gorgeous than he already is. His long wavy dark brown hair is pulled back, accentuating the masculine angles of his face, and his delectable full lips widen even more, putting his straight white teeth on display. "Good thing I like it rough then."

I choke on my chuckle and mentally try to redirect all the blood in my body from trying to pool between my thighs. Fuck, that was hot, and once again the last thing I need to be thinking about right now. I turn away from Bastien's panty-melting smile, and my eyes land on Torrez. His nostrils flare slightly, and a knowing smile sneaks across his face. *Shit*, he can probably smell my wet underwear from there. I fixate on a tree to my right, deeming it the only safe place to rest my gaze as I try to regain my composure. I karate chop my surge of lust down and focus again on the task at hand.

"I'm not sure how the source of your magic feels to you, but to me, it feels like a dark cave that sits in the center of my chest. It feels endless to me but not empty. I visualize which branch of magic I want and then call on it. I then weave the magic with my intention and desire. When I feel like I have exactly what I want, I push it out into the world."

At my use of the word *desire*, a low grumble sounds off, but I ignore it instead of figuring out the source. My money is on Torrez or maybe Bastien, but I don't want to dip my toe in that pool. Fuck knows I don't need anything else getting wet right now.

"Does that make sense to everyone?" I ask, and I'm surprised when everyone nods their head yes. "Sweet. I want each of you to call on your Sentinel magic and then picture pushing that magic into the runes of the weapon or ability you decided to call upon first," I explain. "Push a small amount at a time until you can feel the runes wake up. You'll feel the markings almost begin to siphon off the magic you're holding, until they're full and an ability flares or a weapon materializes where you instruct it to."

A staff materializes in the air and drops in front of Enoch. He snags it mid-fall and stares at the weapon in his hand, his eyes filled with awe and his smile proud.

"Fucking show off," fills my head, and I chuckle and look at Sabin. I give him a nod, letting him know I heard him, before my eyes move around the rest of the group.

Slowly knives appear and then disappear just as fast. Knox lets out a shout of excitement when a long sword appears in his hand, and he's holding the hilt instead of the blade. Kallan looks shocked as fuck when a whip appears in his hand, and it makes me do a double take, too. I guess that's what the rune on the side of my hand does. I quickly run through my memory to see if Kallan had any other runes besides that one, but I can't remember if he did or not. I only remember him showing me that one.

An image of Valen pressing into me on a bed pops into my mind. His knee moves up between my spread thighs, and he rubs against the sweet spot at the apex. I moan and grind down against his thigh, chasing the sensations that the delicious friction causes. Valen leans over me and kisses me, his tongue teasing mine, stoking my need even more. I moan into his mouth, and he pinches a nipple between his thumb and forefinger. And then just as quickly as it appeared, the image disappears, and I'm left hollow and unsatisfied.

My head snaps to Valen, and I find his gaze hooded and his head tilted to the side as he drinks me in with a molten look. "Just a small reminder of some things that need to be done before we rush off to kill bad guys," he shouts across the field. I give an awkward nod, letting him know that his image and words came through loud and clear.

I swallow hard as an echo of his mouth on mine, his

fingers pumping in and out of me as strikes of purple magic push us both into an orgasm, rises up from my memories. As turned on as I am, I also realize just how right he is. I need to make sure all of my Chosen are as strong as possible. *Must find time to fuck Valen, Sabin, and Torrez,* I tell myself and then try not to giggle like a fucking idiot at my *To Do* list. *By the moons, Vinna, get it together. Wasn't I just droning on about how all of this is life and death shit, and here I am having naughty daydreams about when and where I can seal the deal with my Chosen.*

I shake away my distracted thoughts and spend the next four hours walking everyone through calling on the runes that they have, until it starts to appear like it's second nature to them. The satisfaction that's bubbling up inside of me fizzles when Kallan yelps in pain and grabs onto his bleeding palm with his other hand. Ryker is there in seconds, knitting up the wound.

"Thank you," Kallan offers absently as he wipes the remaining blood on the leg of his jeans. I'm trying to figure out what the hell sliced up his hand, since I didn't think he had runes for any of my swords or... And that's when it hits me.

I burst into laughter, not able to help it. Kallan's serious face when he's in Drill Instructor mode flashes through my mind, and it sends me deeper into a howling fit of giggles. Everyone is staring at me like I've lost my mind, and I work hard to calm down long enough to explain what the fuck is wrong with me.

"Kallan?" I ask on a choked laugh. "What other runes do you have?"

Kallan narrows his eyes at me, and I lose it again, tears dripping down my face.

"You got the ass daggers, didn't you?" I question, my voice a high-pitched squeal of pure delight.

"I don't want to talk about it," he tells me through gritted teeth.

Our collective audience starts to chuckle as the source of my amusement is finally revealed.

"Let me see," I beg him, and he gives me an affronted glare.

"No," he argues and drops both of his hands to cover himself like I can see right through his black workout pants. That makes me laugh even harder. I stare at his bubble butt and try to picture what the runes look like on the bottom of his ass cheeks.

"Quit being a perv," he demands, and he pivots so I can only see his front. I can tell he's trying hard not to crack up now too, and I wipe the laugh tears from my face.

"Oh my stars, I fucking needed that," I admit and give Kallan a grateful smile. "All ass dagger jokes aside, it's one of the most useful weapons I have," I reassure him, and he puffs up a little prouder and drops his hands from where they're hiding his sweet cheek runes.

Bastien pulls his phone from his pocket and swipes it open. "Silva says lunch is ready." The words aren't even out of Bastien's mouth before he and Knox start outright sprinting toward the middle house. I laugh again before the thought of eating a meal with Silva sobers me. "Who wants to volunteer to check mine for poison first?" I ask, only half joking.

"Ours too," Nash announces as he glares after Bastien and Knox.

I give him a small smile, and before any of my Chosen can interfere, Nash asks, "Can we talk?" The look on his face is so earnest and worried. I instantly feel like shit for not seeking him and his coven out sooner and making sure they were okay. There are just too many egos to stroke and too many guys to keep happy. I can't keep track of fuck-all at this point.

"Of course," I tell him and then shoot Valen and the others a pointed look. Valen seems hesitant to leave me alone, so I motion for Nash, Enoch, and Kallan to follow me, and I walk away from the other four who are dawdling instead of leaving to go fuel up on whatever's been prepared for lunch. I don't spare a backwards glance as I move closer to the tree line, Nash and the others close on my heels. I get far enough away that none of the others should be able to hear, unless some of them have figured out the runes on their ears already.

"How are you guys holding up? I'm sorry I haven't asked before now. There's a lot of crap going down, but that was shitty of me."

Kallan leans against the trunk of a large pine tree and gives me a forgiving smile. Nash just nods his head in understanding, and Enoch watches me intensely, his feet spread and his arms crossed. No one seems eager to say anything, and I can't help but feel squirmy under Enoch's gaze.

"Bro, blink, you're creeping me out," I mumble, and Enoch and Kallan both snort out a laugh. "Anyone heard from Becket?" I ask, not able to help myself. I haven't spent as much time worrying about him as I probably should have, given that I played a part in his current messed up situation, but staring at Becket's coven, minus him, is weird.

"He's not answering any of our calls. My dad said he's being cooperative and that they don't think Becket was involved or aware of anything that his dad had been up to," Enoch tells me, and a small weight of uncertainty falls away from my chest. "Speaking of, my dad gave me a play by play of what happened that night. Are you okay?"

I shrug, not sure how to answer Enoch's question.

"Killing has never really stuck with me the way it maybe should. I mean, I kill in self-defense or the defense of others, so I always felt justified. But this is the first time I've spent any time thinking about the families or loved ones of those I've ended. I don't feel bad about what I did, but I feel for Becket, and it sucks that something I did hurt him."

"His dad made the choices he did, and he's the one to blame for what Becket is going through. Not you, Vinna. You did what needed to be done, and Becket will see that when everything comes to light." Enoch steps forward and pulls me into a side hug. I give him a weak smile, wishing his words could chase away the guilt that's been gnawing at me.

"Unless you want to lose an arm, you should probably take a step away from her," Nash advises.

Enoch lets out a frustrated growl but listens to his coven mate. "They're being ridiculous, and when we figure out how we got marked and exactly what it means, they're going to have to just suck it up," Enoch grumbles.

Something in Enoch's tone triggers a warning inside of me, and I look at him for a second, trying to put my finger on what it is. "Enoch, I meant it when I told them that I don't think you guys are Chosen." Something flashes in Enoch's eyes, but I can't identify what it is. I look at the others, and I'm surprised to see something similar in Kallan's eyes too.

"What makes you say that?" Nash asks me, with no hint of emotion indicating how he feels about things one way or another.

I look at each of them in turn and try to sift through what I'm feeling. "My connection to you guys feels different than it does with my Chosen. The attraction is different."

"So you're not attracted to us?" Nash asks, confusion lacing his voice.

"No, I mean, you all are hot, don't get me wrong, but with them, it was like I was body slammed by it. Everything clicked and felt so easy and right."

"So you want us to be easier? Because I'm game..." Kallan announces as his face lights up with a cheeky smile.

I roll my eyes at him and bite back a chuckle. "No, fuck, why is this so hard to explain? Things are easy with you guys, too, but not in the same way. It's like how I am with Mave."

Kallan pretends to take a knife to the heart while croaking out, "Friend-zoned." He's still smiling that smart-ass smile, but there's hurt in his eyes.

"Is that because you just refuse to look at us that way, Vinna? I mean, with what happened with the shifters when we first met and then being taken by the lamia, there's always some kind of drama getting in the way. Don't you think that could be clouding how you see us? What if your magic has chosen us too? If we asked you a month ago if you'd have any more mates, you would have insisted the answer was no, but now you have Torrez," Nash points out.

I snort and shake my head. "That is accurate. I didn't see Torrez coming, but I was a little bit in denial of the pull." I sigh. "I don't know what your markings mean; all I know is it just feels different to me." I look to Enoch, knowing he needs this hammered home more than the others, but I can tell he's not hearing me.

"But, like you just said, you don't know for sure," Nash points out. I fight the urge to glare at him for once again circling back to the fact that I can't give a definitive answer. I honestly don't even know why he's pressing. Nash has never really looked at me like he's at all interested.

"Technically, no, I can't say that I know for sure. But your marks aren't anything like the marks the rest of my Chosen have, and that supports what I'm feeling."

Enoch opens his mouth, and I can practically see the argument on the tip of his tongue. "What if I marked you for someone else? You could be Chosen, just not mine. Have you given that any thought?" I ask them, and Enoch promptly swallows his argument and closes his mouth.

"Maybe," Kallan agrees casually, and then he reaches for my hand. "But how do you explain these then?" he counters as he lines up both of our middle fingers and the identical runes that line them.

"Really rad friendship bracelets," I say, but it comes out like I'm asking a question. Kallan laughs. "Listen, Ass Daggers," I start, and he puts a finger up to my mouth to stop me.

"That is not a thing, don't try to make it a thing. Shitty nicknames can go both ways," he warns, and I smile.

"Fine, Kallan, to answer your question, I don't know, and you already know that because I've said it a billion times already. *I don't know*," I confess, even though I want to crush the words in my throat to keep them from leaking out and giving any of them hope. I want to squash it once and for all and make everything easier on me and them and the guys, but there's nothing else I can say to Kallan's question. As much as I fucking hate it, the reality is I just don't fucking know.

They don't feel like my Chosen...but they could be.

7

Lunch is about as awkward as I thought it would be. Each of my Chosen have questions burning in their eyes, and despite my efforts, I haven't been able to squash the hopeful light that reflects back to me in Enoch's and Kallan's gazes. I have no idea what Nash thinks about anything. Sometimes he pushes like he's on the same page as Enoch and Kallan about wanting to be Chosen, and other times he seems completely indifferent, but it's the least of my problems right now. Silva, Aydin, and Evrin announce that they're going to head out after lunch and might be gone for a day or so depending on where the trail of lamia leads.

I finish off the last of a yummy potato dish, whose name I can't say, and silently wonder if I'll ever eat another thing not cooked by the sisters without missing them. I make a mental note to call them later today, and then I add Mave to the list too. My ears perk up when I hear the mention of the barn area and the words "off limits" spoken in the same sentence. I fight to keep from snorting at Silva's warning to stay away, because if he knew shit about me, he would know he pretty much just lit up a neon sign asking me to snoop through whatever is out there.

"I'm prepping some spells with the shifter toxin you all brought, and I don't want to risk anything messing up the volatile potion until it's ready," Silva tells the twins casually, and they nod in understanding.

Knox inquires about what kind of spells Silva is working on, but as soon as the discussion gets technical, I can't follow what the hell they're talking about anymore. Ratios of ingredients to woven magic, the time it takes to adequately cook a certain potion, the time it takes a spell to settle. It all sounds so intense, and I'm reminded of something Sabin once said about how Spell casters were like chefs. I haven't seen Knox in his element with his branch of magic, but it's not hard to picture him apron-clad and cooking away, with a wide smile on his face as he rocks out to music and adds a pinch of this and a dash of that.

Like he can feel his name in my thoughts, Knox looks over and gives me the same wide smile I was just picturing in my mind. I haven't seen much of that smile in the last forty hours. A part of me wants to seize it and shove it in the pockets of my soul so I can pull it out whenever I need it and Knox isn't feeling obliged to send a new one my way. Aydin pushes his chair back from the table and stands up, his eyes jumping to each of us briefly.

I don't know what it is about Silva and this entire situation that has me feeling leery, but I can't shake the feeling. I didn't miss that he never answered my question about how he and Lachlan and Keegan ended up here, and I decide to see if I can find some answers for myself as soon as Silva, Aydin and Evrin leave. I debate for a moment about including the others in my hunt for clues, but with all the tension and bickering still going on, I decide it will just be easier if I check things out on my own first.

"If we need anything, we'll call. If shit goes down, I'll send a sign. If neither of those things happen, then we'll see you soon." Aydin laughs, and it's joined by a couple chuckles here and there, but I'm not in a laughing mood. I don't think that doing the very thing that got Lachlan and Keegan caught by the lamia is exactly the soundest of plans, but I doubt Silva would listen to anything I have to say about that. I keep my reservations to myself and my mouth shut as Evrin and Silva join Aydin in standing up. They all say a brief goodbye and then stalk out of the room.

I turn to Sabin and trace my finger over one of the trees tattooed on his arm to get his attention. His forest-green eyes meet mine, and his plump lips offer me a sweet smile.

"When everyone's done eating, we need to continue training. I'll meet you back there, but will you run them through the same exercises we were doing earlier?" I ask.

"Of course. You okay?" he queries, and I nod and give him a demure smile before pushing away from the table. A few of the guys watch me leave, but no one says anything, which I'm grateful for. It means I can save my diarrhea cover story for some other time. I sneak through the main house and out the back door with no one the wiser. I check out the back of the house to make sure no one is watching me, but the windows are empty, and the faint sound of the guys talking is still coming from the direction of the dining room.

I slink away from the white stucco walls, out toward the trees, moving in the direction of the roof that I saw earlier when Aydin pointed it out. It's dark out *again*. Apparently, Belarus gets very little daylight in the fall and winter, and we've passed the three-hour window where the sun comes out just long enough to remind us of its existence before it flips us the bird and disappears once more. There are enough flood lights on the back of the property and around the house that training in the dark isn't a problem, but as I move further into the trees, I become more aware of how foreign everything around me is. There's an ominous feel to the forest here, and I don't know if the trees themselves are radiating that or if it's my mind and my suspicions getting the better of me.

The faintest sound of fabric scraping against wood reaches me in the dark, and I freeze. I call on the runes on the helix of my ear and focus past the sound of my own pounding pulse. I scan my surroundings, my knees bent and my body ready for anything that may come my way. But after what feels like forever just standing and listening, I don't see or sense anything out there that poses any threat. I put one foot in front of the other again, and before I know it, I'm walking into a cleared area where an old barn stands.

I feel a magical barrier a few feet away, and I call my Defensive magic forward. I close my eyes, and when I open them, it's with a sheen of magic filtering my view. A coral-colored dome protects the grumpy looking barn. I think back to everything that Becket and Bastien have taught me about barriers, and I filter through my options as I stare at the coral glow of the obstacle in front of me. I don't want Silva to know that I was in here, so shattering or overtaking this protective magic—which is usually my go-to—is a definite no go.

I pull on more Defensive magic from my core and direct it to pool in my hands. I crouch down to the base of the barrier and run my index finger in a straight line up the side of the barrier, standing as I move higher. I weave my intention to go unnoticed and leave no trace, with the yellow-orange magic in my hands as I go. My magic coats the magic of Silva's barrier, and a slit in the side of the dome forms directly in front of me. Silva's protections aren't overly strong, and the lack of over the top security measures on the building makes me question whether he's hiding anything in this place.

I step through the slit in the barrier, and as soon as I'm all the way in, all noise of the forest disappears. It's quiet in here, and the sound is distorted like I'm underwater. Why would Silva put sound protections on this place? I file that question away and quickly make my way inside the barn. It's so dark I have to manifest a ball of fire in my hand so I can see through the inky blackness. The fireball lazily floats above my moving palm as I search for a light switch. I spot one just to the left of the door and flip it on, causing the fluorescent lights above me to sluggishly blink to life. The buzz of electricity as it runs through the bulbs fills the quiet of the barn, and I look around, not sure what to expect.

At first glance, the roof is two stories above me, and the inside of the barn has been quartered off. I walk through the room that I'm in and open the door to my left. It swings open with a slight creak and reveals the spells that Silva was talking about, or at least I think that's what's in here. I recognize stoppered bottles of the shifter saliva Sabin and I took from his family's warehouse. I didn't know how many of the bottles survived the shifter attack, but it looks like a couple of cases arrived here unscathed.

I don't walk through the doorway or feel the drive to explore this room. I don't actually know how volatile these spells might be, but it's not worth the risk of accidentally blowing myself up. I close the door, and that same angry creak voices its displeasure at being disturbed. I move to the doorway on the wall to my right. The one light switch must control the illumination in the back rooms of the barn too, because I walk into a bright room with large maps covering two of the four walls. I move closer to one of the maps and run my gaze over the dark green markings that have been made on them.

If I'm reading this layout of Europe correctly, it seems Lachlan, Keegan, and Silva have been tracking lamia movement in Greece, Portugal, Poland, Romania, and Belarus. There are clusters of green Xs in all of these countries and lines connecting the clusters. Without a key or someone to explain what all the writing means, it's impossible to decipher for certain, but I don't miss that the largest cluster of green Xs is just across Belarus's border with Russia. There's a small blue star close to the Kazakhstan–Russia border, and something about its presence niggles at my mind.

No matter how I try to reach for whatever it is that's bugging me, I can't get my mental fingers around it. Sets of computer screens demand my attention, and with a shake of the mouse, the screens come to life. I have no idea what to make of the images I see on them. One looks like ruins of some kind. There are crumbling piles of old stone, and one stubborn wall with a small cut out for a window still fighting against the elements and refusing to topple over. On another screen is a picture of a man or more likely some kind of supe.

He looks older than Lachlan and his coven, but I'm not sure exactly how much higher up his age range would fall. He's handsome, has curly brown hair, and his frown lines seem etched into his skin like a warning. There's nothing familiar about him, and the picture gives no indication of why Silva or anyone else would be interested in him. The third computer screen has a tab that requires a password. I click on the two screens with images on them, but they don't respond to the commands of the mouse, and it's clear that, without the password, I'm not getting any more information about what's on these computers.

I leave them and scan the rest of the room for anything else that might be of interest, but aside from a couple chairs, the desk that takes up most of one wall and only has markers in the drawer, and the computer screens nestled in one corner, this room isn't hiding anything else. I move to the last door. I open it cautiously, and it gives way without a sound.

The room is the same packed dirt as the rest of the barn, but it has dark splotches that mottle the color. There's a bucket in the corner, and something about the smell in the room has my hair standing on end. My gut churns with warning, but I can't place what it is about this space that is setting my internal alarms off. I move to step further inside the room when the telltale creak of the door that leads into the spell room breaks through the silence like a cannon.

My adrenaline spikes, and my heart starts to race. I swallow down my fear and quietly shut the door to the room I'm not going to get to explore. I move soundlessly until my back is pressed against the wall directly next to the door leading into the room. I never shut it behind me when I came in here, but it's closed enough to offer my movements some cover and so that I'll be able to grab whoever pushes the door open before they see me.

I work to slow my breathing and focus on the door and any movement in the other room. Whoever it is, they move as soundlessly as I do, and I'm surprised when a hand appears out of nowhere and pushes the door open. I spot the runes on the ring finger of whichever of my Chosen has decided to follow me, and I'm instantly relieved and irritated at the same time.

"Valen, what the fuck?" I demand, my question exploding into the silence like a firework, and Valen jumps and lets out a small yelp.

"By the stars, Vinna, you scared me."

"You scared me, you ass. Why are you following me around?"

Valen gives me a sheepish smile. "We wanted to know

where you were sneaking off to, and I won the roshambo off."

I chuckle, not able to help myself. "You rock-paper-scissored to see who would follow me?" I ask, my tone exasperated with just a touch of amusement.

"Of course, arm wrestling takes too long," Valen tells me matter-of-factly before his attention turns to the room and its contents. "What are you doing in here?"

"Spying," I admit casually, as I join him in looking around again.

"Find anything good?"

"Not really. I can see where Silva and the others have been tracking lamia, but I have no idea what all the markings on the map mean or where the pictures on the computers are from and what significance they have."

Valen steps further into the room and quietly peruses the map and then the computers. Unlike me, he actually tries to type in a couple of password options, but nothing is correct. He studies the picture of the man just like I did and then looks at me with a shrug of his shoulders.

"Yeah, I got nothing," he admits, and we both step back to the map and stare at it for a minute.

"The thing I still want to know is how did they end up over here? The sisters said they were following up on a lead, but where did that lead come from? Why is Silva being so squirrely about this place. What's he up to?"

"Well, aside from the fact that he doesn't trust you, he also has a tendency to treat Bastien and me like we're still thirteen. He never really tells us about missions or plans because he thinks we're kids and can't handle it. I know there's mutual distrust on your part too, but honestly, he's not behaving out of character."

"Well, you would certainly know him better than I would," I admit.

I turn back toward the weird dirt room that Valen's interruption kept me from looking through, but he reaches out and grabs my hand, keeping me from leaving. I turn around to find worry in his eyes.

"Are you okay?" he asks me, and I'm not sure what to say. "We're worried about you. You're pushing pretty hard, not giving yourself any time to just breathe and process," he tells me, his stunning hazel eyes searching mine. "What's going on in that beautiful head of yours?"

Valen pulls me into him, and I tilt my head back as he brushes stray strands of hair out of my face. His brow is furrowed with concern, and his lush lips are pursed with questions.

"Fuck, Valen, I don't even know," I tell him on a deep sigh. "I feel like if I stop, I'll have to look at all the crazy shit that is my life right now."

"Crazy bad or crazy good?" he asks, his green and brown eyes drinking me in.

"Both," I say, but it sounds more like a question than a statement.

Valen waits patiently for me to collect my thoughts. He doesn't press or try to coax more out of me, but gives me the time and quiet support to put it together on my own. He stands there, lending me his silent strength, happy for me to soak up as much as I need for as long as I need.

"In less than three months, I've learned that I'm not human, and then I learned that I'm not even a caster; I'm some other magical being that no one knew existed anymore. The only living family that I have hates my guts, and I have no idea why. Talon, the one person who did care about me, turned out to be a lamia, but he only clued me into that fact as he was dying in my arms.

"I've been abducted twice now, forced you and your coven into a relationship with me, marked a wolf shifter, and now three other casters have some runes that match mine and some mystery ones. We're here in a country I've never been, to rescue an uncle who wishes I didn't exist, and to deal with the lamia who killed your parents and mine. And..." I hesitate for a moment, a little shocked by the words that sit on my tongue. I debate for a second how smart it is to release them, but I stare at Valen's beautiful face and the understanding look he's giving me, and I decide what the hell.

"I'm fucking scared." As the words tumble out of my mouth uncensored, I can feel the stress and tension I've been carrying slowly lifting. I look into Valen's patient hazel gaze, as the words *I'm scared* spill out, and it's right then and there that I realize how much those two words encompass everything that I'm feeling. Because regardless of whether I'm being attacked by a grizzly shifter or looking into Sabin's dark green eyes when he tells me he loves me, I'm fucking terrified.

I'm terrified of getting too close and too dependent on them. What if Enoch and the others turn out to be Chosen, what will Knox and Bastien do? Will they leave? How will Valen stay if his brother goes? We're quite possibly about to face off with Adriel and his entire nest. What if we don't survive, or worse, what if they don't, but I do? Nothing in my life has ever been stable, and if there's one thing I know for certain, no one ever stays. Not even when they want to.

8

"Is it normal to be *more* freaked out by the good things in life than I am by the bad things?" I ask Valen, my voice small and unsure.

He pulls me even closer, my chest against his, and his eyes skate around my face, looking for something. "I don't know about normal, but it makes sense given the circumstances. When Talon found you and put you up in a safe place to stay, how long did it take before you trusted that situation? Before you started to trust him?"

I mull over his question and push a wayward curl off his cheek. "A couple years, maybe more," I confess, and Valen nods like he expected that this would be my answer.

"And when Laiken would bring you food or help you after Beth hurt you, how long did it take before you stopped being afraid of the help?" he asks me, his voice low and soft, his tender tone sinking right inside of me and messing with my soul.

"I never stopped being scared that Beth would find out. I was always scared for Laiken. Always scared for me."

"You've known us for less than three months," he tells me and pauses while that sinks in. "Yes, we are tied together.

No, we will never walk away," he adds, answering my unvoiced fear. "If it takes you forever to learn how to trust us, then it takes forever. If you never stop being scared, that's okay, because there's six of us now, and each of us will carry the weight of that fear. We'll build the walls of trust for however long we need to." He looks down at me, his eyes swirling with strength and assurance. "You are ours, and we are yours, and that's what it means to be bonded."

I pull Valen's lips down to mine. I don't know a better way to respond to his beautiful words other than to show him what they mean to me. I'm not eloquent when I speak, I like the word *fuck* entirely too much to ever be. But as Valen's full lips meet mine, I realize I can be poetic in the way my tongue dances with his. Reverent when I pull his clothes from his incredible body. Tender as I moan into his mouth. I can love him through my actions and touch in a way I can never seem to get out with words.

Valen sucks my bottom lip into his mouth and pulls up the hem of my shirt. We break away as he pulls it over my head, and then his lips are back on mine. His hands cradle my face, guiding me deeper and deeper into his kiss. He reaches down and circles his arms around my thighs and lifts me onto the desk. I run my hands up his thickly muscled arms, loving the feel of his soft tan skin on my fingertips and the hard strength just underneath. He steps between my legs, kissing me until every nerve ending in my body is coursing with need.

I pull his hair out of the tie that's holding it back. I fan his dark chocolate waves around his strong shoulders and love the silky feel of it. I pull back, tracing his high cheeks and posh nose with my eyes, letting them roam over his chiseled jaw and full lips with pure veneration.

He pulls me into another kiss, his lips filled with the same kind of worship my gaze has. Violet magic appears on my arms, but neither one of us is fazed as it travels from me to him. His groan of pleasure vibrates my whole body, and it makes me ache even more to move things along. I pull off my sports bra, and Valen chuckles as my lips are pulled from his.

"Where's the fire?" he asks on a laugh.

"In my vagina," I announce and then crack up. "That sounded way less sexy than I thought it would."

Valen runs his thumb across my smile, and his hazel eyes flash with heat. "How did I get so lucky to be chosen by you?" he asks, his tone pure worship, and if I had any response, it would have been swallowed up by his kiss and all the want and admiration he pours into it. I tug at his pants, untying the strings to his sweats as he pulls at the waist of my leggings. My underwear goes with them, and he crouches to pull everything slowly down my legs.

I want him to hurry; I miss the feel of his body against mine already, but Valen has other plans as he kisses gently back up my calf, behind my knee, up my thigh. I shiver with anticipation and watch him hungrily as he flicks his tongue out to tease my leg. I grab him by his wavy, dark brown hair and redirect his attention to where I want it to be.

"Ah yes, how could I forget you were suffering with fire crotch?"

I laugh, but it quickly turns into a moan as Valen spreads me and flicks his tongue out against my clit. He teases me with soft strokes, and just when I'm about to throw him on his back and ride his face, he sucks me into his mouth and shoves a finger inside of me. I shout out my approval, and the vibration of his pleased moan sends tingles all the way through my limbs.

Valen pulls away from my clit with a pop and pumps his finger inside of me slowly. "I've been dreaming of doing this since that first night you fell asleep on top of me."

"Mmmmm," is all I can manage as he adds a second finger inside of me and curls them up, hitting a place at the roof of my vagina that I'd like him to spend more time exploring.

"I woke up, and you were straddling me, and I should have flipped you on your back right then and there and fucked you, but I didn't, and it's haunted me every day since," he tells me, his tone deep and velvety.

"So fuck me now," I challenge, and I watch as he circles my clit with his tongue and moves his fingers in and out of me faster and faster.

I writhe with the sensations his mouth and fingers are giving me, and he growls in approval, his eyes fixed on mine. "You like that, sweet Vinna? Show me how much you like it by coming all over my face."

Valen sucks on my clit again and curls and then circles his fingers inside of me. His demand bounces around my mind as I pinch my nipples and happily fall over the edge into a toe-curling orgasm. Valen doesn't stop fingering me, but his mouth takes mercy on my clit, and he moves his face from between my thighs and nuzzles my hand away from my breasts. He pulls a nipple into his mouth and sucks hard, and I ride his hand, the end of my orgasm stretching out inside of me before fluttering away.

"Valen, please," I beg shamelessly as he moves from one nipple to the other.

"Please what, my love?"

"Please get inside of me," I growl, and thank fuck, he pulls his fingers out and replaces them with his cock.

Valen pulls my hips forward off the desk and thrusts into me so hard I scream his name in encouragement. His big hand is splayed on my lower back, and he tilts my hips up as he pulls out and then slams back in.

Fuck. He feels so good, and I have no choice but to throw

my head back and beg for more. He pumps into me harder and faster and then slows his pace as he leans forward and claims a kiss. I taste myself on his tongue, but I can't focus on anything other than how incredible Valen feels inside of me.

"You feel so fucking good," he tells me, echoing my exact thoughts.

Our foreheads press together as we fight for air and chase release. I wrap my arms around Valen's back trying to pull him impossibly closer to me. I want his soul to wrap itself with mine. For us to fuse together in every possible way so that we're never without each other and *nothing* can ever change that. He reaches down between us and plays with my clit, and I fracture into a thousand pieces. Pleasure slams through every inch of me, and I swim in it and feel Valen slam inside of me a couple more times before he shouts out my name and buries himself as deep inside of me as he can go. We pant for a minute, reveling in the feel of each other, and let the tail end of our orgasms cover us like a tingly blanket.

"Well done," I praise and pat Valen on the back, and I lean forward and nip at his chest.

He looks down with a proud smile, and we both start laughing. He grinds his hips against me again and sucks on my bottom lip.

"Now don't go starting things you can't finish," I warn.

"Who says I can't finish?"

"Well, being that you have about twenty minutes, give or take, before you're writhing around in pain, I'd say another round is welcome but unlikely."

"Raincheck then?" he teases against my mouth.

"Yes, please," I whisper at his mouth and kiss him hard until we both have to come up for air. "Let's get you to the room so you can transition there on the mattresses instead of here in the dirt," I tell him as I look down to where we're still connected.

Valen's smile is contagious, and we both press against each other, beaming like fools. "Beautiful and wise," he tells me before pulling out of me and searching for clothes.

He hands me my leggings, bra, and top before collecting his own clothes and pulling them on.

"Should I let Bastien know what's going on so he doesn't get the same scare you did?"

Valen chuckles and gives me a quick kiss. "No, fair is fair. He should live through the same panic I did. Helps us appreciate the other more, especially when one of us is being a stubborn ass."

"Bastien, being a stubborn ass? I don't believe it," I snark, and we both head out of the barn and back out into the cool night.

"Did you find anything suspicious in there?" I ask, jerking my head in the direction of the barn behind us.

"No, just the spells he mentioned, some maps, and one very sexy Sentinel," he tells me and slaps my ass. "What were you thinking you were going to find?"

"I don't know. I didn't have anything specific in mind. I was just hoping to find something that would put all of the pieces together." Valen follows me out of the cut in the barrier. I reach my hand out to where my magic coats Silva's and pull it back inside of my center.

"You're getting good at that," Valen tells me with a nod. "But you should close the access point behind you, or at least set a trip-cast inside of the opening so you know if anyone comes in behind you."

I nod and shoot him a smile, and I make a mental note to practice more protective casts. He grabs my hand and intertwines our fingers as we walk back to the house. The intimacy of it is so simple and yet it feels so huge at the same time.

"What do you mean by put the pieces together?" he asks.

"Like where Lachlan and them got the lead that had them flying to Europe in the first place. Or why Silva has a barrier around this barn to begin with."

"Well, that last part might be easy to answer. They were tracking lamia, so this could just be a precaution in case the lamia caught on and started tracking them. This barrier would have kept the lamia out of the building and prevented them from hearing any plans made inside. Lamia have really good hearing, among other things."

I have to admit that he makes a valid point, but I still can't let go of the doubt and suspicion that there's more here that I'm just not seeing. We stay in the trees and skirt the others who are still training hard behind the house. The sight of them working to master their runes feels amazing, but I shut out the pride that fills my stomach and focus on getting Valen back to the house. We sneak in, and I pull blankets back from the mattresses on the floor.

"You might have time to get a quick shower in, wash off the sex before you're wishing you could black out instead of feeling the runes sear themselves into you."

Valen kisses me and then flicks the tip of my nose. "What a beautiful picture your words paint for me," he deadpans. "And I'm perfectly happy to have your orgasms on my skin until this is over and I can talk you into taking a shower with me."

I chuckle. "Well, you might be waiting a while; I'm pretty sure I have PTSD from the last time I tried to shower with one of you."

We both cringe at the memory of Ryker lying on the shower floor in pain as his runes surfaced slowly on his skin. Valen's eyes soften, and his mouth turns up with a sly smile. "That's all the more reason why we need to reenact it and chase the bad memories away with lots and lots of orgasms."

I clench my thighs against his tempting words, and the movement isn't lost on him. A knowing grin fills his face, and he pulls me in for a thorough kiss. He grunts, but this time I know it's not from pleasure but the first tendrils of pain. Valen falls to his knees, and I go with him. I hate this part, but I'm warmed all over by his efforts to smile through it.

"Bastien will be freaking the fuck out right about now," he grits out, and I laugh and pull Valen into my lap, cradling him as the transition takes its violent hold and works to leave its mark. His hand reaches up to caress my cheek, and I selfishly lean into it, needing the comfort.

"It's okay, Vinna. I've been waiting for this since the night you marked us. It'll be over soon."

"Pretty sure that's what I'm supposed to be saying to you," I tell him on a chuckle.

"Fine, we'll keep saying it to each other until it's over," he relents, a grunt stealing the end of his words.

I brush loose strands of hair out of his face. "How did I get so lucky?" I tell him, parroting his earlier sentiments. And that's all I can think as I watch him go through hell. Bastien comes tearing into the room, takes one look at us, and smiles, relief filling his eyes. He kneels down and takes Valen's hand and starts reciting poems as Valen and I take turns telling each other that it's okay and that it'll be over soon.

9

"That was a cheap fucking shot!" Bastien bellows.

Kallan looks unfazed by Bastien's outrage and readies himself for another attack. "Oh come on, aren't you some big bad Sentinel now? You think everyone is going to fight fair?" he taunts.

"We're training, not fighting right now, but if you want to stop pulling punches, I'm perfectly happy to oblige," Bastien tells him through clenched teeth.

When Kallan yawns, I slam a hand over my mouth to keep hidden the smile that flashes into place.

"Are you done monologuing, or should I take a seat?" Kallan asks, his tone bored.

Bastien curses and does something with his Defensive magic that has Kallan choking. "That's enough bullshit out of you," Bastien goads.

Kallan counteracts Bastien's cast and gulps down air as he flings maroon-tinted magic in return. Bastien rolls to avoid it, but it catches his heel. His hands slam down and stick to his sides, and his legs seem to seal together. He looks like he's doing his best impression of a falling log or some kind of fish out of water as he struggles on the ground.

"Motherfucker!" Kallan shouts out and starts scrubbing at his eyes. "Really, you're going to Magic Mace me? Who's taking cheap shots now?"

I attempt to shove the laugh that's trying to crawl out of my mouth back in, but it just comes out more high-pitched and obvious. Both Bastien and Kallan were doing well with the previous training. I've just paired them up, which based on the banter that's happening, was a genius move.

"Oh, you poor baby, did you think everyone is going to fight fair?" Bastien mocks, and I completely lose it.

Both of their heads snap in my direction, and judging by the scowls on both of their faces, neither of them find my obvious entertainment very amusing. That just makes me laugh even harder. I've been watching them for about an hour, and I'm learning so much as I do. I've read a lot about Offensive and Defensive magic, but reading lines in a book and seeing it with my own eyes are two very different things. So far, with Enoch and his coven, we've focused on Defensive magic and Elemental magic. We were just starting to dip more into the other branches when I had my awakening, so it's been awesome to see these two go at it. I get to see some of the things that I've learned, used against a branch of magic I haven't tapped much into and it's incredible.

Offensive magic and its casts primarily mess with an opponent's senses or body in some way. Casters do this by either overloading their opponent with pain or nulling them and stealing their senses. Kallan hasn't tapped into the pain aspect too much, but everything else has been fair game. They're both so creative in how they attack and defend, it's mesmerizing, but the commentary is what's been keeping me glued to this spot. I don't think I've laughed this hard in who knows how long. I have tears streaming down my face from the hilarious bickering they've been doing back and forth.

"Is she laughing at us?" Kallan asks.

"She certainly is," Bastien confirms.

I wipe tears from my eyes and look up to see that they're both on their feet now and staring at me, the look in both of their eyes incredulous.

"Don't mind me, carry on," I manage to squeak out between peals of laughter.

"Do we amuse you, Bruiser?" Bastien asks me, but I know that tone.

He's going to try and come for me, and the way he's moved his weight to the balls of his feet confirms my suspicions. *Good*. They're using too much magic and not enough of the weapons they're *supposed* to be calling and using against each other. I know Kallan doesn't want to talk about the runes cupping his ass cheeks, but he needs to start using them. I pull up a barrier just as Bastien shoves his sunset-orange magic at me. It hits my barrier, causing it to shatter, but I'm already moving.

I know my shields pretty much work as a failsafe, but I don't want to test their infallibility, so I've been working hard on different barriers. I call a new one into place, the orange-yellow sheen glimmering around me. I drop it for a heartbeat and send three daggers flying toward different parts of Bastien's body. Warmth slams into me from behind, and I'm forced forward by Kallan's unsurprising tackle. I use Elemental magic to create a forceful gust and blow myself out from underneath him. He swears as he slams into the hard dirt minus my body to cushion his fall.

I twist cat-like mid-air, landing upright, and send daggers flying toward Kallan on the ground. He rolls to avoid them and kips up onto his feet. Bastien comes up on his side, and they both rush me. I palm two daggers, and in a blink, the three of us are caught up in a dance of movement. Lunging, twisting, striking, looking for access to each other, one tiny opening where we can land a hit or a blade and win.

I breathe in with each defensive move I make, and out with each attack I deliver. The three of us are a blur of action, and we all move so well together, as we evade and assault one another, that if I didn't know better, I'd think this was choreographed. I lean back to avoid a kick Kallan sends my way, and I realize too late that I've left my stomach exposed to Bastien. He doesn't capitalize on the opening, and I know he saw it. His eyes flit from my stomach to my legs where he then tries to sweep my feet out from underneath me while I'm off balance.

This fucker isn't going for the kill shot.

I pull on my Sentinel magic and send a pulse out that throws Kallan and Bastien away from me. I stomp over to Bastien on the ground, who's slowly getting up and shaking the rattling my magic just gave him out of his limbs.

"Are you fucking pulling punches?" I demand.

"What the hell, Bruiser?"

"Don't what the hell me; are you pulling your hits?"

Bastien doesn't answer, but I didn't really need him to.

"My stomach was open. You should have shoved a blade into my side and given yourself the upper hand, but you didn't. Why?"

I'm in his face and shouting, and the other guys have stopped their training to watch.

"I'm not going to fucking stab you, Bruiser. Shoving a dagger into your stomach isn't going to make us better fighters. I don't have to actually beat the shit out of you to prove that I can."

"You need to know what it feels like to go for the kill so that you can rebound accordingly. You need to be prepared for how your opponent will respond to being hurt."

"Bruiser, that's not how training works. We execute

supes as paladin, but they don't have us actually kill them in training as conscripts to guarantee that we know how."

"They're producing subpar paladin then," I argue.

"Bruiser, I appreciate your bloodlust—it's hot as fuck—but you're wrong on this. Repetition of movement and muscle memory, that's more important than actually shoving a knife, sword, mace, arrow, or any of the other magical weapons we can conjure up, into someone so that we know what it feels like."

I know Bastien is still talking to me, but this situation triggers the memory of the first time Talon ever hit me in training. One minute I'm with Bastien in Belarus, and the next I'm with Talon in the ring.

I wipe at blood from my split lip and stare at Talon in shock.

"You fucking hit me?"

"And?" Talon asks, his breath even in spite of the hours we've been sparring.

"We're training," I tell him, confused.

"Yeah, and you need to know how to shake off a hit."

Beth's rage-filled face pops up in my mind, and I try to shove it away. "I know how to take a hit," I tell him, my voice low, my eyes filled with fire.

"No, you know how to mentally and physically protect yourself while taking a beating. What I'm teaching you is how to work through the pain of a hit so hard it scrambles your senses. I'm teaching you how to navigate that so you can strike back through it. If you can learn to do that, then there will be no more beatings that you have to protect yourself from anymore, because you'll be the lethal one doling them out."

I shake away the echoes of Talon's voice in my mind and the pain that bubbles to the surface of my soul with it and snap back into the here and now.

"Killer, we told you before that none of us will physically hurt you in a fight. It's not about you; we wouldn't do that to each other either. Because just like Bastien said, it's not necessary," Knox argues.

"It will make you better fighters. All of us need to be the best we possibly can be. What don't you get about that?" I throw my arms out in frustration. "We have just a couple more hours of daylight, and you are wasting time. Let's go!" I clap my hands together like some kind of sports coach, but none of them break away ready for action.

"Squeaks, we know you pushed hard before. You were alone, and you did what you had to do, but you're not alone anymore; you have all of us now."

"Yeah, that's all fine and dandy until they wait for us not to be together to attack. Sabin and I were just grabbing supplies when those shifters came after us. I tried to do what I could, but there was just one of *me*. You all need to be able to do what I can do, and that includes fighting through pain and following through on all your hits in training. We can get healed; it's not like we're inflicting legitimate mortal wounds or something," I argue, and I wince at the panic I can hear in my voice.

Sabin separates from the group and walks toward the house we're staying in. I don't catch a glimpse of his face, so I can't tell if he's pissed, irritated, or just has to pee.

"Vinna, you know what sticklers we are about training," Kallan tells me, motioning to Enoch and Nash. "And how important the *three* of us think it is that you get as caught up as you can when it comes to your abilities."

"What's that supposed to mean?" Ryker demands. "You three aren't the only ones who care about her training."

"Could have fooled me," Nash mumbles, but it's just loud enough that everyone hears it.

"We are her Chosen. We care about her more than anyone or anything on this planet," Knox snarls as he takes a menacing step closer to Nash.

Valen shoots a hand out to keep Knox from charging, and I throw my head back in irritation that these fuckers are arguing again. Sabin rounds the corner from the front of the house, carrying what looks like a blanket, and makes his way back to where we're all standing. Their yelling is getting louder, their insults sharper as these fuckers face off again. Sabin walks toward the churning display of testosterone, but instead of jumping in the middle of it to help break it up, he just bypasses it, grabs my hand, and starts pulling me toward the trees.

"Um...what are you doing?" I ask confused, but not at all upset at being pulled away from these boys and their fucking drama. We've been here almost two weeks now, and not a day goes by where they're not sniping at each other about something.

"We're going to find a good spot in the woods, lay this blanket down, and then we're going to fuck," Sabin announces.

My head snaps to him, but he's tracing a path through the trees with his eyes and not looking at me. *Holy shit.* A flash of heat sparks through me, pooling at the apex of my thighs, and I quickly recall the few times Sabin's even kissed me.

"Why now?" I ask, not sure what the sudden rush is, not that I'm complaining, but I just figured he'd be the last and hardest to coax into this.

"Because you're right. Well, partially right anyway. I agree with Bastien that we don't have to stab each other to be the best possible fighters we can be. But I do agree that our enemies aren't going to come when we're at our strongest. They'll try to pick us off or come for the weak links."

Leaves crunch under our feet as we weave through the trees, and Sabin holds my hand firmly in his as he leads us further away from the houses.

"That night with the shifters and Elder Albrecht, I was the weakest link. I never want to be that again. I love you. You love me—even if it freaks you out to say it—I know you do. So I just don't see the point in holding off. We need to be united and as strong as we possibly can be."

I can't argue with the logic behind Sabin's words, but they don't exactly make me feel all warm and glowy either. I stop, and it yanks my hand from his when he keeps moving forward. Sabin looks back, his brow furrowed in question.

"So your sudden desire to fuck is all about duty and the greater good?" I ask flatly.

Sabin's forest-green eyes flit back and forth between my seafoam green irises. He takes a step closer to me, and the quiet intensity that surrounds him makes me shiver.

"My desire for you is not sudden or based on any sense of duty. I've wanted inside of you from the minute I walked in on you, Ryker and Valen in the closet. It was all I could do not to unfold that towel around your wet body and lick every drop of water from your skin. I've wanted to fuck you among the trees since the second I pulled you off of a runaway Darcy. Then I had to deal with the torture of riding back on Bennet, with you rubbing back against me with every hoof-fall. It would have been easy to reach around, unbutton your pants, and make you moan my name while we slowly made our way back."

Goosebumps breakout over my skin, and my nipples grow hard and needy with every word out of Sabin's mouth. He steps closer to me.

"I wanted to be inside of you when I told you I loved you and that you were more than I could have ever wished for. I should have been thrusting in and out of you when I confessed what a dumbass I was for not seeing that clear as crystal right away. I should have been begging for your forgiveness, with deep kisses while you were underneath me, your pussy tightening around my cock and begging for release."

Wind pushes a strand of hair in my face, and Sabin twirls it around his finger and watches the effect his words have on me. My eyes drop to his lips, and I step into him, the tips of my fingers lightly grazing the muscles of his stomach. My pussy clenches at the feel of him against my hands, his body brushing up against my peaked breasts, his breath on my face. I take the blanket from his pliant hands and move to spread it out.

There's a tree trunk practically at each corner, and it's not the most spacious or private, but it will have to do. I turn around to find Sabin's dark green eyes fixed on my every move. I kick off my shoes and step back onto the blanket, pulling my shirt up and over my head.

"O Captain! My Captain—" I don't get another word out of my mouth before Sabin's lips are on mine, his kiss drinking up my unvoiced invitation, his tongue lapping up my desire. I moan his name into his mouth as he pinches my sensitive nipples through my sports bra, and he hums in appreciation when I suck on his bottom lip the way I want him to be sucking on my breasts right now.

With no further direction needed, he whips my bra off, picks me up and lays me on my back on the blanket. His hot mouth latches onto my breast, and he sucks hard as he simultaneously flicks the tip of his tongue against my nipple. It sends zings of sensation from my chest to my clit, and I writhe underneath him, needing more. Sabin trades nipples and shoves his hand between my legs to rub my slit over my pants. I ride that friction as I yank his shirt off and push at the waist of his pants.

Sabin leans back, fire banked in his gaze, and he methodically slips his pants down his thighs and off. I run my greedy and appreciative eyes over his incredible body as he does. His creamy, smooth skin is a gorgeous contrast to the dark tattoo that runs up his left arm, and I want to trace every inch of muscle on his body with my tongue. I free myself of my bottoms, and the cool air against my wet pussy makes me ache for him even more. I spread my legs, and Sabin licks his luscious lips. He leans down to lick me, but I sit up and pull at his face.

"I need you to fuck me *now*."

A flash of violet magic sparks from me to him, but Sabin doesn't question it, he just smiles and then kisses me so deeply and thoroughly that nothing else matters right now. He nudges the tip of his cock against me, and as irritated as I am that he's not inside of me right now, he keeps hitting my clit in this delicious way, and it's distracting the fuck out of me. Out of nowhere, a wall of leaves flies up into the air and starts to swirl all around us, shielding us from the outside and instantly creating an intimate and stunning atmosphere. Reds, golds and purples cyclone around us, and I'm momentarily mesmerized by how breathtakingly beautiful it is.

Sabin rubs against my clit again, and I'm brought out of my trance by the feel of him all over my body.

I lean away from his kiss and smile. "Always the romantic, you and your leaf sanctuary."

He laughs and nips at my jaw. "Just in case we're not as alone out here as we thought. I don't want any distractions while I'm buried deep inside of you and you're screaming my name."

With that, I use my heel to kick him in his incredible ass. "Let's go then," I tell him and then click with my tongue the same way I do when I'm trying to get Darcy to pick up the pace.

He brushes a lock of hair out of my face, and then he watches my reaction as he slowly pushes inside of me. It's so torturous and perfect, and I can't help but close my eyes and revel in the feel of him filling me up. His hips meet my inner thighs as he releases a deep groan, and I kick him in the ass again, my need for him to speed the fuck up clear. Sabin laughs, and then he obliges.

I'm so lost in how good he feels I have no idea what I'm rambling, all I know is that I am. Sabin doesn't seem bothered by my incoherent encouragements; he just works me harder until he's fucking his name out of my mouth over and over again. His face is scrunched in concentration, and I suspect that he's trying to hold off his release, but my orgasm is just on the brink as he pounds into me deeply.

He watches me bring my hands up to pinch my nipples, and a few thrusts later he reaches between us and pinches my clit. Just like that, I explode and swirl exactly like the multicolored leaves still cocooning us, riding my orgasm like it's a whirlpool. Sabin presses his face into the crook of my neck and shoulder, purple magic crackling from me to him, and then he buries himself as deeply as he can get, the words, "I love you, Vinna," painting his orgasm.

10

"So, how long does it take usually?" Sabin asks as he pulls up his pants.

"Anywhere between twenty to forty minutes. Knox and Ryker seemed to have the biggest gap between *sealing our bond*," I tell him, using air quotes, "and getting their runes. Bastien's runes showed up around the twenty-minute mark, and so did Valen's. It's kind of a crap shoot," I offer with a shrug.

I pull my sports bra back on and watch the leaves still swirling around us as we both get dressed.

"I wonder why it's different?" Sabin muses to himself, but I don't say anything. Primarily because I have zero answers, but also because, in the grand list of questions I want answers to, this one just doesn't rank very high. I straighten my shirt on my body and lie back down on the soft blanket that barely pads the hard earth underneath us. I know we need to get back to the others and continue to work our asses off, but I just don't want to yet.

"What's the sigh for?" Sabin asks me, caressing my cheek with the back of his fingers.

"I'm not looking forward to going back to the cluster

fuck that is our training sessions," I tell him as I trace the shadowed trees that make up the tattoo on his arm with my fingers. "We take five steps forward and twenty back practically every day, and I don't know what to do about it."

"They're big boys, Vinna, they'll figure it out."

I snort humorlessly. "If by figure it out, you mean *take* each other out of the equation, then yes, I believe that's accurate."

Sabin chuckles and shakes his head. He watches the leaves that are still swirling all around us for a minute. "Enoch's coven is just a sore spot for all of us for one reason or another. We're a coven, and if you fuck with one of us, you fuck with all of us. For the twins, it started when the council made it very difficult for Lachlan or anyone else to go looking for the missing paladin. We know now that Elder Albrecht was working with Adriel all along, but we didn't know that then. The council dragging their feet and not sanctioning searches created a lot of issues between Lachlan's coven of paladin and the council."

Sabin's eyes fix on mine, and I nod with understanding.

"The twins carried the issues and frustrations that Silva and the others were experiencing and set them right at Enoch and his coven's feet. It wasn't fair, but the twins directed their frustrations at Enoch and Becket because of their fathers. Then there was the whole thing that went down with Ryker and his needing to be taken away from his dad. We're two of the most powerful covens our age, which has always put us head-to-head against each other for things like mates and our place as Paladin Conscripts.

"I'm not saying Enoch and his coven mates aren't responsible for this feud we have going on too. They've perpetuated this bullshit just as much as we have, but now to have *you* in the middle of it all and...well, cluster fuck. The covens have never trusted each other. Never had to work together, and the circumstances around Enoch, Nash, Kallan, and Becket being marked are suspicious as fuck."

"I know that, and I get it, but we don't have time for this petty shit. We could face off with Adriel any day now, and I'm worried if we do that, they'll be looking for opportunities to eliminate each other instead of the enemy. It's stressing me the fuck out."

Sabin sits up and pulls me into his lap, and I soak up the comfort. "Vinna, we know what's at stake here, but we all need time to adjust. Not only to each other, but to our bond with you and our new abilities. It's a lot."

"I get that, Sabin. I *really* fucking get that, but time is the one thing we just don't have."

He nods and then shakes his head. "Fuck, maybe we should do some trust exercises or something. I mean, shit, it couldn't hurt at this point," he mumbles.

I picture the guys all trust-falling backwards into each other's arms, and I crack up. "We'll throw yoga and group meditation into the mix too. I mean, worst case scenario, if they all kill each other off, I can at least start a pretty sweet resort here."

Sabin pulls me in for a laugh-filled kiss. He hisses when I pull away and nip at his bottom lip, but it's not the sexy kind of hiss a girl wants to hear when she's doing that. I climb out of his lap, and Sabin leans all the way forward like he's trying to crumble in on himself. I guide him onto his side and notice in my periphery that the leaves are no longer swirling around us but floating slowly down to the ground.

Movement to my right sends my heart racing, and alarms blare through my brain. *Fuck, not again, not when he's hurting*, I plea with the universe. In a blink, I have short swords gripped in each hand and am on my feet standing protectively over Sabin. He's rocking and groaning in pain on the ground, and I let anger fuel the rising fight in me. I'm fucking pissed that I'm dealing with some other shit instead of being there for Sabin when he's hurting.

I tap into the runes on my ring finger and signal to the guys that I need them. A naked man with long curly ash-brown hair seems as surprised to see me as I am to see him. He doesn't try to cover himself up; he simply tilts his head to the side and inhales deeply.

Shifter.

My mind identifies that much, but I have no idea what kind. He says something to me in a language that could be Russian, Belarusian, or fucking Swedish for all I know. I watch him and call on the runes to increase my hearing. The naked shifter repeats whatever he just said to me, but I focus on the sounds around me instead of his voice. I don't want to take my eyes off of him, but I need to make sure no one is sneaking up on Sabin and me from behind. The stranger takes a step forward, and I crouch automatically.

"I wouldn't do that if I were you," I warn him, and he stops.

Sabin cries out through clenched teeth, and the shifter's eyes drop to him, confused. I want to comfort Sabin like I've done with all the others, but locked in this weird standoff with this guy, all I can do is lamely tell Sabin, it's okay. I hear something moving fast toward me, and I flash a barrier over Sabin and me and prepare to have something slam up against it. Torrez's massive charcoal-gray wolf leaps out of the trees and lands in front of me.

The second the naked shifter sees him, he also shifts into a wolf. This guy's wolf is smaller, and his coat is primarily white and gray with touches of gold on his chest and his muzzle. They both flatten their ears, pull their lips back off their teeth, and release menacing growls at one another. They do this for what feels like a lifetime—but in reality is probably only twenty seconds—before they both stop and just stare unblinking at each other.

The tricolored shifter's eyes move to mine for a fraction of a heartbeat, and another growl vibrates out of Torrez. The shifter's yellow gaze snaps back to Torrez, and he lowers his head slightly like he's apologizing. They face off like statues for another beat before the shifter turns around and trots away.

I drop my barrier, and Torrez moves in a circle around me, sniffing at the air and the ground before he comes back to me and rubs up against my side. My short swords disappear, and I shove my hands into his thick dark fur. Adrenaline pumps through me, and I try to calm myself down now that the immediate threat seems to have passed. Or at least I think it has, judging by Torrez's sudden affectionate behavior. Bastien, Valen, Ryker, and Knox come running through the trees into the small little clearing, and Enoch, Kallan and Nash are right on their tail.

"What the fuck happened?"

"Are you okay?"

"Fuck, he's fast."

All sound off at the same time as everyone runs their gazes over me, Sabin who is clearly suffering on the ground, Torrez the wolf, and the woods all around us.

"I'm fine," I tell Ryker, answering his question first. "A shifter showed up out of nowhere. He surprised the fuck out of me just when Sabin's transference started," I tell Enoch, answering his question, and I ignore Knox's comment, figuring it was more a statement than anything that needs to be addressed.

"Where's the shifter?" Valen asks, his gaze moving through the trees around us.

Torrez flashes from his wolf into himself, and it's accompanied by groans and the others shielding their eyes.

"Come on, man, no one wants to see that," Knox whines as he fixes his eyes on the sky.

"You could have warned us or something," Bastien grumbles. I try not to laugh or stare too hard at Torrez's dick or his muscles or at Torrez at all, because Sabin is on the ground suffering from our bond, and the last thing I should be thinking of is where to pin the dick on the Sentinel. Torrez turns to me with a smirk, and I want to punch him in his overly sensitive nose for always knowing what I'm thinking because of how I smell. Traitorous fucking hormones—or whatever it is that makes me smell.

"We're on the edge of a pack's territory," Torrez announces, his heated eyes never leaving mine. "Muriel was patrolling when something about leaves caught his attention. I'm not sure what he meant; he has a pretty heavy accent."

I snort at the name Muriel, and Torrez looks at me, perplexed. "Muriel," I tell him, because really that's explanation enough, but it's clear he doesn't get it. "Just seems like a funny name for a big bad wolf shifter," I add. I look around to the other guys for support, but it seems I'm the only one amused by the revelation.

"Bunch of grumpy fuckers," I mumble to myself.

"Anyway," Torrez continues, gesturing to me and Sabin. "He ran into these two, asked them what they were doing, I showed up and explained, and we're now invited to dinner on Sunday." Torrez moves past me, his warm arm brushing mine, and it starts a delicious fluttering in my stomach and leaves a trail of goosebumps on my arm.

"Wait, what do you mean we're invited for dinner?" Kallan asks as Torrez moves further away from the group.

"Well, not you guys, I should say. Just Vinna and I," Torrez answers casually, like this is no big deal and none of the other guys should take any issue with it.

I count down in my head: *three, two, one...*

"Yeah, that's not fucking happening," Enoch and Bastien say at the exact same time.

"Jinx," I throw out on a chuckle, but once again, I seem to be the only one amused by what just happened. I sigh when both Enoch and Bastien just glare at each other.

"It's a formality that has to happen if we don't want issues with that pack. I'm a shifter who's staying close to their land with my mate, and it's polite to introduce yourself to the neighbors so they don't try to rip your throat out," Torrez tells them, as if that settles any argument they may have.

"Have you not seen the trouble that finds Vinna whenever she pairs off or tries to do anything alone?" Valen asks him.

My first reaction is to object to Valen's words, but as irritating as it is, he's fucking right. Torrez fixes his dark brown eyes on me, and the corner of his mouth twists up in a smirk. "She is a little trouble magnet, but I'm fast and strong and can more than hold my own, and she's...Vinna. We won't have any problems."

"You don't know anything about this pack. They could very well be working with Adriel, and you two are about to casually walk into a trap," Knox argues.

"Muriel's pack does not interact with lamia. I asked him, and he answered truthfully. Lamia know better than to try and breach an unfriendly pack's territory," Torrez states.

"Sorik," is all Bastien says, and Torrez turns to him, confused.

"Bless you," Torrez tells him after a beat.

Bastien rolls his eyes. "No, that's the name of the lamia who breached your pack territory to talk to Vinna."

A deep growl pours out of Torrez. "A certain trouble magnet was not very forthcoming with any information about that incident. She was too busy being stabby," he accuses.

"I was only stabby because your furry ass was being handsy," I defend.

"Lamia had just breached the pack boundary, for the first time in history, to get to you. I was making sure you were okay."

"You were fucking handsy, bro."

"You were my mate!" he exclaims, his tone exasperated.

"I...didn't know that at the time!"

"You two can fuck this out later; the point is that lamia can and will breach a pack's territory with the proper motivation," Bastien announces, and I don't miss the glint of amusement in his eyes.

Fucking weirdo.

"Vinna went with that lamia, Sorik," Torrez growls out the name. "He didn't attack a pack of shifters to get to her. So if she agrees not to go wandering off looking for trouble, all should be fine."

I roll my eyes.

"You all can stand on the border of their territory if it makes you feel any better, but I guarantee the pack isn't going to let you get any closer than that. And whether you like it or not, the Witch and I have to do this. I'm not sure how large the pack is, but even if they're relatively small, it's a bad idea to piss them off. The last thing we need is to add another enemy to our list. The invitation to join them for a meal has been extended, and we're going."

With that, Torrez walks away. "Stop looking at my furry ass, Witch," he shouts over his shoulder.

My eyes snap up from his completely bitable—and hairless—ass, and I adopt a completely innocent mien. Torrez flashes into a wolf and trots back in the direction of the houses like he doesn't have a care in the world. Ryker and

Knox both crack up, and I mentally chant *nothing to see here, folks*. I look down and find Sabin's forest-green eyes waiting for mine. I'm still standing over him, and I crouch to wipe sweat from his forehead.

"Fuck, are you okay?" I ask as I scan his face for any more hints of pain, then breathe a sigh of relief when I don't find any.

"Yeah," Sabin tells me, a slight tremor in his voice. "I think we shouldn't be allowed to wander off on our own anymore," he teases, and I can't help the chuckle that sneaks out of my mouth.

"Group sex it is," I tell him, and he barks out a laugh as I help him stand up.

"I'm totally making a t-shirt for you that says Trouble Magnet," Sabin teases.

"Make it black so it matches the Captain Cockblock shirt I'm making for you. Then we can walk around hand in hand, like one of those annoying matchy-matchy couples, kissing each other with too much tongue and freaking people out."

Sabin gets to his feet shakily, and Valen and Ryker reach out to steady him and help him back to the house. He shakes his head with a snort and looks back over his shoulder at me. "Like I said, you're trouble."

I rub a tired hand over my face as I watch them walk away and I can't help the chuckle that escapes me at Sabin's words. "You know you like it," I shout out as they disappear into the trees.

A distant but distinct, "Fuck yeah I do," reaches me through the foliage, and it tugs my tired, stressed out face into a smile.

11

We all stand in the middle of nowhere, running our eyes over everything we can see with the aid of flashlights and a gas lantern. Despite multiple arguments against it over the past three days, all of us stand in an awkward cluster near the border of the Volkov pack's territory. Muriel stands on the other side of the invisible line, patiently waiting for us to break apart.

"Are you fucking sure this is going to be okay?" Bastien asks Torrez for the nine millionth time today.

"It will be fine. If anything attacks the pack, you all can rush in and save the day. Stop worrying so much." Torrez pats Bastien on the back a couple times and then laces his fingers with mine.

I've never held his hand before, and it feels weird as fuck. The fact that I feel weird about it at all doesn't make a whole lot of sense to me because I'm pretty close to dry humping him at any given moment, so you wouldn't think hand holding would be a pearl clutching situation, but apparently it is. I feel like I'm about to go on a first date, although I guess I kind of *am* about to go on a first date. Torrez pulls me over the invisible line delineating the pack territory, and Muriel turns around and leads us away from the guys.

I don't look back or get too dramatic about saying goodbye to them. They're already at DEFCON one, and any sign of nerves or uncertainty from me could have them crossing the line literally and starting some messed up war with these shifters. Or at least that's how Torrez explains it, and since he would know pack rules better than the rest of us, we're deferring to his expertise on the matter.

Torrez lets go of my hand and wraps his arm around my shoulders instead. It makes it awkward to walk since I have my hands fixed to my side, but I relax after a minute and absorb his warm comfort. None of us talk as we make our way further into pack territory, and after about a half an hour, we walk into an open area that has two dozen cabins nestled inside of it. Muriel guides us through the smattering of log housing, and we reach a clearing at the center of all the houses. There are several long tables set up with benches that are full of the Volkov pack, who are already gathered and waiting for us.

The talking and boisterousness calms as Muriel leads us toward the rows of tables, and I try not to squirm as I feel the pack watching us and taking our measure. I take a deep breath and tell my nerves to fuck off. It may be Torrez that's making me nervous, but they won't know that. They'll just smell the unease, and I don't want to offend or put a target on my back. I shake off any anxiety and slip my game face on. Torrez gives me an approving squeeze, and I wrap the arm that's sandwiched awkwardly between us around his lower back. Torrez dips his head down and breathes me in, and as odd as that may be, it helps to fortify me for some reason.

Two people stand up from the center of the last row of tables, and Muriel leads us to them.

"Welcome, welcome, we are so very happy to have you. We don't get visitors often, so this is a treat for us," the large man standing bellows at us.

He looks like the human version of the Ghost of Christmas Present from *The Muppet Christmas Carol*. His red beard sways as he talks, and he bounces on the balls of his feet like he can barely contain his enthusiasm. I immediately like him.

"My name is Fedor Volkov. I am the alpha of this pack, and this is my mate, Manya Volkov."

He gestures to a tall lean woman with silvery-blonde hair and dark depthless eyes. She smiles sweetly at us and dips into a tiny little curtsey.

"I'm Mateo Torrez, formerly of the Silas pack, and this is my mate, Vinna Aylin," Torrez introduces in return.

"Oh, Aylin is it?" Manya asks, and her focus on my last name makes my hackles rise with worry. "You didn't take your mate's last name?"

I breathe through the rush of adrenaline, "Um, no I didn't," I tell her stiffly, and she nods at me politely.

"Come, sit, we're just getting ready to serve the first course," Fedor commands, and he motions to a space on the bench directly across from him. "Muriel informed us that you've only been in Belarus for a couple weeks; what brings you to this part of the world?" Fedor asks us as he settles himself on his side of the table.

I'm shocked how easily I understand Fedor and his wife. They have accents, but they're not so thick that it's a struggle to follow what they're saying. I'm insanely curious how their English is so good, but I don't want to be an asshole and risk being rude by asking them.

"Um, we're here to join some family that was checking out the area," I answer Fedor's question vaguely.

I sit down, and Torrez wraps his hands around my waist

and pulls me closer to him, which makes Fedor and his mate chuckle. I look around the table, and everyone is sneaking peeks at us and chatting quietly. Manya raises her hand, and on cue, people pour out of the closest cabin, carrying trays overflowing with food. They spread out around the tables that are filled with shifters and start handing out plates. A bread bowl with some type of thick soup or stew is set in front of me, and steam rises off the top, tempting me with its delicious smell. I move to grab the spoon that's been set next to the plate, but Torrez stills my hand, covering up the movement by intertwining his fingers with mine and bringing our hands back under the table.

I look at him curiously, but he just jerks his head in the direction of the alpha. I pause to look around and realize that everyone is watching him and waiting. Alpha Volkov scoops up the thick soup and shovels a bite into his mouth. He savors it for a moment and then swallows it. He turns to his mate and watches as she does the same thing. When Manya is done with her mouthful of food, the alpha gives a nod, and everyone else sitting at the tables digs into their meal. Torrez releases my hand and reaches for his spoon.

I take a cautious bite of the soup, and it's all I can do not to spit it out. It's fucking hot as hell! I form an O with my lips and breathe rapidly, hoping the cool night air might somehow help the molten food on my tongue burn a little less. *Motherfucker.* I blink away the water in my eyes and grab the cup in front of me to help ease the second degree burn I just gave my tongue. The smell of beer hits my nose as I take a deep pull from the cup, but the liquid is cool, and I'm pretty sure I just scalded off all of my taste buds, so this beer could taste like rotten piss, and I'm none the wiser.

I don't miss Torrez's snicker as he blows on his spoonful of soup and watches me wiggle in discomfort. "The food was steaming, you know. That's usually an indication that it's hot," he teases.

"I'll have you know that I was lulled into a false sense of security by the big ass bites Fedor and Manya took," I whisper yell at Torrez, while I try to discreetly fan my tongue with my hand.

A laugh rumbles from his chest, and I ignore what the sound does to my body. I manage to eat the rest of my soup and part of the bread bowl without incident, but I have no idea how it tastes. I suppose that could be one good thing about permanently damaging my ability to assess flavor. Even if they feed me something horrible, I won't offend them by not eating it because it all tastes like numbness to me.

"So, Torrez, you mentioned that you were *formerly* of the Silas pack. May I ask why you are not *currently* part of the Silas pack?" Fedor asks. He wipes his mouth with a cloth napkin and pushes away from the table to give his full stomach a little more room to breathe.

"Well, Alpha, I'm not sure what your pack rules are, but in my former pack, matings were only permitted between shifters. Because Vinna isn't a shifter, I had to leave the pack to pursue the mating."

I wave off the guilt that starts to creep into my mind at his words and instead focus on the alpha's response to Torrez's explanation.

"Ah I see. We don't put any major stipulations on our pairings so long as it can result in offspring," Fedor explains. "Although there are mostly shifters in these parts of the world, so we don't see as many inter-magic relationships, regardless of the fact that we're not opposed to them."

I open my mouth to ask what he means about the relationships having to result in offspring, but Manya cuts me off.

"We noticed she doesn't carry your scent; is it different for other supes than it is for shifters?" she asks, and I furrow my brow, perplexed by what she means.

Torrez stutters for a moment, and I turn to him, even more confused by his reaction to her question.

"Forgive my mate's boldness," Fedor apologizes. "She's always been curious and spoken her mind."

"It's fine," Torrez waves away the apology and takes a sip of beer. "Um, it's just that Vinna and I haven't completed the mating yet, so that's why her scent doesn't carry mine," he explains sheepishly.

Fuck, even I feel embarrassed by what he's saying, and I didn't even know this was a thing. Why do I feel like I just got caught doing something I'm not supposed to, or maybe in this case, caught *not* doing something I was supposed to?

Manya's head snaps in my direction, shock written all over her face. "You haven't completed the mating yet? Why in the world not?" she asks, just like that. Fedor doesn't jump in this time to apologize for his mate; he looks just as curious and shocked as his wife does.

"Uh...well...I mean...this just happened a couple weeks ago. I didn't really know how I felt about it, and there's been a ton of shit going down since then..."

"You don't agree with the pairing?" Fedor interjects, the judgement clear in his tone.

"No, it's not that. Yeah, in the beginning I didn't see it, but then...well...anyway, I'm on board now, but like I said, there's a lot going on, and there hasn't been time..." I trail off as Manya's eyes widen in horror, and she shakes her head at my explanation.

"We have a den we'd be happy to offer to you," she tells us, and I sputter on the sip of tasteless beer I'm currently trying to swallow. Torrez pats my back hard a couple times and tries to cover up the smile on his face.

"That's very nice of you, but we're okay. We're just taking things slow, getting to know each other, you know." It's clear by the looks they're both wearing that they do not, in fact, know at all.

"Why would you reject such a good mate?" a woman further down the table asks me, her tone baffled.

"I'm not rejecting him," I defend. "Is it hot out here?" I ask, and I turn to look around. "Is it suddenly hot to anyone else, or is it just me?" I fan my face and glare at Torrez as he chuckles into his cup while he steals another sip.

"You had to be a beta in your last pack," a man to my left announces, like that solves it all.

"I was," Torrez informs him.

"Dominant *and* good looking, what's wrong with you?" another woman asks me.

Animated chatter takes over the table, and I can't keep track of anything they're saying as it's a mixture of English and what sounds like a couple of other languages.

I look to Torrez to defend me against their crazy, but his smile grows wider, and he just shrugs like there's nothing he can do.

"Well, if you don't want him, I do," a large woman announces as she stands at the next table over. She's massive and looks like one of those heavy weight lifters you see in the Olympics, the ones with the tree trunk thighs and the bulldog face.

"You can't just challenge me for my mate!" I declare. "He's mine," I answer back, my tone a little whinier than I want.

"Technically she can. You aren't actually mated until it's consummated, and since you aren't interested in doing that right now, the challenge is fair," Fedor tells me and then looks at Torrez. "Brun would make a fine match; she'd bear you nothing but alphas, I'm sure."

It's all I can do not to tell Fedor he can shove that matchmaker shit up his alpha ass, but being that I'm already in enough trouble with this pack at the moment, I manage to keep my mouth shut. Torrez nods at the alpha like he's contemplating the offer of Brun and her alpha baby-making skills. I glare at him. The entire pack is already pushing tables out of the way to make a space in the middle of the clearing where it looks like this fight is about to go down. Brun is already on one side of the clearing, hopping up and down and stretching out.

"Is this for fucking real?" I whisper-screech at Torrez, and I look around to take in the growing excitement of the shifters all around us.

"Looks like it, Witch," Torrez tells me, with way too much amusement in his voice and sparkling in his eyes.

He's fucking loving this.

"I should just let Brun have you," I growl at him. "She'd probably break you in half with just her vagina, and then we'd see how funny you think all of this is," I grumble, and Torrez just smiles even bigger.

"Kinky," he retorts and then skips away before I can deck him.

"What are the terms of this challenge?" Fedor yells out, and the excitable shifters quiet down to hear him.

"No magic," Brun shouts out.

"Then no shifting," I call back.

"Winner is mated before sunrise, or they're open to challenge again," Manya announces, and I shoot her a *fuck off* look that doesn't faze her at all.

I watch Brun do the last of her stretches, and look down at what I'm wearing. Skinny jeans and a sweater do not make for the best gear to fight in, and I don't need to risk my range of motion being limited. I kick off my ankle boots, unbutton my pants and shimmy out of them.

"What are you doing?" Torrez hisses at me.

"Making it easier to move around," I hiss back.

I pull my sweater off over my head, leaving me in a tank top, bra and underwear. A few appreciative whistles sound off in the crowd, and Torrez releases a warning growl and puffs up in challenge. I can't help but appreciate the dose he's getting of his own medicine—and his nice pecs. Torrez sniffs at the air and turns his heated gaze on me.

"Fucking wolf nose," I grumble to myself, but apparently not quietly enough, because Torrez releases a bark of laughter.

He slaps me hard on the ass and pushes me forward. "Go win me," he instructs as I move closer to Brun.

I want to glare at him, but I'm too busy explaining to my vagina that we have to *not die* before we can fuck the annoying smile off his face. I'm pretty sure the scent of my arousal is perfuming the air all around me, and I attempt to mask it with anger as I hype myself up for this match. I assess Brun as I start to stretch out, but I'm mostly chanting in my head about all the things pissing me off at the moment and inviting the rage and bloodlust into my veins.

I go through all the shit with my Chosen and Enoch's coven, playing back every stupid fight and snipe they've made at each other. I tap into Silva and his disgust, and then shovel Lachlan's hate onto my pile of burning fury. I pick at every question I have that I'll probably never get the answers to, until they open up and bleed frustration into me. And when I repeat over and over again how this bitch is trying to steal what's *mine*, my game face slams down, my beastmode in full effect, and my soul cries out for blood and penance.

I go still on my side of the clearing and wait to be set loose. Fedor announces a bunch of shit I don't pay attention to because, instead, I'm picturing ripping this chick's head off on repeat in my mind. I'm so fucking keyed up that as soon as Fedor whistles, indicating the start of the fight, I charge.

I sprint toward Brun, who seems shocked by my move, but that's exactly why I did it. This big ass woman is probably used to fighting others who take their time and look for an opening to counteract her strength and size. But I don't fucking care if she hurts me, because I know I'm going to hurt her a hell of a lot worse. When I'm a couple feet away from Brun, who is now also running full speed toward me, I bend down as low as I can and tackle her around the thighs. We fall to the ground, and as her back slams into the dirt, I knee her between the legs.

Guys think they hold the pain rights to that move, but it fucking hurts for women, too. Brun shouts out and then growls at me. She uses her brute strength to roll me over, switching our positions, and tries to claim the advantage of being on top. I manage to get my bent legs between us, and when I feel the grit of dirt against my back, I push to straighten my legs and move Brun's big ass body away from me. I can't throw her completely off, but I can get her far enough away from me to land some head shots.

I hold her in the air with my legs, in some fucked up Superman pose, and pummel her face and neck with punches. She can't even manage a swipe in my direction because she's too busy guarding her head from my attack. She scrambles off of me, and I kip up onto my feet. She wipes blood from her nose and mouth with the sleeve of her shirt and spits blood at me, enraged. The insult falls short of where I'm standing, and I smirk at her. She comes for me, and I crouch down, making it look like I'm going for her legs again. She bends lower so as not to give me the advantage again, but at the last minute, I spring up and throw my arm out to clothesline her.

The hit rattles me, and I'm pretty sure I just fucked up my shoulder and forearm. Brun screams and scrubs at her face, trying to get her eyes clear of the dirt I just threw at her. I'm flung around onto her back from the momentum caused by Brun running and me throwing an unmoving arm in her way. I was trying to get her to go down again, but I can work with this too. I wrap my fucked up arm around her neck, my inner elbow tucked under her chin, and use my good arm to pull the headlock tighter. It fucking hurts, and I'm about seventy percent sure I've broken something, but I'll ride the pain in order to fucking end this bitch.

Brun scratches at my arms, and I bring up my legs to pin her arms down as she falls to her knees. I squeeze harder and feel a couple taps on my calf, but I ignore them. If she thinks I'm going to release her after she tried to take my motherfucking wolf, she's in for a rude fucking awakening. Brun falls to her side, and I go with her, but I'm locked in tight, and there's no way she's getting out of this. I squeeze until I feel her start to go limp, and then I move my hand under her chin so I can snap her neck.

"*Witch!*" Torrez yells at me, and I look up to find him only a couple feet away. "Stop. You won. This isn't a fight to the death; you can let her go," he tells me, but his words swim slowly in my brain, not making much sense.

He takes a step toward me, and I narrow my eyes at him and practically growl. Gasps sound off around me, but Torrez just smiles.

"You forget, Witch, the kill is not the prize tonight. I am. Let's do something else with all that aggression streaming through you." Torrez's tongue darts out to lick his full lips, and I track the movement and find myself mirroring it. His molten brown eyes dip down to my mouth, and he gives a little growl of approval. He offers his arm, and I debate for a second, my hand gripping Brun's chin, before letting go and setting my palm inside Torrez's.

"That's my girl," he coos at me before he throws me over his shoulder and slaps my ass hard. "Now, let's go make you mine."

12

Torrez practically kicks the door down, but I don't say anything about it since I find it hot as fuck. The *den* the Volkovs have provided is a small log cabin tucked back in the trees, away from all the other houses. I try not to think of it as *the house of fuck*, even though it's clear that's all this place is used for. I'd guess every mated pair in this pack sealed the deal in this place, and I try to not get the heebie-jeebies. I take in the rustic furniture and the big wood-framed bed and try not to think about what a blacklight would find in this place.

Torrez sets me on my feet and closes the door. He turns back to me, and that same predatory gleam is in his eyes that was there the other day when I ran from him. It once again sends flurries of anticipation and excitement blazing through me. He scents my emotions in the air immediately, and the corners of his mouth tilt up in a smirk.

"You going to run from me again, Witch? Let me show you how dominant I can be?" he asks, and my stomach flip flops at the gravel in his tone and the images his questions conjure.

"You want me to make you work for it, Wolf? Is that what

you need?" I ask curiously, hunger in my voice and wetness pooling between my thighs.

"I think you need me to earn it," he counters.

I contemplate those words and realize he might be right. I'm not sure why that is. I haven't felt that way with the others, but my relationship with Torrez has been different from the start. More aggressive. He brings out this side of me that I usually tuck away when I'm not fighting, and I like it. I eye him up and down and then meet his gaze with a teasing smile.

"So earn it then," I tell him, and then I leap toward the bed in an effort to get away from him.

I want the higher ground that the bed provides to defend myself better, but I clearly need to come up with a plan B because Torrez plucks me out of the air like a fucking frisbee and pulls me into him. Excitement squeaks out of me, but I bite down on it and push to get out of Torrez's arms. He nips at my neck in response to my half-hearted efforts, and my nipples grow hard. I bite him on the shoulder, and he growls and proceeds to back me into the wall.

"Sure you don't have any shifter in you?" Torrez asks me huskily.

"No idea," I answer, just as breathless.

Torrez licks the shell of my ear and then whispers, "You're about to."

I laugh at the awful pick-up line, and his eyes light up with mirth.

"Now kiss me, Witch," he orders as his hands skim up my sides, and he pins me against the wall with his hips. He pulls up the bottom of my tank top and whips it off over my head. I grab the back of his neck and pull his lips to mine. We fight for control of the kiss and battle for dominance over each other's mouths. I bite Torrez's lip, but he doesn't even flinch when I draw a small amount of blood.

He just growls into my mouth and grinds up into my spread thighs.

He paws the front of my bra and tugs it away from my body. I wore actual clothes for this dinner instead of workout gear and, therefore, a proper bra, clasps and all. I pull away from his bruising kiss. "Don't fucking rip it," I warn him. "I only have so many good bras on this trip."

He groans and kisses his way across my jaw. "I've never been good at these evil little contraptions," he tells me between kisses, pulling on the front of it again.

I laugh. "You're telling me the big bad wolf has been bested by a bra?"

Torrez smiles at my teasing challenge and then rips the bra off me in one quick pull. "Not anymore," he tells me with a smirk.

"You fucking prick," I yell at him and push off against the wall with my good arm in an effort to unpin myself. "You did not just do that after I told you not to!" I try to push him away from me, needing adequate distance so I can yell at him, but he fights to keep me pinned. I ignore how much I like that and focus on my outrage over the battered garment that's been flung to the ground. We wrestle back and forth, me gaining some space between us, and him slamming me back against the wall and pressing into me.

I realize I've been duped into thinking I'm going to gain the upper hand, when I shimmy up high on the wall and try to kick out at Torrez. He simply smiles the epitome of a wolfish grin, grabs my leg, puts his big hands under my ass and pulls my center right to his face. He nuzzles my wet panties and sniffs deeply.

I slap his arm. "Quit being fucking weird," I growl at him and then bite back a moan when the tip of his nose circles my needy clit.

He brings one hand out from where it's supporting me

high upon the wall and grabs the side of my panties and rips them off too. *This motherfucker better believe he's buying me new underwear.* Torrez latches onto my clit and starts to suck on it, and all thoughts of underwear shopping go flying out of my sex-hazed brain.

I crack my head against the log wall when I throw it back to shout out a "fuck yes!" Torrez eats, sucks, and licks me like he's trying to win a pie eating contest, and my pussy is the pie. And not just any pie, like the best pie he's ever tasted, and he's determined that no morsel should be left behind. I come so hard that I unashamedly grab Torrez by the back of his neck and grind against his greedy mouth as I ride out my orgasm. He growls in approval, and the vibration of it sends me up and over into another orgasm that leaves me jelly-like and has me practically melting into the wall with satisfaction.

Torrez slides my body down his, and I realize he's still completely dressed. I'm two orgasms in and blissed out, and I haven't even managed to get him naked yet. I reach for his shirt and pull it off, needing to feel his warm skin against mine immediately. I hurry to unbutton his pants, ignoring the twinge it causes in my shoulder and forearm. I push them down his hips, and his erection springs out like an aggressive beacon of promised pleasure. I blame my post-orgasm brain, because the next thing I know, I'm kissing the tip of Torrez's cock and thanking it in advance for what it's about to do.

"Did you just thank my cock?" Torrez asks on a choked laugh.

I pause for a minute and try to come up with some logical explanation for what I just did, but there just isn't one.

"I did," I admit as I straighten up to admire my handiwork.

Naked Torrez is a feast for the eyes. Silky bronze skin, muscles for days, a smattering of black chest hair that trails down to a cock apparently worthy of worship. My mouth and vagina water as I take him in. He stands proudly, an amused smile on his face, happy for me to eye fuck him for as long as I want. He trails a finger down the runes on my sternum, and my nipples get even harder at the soft touch.

"Turn around, my Witch, and face the wall."

I spend about three milliseconds debating if I'm going to fight his command, but who am I kidding, I'm fucking dripping I'm so into what's happening right now. So I do as I'm told and turn to face the wall, delicious anticipation unfurling in my stomach. Torrez pushes all my hair over my right shoulder and skims his lips over the runes on the top of my left shoulder. Sentinel magic flashes to life on my arms, and Torrez tenses for a moment.

"It's okay," I reassure him. "It's part of completing the bond. It won't hurt."

I reach back and take Torrez's hand and slowly bring it in contact with a flash of purple magic. It does what it has with the rest of my Chosen and sinks into him, eliciting a pleasure-filled groan from Torrez's full lips.

"See," I tell him, and he nips at my neck, making me moan in response.

Torrez trails his hands up the runes on my arms, soaking in all the violet strikes of magic that flash from me to him. He traces the runes on my ribs and then runs a hand up the runes that frame my spine. I'm so worked up that I'm on the verge of begging by the time he places a large palm between my shoulder blades and applies pressure. He pushes my upper back forward with one hand and pulls my hips back toward him with the other. My ass is now pressed even more snuggly against his hard cock, and I rub against the length, not able to help myself.

"I've been dreaming about bending you over just like this and fucking you just like this since you sauntered into the ring and challenged me."

Torrez thrusts into me hard on the word "fucking," and I have to press my hands against the wall to keep from careening into it. He buries himself deep inside of me, and we both groan appreciatively. Torrez doesn't move right away, and I'm torn between needing him to and trying to figure out what he's going to do next. He keeps one hand on my hip, and the other trails around my side, up my ribs, and stops at my throat. He bows my body until my back is flush with his powerful chest and then whispers into my ear.

"You feel even better than I thought you would, *mate*," and with that, he starts to piston in and out of me at a perfect, punishing pace.

I reach one hand back and sink my fingers into his thick short black hair as he arches my body and fucks me so hard and so good that I can only hold on for the ride. His hand drops from my throat and cups my heavy breasts, kneading and pinching each one, sending more strikes of pleasure through me as he does. My whole body ripples in pleasure with each deep thrust Torrez perfectly delivers, and I'm torn between never wanting him to stop and begging for the building orgasm inside of me to pull me under already.

His hand drops from my breasts, and he reaches down and starts playing with my clit. I shout out, and Torrez growls encouragingly in my ear. "Scream for me, Witch. Scream your mate's name while I mark you and make you mine forever."

I open my mouth to call him a *bossy fucker*, but pain tears through the top of my left shoulder, and then an orgasm slams into me like a freight train. I scream Torrez's name, not able to help it, and I have no idea if it's from the pain he's responsible for or the pleasure. He slams into me one last time, calling out my name as his release flashes through him. We both ride our waves of pleasure, connected by body and now soul, and I sag against him as my release ebbs and my body tingles with satisfaction. He licks at my shoulder, and it soothes some of the pain he just inflicted there.

I look down to figure out what the hell hurt so bad. "Did you fucking bite me, Wolf?" I demand, swiping at my shoulder and the blood that's seeping out of the puncture wounds there.

"It's part of mating with a shifter," he tells me casually as he kisses over the wounds that must be on the back of my shoulder too. "I have to mark you in order for our magic to blend and the bond on my side to be complete."

"Well, warn a girl next time, will ya? That's the second time you've bitten me, and it fucking hurts."

Torrez chuckles and runs the fingers he still has buried in my folds in a slow circle around my clit. I squirm to get away from him, feeling oversensitive, like any touch is just too much right now.

"You'll like it now that the bond is sealed," he tells me, absently pulling my face to his for a soft kiss. "My wolf instincts will push me to mark you, but it won't hurt you now. Many mated females say it makes them orgasm right away."

Torrez pulls out of me, and I clench around the absence of him, a little sore. We both move to the ensuite bathroom to clean up, and I run my eyes over the runes on his sternum and swallow down the worry that starts to bubble up inside of me. I'm not sure if I fucked something up when I marked him. I hope that Ryker's orgasm theory is right and what we just did together solidifies the connection just like it has with the others, but I can't help but worry that it might not. I take the appearance of my Sentinel magic while we were together as a good thing and figure it's all a waiting game at this point. One way or another, we'll know soon enough.

I look up from where I'm washing my hands in the sink, and Torrez is watching me in the mirror.

"What?" I ask, my eyes bouncing back and forth between his deep brown irises.

"I just can't believe that I found you. That I finally have a mate," he tells me, his eyes soft and his voice filled with wonder.

I give him a sweet smile. "Am I up to snuff, everything you hoped I'd be and more?" I tease.

Torrez chuckles and runs a soft finger over the bite I now sport on my left shoulder. "You know, it's weird, but I never could picture what my mate might be like or if I would ever find one. I felt inside like I was meant for more. That probably makes no sense, but I just felt like there was more out there for me than pack life and raising pups. I used to think maybe that was just my ego talking, but now, as I sit here staring at you, it all just makes sense to me."

Torrez's words soak into me, and they spread warmth as they move from my mind to my soul.

"It makes sense to me too," I admit. "I never fit in any kind of way in the non world. I saw glimpses of more, and I knew I was meant for that; I just couldn't seem to get there."

Torrez nods his head, and I can feel the understanding radiating off of him.

"It's strange that I'm all over here, like don't mind me and my six mates, and somehow none of that actually feels weird to me at all. Is it weird for you?" I ask, watching him in the mirror. "You thought you'd have one mate and probably never thought that you'd have to share her with five other guys."

He shrugs. "So you're greedy. There are worse traits in a mate."

I laugh and turn to punch him in the shoulder. He captures my hand and pulls me out of the bathroom and toward the bed.

"Um, there is no chance in hell that I'm getting in that bed," I tell him and try to tug my hand out of his grip.

"They get a new mattress and new sheets after every mated couple. They give the couple the mattress and sheets for their own use as a present."

I furrow my brow in doubt at his statement.

"Everything smells clean," he tells me, folding back the bedding and pulling me hesitantly into the sheets.

They're cool and soft and smell like pine trees. Torrez's warm body is inviting, and I press into him for warmth and a much needed distraction from lying in an unknown bed, in an unknown country, in an unknown pack's territory. He nestles me under his arm, our naked chests pressed together, and plays with the ends of my long hair down my back as we settle in.

"So, Torrez—"

"Teo, call me Teo," he interrupts.

"But I know you as Torrez."

"Yeah, but that's my last name, and we're all mated for life and shit, so you should call me Teo."

I'm quiet for a beat, mulling over how weird it would be not to think of him as just Torrez. "So, Wolf," I say instead.

He laughs. "Fair enough," he concedes. "Yes, Witch?"

I chuckle at the equally hideous pet name. "Like you said, we're all mated and shit, so we should probably, you know, get to know each other?" My statement comes out more like a question, and he vibrates with laughter against my body.

"What, you're telling me you want to know all about my childhood and every detail of my life until now? We might be here for a while," he teases and then presses my body tighter against him. "Although I suppose there's nothing wrong with being here for a while," he admits, his voice lowering seductively.

I run my fingers through the short black hair on his chest and laugh. "No, nothing wrong with that at all," I agree. "I don't need every detail; I'm sure there's a lot of time spent on the toilet that's not pertinent to our future lives together, and in your case, a good chunk of time scratching yourself in wolf form. You can skip all of that," I tell him.

He laughs even harder and slaps my ass. I squeak in surprise and clench my thighs together as the sting moves from my cheek to my clit. I can practically smell the arousal that suddenly perfumes the room, but Torrez doesn't acknowledge it.

"You want details, but not too many." He trails off for a second. "Let's see... I'm originally from a pack in Canada, but most of that pack, including my parents and four brothers, were wiped out in a fight over land with another pack."

I sit up to stare at Torrez's face, but he's not wearing any hurt or sadness. He's just stating the loss of his family as fact, just a part of his story. I run my hand over his cheek, and he leans into it slightly and nuzzles my palm. I rest my head back down on his chest and wait for him to say more.

"I migrated south with other survivors of my pack and broke off on my own with a couple of other bachelors when we came of age. We traveled a lot and ended up in Maine somehow. One of our group met his mate in the Silas pack. I was tired of roaming, so I petitioned Silas to join, and I've been there for about forty years now."

I choke on air and sit up to cough. "You what? How old are you?"

"I'll be 109 in January."

13

"Holy shit!" I exclaim and try and then fail to process that number.

"Shifters live about four times the lifespan of humans. We age at the same rate as most nons until we hit puberty, and then it slows down. Did you not know that?" he asks confused.

He sits up next to me and watches my face. "I did *not* know that. I mean, it is what it is, but what are you doing with a twenty-two-year-old? Don't you want to be with someone who can talk about the good ol' days of prohibition and the discovery of the Americas and shit?"

He narrows his eyes at me and then pounces. He presses me back against the bed, and I laugh hysterically. He starts to tickle me, and I squeal and writhe to get away from him.

"*The discovery of the Americas*, really?" he demands.

"It's not my fault you're old!" I shout at him and wiggle to get away from his hands.

"I'm not old; by shifters' standards, I'm like twenty-eight."

"Yeah, but by my standards, you're ancient as fuck. Oh

man, just wait until the others find out. I can hear the geriatric jokes now."

"Ancient or not, I can still kick all of your asses, so bring it," he challenges.

"Pshhhh, I seem to recall fucking with that undefeated record you were so proud of."

"I demand a rematch. I was too busy checking you out to fight properly," he defends.

"Oh please, don't make me break your jaw again. I can think of way better things I'd rather do with your mouth." My smile is salacious, and I wag my eyebrows at him.

Heat replaces the amusement in Torrez's eyes, and he leans down. "Is that right, Witch?" he asks against my lips.

I flick the seam of his lips with my tongue and reach down and palm his hardening cock. "Mmmm, so many better uses for that mouth of yours," I tell him, and then I flip him onto his back.

He growls in approval, and I waste no time in lining him up and dropping myself down his thick length at a maddeningly slow pace. I watch as Torrez's eyes grow hooded, his gaze fixed on where I'm connecting us. He loses his patience with my teasing pace and lifts his hips off the bed, pushing deep inside of me. I moan his name and push him back down on the bed. I lean forward and bite at his earlobe.

"You got to be bossy last time. It's my turn," I whisper in his ear.

I roll my hips back until he slides almost all the way out of me and then curl them forward until I'm clenched around the base of him again. I skim my lips over his jaw and then bite his neck, leaving satisfying imprints of my teeth in his beautiful bronze skin. I push against his chest with my palms and sit up so I can lift my hips and drop them back down over and over again.

Our eyes are locked on each other, heated and intense,

and I fucking love the worship and pleasure pouring out of his molten chocolate gaze. He calls out my name, and the sound of it on his lips spurs me on. I grab his hands where they're gripping my waist and move his palms up to my breasts. I knead them over his hands until he starts touching me exactly the way I want him to, and I drop a hand down to play with my clit as I ride my Wolf with wild abandon.

I cry out as he pinches my nipples hard, and I rub my clit faster, causing the tingles in my limbs to move into my core ready and waiting to explode out again.

"Fuck, you feel good, Wolf," I tell him, and with that, he thrusts up into me and practically howls out his release.

I grind down onto him, and just as I'm about to go over the edge, pain punches me right in the chest, and my lungs deflate from the force of it. I collapse on Torrez with a whimper, and I realize through the fog of searing, white hot burning, that every muscle in Torrez's body is taut and strained and probably experiencing the same brutal hurt that I am right now. I can't move, and if I don't get air to inflate my lungs soon, I'm going to pass out. Torrez screams out, but it quickly turns into a snarl, and in the back of my mind, I wish I could comfort him, but I'm just as fucked right now as he is.

Between my strangled cries, I try to tell myself that this is good. I'm hurting because the bond with him is working, and his runes are searing themselves exactly where they always should have been. I didn't fuck up the connection. I wish I could feel relief about that right now, but all I feel is pain, and it seems like it's lasting way longer than it did when I got my first Chosen runes. I bite down on another wave of agony and taste blood in my mouth. I know I'm not going to die, but I know I'm reaching the threshold of what my body can take.

Arms wrap around me, and I scream, not able to hold it

in anymore. I'm faintly aware of the fact that Torrez is still deep inside of me, and with that thought, I hear Torrez say something to me, and then I feel his teeth sink into my arm. An orgasm shoots through me, battling the white hot pain in my body for my attention. It's too much, the feel of so many conflicting sensations in one body, and I feel myself rapidly shutting down before everything blinks black.

* * *

I feel like I'm underwater. Everything sounds muffled and fuzzy. I can hear my heart beating steadily in my chest and feel an echo of pain that's resonating in every inch of my body. I release a small moan that seemed to be trapped in my throat, and Torrez brushes damp hair out of my face and tenderly kisses my lips.

"Fuck, you scared me," he tells me, and it's almost as if I can taste his worry on the back of my tongue.

"That was the weirdest orgasm in the history of orgasms. Never do that again," I croak, and Torrez laughs and helps me sit up in his lap.

The realization of what just happened flashes through me, and I look down at my shaky hands in panic. A new black rune sits on the knuckle of my ring finger, and it's a perfect match to the rune that sits under the eight-pointed star on Torrez's ring finger. I breathe out a sigh of relief and quickly go through the checklist to make sure everything is working as it should. I tap into Torrez's rune in the line of runes on my head behind my ear.

"Can you hear me?" I ask, and his eyes go wide.

"Did we form a pack link?" he asks me in shock. "I didn't know that could happen with mates that had different magic," he confesses, and there's a spark of excitement in his eyes.

"I'm not sure how a pack link works, but I can do this with my Chosen. The runes that are now behind your ear, this is what they do. We can talk individually, or you can call on all of them and we'll all be linked and able to talk at the same time."

I release the magic in the runes on my head and activate the runes on my chest. "Can you feel what I'm feeling?" I ask. I watch his face as it scrunches up in confusion and then surprise.

"You feel relieved and tired..." Torrez tilts his head to the side in thought, and the corner of his mouth lifts up in a wry smile. "How are you horny right now?"

I shut the runes on my chest down, slamming the door on the connection. Torrez laughs.

"Like you said, I'm greedy," I announce defensively, and he laughs even harder. I shake my head at him and fight the smile that wants to take over my face. "Don't be jealous of my super powers," I tell him, and he completely loses it. Tears spill out of his eyes and down his cheeks, and he's so fucking beautiful in this moment, I almost can't take it.

"Seriously, give me a cape, and I'd be legit as fuck," I tell him.

"Edna says no capes," he deadpans, and it's my turn to crack up.

"Fine," I announce through my laughter, "give me some knee high boots and an armored bikini. I'm pretty sure that's what most female superheroes are allowed to wear these days anyway."

"And then what do we call you?" he asks, wiping tears from his cheeks.

I think about it for a minute and then lose myself in hysterical laughter. After a couple minutes, I get myself under control enough to say, "You can call me The Greedy Vagina." I crack up again, laughing so hard my cheeks and stomach hurt. "Watch out, world, here comes The Greedy Vagina and The Geriatric Wolf."

Torrez throws his head back and bellows out his laughter, and I join him, not able to help it. "Worst...fucking...superhero...names...ever!" he pants between chortles of laughter.

"I know," I agree. "I should never...be allowed...to name anything...ever again!"

Realization hits me, and I slap a hand to my forehead. "I am the worst mate ever!" I call on the runes for all of my Chosen behind my ear.

"Are you guys okay?"

"You're a little late, Squeaks; we've all been recovering for a good forty minutes," Ryker announces, and I instantly feel like shit.

"I'm so fucking sorry, you guys! I sort of passed out and woke up a little loopy," I admit.

"It's all good, Killer. It freaked the fuck out of Enoch, Kallan, and Nash, so totally worth it." I laugh at the glee in Knox's tone, but I feel bad for Kallan and the others. Watching all of my guys drop in pain for no reason would be scary as hell.

"So I take it the transference went okay with Torrez?" Bastien asks, and before I can answer that it did, Torrez speaks up.

"Yup, I'm officially part of the crew," he announces, and my mind fills up with *"welcomes"* and *"congratulations."* My soul feels like it's practically glowing with the exchange, and I realize that even though I've been terrified to label the things that I'm feeling, it doesn't change the fact that those feelings have taken root and are blooming on their own. This little flower doesn't give a fuck if I want to look at it or not; it's growing, regardless of my desire to acknowledge its existence.

"*Everyone have new runes?*" I double-check, needing to make sure that nothing is missing.

"*We sure do. Everyone is connected to Torrez now, and what's even better is that Enoch and his boys are still rocking the runes they had before, which further confirms that they're not Chosen.*" I can hear the relief and happiness in Valen's voice, and I hope that this realization helps all of them get their heads in the game and has them spending less time worrying about shit that's out of our control.

"Well, we're going to, um...get dressed, and then we'll head your way," I tell them awkwardly. I know they don't seem to care about which one of them I'm fucking, but it still feels weird to be so casual about it.

"*You're evil, Vinna, making all of us think about you naked right now,*" Sabin mock-scolds.

I laugh. "*Sorry, not sorry,*" I tease and then instantly regret it as I'm flooded with images from each of them of exactly what they'd like to do to me in my current state.

"*You sneaky fuckers!*" I shout out as I tear away from the connection and have to immediately start talking my libido down.

Torrez cracks up when I shoot out of his lap and speed walk to the bathroom. "You have some very creative mates," he calls after me. "I'm just bursting with all kinds of new ideas and plans now."

I slam the bathroom door behind me and lean against it, breathing heavily. I swipe at my face with my hands and chuckle at just how unhinged I am from their delectably dirty minds. I flip on the light and turn to the sink to splash water on my heated face. It doesn't help. Fuck, maybe I need to take a freezing cold shower in order to deal with the hormones that are currently surging inside of me. I look up at my reflection and immediately my eyes land on the new runes I have on my left shoulder.

"What the hell?" I ask absently, as I lean forward to get a better look at the new symbols that are now marked in my skin. There are eight of them, and they form a sort of half-moon shape. I realize quickly that it's not actually a half-moon that they're forming, more like there's a rune in each place where every tooth pierced my skin when Torrez bit me. I turn around and find eight more runes on the back of my shoulder, too. I open the door and poke my head out.

"Just out of curiosity, how does it work when you mark me?" I ask, going for nonchalant, but coming across squeaky.

"Um, it's kind of complicated, but the simple version is that shifters sort of partially shift, or at least our mouths do, and we bite our mates. Why?"

"Um, because this happened," I tell him, stepping out and pointing to the new runes on my shoulder.

"Yeah, those showed up a couple minutes after you passed out. Do you know what they do?" he asks, and I do what I always do when I have no fucking clue about anything, I shrug. I look down and run the pad of my index finger over one of the new runes, tracing the symbol as I contemplate.

"I guess we'll find out, but I don't know that this place is the best environment to do that," I tell him as I motion to the cabin we're currently holed up in.

"Do you think you might be able to shift?" Torrez asks, and I don't miss the eager glint in his eyes.

"Honestly, your guess is as good as mine at this point," I admit and then rub at my temples. I look around the room, and as much as I want to crawl back into the bed and have a little nakey-nap, the others are waiting for us, and we've gotta go. "Any chance you have my jeans and sweater?"

"Oh, you mean the ones you stripped out of before the challenge?" he asks, his tone clearly stating his disapproval.

"I wouldn't have been able to move like I needed to," I defend. "You could be in here right now with Brun, so you just think about that before you go trying to get all territorial on me," I scold, and he laughs.

Torrez walks over to a chair in the corner and picks up my neatly folded clothes, handing them to me. I'm not sure what time it is, but I'm hoping it's late enough that the pack is asleep, and we can just sneak off without having to do a walk of shame. I snag Torrez's jeans off the ground and reach inside to steal his underwear. I pull out a pair of black boxer-briefs and shake them at him.

"If I have to go commando, so do you," I declare, and annoyingly, Torrez seems more amused by this than he is upset. He smiles at me the whole time we're both getting dressed. I pick up my shredded under clothes and stuff them in Torrez's pockets. He breathes me in deeply as I manhandle him and pulls me in for a soft kiss before I can step away. I almost give a contented sigh against his lips, and then I remember that I'm irritated that I have no comfy and supportive undergarments on. I narrow my eyes at Torrez, and he laughs. It's clear he knows the effect he has on me, and he's playing dirty.

"Careful, Wolf," I warn, my tone seductive as I trail a finger down my chest. "Two can play that game." He pulls me closer, and I lean in toward his mouth, loving the heat in his eyes. At the last minute, I veer to the side, denying him a kiss, and whisper in his ear, "Let's be super quiet as we sneak out of here; maybe they won't notice that we've left." I don't wait for him to answer before I'm reaching for the door and pulling it open. He growls irritably and reaches for me, and I laugh quietly and make a run for it.

I freeze just outside of the doorway, and Torrez slams into me. "Shit," Torrez swears as he grabs my waist and keeps me from tumbling down the front stairs. "You can't just stop..." he starts to tell me, and then he stops talking as he sees what I'm seeing. A couple of female shifters and a handful of males all straighten up as we stumble out of the door. All of them sniff at the air, and I watch as each of their faces fall, and a couple of them make irritated noises before walking away.

"Um, what the fuck was that?" I ask Torrez, who moves to stand shoulder to shoulder with me.

"Those were the members of the pack who were hoping to give challenge, just in case your mating wasn't sealed," Manya explains as she and Fedor walk toward us from the surrounding trees. "But it looks, and smells, like everything is in order. Congratulations, you two," she exclaims, opening her arms and pulling Torrez and me in for a hug.

"She's no Brun, but she's stronger than she looks," Fedor tells Torrez, with some hard slaps to his back, like he needs the words of encouragement or consolation.

Torrez looks down at me, and I can just tell he's silently warning me not to nut punch the alpha. *"She's no Brun,"* I mock in my head and then jump when Torrez sneakily drops his hand from around my waist and pinches my ass. "Don't do it, TGV," he warns me casually.

I choke on a laugh at the abbreviation of my horrible superhero name as Torrez leads me away from the alpha couple.

Yep, I should never be allowed to choose names for anything...ever.

14

My phone vibrates, pulling me out of that in-between gray world that exists when you're trying to sleep, but you're not, and yet you're not completely awake either. I look at the incoming text and smile, quickly gauging how difficult it will be to sneak out of here without waking anyone up. Bastien's hand is resting on my hip, and I gingerly lift it and set it on the mattress next to his warm body. Then I untangle my legs from Ryker's and have to unthread Knox's fingers from out of my hair. Sabin, one bookend to this little cuddle party, has his back to me. While Valen, who's on the other end, is holding the corner of my long pillow with an outstretched hand. The room is filled with the slow, deep breaths of sleep, and I tiptoe my way out of the room, trying not to jostle anyone too much.

I discovered one night when I had to get up to pee, that Torrez likes to run as a wolf at night. So I'm not overly surprised that he's not fast asleep like the others. I don't know how he's not a walking zombie all the time, between training all day and running at night. He's been pushing hard to catch up with the rest of my Chosen since he got all of his Sentinel runes, and I figured he'd crash at the end of the day like the rest of us. I guess there's no hitting the snooze button when it's time to *feed the beast*, as Torrez likes to call it.

I make my way out the front door and circle to the back of the house. My phone lights up when I unlock it, and I click on the text message that brought me out here in the first place. I send a quick reply as I move toward the trunk of a fallen tree just inside the tree line behind the house. I click on the contact and press the green phone button, bringing my phone up to my ear.

"Hey, Vin, did I wake you up?"

"Na, I was pretty much up but trying to convince my brain not to be. What are you up to? It's getting kind of late there, isn't it?"

"It's only nine thirty, and I'll go to bed soon. I was just working through the last video you sent, and I had a question."

"What's up?" I ask as I settle against the big log.

"Okay, so you talk about combos and then show me a couple of different ways I can hit someone multiple times without giving them a chance to hit me. But in the fourth combo you do, would it work if, when I spin, I throw an elbow into their side and then deliver the kick, or would that mess with my momentum or something?"

I chuckle. Who knew Captain Cockblock had such a kickass little sister? Cyndol and I have been texting back and forth since I met her. She's filled me in on her *mean girl* problem, and I've been talking to her about self-defense and radiating *don't fuck with me* vibes. When the guys and I started training here, I saw the perfect opportunity to send her some visuals. I'm pretty sure the guys think I'm crazy when I force them to practice the basics at the beginning of every training session we do. I always spout some bullshit about how brushing up on the basics makes us better at everything else, and they just go with it.

What they don't know is I record our *back to basics* sessions and send them to Cyndol every afternoon so she can practice. Sabin's going to go mental when he finds out about this, but I figure by then, Cyndol will be able to take him, so it's all good.

"So combos can be tailored to what feels right for you. It's important to follow your instincts when you're practicing and getting a feel for the flow of the hits, because what may feel natural to me will be different for someone bigger and stronger than me or someone smaller than me," I tell her.

"Okay, that makes sense. I just wish I knew how it feels to actually hit something. I mean, just practicing the movement is good, but how will I know if an elbow will work without actually throwing an elbow to see if it messes with my balance or momentum?"

I beam at her question and send her a mental hug through the phone. If only I could get my Chosen to think the way Cyndol does.

"That's why I ordered you a combat dummy," I tell her, and I'm so fucking excited about it that you'd think I was the one getting a present.

"No way! Are you serious? Oh my heck, you are the freakin' best, Vin. I can't wait!" I can hear Cyndol jumping up and down and squealing excitedly as she does. It makes my heart so fucking happy that I'm resisting the urge to jump up and down myself.

"It should be arriving at my house in the next couple of days," I tell her, and we both squeal again. "I already talked with the sisters, and they're going to call you and arrange a time to sneak it into your room. So keep an eye out for their call, okay?"

"Crap, I think my screaming woke up one of my dads. I

gotta go. I'll text you later, you're the freaking best, Vin, love ya!"

"Night, Cyn, love you too!"

The call ends, and I stare at it, smiling for a couple of seconds before pulling up another number and calling that.

"You okay?" Mave croaks, and I chuckle.

"What are you doing in bed? It's not even ten there," I ask as I pick at the bark on the tree I'm sitting on.

"It's been a long couple of days. I miss you. When are you coming back?" she asks me.

I sigh. "I don't know. Training is coming along pretty well actually, which is a massive relief, but the paladin are still tracking the lamia and trying to figure out where Lachlan and Keegan might be. So far, they've got nothing, and the rest of us are just waiting."

I look out toward the barn, and surprisingly, I can see a light on inside through the trees. Aydin, Evrin and Silva must have gotten home after we went to bed.

"Are they still trying to rip each other apart?" Mave asks.

I look back toward the houses. "It comes and goes. They'll be good for a couple days, and then something will set one of them off." I shrug and then realize that Mave can't see it. "Oh by the way, you're fired from Best Friend status," I tell her casually.

"What? No, what did I do?"

"How the hell did you not tell me that Torrez was going to bite the shit out of me when we mated? As a shifter and my bestie, you should have fucking warned me or something," I scold.

Mave screams with excitement, and I can't help but laugh. "You finally mated Torrez! I need details! Was it good? What am I saying, of course it was good, have you seen that body? What did your harem say? Any Bitter Bettys about it?"

I laugh even harder as she shoots one question after another at me. "No Bitter Bettys, they were actually encouraging it, believe it or not." I chuckle, and Mave releases a dreamy sigh.

"Man, you're one lucky girl, Vin. If I didn't like you so much, I'd have to hate you on principle. So...how many times, what orifices were explored, are you covered in bites?"

I sputter out a laugh and clench my thighs against the heat building at their apex. "Please, you think I'm going to tell you shit when I'm still waiting for you to spill the tea about Pebble?"

Mave groans, and I can hear her throw herself back onto her pillow in exasperation. "That is complicated."

"How so?"

"Well, you sleep with a dude once and they think they own you. It's like sorry, bro, but a couple orgasms does not a mate make."

"Oh, only a couple orgasms?" a gravelly male voice asks on her end of the phone.

My smile turns into an open-mouthed *O* of shock.

"Mave, are you in bed with Pebble right now?" I whisper shout, my voice getting all kinds of high-pitched and squeaky.

"I told you—I like your dick, not you," she chastises Pebble, ignoring me.

"Anyway," Mave redirects. "So that means you have four mates down and two to go, right?"

"Um," I giggle. "No more to go; I'm officially six for six, but if you think I'm going to be distracted that easily, then you have another thing coming, young lady."

"By the moons, Vinna, you're not wasting any time with those boys, are you? I'm seriously so fucking proud of you right now. Makes me want to go out there and find my own harem." Mave yells out an objection, and I hear noise over the phone that tells me someone has taken it away.

"Vinna," Pebble's clear voice rings out over the line. "You're a bad influence. Now Mave needs to go and be reminded of why one mate is plenty for her."

I can hear Mave fighting for the phone in the background, and then a feminine moan reaches me through the phone. I snicker.

"Mave, you follow your harem hunting heart," I yell through the phone.

She laughs. "I'll call you later, Vin, miss you and love you!" She squeals, and the line disconnects. I shake my head, smiling, and push off of the tree trunk to head back inside. I jump when, out of nowhere, Enoch steps out of the darkness between the trees across from me.

"Fuck, you scared me," I accuse, and I slam a palm over my chest and try to slow my rapidly beating heart.

Enoch chuckles and starts walking toward me. "Sorry. Try yelling about harem hunting a little quieter next time, and you'll hear me coming," he teases.

I snort and shake my head. It's annoying, but he's right, I should have been more on guard and alert than I just was.

"What are you doing out here?" I ask, looking around to see if there's anyone else with him.

"Same thing as you," he tells me, holding up his phone. "I check in with my dad every couple of days."

I almost spit out an "of course you do," but I manage to swallow it down before it can escape.

"No watch dogs?" Enoch asks, looking around me for any of the guys.

I jerk my chin to the house. "No, they're all sleeping. Well, everyone except for Torrez, who's probably out peeing on shit and hunting rabbits or whatever it is his wolf likes to do out here every night."

Enoch chuckles and brushes a hand through his light blond hair. I study him for probably the first time since he and his coven were marked and showed up at my house. He looks fucking exhausted. There are no bags or dark circles under his eyes to make his fatigue more obvious, but it's in the pull of the corners of his mouth, his anxious blue eyes, and the sigh I can practically feel on the tip of his tongue.

"How are you guys doing?" I ask lamely, turning to face him on the log and giving him my undivided attention.

He looks at me for a minute, like he's trying to gauge if I really care, and then releases that sigh I knew he was holding in his mouth. "We're okay. All of this has just been a lot," he confesses, and I wait patiently for him to say more. "My coven and I weren't exactly doing great before the runes, not since I dropped the Sentinel bomb. Nash knew, but they didn't, and that didn't sit well with Kallan and Becket. Next thing you know, this happened." He gestures to the runes on his middle finger. "Then the shit with Becket's dad, and now we're here where we're barely allowed to breathe, let alone get too close to you, without triggering some bullshit caveman response from someone."

I chuckle, but it's hollow. "Yeah, *a lot* is probably an understatement for everything that's happening," I admit. "For what it's worth, I'm really fucking sorry that you guys have been dragged into all of this. It's not easy by any stretch of the imagination."

Enoch reaches out and sets his hand on mine. "Don't. Don't be sorry. We're glad we're here. I'm glad we're whatever we are to you; it's just hard to be in the dark about everything."

I turn my hand over from where it was sitting on the log and trace my finger over the mystery runes before I take his hand in mine. "Tell me about it. That's been the story of my fucking life up until now. I wish I had answers for everyone.

I have about a billion questions in my mind that I'd love the answers to, but the reality is we're probably never going to get them. It fucking sucks, but there's nothing we can do to change that," I tell him, and I give his hand a comforting squeeze.

He squeezes back, and it makes me smile. I used to be so awkward about physical affection, and in this moment, I'm proud that I can offer comfort and not feel weird about it. It feels natural.

"So what do we do?" Enoch asks, his eyes searching mine. "Do we just leave things as they are, open-ended and unsure? Or do we try to find what answers we can?"

"What do you mean?" I ask, confused.

"We have some of your runes, but not all," he recaps, and I nod. "None of us know what that means, but there is a way that we could find out whether or not Nash, Kallan, Becket and I are in fact Chosen. Torrez had runes that you guys didn't have until you completed the bond."

I stare at him for a beat as his words circle around my mind. I pull my hand back, and Enoch furrows his brow in frustration.

"You want to fuck?" I ask, making sure I'm clear about what he's saying.

"I'm not saying right here and right now. All I'm saying is that we all want answers, and whether the others like it or not, there is a way to find out if somehow we have a partial connection that would be completed if we mated. We would know for sure if we were Chosen or somehow something else to you."

I run my gaze over his face and try to think through how I feel about what he's saying. I study his lips and try to picture what it would be like to kiss him, to have his body pressed into mine, moving in and out of me. He's attractive, there's no denying that, but is that enough?

I pull my eyes from his mouth and move them up to meet his stormy gaze. "And if I said okay, let's see what happens right here and right now, what would you say?"

Enoch leans into me slightly, and he searches my face for something, his eyes bouncing from my sea-green gaze to my parted lips and back up again. "I would say yes," he tells me, and then he moves to close the distance between our lips.

I put my hand on his chest as he leans into me and press him back gently, stopping him. "See, that's the problem, Enoch." His eyes fill with confusion. "We could fuck out here in the dark, test whatever connection we may or may not have, but then what happens?"

"We would know," Enoch counters.

"Yeah, but at what cost?" I implore. "Let's give your theory the benefit of the doubt. We fuck, somehow seal the bond, and you are in fact Chosen. What happens tomorrow when you walk out to train with your Sentinel runes? You think just those markings alone will make my other Chosen accept you?" I shake my head. "It would fracture us. They would continue to think you're untrustworthy, and they would turn those same eyes on to me too."

"They accepted Torrez," he argues.

"Torrez was very different."

"How?" he challenges.

"Torrez came to them first. He told them that he wanted to be a mate, and then he backed off and waited for a decision. They didn't object to him like they do to you. Maybe that's not fair in your eyes, but it is what it is. I didn't know how I felt about Torrez until I had to look at a future without him in it."

"But you say you don't know how you feel about us too," Enoch points out.

"No, I say that the bond with you, Kallan, and Nash

doesn't feel the same as my bonds with my Chosen. It feels different to me."

"Yeah, but you felt different about Torrez, too. You rejected him in the beginning just like you're rejecting us now."

"No, Enoch, it's not the same." I run my fingers through my hair and try to select the words that will help put all the pieces in place for him and for me. "Torrez and I had a connection from the very beginning, but I didn't know myself well enough then to identify what that meant. I know myself better now, and what I wanted from Torrez was different from what I want from you, Kallan, and Nash."

Enoch turns his head away from me to stare off into the dark, and I put a hand on his cheek and move his eyes back to mine. "I feel a connection with you, Enoch. We train well together, we think similarly in how we fight, our drive to win is the same. You push me to be better, and then you show me how to achieve that. I'm comfortable around you, it's easy to be in your presence, and I trust you. You feel...I don't know...like family maybe, like we'll always be friends, always watch each other's backs," I explain, my eyes begging his to understand.

He sighs. "So I've been friend-zoned," he quips, and I roll my eyes.

"Honestly, Enoch, I think if you really look inside your soul and study the truth there, you'd realize that you don't actually want me. You want these." I point to the runes on my arms and hands.

Enoch's blue eyes frost over, and he opens his mouth to argue.

"Fine, you want me in all of my glory, and the runes mean nothing to you?" I challenge. "Then don't you want to win me the right way? By proving yourself to my Chosen, by earning their unwavering trust and loyalty? If you had that, then why would they object to us *fucking for answers*. If you had that, and it turned out you were right all along about being Chosen, they would welcome you with open arms. You'd have *earned* a place as one of them, instead of stealing it in the night, behind their backs, knowing how they would feel about it."

He watches me for a moment and then nods his head.

"Okay, I'll earn you then, Vinna."

And with that, he pushes off the fallen tree and disappears back into the night.

15

I take a deep breath. "Okay, but what if I turn into a wolf?" I ask again for the tenth time, and Torrez shakes his head.

"Would that really be the worst thing?" Torrez asks.

"No, it would probably be amazing, but I just don't think I can deal with that on top of everything else going on right now," I tell him, my tone a little more hysterical than I mean for it to be. After my talk with Enoch, I couldn't go back to sleep, so I blame that for my current state of panic.

"Listen, Witch, the only thing you need to fear turning into right now is a chicken. So stop clucking, and let's see what your new runes do."

"You suck at pep talks," I snark.

Valen grabs the back of my neck and pulls me toward him. "Sentinel up, or none of us will be sucking on anything for the next week." He lets go of my neck, and I lean back to glare at him.

"Fine, be that way!" I growl and then stomp away from all of them. *Have lots of mates, they say. It'll be so much fun, they say. Yeah, until the fuckers gang up against you, and you never win an argument again,* I grumble.

"You're right; sex, or the lack thereof, really motivates her," Valen observes, and then he proceeds to fist bump Torrez.

I point an aggressive finger in their direction. "There will be no *bro-ing* out. And consider yourself warned—if I wolf out, I'm biting both of you."

"Ooh, your kinky is showing again, Bruiser," Bastien announces as he joins Valen and Torrez. "Why is she all riled?" he asks casually.

"We threatened her with no sex for a week," Valen fills his twin in.

"Yup, that'll do it," Bastien chuckles.

"I can fucking hear you," I shout at them.

"None of us care," Bastien shouts back.

I glare at each of them in turn as I pull magic from my core and feed it into the new runes I now have from Torrez's mating mark. I feed the magic into the new runes slowly and from one blink to the next, everything changes.

My vision sharpens and alters. I'm assaulted by what feels like a billion different smells. I can see so much more in my periphery than I could before, and I can't seem to decide where I want to focus.

"Whoa," Torrez comments offhandedly, and I don't know if that freaks me out or makes me excited.

"Am I a wolf?" I ask, unsure. I look down at my hands, and all I see are my hands, although now I feel like I could count every hair on my arm. When did I get so hairy? Does Torrez see himself as a wolf when he's in wolf form, or is this what his body looks like to him even though he looks like a wolf to everyone else? Man, this is trippy. I wonder what color my coat is. Black maybe?

"You're not a wolf," Torrez tells me, stepping closer. "Well, not a fully shifted one anyway."

"Uh, what the hell does that mean?"

"Your eyes have shifted. They're still the same green, but they're wolf eyes right now, not your regular eyes."

"Oh, well that explains this change in my vision then. Am I hairier?"

The three of them laugh.

"No, but you can probably make out the details of your body much better than you could before," Torrez tells me, and I breathe out a sigh of relief.

Time to magically shave again.

"Anything else different?" Valen asks. He bends over to get a better look at my new wolf eyes, and I snap at him for shits and giggles. He doesn't even so much as flinch or make a noise of surprise. Lame.

"You don't scare me, love," he teases, and I don't miss his use of that word again. It slipped out a few times when we were getting it on in the barn. I chalked it up to an in-the-moment term of endearment, but it seems I was wrong. I've got Chosen dropping *L* bombs like I drop *F* bombs, and I'm not sure what to think about all of that. Or maybe I do know what I think about all of that, and I just need to work on the logistics of what I want to do about it.

"What I smell has changed," I tell them. "It's more overwhelming than the eyes. I can pick up a ton of things I couldn't before, but I'm not sure what everything is."

Torrez brushes my cheek with the back of his hand, and I lean into it. "Yeah, that makes sense. It will take time for you to catalogue different scents in order to identify them later."

"Does this mean I'll be able to smell lies and emotions, too?" I ask, excited.

"Yup," Torrez admits, and I can't tell if he thinks that's a good thing or bad thing.

"We'll have to start introducing smells to you right away

so you can learn. Your wolf eyes will be most useful at night. Our night vision is incredible, so that will definitely be a handy tool. What about your hearing, any changes there?"

"I already had runes for that," I confess, and I hear Bastien and Valen both sputter out, "What?"

"Where are your runes for that?" they ask in unison.

I point to the helix of my ear. They both grow quiet with concentration, and I know they're testing those tiny runes out. They're easy to forget about, and I've been purposely not pointing them out to any of them.

"Holy shit," Bastien blurts, his tone filled with awe. "I can hear Aydin and Evrin all the way in the house."

I tap into the runes on the helix of my ear and focus on the main house where Silva, Evrin and Aydin are staying. I hear someone in the kitchen working and figure that's who's responsible for our tasty meals, even though I've never seen them. The table just seems to always be filled with food.

"That group that kept visiting that house just out of town has stopped. I'm not sure if they got what they wanted from there, or if somehow they spotted me, but we should probably check out what it is now that there's less of a risk of getting caught and we've lost the trail of the lamia who were visiting there regularly," Aydin announces.

"When do you want to go in? Tonight?" Evrin asks.

"It's better to check it out sooner rather than later. It's probably our best lead at this point. Is Silva back yet from his assignment? We'll need him on this one for sure," Aydin tells him, and then the room fills with the rustling of papers.

"He was here when I got back last night," Evrin tells him. "I haven't seen him yet this morning. I think he's in the barn again."

"Are the spells ready yet?" Aydin queries as he messes with more papers.

"I told him to have Knox look at them since that's his area of expertise, but I don't know if he has or not."

Evrin and Aydin's words niggle at the back of my mind. I thought they were surveilling with Silva, but it's clear Aydin and Evrin were off on their own. Why would they separate?

"Earth to Vinna," rings in my ears and pulls my focus, and Bastien steps into my line of sight. I let go of the magic in all of the runes I currently have activated. My regular vision snaps back into place. I'm no longer bombarded by different smells, and I realize that it's easier for me to focus when my sense of smell isn't so heightened.

"So, Bruiser, how often did you use this little skill to spy on us?" Bastien asks me, a naughty glint in his eyes.

I laugh. "Only a couple of times, and usually you guys weren't saying anything interesting. I mostly use it to track where people are," I admit.

"So that's how you kept avoiding us," Valen exclaims, and pieces of something that must have been bugging him come together.

I shrug.

Shouting kicks off behind the guys, and we all move to see what's going on.

"You fucking cut me, you asshole," Knox roars at Nash.

"It was an accident, you baby. Give me your arm, and I'll heal it," Nash offers, disdain dripping from his tone.

"Fuck you, we have our own healer. But you should get the hell away from me before Ryker is done, or I'll fuck you up so bad it'll take a healer days to fix you," Knox threatens, and I start walking toward them ready, yet again, to break up their drama.

Knox extends his arm to Ryker, and I watch as blood drips freely from his arm and lands on the packed dirt below him. I don't know why, in that moment, everything clicks together, but it does. All the uneasiness and warnings that my instincts have been hammering me with since before we got here fall into place, and I see a horrifyingly clear picture. Maybe it was Aydin and Evrin talking about how Silva came home before them, and the lights I noticed were on in the barn late last night. Or maybe it's the color of the dirt as it soaks up Knox's blood, creating a mottled splotch that looks eerily familiar, but I suddenly know where Lachlan and the others have been getting their leads. And I'm fucking pissed.

I take off for the tree line behind us, sprinting hard and pumping magic into my runes so I can move even faster. I hear shouts behind me, but I don't have a second to lose to stop and explain what I just realized. I flash through the trees until I see the barrier and the barn. I wrap my hands in Defensive magic, and they glow from the orange-yellow magical casing. I lace that with Sentinel magic and run at the barrier full out. I punch out at the barrier when I'm close enough, and I feel it shatter beneath my fist. I run through the shards of magic as they crumble into nothing, and I ready myself for what I know I'm about to find.

I blow the front door off its hinges with Elemental magic and run through, doing the same to the second door, before Silva emerges from the dirt room I knew he'd be in. Our eyes lock, and I see surprise there for a second before his gaze fills with indignation.

"What the hell do you think you're doing?" he demands.

I take menacing steps toward him. "What the fuck do you think *you're* doing? Did you not fucking learn from the last time you did this? Did you really think I would just sit by and let you do it again?" I throw an arm out in the direction of the dirt room he just walked out of. "Move," I order.

"I have every right to use all means at my disposal to find out—" Silva defends, but I cut off the bullshit justifications, and I slam him with air, forcing him to get out of my way.

Silva has a protective barrier up around him in a blink, and he doesn't budge.

"You don't want to do this, little girl," Silva warns me.

"Not true actually. You've fucking earned this fair and square."

I push harder at him with air and then throw another barrier on top of the one he already has around him. I check for weak spots in his cast and compress my barrier around him. It seals under his feet, and I use the Elemental magic I'm already directing at him to start to lift him up and out of my way. Silva starts to chant something and then he claps his hands together and a white light shoots out from his palms, melting my barrier and dropping him back into place. A small sound of annoyance slips out of me, and Silva smirks in my direction at the sound of it.

I click my tongue at him with disappointment. "Silva, you didn't think that was all I had, did you? I've been working hard while you've been away," I tell him sweetly.

I infuse an Offensive cast with the air magic I'm calling on and then braid it all together with a Defensive cast. My magic flashes out like a whip and wraps around Silva's barrier. His smug look turns worried when I pull back on my threads and his barrier crumbles around him. I tighten the cast around him and yank him out of my way.

Silva slams into the wall of maps and crashes down on the desk that Valen and I christened. I debate for a second which weapon I want to reach for, but I decide, for this asshole, we'll go old school. I run at him as he pushes himself off the desk to stand, and I punch him in the stomach. Silva rallies and kicks out at my knee, but I twist, and he gets my lower thigh instead. He grabs the computer screen and throws it at me, but it ricochets off the barrier I just called on and slams to the ground.

Silva and I trade hits and misses, but he could learn a

thing or two from his nephews, as they are way better at hand-to-hand than he is.

"Ten years ago, you tortured a lamia looking for my dad and the others who went missing," I grind out as my fist lands on Silva's ribs, and I spin to avoid another kick to my lower body. "You dumbasses let that lamia convince you that a baby killed Lachlan's brother and was somehow responsible for all of your problems in life."

I punctuate my statement with a knee to his thigh, a cuff on his ears, and another hit to his ribs. He reaches out, trying to land a jab, but I grab his forearm with one hand and thrust my other hand up at his elbow. Silva screams as I break his arm, but his pain doesn't mean shit to me. I grab him by his pony tail and kick his feet out from under him.

"You want someone to blame for all your problems? Blame that fucker," I seethe at him as I hold his face above the black, broken computer screen. Silva's reflection stares up at him through the spidering cracks of the monitor.

"You're fucking lucky your nephews are about to run through the front door and stop me from killing you. Maybe someday you can pull your head out of your ass long enough to realize how lucky you are to have them. Until then, you better stay the fuck away from me." I smash Silva's head against the desk, and he crumbles to the ground, out cold.

"What the hell, Vinna?" Bastien yells from the front of the barn.

Good. He and Valen can deal with their fucked up uncle. I'm already across the room and gripping the door knob that leads to the dirt room, whose purpose I couldn't figure out until five minutes ago. I push the door open, and sure enough, exactly as I feared, there is a lamia that's bruised, battered, dripping blood, and tied to a chair.

He looks up toward the doorway as I step through it, and

I throw a hand over my mouth to stop the sound of a gasp from traveling too far. Brown hair, olive skin, and stunning crystal-blue eyes look up at me. I recognize him instantly. It's the lamia that was with Sorik that day on Silas's pack territory.

How the hell did he get here?

16

"What are you doing here?" hisses out of both of our mouths at exactly the same time.

I step toward him, taking in his state, and I tear off my shirt and press it against the deep cuts lining his right arm. He throws his head back and hisses in pain when I apply more pressure, and I apologize as I look for any more damage to his body that needs immediate attention.

"By the stars, what was he doing to you?" I ask absently as I take in all the bruises.

"We graduated from beating to cutting about an hour ago," he informs me.

Rage simmers inside of me, and I hope the twins get Silva the hell out of here, or I might press for a round two with him. I run my eyes over the chair the lamia is strapped into, and it looks like Silva or one of the others made it. Pieces look welded together and constructed just for this purpose, and my stomach roils when I wonder how many lamia they've done this to.

"What the fuck?" Knox asks from the doorway before he rushes forward to help.

"They were still doing it," I tell him, shaking my head as we search for a way to release the constraints.

Blood is starting to soak through the shirt I have wrapped around this lamia's arm, and I notice that he's just sitting here, watching me warily.

"Knox, I need your shirt. Do you know anything about lamia, like how to stop them from bleeding to death?" I ask.

Knox whips off his shirt and hands it to me, and then he starts messing with a chain under the arm on his side of the chair. Enoch, Kallan, Nash and Sabin pour into the room, and everyone but Sabin's eyes harden when they take in what's going on.

"Vinna, what are you doing?" Enoch asks me, stepping forward and reaching for me. Sabin grabs him and stops him from pulling me away, and they start arguing.

"I need something that's going to dilute the shifter venom that he put in all of my cuts and that I've been dosed with since I was brought here. Then I need to feed, so I can start to heal," the lamia informs us.

"I can put something together for the toxin," Knox tells me, and then he motions for Sabin to come over and take his place. Sabin steps in and starts working on the same chain that Knox just was.

"Are you guys crazy? Are you forgetting that lamia kidnapped us, Vinna, and killed your friend?" Nash asks from the corner of the room he's standing in as he takes in everything with disdain.

I shoot him a glare. "Not this lamia, Nash. He didn't take us." Nash shakes his head in obvious disapproval, and disappointment wells up inside of me. "I was taken by casters, too; should I also assume every caster I meet is bad and deserves to be tortured and brutalized?" I ask him casually. I turn to Enoch who I can see is having the same issue with this situation as Nash. "I refuse to generalize a whole species based off the actions of a few."

"That's probably because you have very limited experience with this particular species," Enoch grumbles.

"Well, being that I'm alive and pretty much everything that I am today because of a lamia, I'm going to say I probably have more legitimate experience than you do," I argue.

I turn back to the crystal-blue eyes of the lamia that's still strapped to the chair. "So the whole feeding thing is new to me. Do you prefer a neck, wrist, blood in a cup? What works best for you?"

His eyes widen in shock, and they move cautiously from me to the others in the room. "You...you would feed me?" he asks, his voice low and just shy of a whisper.

"You said you needed to feed, right?" I ask, confused. Do they not drink from people like I thought they did? Shit, did I just offend him? "Sorry, maybe I've seen too many vampire shows. I didn't mean to be an asshole," I rush to tell him.

His ice-blue eyes search my gaze, and his lips seem to be fighting not to show any hint of amusement. "No, they pretty much have it right. Well, my face doesn't morph into that of a demonic shar-pei, but we do drink from people when we can."

Sabin gets the metal on the lamia's arm unlatched and moves to do the same to his leg.

"What's your name?" I ask him as I place my wrist in front of his face.

Sabin gets one leg unchained and relocates to my side of the chair to finish working.

"Siah," he answers, and I notice that his pupils start to dilate as I push my wrist closer to his mouth. I nod in encouragement and press closer to his mouth. He abandons the obvious wariness he's feeling about this situation and sinks two sharp canines into my wrist. He pulls his fangs from the new wound quickly and then seals his mouth around the punctures and sucks hard at them, his eyes never leaving mine the whole time.

I'm oddly fascinated by what he's doing and very aware that we're being watched by disapproving eyes, but helping him is the least I can do after what Silva just did to him. I turn away from the sight of this lamia feeding from me and focus on the others in the room. Ryker is standing in the doorway, waiting to be told what we need.

"Where are the others?" I ask, ignoring the strange pull at my wrist.

"Valen, Bastien and Torrez are taking Silva to the main house and making sure that Aydin and Evrin don't leave. Knox is making something in the other room."

Out of nowhere, purple magic sparks to life on my forearm, and before either of us can pull away, the magic strikes out at Siah as he's drinking from me. His eyes widen with fear, but as he absorbs the magic, his eyes close, and his face relaxes the tiniest amount. I don't hear his moan, but I can feel it where his mouth is attached to my wrist. The next thing I know, pleasure is surging through me, and I tilt my head back, reveling in the feeling of it.

"Does that mean what I think it means?" Sabin asks, his tone pure shock.

Siah flinches back from my arm, and just like that, the euphoria is yanked from me too. My head snaps down, my eyes immediately landing on his, and we both just watch each other for a beat. The last chain on the chair is loosened, and just as Siah pulls his arm free, Knox pushes past Ryker with a bottle of blue liquid in his hand. I step away from the lamia as Sabin and Knox start administering the blue liquid to his wounds, but as I watch, I start to feel oddly fuzzy all of a sudden. I hold out my arm and move toward Ryker so he can heal me, when the world tilts out from underneath me, and I watch as the ground rushes up at me. I'm yanked away from the pain the ground promises and wrapped up in someone's arms. I feel the telltale tickle of magic moving over my body, and then everything goes numb...and then dark.

* * *

I'm warm when I come to, wrapped in strong arms, safe, confused, and surrounded by people. Voices dance around me, and I feel like I could almost float on the anger in the room as they argue. I nuzzle the chest my cheek is pressed against, and soft lips kiss my forehead. I blink slowly, my eyes adjusting to the light in the room. Ryker's sweet smile looks down at me, and I can't help but return it.

"My hero," I sigh dreamily, and his chest rumbles with a laugh that vibrates through me. "Thanks for catching me," I tell him and pull his lips down to mine for a quick kiss.

"Wish I could claim the save, but the lamia caught you," Ryker tells me, his face so close that all I can focus on is how much I want to turn that quick kiss into so much more. "Then Torrez almost ripped him apart when he walked into the room to find an unconscious you in the arms of some lamia no one knew. It got worse when Torrez caught his scent and realized he was one of the lamia that breached his old pack's territory."

I exhale a long tired breath and reach up to push hair out of Ryker's face. "Think if I just close my eyes and stay like this with you, they'll work it all out on their own?" I ask hopefully.

He scrunches up his face adorably with doubt. "It's not looking likely," he confesses, rubbing the tip of his nose against mine.

I pull him in for another kiss. "Well, thanks for the

cuddles then. Let's work some serious make out time into the schedule soon, okay?"

His laughter washes over me, and I sit up with the feel of his happiness on my skin. The arguing in the room pauses as attention is turned to me. My eyes land on Aydin, and a spike of pain slams into me.

"Did you know?" I croak, not sure what I'll do if he says yes.

"No. Evrin and I had no idea they were still doing that."

I nod and stand up, shoving a heavy weight off my chest with his words. "Silva?" I ask as I get up, my legs shaky.

"He's upstairs. Ryker and I refused to heal him, so he's recovering the old fashioned way," Evrin supplies. His tone and features are pissed, and I'm pretty sure he mumbles "stupid prick," but it's so quiet I can't be sure.

"You okay, Killer?" Knox asks me from where he's leaning against a wall on the other side of the living room we're all gathered in.

"I think so," I tell him. He pushes off the wall and makes his way to me. Knox pulls me into a hug, and I realize right now in this moment, how much I've missed him. He's been so serious and frustrated since Enoch and his coven showed up, and I hate that he feels more guarded to me now. I know he's still ride or die, but it sucks that he's not as carefree as he usually is.

"Miss you," I tell him quietly, when he cups my cheeks and searches my eyes.

"I'm here, Killer."

I nod and give him a small smile before I turn back to the rest of the room. Knox wraps me up in his arms, and I lean back into him, happy to use his strength right now instead of trying to pull my own armor up and over me.

"Your...uh...magic went a little crazy when you passed out. Any clue what happened?" Valen asks me.

"Sentinel magic," I fill in, and Valen looks around like he's hoping Siah didn't just catch my mistake. "It's okay," I reassure. "Sorik trusts him, and he already knows. Sorik talked about being Chosen and his runes even though Siah was there. I figure the Sentinel cat's out of the bag."

"We don't even know if we can trust Sorik yet, Vinna," Valen warns me.

"You can trust Sorik," Siah speaks up from the big chair he's sitting in. He looks completely healed. "I've yet to meet a more decent being than Sorik. We've been close since we were brought into this world"—Siah motions to us—"but he kept your mother's secret, their secret, until he had no other choice. He needed help getting to you, and I know he's been working tirelessly on arrangements for you since."

My features must fill with obvious question, because Siah shakes his head.

"I don't know what the arrangements are; it was safer if I didn't know. All I have pieced together is that he's searching for something, and I'm watching his back while he's doing that."

"Why would you help him?" Evrin asks, his tone suspicious.

"Because regardless of the fact that we've been sired into Adriel's nest, it doesn't mean we all agree with his obsessions."

"Then why not leave?" Bastien asks, and there's no missing the accusation in that question.

"And go where?" Siah demands. "We're not a beloved supernatural species. No one is throwing their doors open to welcome us and offer a safe haven from the mad masters that rule us. There's too much bad blood and prejudice out there for us to survive on our own. Not to mention that we'd be hunted down by our own kind for breaking from our sires without permission." Siah narrows his eyes at Bastien. "So you tell me where we're supposed to go."

The room falls quiet, everyone's gazes locked on each other. Uncertainty and tension wafts around each of us as we all try to work out what happens now.

"So how do we stop him?" Sabin finally asks.

"I don't know if you can. He's obliterated much larger numbers than you have, so attacking him won't go well." He jerks his chin in my direction. "As soon as he finds out that she's this close, he'll throw everything he has at you in order to get to her."

"Then we make sure he doesn't find out," Bastien announces, glaring at Siah.

"I'm not going to tell him, if that's what you're getting at, but they haven't exactly been discreet in their hunting." Siah jerks his chin in the direction of Aydin and Evrin. "It's only a matter of time before someone recognizes who they are and lamia are sent to investigate."

"Will he trade for Lachlan and Keegan?" I ask Siah.

"Trade what?" Aydin asks confused.

I take a deep breath. "Me."

The word is barely out of my mouth before the whole room explodes with arguing. I wait silently as they fling their objections my way. But their promises that we'll find another way, or the reasons they have for why it's a bad idea, slide right off of me as I watch the crystal-blue eyes that are watching me.

"Your friends are the only leverage Adriel has right now. He would say he'd exchange them, but he won't. He'll use it as a way to lure you out, take you, and then use them against you. Even if they managed to escape somehow, he'll hunt anyone and everyone you've ever known. He'll dangle each and every one of them in front of you until they're dead or he gets what he wants."

"Fucking hell," Knox breathes out, and the frustration in his words tickles my ear as it passes by.

I watch Siah as I mentally flip through the options for other plans of attack. Violet magic sparks on my hands, and I mentally curse it and shake them until the flashes sputter out. Ryker gives me a questioning raised eyebrow, and I huff out a breath and shake my head.

"We'll talk about that later," I tell him, and he snorts out an exasperated breath of his own.

Keep the flirting and the Chosen marking to yourself, magic. We've got enough shit to deal with right now; you and your hoarding can just fucking wait, I scold, and then once again feel like a dumbass for lecturing something that's essentially me. Although I swear it has to have a mind of its own.

"So what if we attack from all angles?" Kallan asks absently, and all eyes in the room move to him.

"Meaning?" Valen asks.

"Meaning, what if Vinna gives herself up—" The rest of Kallan's words are swallowed up by shouting. Everyone starts to square off, and I begin to feel like the aggression in the room is about to boil me alive. I push out of Knox's arms, which isn't hard to do because he wants in on the beat down that sits like a promise in the eyes of all of my Chosen.

"*Stop!*" I yell out, and the command is punctuated by a pulse of Sentinel magic that shoots out in a purple arc that slams into everyone. Enoch, Nash, and Kallan drop to their knees, and everyone else in the room hisses as the magic rushes through them and out through the walls. I look down at my hands, a little surprised by what just happened.

Well, fuck.

Looks like my magic is done messing around. I brush off my surprise and try to adopt a *I totally meant to do that* mien. Based on Torrez and Knox's snickers, I'm not pulling it off as well as I was hoping for. I shoot them both a look and then focus on Kallan. He struggles to look up at me.

"Uh, are you okay?" I ask warily, completely shattering any illusion that I know what I'm doing. I offer him a hand, and as soon as I do, it's like whatever hold was keeping Kallan and his coven on the ground breaks. They all get up, their eyes bouncing from their limbs to me like they can't figure out who or what betrayed them.

"What were you saying before about attacking from all angles?" I ask before the room can break out in another yelling match now that the effects of my magical bitch slap seem to have worn off.

"I was saying, if you give yourself to Adriel, that means we have you, Lachlan, and Keegan on the inside." Kallan points to Siah. "If *he* can gather the lamia who want out from underneath Adriel's thumb, then we'd have another group on the inside too. If we could coordinate something with us on the outside and you all on the inside, we could attack from all angles."

"Has anyone ever done that before?" I turn and ask Siah.

"No, at least not like how he's suggesting. When your mother escaped, the prisoners were capitalizing on an attack that was happening, but the attacking group and the escaping group weren't working together."

"Do you think you could get other lamia to join in the fight against Adriel?" Aydin asks.

Siah shrugs. "There are some I know that would, but it's hard to say how many would actually fight other members of the nest. It would also be very tricky to try to more or less plan a rebellion without it being whispered into the wrong ears or brought to light by a weaker member wanting to win favor with Adriel."

I nod my head in understanding and lose myself in thought for a moment. "Wolf?" Torrez's eyes move from Siah to me, and I see a hint of something I can't identify in his gaze. "Do you think you could convince the Volkovs and any other packs they know to fight with us?"

"I don't think they'd take much convincing," he tells me with a grin. I smile and nod back at him, they were pretty amped for a good fight.

"How many lamia are in Adriel's nest?" Enoch asks Siah.

"About two hundred and fifty, give or take. A third of that number is actually skilled fighters. He sends out hunting parties all of the time, so there could be anywhere from ten to sixty battle-ready lamia gone at any given time."

I look around the room as Siah talks about the size of the nest. There are fourteen of us. How the fuck are we going to take on those numbers in a head-to-head fight? Kallan's suggestion just became the best shot we've got. If we can get the Volkov pack to fight with us, then we'd be a hell of a lot more evenly matched.

"Is the nest predominantly male?" Valen queries, and I can see the spark of calculation in his eyes.

"The ratio is about seventy-thirty, but the females are just as deadly as the males, if not more so. It can be hard for other supes to kill women, and female lamia will use that to their advantage."

I look around the room. "Anyone else have a better plan?" I ask, meeting each of their eyes in turn. Every single one of them hesitantly shake their heads slowly or answer no after a beat or two.

"Then, let's do this."

17

Bouncing around the room is a cacophony of: "Wait, what?"; "Fuck no,"; "Killer!"; "Think again, Witch." Aydin, Evrin, and Kallan move to block the door. When Siah stands up, a handful of voices yell at him to sit the fuck back down. It would be kind of funny if everything about this situation wasn't deadly serious.

"We've talked for all of ten minutes, and you're ready to just walk up to Adriel's front door and ring the bell?" Valen demands, stepping closer to me, his irritation pushing uncomfortably up against me.

"What's left to work out?" I challenge. "You guys continue to train, Torrez is going to get the pack involved, Siah is going to rally as many lamia as he can, and I'm going to pretend to get taken and wait for my chance to kill Adriel."

"Oh, just like that, huh?" Sabin argues, and I try really fucking hard not to roll my eyes.

"Excuse us, we're going to go have a little chat with our mate," Knox announces to the room and then picks me up and starts to carry me out.

Enoch moves to follow, and Bastien steps in his way.

"Chosen only," he growls at him. A tic starts in Enoch's jaw, but he doesn't argue or move. Siah watches Knox manhandle me out of the room, and the rest of my Chosen fall in line behind us.

"You're lucky I like being carried around, or all of you'd be begging Ryker to heal more knife wounds," I tell all of them with a huff.

Knox carries me out of the big house and over into the little side house we've been staying in. He bypasses the small sitting room and stomps to the room where we sleep. He flips me over his shoulder and drops me onto my back. I bounce on the mattresses we have pushed together on the floor, and Knox immediately climbs over me and crashes his lips to mine in a hard, demanding kiss. I spread my legs automatically for him, and his large muscular body settles perfectly where I want it.

Someone clears their throat, and I smile against Knox's mouth. He makes an irritated noise and sucks on my tongue, pulling away to growl over his shoulder.

"Wait your turn," he grumbles before grinding between my thighs and turning back to kiss me deeper. Chuckles reverberate off the walls of the room, and someone else makes a satisfied *mmmm* sound.

"I didn't know exactly how I'd feel about watching her be with someone else, but it's actually fucking hot," Torrez announces.

"It is, isn't it?" Ryker agrees. "I, for one, never thought I'd be okay with group stuff outside of the Bonding Ceremony, but watching definitely has its own appeal."

Murmurs of agreement sound off around me, and I snort super unattractively into Knox's mouth and push him back.

"You guys are all fucking weirdos," I announce as I wiggle into a sitting position, ignoring Knox's objections.

"You know you like it, Bruiser. You pretend to be weirded

out by group sex, but we all know you're game. You're not fooling anyone."

I look at Bastien, incredulous. "I am weirded out by group sex. There are six of you and one of me, and I just can't work out the logistics of that."

"Seven," Sabin blurts, and all heads swivel to him. "Based on what's going on with her magic, I suspect that the lamia might be lucky number 7, either that or he's one of whatever Enoch and his coven are," he explains.

"Well, shit, Bruiser, another one?" Bastien whines.

I let out a loud irritated moan. "My magic and I have already had a little chat and agreed it needs to go to rehab for hoarding."

"Greedy vagina, greedy magic...we might be screwed, fellas," Torrez throws out.

"Not often enough if she keeps adding mates," Knox grumbles, and I glare at him.

"We need to trust the magic. If he's lucky number seven, it is what it is," Sabin argues.

"I agree," Ryker and Valen add.

"Well, I am not looking to keep adding mates. Enough is fucking enough."

"No amount of fucking is ever enough," Knox counters with a smirk, and I roll my eyes.

"That is not what I mean, and you know it."

I turn back to the others. I'm completely perplexed by the fact that they're discussing this like it's all just no big deal. *Don't mind us, we're just deciding whether you need to add another mate, no biggie.*

"Why do you guys seem so casual about this anyway? You all went berserk when Enoch and his coven showed up on our doorstep. My Sentinel magic lights up for some random dude, and you all are just chill about it?"

"Because Enoch, Kallan, Nash, and Becket don't feel right as your Chosen," Valen defends.

"Oh, but this lamia none of us even knows shit about does?" I challenge.

"Your magic seems to think so," Sabin argues.

"My magic is out of control and needs to be forced into a chastity belt," I inform him, and laughter bounces around the room.

"So if you guys are all kumbaya with whatever my magic chooses for us, then why do all of you reject the possibility that my magic chose Kallan, Nash, Becket and Enoch?"

"Nope, it's different," Ryker tells me, shaking his head. "We can feel it, and we know you can too. You said from the beginning that they didn't feel like Chosen to you. Has that changed?"

"No," I answer without having to give it any thought.

"What does Siah feel like to you?" Sabin asks.

"I don't know. I haven't even really thought about it. You know, with being busy trying to figure out how we can kill Adriel and shit," I snark.

"Why did you feed him, then?" Ryker probes.

"I would have done that for any lamia in his situation. He was being tortured and needed help to heal. That has nothing to do with my magic going all swoony over his eyes."

"Called it," Bastien announces, and the other guys grumble and swear.

"Called what?" I ask, confused.

"I said his eyes would be the first thing you'd admit to liking. Knox said muscles, Ryker said lips, Valen refused to play, Sabin said his mysterious air, and Torrez said you wouldn't admit anything until you were called out, which I guess technically is right in this case too, since we're all calling you out right now."

Torrez smiles, and he and Bastien fist bump.

"What did you win?" I ask, irritated by how amusing they think this is.

"Cuddle rights at night for a week."

I slap a palm to my forehead and shake my head. "I thought you three didn't want another mate?"

"Your magic keeps trying to spark up and mark him as something. I don't know that any of us have much of a choice, including you, Bruiser," Bastien teases.

"I still get my night in the rotation, though, because I didn't play your dumb game," Valen warns his brother.

"Party pooper," Knox cough-accuses.

Valen flips him the bird. "Nope, I'm the smart one. You're going to be all cold and cuddling your compeer for the next seven days, and I'll still be in the rotation to have my arms wrapped around our mate's tight body, twice this week."

My skin heats at Valen's words, and I try not to yell out "nap time." Torrez chuckles, and when I look at him, he taps at his nose.

Busted!

Torrez rearranges what is clearly his hardening dick in his pants, and I lick my lips as I watch him, completely unashamed of the fact that I'm perving out. Maybe they're right, and I'm not as opposed to this whole group situation as I thought. *I wonder how many orgasms a female body can handle before it combusts into flames?*

"She's thinking about sex again, isn't she?" Knox asks Torrez.

"Oh yeah, this room just filled up with so much lust, I'm going to be hard for the rest of the day," Torrez informs him.

"By the moon, will you all stop distracting me? We're not here to talk about group sex, or adding mates, cuddle parties, or erections that last all day. We're here to argue about the Adriel plan until you all realize that the plan we just came up with is the best and possibly *the only* way."

"It's not the only way," Sabin insists, and I blow out an irritated breath.

"Okay, so what's the alternative?"

I wait patiently for them to say anything, but everyone's quiet.

"What if we have Siah go back, work things from the inside like he's planning now, and we still attack from the outside? That plan is the same, just without you in the middle or in any extra danger we might not be able to get you out of."

"That could work, but if I were there, it would be a useful distraction. Siah said it will be hard to organize the lamia. I imagine it will be even harder if all eyes are on him. You all know we can't just attack from outside. The paladin have been there and done that; somehow Adriel gets the upper hand. You guys are here to rescue Lachlan and Keegan. I'm here to kill Adriel. Our best way of accomplishing what each of us wants is this way," I explain.

"I don't like it, Killer. You said yourself that we should stick together. If we split up, we're weaker targets," Knox pleads.

"Adriel doesn't want me dead. He wants my abilities. He'll be focused on trying to get what he wants from me, and it will leave him vulnerable in other places. He's not going to kill me, and I may be there dealing with him alone for a little while, but we're all connected," I tell them motioning to each of them in the room. "I can talk with you, feed you information, help you fine tune the attack. This really is our best option."

"You act like death is the worst thing he can do to you," Valen speaks up. "We don't know what his tactics are like. You're assuming he's going to take his time trying to win you over, but what if he just tries to take them from you. What are we supposed to do if that's what goes down? You'll be on your own, no buffer, no protection."

I take a deep breath and consider what he's saying. My eyes focus on Valen's hazel gaze, and I wish I could smooth away all the worry I see in his face. "You're right, we don't know how I'll be treated once I'm in Adriel's hands. All I do know is that, as long as he's alive, I will never stop being hunted. *We* will never be safe. I know he's a monster. I know not to let my guard down. I am not defenseless. I *can* do this," I reassure them, and I feel the truth of those words settling deep in my veins.

Valen looks away from me, and I watch as he and the rest of my Chosen each lock eyes in turn.

"She'll have Sorik and Siah in there too. I'm not sure what condition Lachlan and Keegan will be in, but they'll fight if they can," Ryker adds, and they all nod their heads in agreement, even though they seem lost in thought.

"Fuck, I wish there was a different way," Bastien grumbles out, and I honestly wish there was too.

This plan is better than the *trade myself* plan I've been wrestling with since Aydin told us what happened, but I still don't like walking into this situation with so many unknowns. Then again, unknowns seem to be the way of life for me these days, so I should probably just get used to it. I blow out a deep breath and look around the room. I feel this sudden drive to commit the space to memory since I'll probably never see it again. If we win, we'll go home, and if we lose… I shove that thought away, not even willing to entertain the possibility.

"Okay, well, it looks like we're doing this," Valen announces, and when no one argues with his statement, I push off the mattress I'm sitting on and stand up.

"Right now?" Knox questions, tugging at my hand to try and pull me down into his lap.

"No time like the present," I tell him and pull away to move to the doorway.

The atmosphere in the room is solemn and suddenly heavy. This overwhelming feeling surges through me that I can't leave like this. I've left too many moments open-ended, shoved away too many emotions I wasn't sure how to interpret or communicate, but I can't walk out of here leaving any possibility of doubt.

"I love you," I announce, turning around at the door. "I know it's fast, and I know the feelings I have for each of you will deepen with time, but I just wanted you to know." I look up at them finally as I run out of words, and I see smiles, looks of shock, and one really pissed off face.

"Did you just *in case I never see you again* love bomb us?" Bastien asks me angrily.

"Um..." I say as I search for the answer.

Shit, did I?

"No," I finally say. "I just figured that each of you deserved to hear it now that I've realized that's how I've been feeling. Like I said, it's new," I stammer on. "No pressure though, you don't need to feel like you have to say that to me just because I said it," I ramble, and then I bite down to keep myself from saying anything else. Fuck, why am I making this so awkward?

"Well, take it back," Bastien demands. He's pissed, and I'm not really sure how to feel about that.

"You can tell me that when we see each other again. When I can feel it in your kiss and in the way your body feels against mine. Not as some afterthought as you walk out the door, worried that something could go wrong."

I narrow my eyes at him. "It's not an afterthought. I felt

like I needed to say it, so I fucking said it. I won't take it back, so you can just shove it up your ass."

Knox snorts. "Did you just tell him to shove *I love you* up his ass?"

"Yup, and if any of the rest of you want to treat my expressing feelings as a declaration of war, you can shove it up your ass, too."

I turn around and stomp out of the room, reeling. I figured there might be surprise when I finally admitted how I was feeling, but I didn't fucking think any of them would get pissed. They say females are confusing, but fuck that shit, males take the cake. I shove out of the front door, and I'm once again greeted by the night. Man, I miss the sun. I never knew how attached I was to that fiery little orb until I barely got to see it anymore.

A hand seizes mine, and I'm yanked back and spun around. Lips press against mine, and I'm wrapped in strong, warm arms as I'm kissed senseless. I thread my hands in his thick wavy tresses and pull him impossibly closer to me. "I love you, Vinna. Bastien does too, he's just scared." I nod in understanding and kiss Valen tenderly one more time before he steps back to make room for Ryker.

"I love you, Squeaks, be safe and come back to us." I smile at him, and he cups my cheeks in his hands and guides my mouth to his. His lips are soft, his tongue expressive, and I can taste his reverence and his declaration on it. Ryker pulls away, and Knox shoves his way in.

Knox picks me up, and I wrap my legs around his waist and hold on to his big shoulders. "I'm sorry, Killer. I'm sorry for being distant the past couple of weeks. Just know I'm always here. I love you. I always will, and we'll figure everything out together, okay?"

"Okay," I tell him, and he hugs me tightly.

Knox kisses me slowly, tenderly, before he pulls away,

sets me on my feet and moves back to make room for the next Chosen. It's like a love assembly line where they each take a turn adding a piece to me until I'm battle ready.

"You love me, Witch?"

"I do, Wolf."

"Well then, come kiss me before I huff and I puff and I blow your house down," Torrez threatens, and I laugh.

"Lame, Wolf, I can think of way better things you can blow," I counter, and Torrez growls in appreciation of my statement.

He kisses me with wild abandon and then moves to my shoulder where he nips at the runes that are there because of his mark. I moan a little when he does, and he pulls away with a salacious smile. "There's my greedy girl," he tells me, and then he pulls my lips to his again.

The problem with this method of saying goodbye is that now I don't want to actually say goodbye. I want to drag each and every one of them back to the room and say, "Fuck it, group sex it is." Torrez steps away from me, knowing full well what he's done to my body, and he fucking loves it. Dick. Shit, I can't even curse him in my mind without getting even more hot and bothered. Sabin steps up to me, and his eyes are so full of love, his smile so full of happiness, that I can't help but beam right back up at him.

"You looove me. You want to bond with me, make love and have babies," he singsongs to me, and I laugh and then choke on the word babies.

"Babies are a hard pass, bro," I tell him, and he smiles at me like I've said nothing. "For real, Sabin," I warn him, but he just kisses me.

He kisses me stupid, and for a minute, I have to remind myself why I was irritated.

"You know how I feel about you, Vinna. You're the best

thing that's ever happened to us. So let's kill this fucking lamia and start living the life we all deserve, together."

Joy takes over my face, and I have to squeeze my thighs together at Sabin's words. "Fuck, it's hot when you get all ruthless and shit," I admit, and Sabin laughs. I salute him as he steps away. "Keep 'em in line, Captain Cockblock. You all need to be training every possible second of the day." Sabin shakes his head at the nickname but gives me a weak salute back.

Bastien charges me like an angry bull, and my stomach flips with excitement by the challenge pouring out of his eyes. *I'm a weirdo.* He stops when his chest is pressed against mine, the tip of his nose skimming the tip of mine, both of us breathing heavily.

"No goodbye kisses and professions of love from me, Bruiser. You can have them when I see you again and I'm deep inside of you. You can scream my name and confess your love as your pussy clenches around my cock. I'll show you what you mean to me then, when you can feel me loving you as I say it. Until then, stay safe and come back to us."

Bastien's hazel eyes are molten, and I'm pretty sure if he says cock one more time, I'm going to come. He steps back, and I immediately feel the absence of all of them. They stand in a line, shoulder to shoulder. My Chosen. More than I could have ever hoped for, and I realize I don't want to go. I'm not sure how to process my hesitancy, because normally I'm bloodthirsty and ready for any fight. I revel in the anticipation of a good match, but as I stare at each of them, feel the ghost of their lips on mine, and hear the echo of their words in my head, I'm aware that for the first time in my life, I have so much to lose.

It's terrifying and uplifting all at the same time, and I don't know what to do. I take a deep breath, searing this moment into my soul. I tell myself that I have to do this for them just as much as I have to do this for me. Killing Adriel is not just about revenge or justice anymore; I need my Chosen to be safe. I want a life with them, and the only way that's going to happen is if I rip this fucking lamia apart.

For us.

18

I wake up with the taste of goodbye on my tongue. I can still feel my Chosen's lips on mine, feel Aydin's big arms around me as he crushed me in a hug and made me promise not to get hurt. The brush of Evrin's reassurances that this will all be over soon tickle at my ear. And the concerned look that Enoch and his coven wore as I climbed into the sedan with a lamia I don't really know and drove off into the dark of day, sit heavy on my shoulders.

The sound of tires against pavement are like a siren's song, lulling me back to sleep, but I blink away the call to unconsciousness. I sit up, instantly missing the feel of the cool car window against my face. It's roasting in here. I run my sleepy gaze over the setting for the heater and notice it's on high.

"Do you mind if I turn this down?" I ask Siah, whose light blue eyes are trained on the dark road in front of us.

"Go ahead. I didn't want you to get cold," is all he says, and I nod while turning the temperature down.

I crack my window a little and sigh at the relief I feel when cool air sneaks in to brush over me. "How close?" I ask, my voice feeling like a violation of the quiet that's been shrouding us since we left.

"Another hour."

Siah falls quiet once again. I don't typically feel the urge to fill silence with small talk, but seeing as how we're going to be depending on each other to get out of this situation as unscathed as possible, I feel the need to find out more about him. I don't know much about lamia aside from the vampire comparison that's been made and what they look like when they die, but I'm not sure if it's okay to ask much about that.

"So, you and Sorik are close?" I ask, figuring that's a better place to start than *tell me every detail about your life from birth until now, ready...set...go!*

"We are."

I wait for him to elaborate, but he doesn't. "I appreciate that the silent broody thing you've got on lock probably does it for a lot of ladies, but I'm going to need you to shed your monosyllabic cocoon for the next hour. I'd like to get some idea of what I'm walking into and exactly how you fit in all of it," I tell him and watch as his face remains stone-like and focused on the road.

He waits a few seconds past uncomfortable silence before he starts to speak again. "Sorik and I were blooded about a year apart, from the same sire. He helped me navigate my new life, and we moved up in the ranks together."

"Blooded?" I interrupt, not able to help myself.

Siah looks at me curiously for a beat before turning his eyes forward again.

"Did Talon not teach you about our kind?" he asks me, and I wince.

I try to cover it up, but hearing Talon's name out of nowhere feels like a slash against my heart. It's like I forget that Talon was a lamia or the fact that he is from the same nest until it's shoved in my face. Then as soon as I remember, his confession in the back of that SUV cuts me open all over again.

"He only told me what he was when he was dying," I admit, and Siah looks at me surprised.

"What about what you were?" he queries.

"He never told me that. I found out at my reading after Talon arranged for me to be found by my uncle."

Siah's eyes narrow, and he shakes his head with obvious repugnance. It's funny because the reality of what Talon kept from me pisses me off, but seeing someone else judging him for it makes me feel defensive of Talon and the decisions he made.

"I guess I'll start with lamia 101, then," Siah grumbles. "I'm sure you've heard our race being compared to that of mythological vampires. We are where that legend finds roots, and there are some truths to the lore, but there are also extreme exaggerations."

I nod in understanding and quickly run through every stereotypical vampire ability I can think of.

"We feed off other creatures, but probably not in the way that you think. We feed on their magic. We need it to survive and replenish our stores when they get low. If we lose too much magic, we can die; if too much magic is forced into us at one time, we can die. And then there's the good ol' tried and true decapitation."

I think back to the way I killed my first handful of lamia. I must have overloaded them with magic, and that's what saved me. I didn't know at the time how it all worked, but it makes sense.

"Blood is the quickest way for us to access another being's magic, hence the fangs." Siah gives me a cold smile, and I can just make out the hint of sharp canines amongst his straight, white teeth. "We're one of the few supernatural creatures that are made, not born."

"How does that work?" I ask, curiosity winning out over not wanting to be rude.

"We're drained of all of our natural magic, and then fed the magic of our sire. Their magic either kills us outright or changes us."

"They can do this to anyone?" I ask, alarm in my tone.

"I suppose in theory it's possible, but it's technically very complicated. Humans have the highest success rates when it comes to being blooded. All creatures have some form of magic in them, and humans are really no exception. For the most part, their magic is so dormant and diluted, many of them are barely worth the feeding, but some have more than others. Sires are typically older lamia, ones who have built up greater magic stores within themselves over time. When they make another lamia, they need to pull all the magic from the being they're draining but not overload themselves so that it will kill them. They then need to force their magic into the drained but not deplete their stores so much that it results in death too."

Siah looks over at me, and I can tell he's trying to gauge if I understand what he's explaining. I give him a nod as my eyes tell him to *keep going.*

"It's a complicated process, and successful sires have it down to almost an exact science. Creatures outside of the non classification are harder to drain and change. It's not impossible, but it's incredibly risky and therefore not attempted often."

I look out the window into the shadows that flash past us as we drive, and mull over everything he's just said.

"As I was saying, Sorik and I were blooded not far apart from each other. We were both new to this world and leaned on each other in an effort to survive it. Our sire, Payter, was a trusted member of Adriel's commanders. Because of that, we were trusted with tasks and responsibilities that were sensitive and important to Adriel. Which is how Sorik and I met Grier, your mother."

My breath hitches when he speaks my mother's name, but he either doesn't notice or doesn't care about the reaction I have to hearing him talk about her.

"We were part of a group of guards that Grier always had assigned to her. The rest I think you know, based on what Sorik explained the last time you both saw one another."

I nod, putting the pieces together. They were with my mother all of the time. It makes sense that Sorik, just like Talon, grew attached to her.

"But Sorik didn't tell you that he and my mother..." I trail off.

"I knew they were close. I watched out for Sorik many times so that he and Grier could have time together, but I didn't know until he asked for help with you about how deep the connection between Grier and Sorik was."

"You never noticed the runes or questioned the random injuries to his hands?" I probe.

"The scars on his fingers showed up after we were attacked by another nest. It's not unheard of for lamia to get injured and scarred in a battle. Most supes know what shifter saliva does to us. They'll coat weapons in it or carry vials of it to use against us in a fight. His injuries weren't unexplainable. There was never a reason for me to see him with his clothes off, so I had no way of knowing."

"Do you know why Adriel is so obsessed with Sentinels?" I ask, hoping he has this confusing missing piece that helps explain why all of this happened in the first place.

"We were trusted with assignments, but we were never in Adriel's circle of confidants. I'm not sure of his exact reasons or how he even knew what Sentinels were, but it fits with what I do know about him. He's power-hungry and insatiable. He's obsessed with being the biggest, baddest being on the planet, and I'm not just talking when it comes to lamia. He wants to rule every supe and non alike. The scary thing about him is that he can convince you that you want the same thing. When he talks to the nest, pumps us up, we walk away feeling like gods, like we own the world and rightfully so. It's taken me a long time to see the manipulations for what they are. He's a being that gets what he wants, one way or another."

"Not always," I counter. "My mother held out against him."

"True, as did the two other Sentinel females he captured before her. But every time he fails, he still learns something new about your kind, and he gets that much closer to getting what he wants from the next one he catches."

My eyes widen in surprise at that admission. "He has other Sentinels?" I ask, my heart pounding harder and faster in my chest.

"He *had* other Sentinels. I'm not sure if he acquired more before the ones I know about. Like I said, I'm not in his confidence, and it's not the kind of place you can just go around asking questions about Adriel and what he's been up to."

"What happened to the ones before?" I ask, even though I already know.

"The first he killed within a week. He lost his temper. The second lasted longer but died in an interrogation with one of Adriel's enforcers. Adriel had the most patience with your mother, but by the time he found her, there'd been almost a hundred years between his last capture and hers. Plenty of time for him to improve at getting what he wanted."

"Does he ever find male Sentinels?" I ask, finding it weird that he keeps stumbling upon only females.

"That's what the hunt order is for, females."

"Where does he hunt them?"

"Everywhere. He has teams dedicated to looking for your kind."

I grow quiet as I think about that. I have so many questions about how Adriel's finding Sentinels and where. Does he just let the males keep it moving? I mean, he has to have come across at least one, you'd think, in all the time he's been doing this. I'm nervous about meeting this big bad lamia, and yet at the same time, there's a thrill of excitement working its way through my nerves. Does Adriel have answers to the thousands of questions that sit in my chest? Can I get him to tell me what he knows about Sentinels before I rip his head off?

"So we know what the plan is once Adriel has me, but exactly what are we telling him about how you're handing me over?" I ask, realizing that we never really worked out that part of the plan.

"I'll tell him that you're there to trade yourself for the two paladin we captured."

"And he won't find that suspicious?"

"He'll be so focused on the fact that you're there, I doubt he'll question much," Siah tells me, his tone confident and dismissive.

The road we're on winds to the right, and we drive into an area that's cleared of trees. The road splits the man-made clearing, and we drive deeper into the dark. I spot something that looks rock-like in the distance. We drive closer, and the rocks turn into some kind of ruin. The remnants of some ancient crumbling castle-like structure loom in front of us, and I'm instantly confused by what's clearly our destination.

"What is this place?" I ask. I lean forward in my seat to take in the decaying structure.

"Who knows," Siah tells me on a shrug. "Some long-forgotten fortress whose name has disappeared from history." The brakes give a slight squeak of protest as we slow down and come to a stop in front of the decaying building. Siah climbs out of the car, and I follow him. I spin and take in my surroundings, alert and unsure of what's going to happen now. Siah walks slowly to me and pulls something out of his back pocket. He unfolds the black square of fabric and offers me the hood.

"Where the hell did you get this?" I ask, confused, and I watch as he searches the far-off tree line.

"You'll need to put that on."

I open my mouth to ask him why, but a flash of movement to my right pulls my attention away. I snap my head in the direction of the movement, but I don't see anything.

"We're being watched by the guards. Put this on, and we'll be escorted in," Siah demands again, and I narrow my eyes at him.

Why the fuck do I need to put on a hood? If we're going to be attacking this place soon, I'll need to be able to relay as much detail about it as I possibly can. Evrin put a tracker on the car itself, so they'll already know the location, but information about the layout inside will help them. Doubt claws at me, but out here in the middle of nowhere, I'm not sure what to do about it. I take a step back from Siah, and he tenses.

"What the hell is going on?" I ask him, suspicion saturating every syllable.

"What do you mean?" he asks, taking a step in my direction, and I immediately flash a short sword and longsword into my hands.

"Vinna, what are you doing?" Siah demands, but I'm no

longer focused on him, I'm focused on my surroundings, waiting for whatever it is that's making my skin crawl to happen. I tap into the runes behind my ear and reach out to the guys.

"Something's wrong," I begin to tell them and then immediately fall silent when laughter starts to bounce around the crumbling walls of the dead building around me.

The hair on my arms stands on end, and I don't miss the cringe that flashes quickly over Siah's face before it's replaced with stony features and soulless eyes.

"Will you just look at her. She's magnificent!" a deep voice slithers out at me from the darkness. A shadowed figure steps out from behind a disintegrating wall and casually strolls toward us.

"I wondered how far your misplaced trust would take you," the figure tells me, the deep bass in his voice trying to tempt me into a sense of warmth and calm. It's like I can feel the tendrils of his timber caressing over me and trying to sink in. I ready myself, my feet shoulder width apart, my eyes trained on the being I can sense is the biggest threat to me. My Chosen bombard me with questions in my mind, but I can't answer them right now. I know if I take any focus away from the figure slowly stepping out of the shroud of shadows, I'll regret it.

Adriel steps out of the cloak of darkness, and the blackness of night falls away from his face like a hood he just pushed back. He smiles at me sweetly, and it lights up his face and sets his eyes aglow. He's gorgeous in the way that all lamia seem to be, and yet his coloring is completely unique and different from anyone I've ever seen before. His hair is modern and styled like he just came from a salon, each follicle in place as it's quaffed voluminously up and just to the side. The shade is a very dark brown that leans to red, and for some reason, it has me picturing blood mixed with rich soil.

He has a beard that's short and neatly trimmed and freckles that have been generously sprinkled all over his face. The strange shade of his golden-red eyes is what probably sets him apart the most. They're luminescent like a cat's, and the molten glow seems to threaten to suck you into them and promises to never let you go. Fair skin with just a kiss of a tan rounds off his unusual coloring. He's complemented the red tones in his hair, eyes and freckles with a navy blue suit that fits his lean yet muscular body like a glove, and a crisp white shirt that's casually unbuttoned at the collar tries to make him look less a threat but fails.

He takes another step closer, and my grip tightens on my weapons.

"Did everything go as planned?" Adriel asks, his eyes locked on mine, and my eyebrows scrunch up with confusion.

"Yes, I laid everything out just as you instructed," Siah tells him, and I try to fight against the panic that starts to rise inside of me at his words.

"Did any of her companions suspect anything?" Adriel presses, and Siah shakes his head.

"No. I put up the right amount of fight for the paladin that took me, and the rest fell into place very easily. She volunteered to trade herself for her family just like you said she would," Siah tells him.

"Typical Sentinel," Adriel jeers. "They always play the hero." Siah and Adriel both scoff at the same time, and indignation burns through me.

"Sorik and his hunters are back there, waiting for my call so they can dispatch the others," Siah relays nonchalantly, like they're talking about the weather and not murdering everyone I love.

"Run!" I shout in my head at my Chosen, putting every ounce of terror and urgency I can into the word.

"You motherfucker," I seethe at Siah simultaneously, and then I leap for him.

He moves like a blink out of my way, and I'm just able to nick him with my longsword as I swing out at the blur of movement to my left. Adriel's laughter dances around my attack like a tornado, and I pump magic into all of my limbs, demanding they move faster so I can keep up with Siah's speed. He growls at me and swipes at his side, his hand coming away streaked with crimson. I let go of my swords and flash throwing knives into my grip, pelting every flash of movement I catch with a blade in that direction.

I am a streak of movement just like Siah is, and rage is thundering through me, demanding more blood for his betrayal. Lamia pour out of the ruins like ants from an anthill, and I start snapping blades all around me to keep them at bay. I send pulses of Offensive magic and Sentinel magic out into the gathering lamia, and I smile as I watch hordes of them light up and then crumble into ash. I track the flash that I think is Siah as it tries to circle behind me and spin to keep him in my sights while I send ripples of magic out to protect my back.

Laughter and snarls drown my senses, but I keep my eyes fixed on the betraying asshole, waiting for the opening, for the kill shot that I know is just about to present itself. He's moving in a predictable way, and I know in just another heartbeat where he'll flash and my dagger will be there waiting for his heart. Satisfaction bubbles inside of me at the knowledge that two seconds after this dagger sinks into Siah's chest, I'll be there to cut off his head. I cock my arm back for the throw, and out of nowhere, something snaps around my neck.

Whatever it is clicks together, and the next thing I know,

my throat is being shredded by blood curdling screams, and my body burns from the inside out. My vision tunnels as I become nothing but pain, and I beg for the encroaching blackness to take me.

"There's my pet," a deep voice whispers into my ear. "You're mine now."

19

Gentle fingers caress my forehead as they brush hair out of my face. I try to lean into the comforting touch as it brushes against my cheek. Too quickly it's gone, and a strangled groan of protest sounds in my throat. I bring a weak hand up to massage the pain I'm feeling there, but my hand hits metal, and brutal reality kicks me in the chest. My eyes snap open, and I try to sit up, wincing at the incredible pain and fatigue I'm feeling all over.

"Slowly," a voice commands me, and a cup is pressed to my lips.

I stare into cold, ice-blue eyes, and I have to blink away the hate and betrayal that starts to well up in my own. I clamp my lips shut against the rim of the metal cup, and a flash of something streaks across Siah's eyes too fast for me to identify.

"This will help you heal," he tells me gently, but I know now not to fall for that passive tone. "With what the collar did to you, Adriel thinks you'll be drained for weeks. This will help you recover faster," he tries again as he presses the cup more firmly against my mouth.

I don't know what game this fucker is playing at, but I don't believe for a second that he's trying to help me. I clench my jaw against his efforts, defiance settling in my features. "Do I need to force it down your throat? Is that what you want, because one way or another, you need to drink this. I know what you think of me right now, and I accept it, but you need to heal and you need to do it quickly."

I try to pull my head away from him, but as fast as a striking cobra, he's holding me against his chest, keeping my head still with one hand and pressing the cup forcefully against my mouth with the other. I choke out a protest and immediately call on every weapon I have that I can stab this fucker with. Pain slices through me, and I flinch away from my magic and bite back a pained cry.

What the fuck did they do to me?

I know I didn't ask the question out loud because talking makes my throat feel like it's filled with broken glass, but I must be wearing my worry on my face because Siah addresses it.

"It's the collar. It makes it painful for you to use your magic. You were using so much of it when Adriel put it on you that he thought he killed you. He took out a good chunk of his elite guard in a fit when you collapsed and wouldn't wake up."

I huff out a tired breath, and the fight I'm trying to put up goes with it. A tear drops down my cheek, and I struggle to swallow down the frustration and anger that's attempting to escape without my permission. I want to ask about my Chosen, about Aydin and the others, but I trample my need to know. I doubt he would tell me the truth anyway.

"Drink this," Siah demands again, pressing the cup against my surrendering lips.

Liquid fills my mouth, and I'm surprised when it's not

the water I was expecting it to be. The consistency is thicker, and the flavor is somewhat sweet. I swallow it down, and Siah forces another mouthful. It dawns on me what I'm drinking, and I try to jerk my head away and close my mouth, but Siah has the cup wedged between my teeth, and I can't clamp them down all the way. He tilts my head back and forces more liquid into my mouth. I cough and sputter and swallow more of the blood he's forcing down my throat, and I feel some of it spill out of my mouth and drip down the side of my face.

When I'm choking on the last of the cup's contents, Siah releases his strong hold and backs away from me.

"Why the fuck are you forcing me to drink blood?" I accuse, my painful, barely there voice not expressing the amount of rage I'm currently experiencing right now.

"Like I said, it will help you recover much quicker. You'll be able to replenish the magic that was stripped from you faster, and you're going to need that."

Like his words just magically ignited the blood I choked down, a tingle works its way through me, and with each second that passes, I start to feel better. Siah gives me a look that smugly communicates an *I told you so*, but I refuse to recognize that he was right, not when he's the reason I'm here. He betrayed us. I was a fucking idiot for believing a stranger. With that thought, I push at the parameters of my *feeling better* and try to call on the runes behind my ear. My breath hitches when the pain slams into me, and I quickly abandon trying to contact my Chosen.

Sorrow floods me, rushing in to mix with my bitterness and fury, and I can feel the sobs forming in my chest. I glare at Siah and shake my head. "Why?" is all I can croak out before I slam down the floodgates on my surging emotions. I will not cry in front of this fucker. I will not let him see one millisecond of weakness from me, I demand from myself. I survived Beth; I can survive this asshole and his psychotic master.

He steps closer to me, and I jerk back away from him when he tries to wipe at the drying trail of blood on my jaw. I glare at him, and once again he's trapping me against him and forcing my compliance. He wipes my face clean, and then when he's done, he just stops and stares at me for a minute, his eyes bouncing back and forth between mine.

"It's not what you think," he whispers, the sound of his soft voice calling goosebumps to rise all over me. His eyes drop to my lips. For a second, I think he's going to try to kiss me, but just as quickly as he pinned my face against him, he flashes away from me and settles himself in the corner. He looks at me like somehow I've wronged *him*, and then his heated gaze morphs into ice, and he fixes his stare on a spot on the wall above my head.

I'm not sure what the fuck just happened or what he meant, but for some reason, I feel like if I speak right now, I'll lose and he'll win. I pull my gaze from the statue impersonation that Siah the asshole is now doing and look around the room. The walls are a rough stone, and the look of them gives me the distinct impression that we're somewhere underground. The lighting is electric but dim, like maybe the connection isn't strong. Or maybe they like it that way. I don't know much about lamia traits and abilities, maybe they have sensitive eyes.

I'm currently perched on a large bed, the gray bedding soft under my palms. A massive dark wood headboard rises up behind me, and a short but chunky footboard sits at the bottom. There is a side table and wardrobe in the room and an arched doorway that I hope leads to a bathroom. The space is stark, masculine, and for some reason smells familiar. I can't place what the scent is, but it's a strange sliver of comfort in all the chaos surrounding me.

Siah's jaw tenses ever so slightly, and the sound of a lock being released fills the room. The large black lacquered door swings open, and in walks a self-satisfied Adriel. His eyes land directly on me, and his lips tilt up in a friendly smile.

"Pet, I'm so relieved you're up. You gave us quite the scare. We'll have to be more careful not to get you so worked up," he teases. He's not at all fazed by the fact that he's the only one amused by any of this. His gaze roves over my face and then moves down my body. When his eyes meet mine again, he studies me for a beat.

"You look like your mother, but you have your father's eyes and dark hair. It's a stunning combination," Adriel observes. I keep my features dead, not sure what he's trying to get out of me.

"I would ask you how you're feeling, but I imagine it's quite an abysmal state you've just woken up in."

I don't miss the satisfied flash that moves through Adriel's features with his words. He loves that he's taken me down, collared me. The piece of shit probably has a hard-on right now. It's clear he likes stealing others' power and not just of the magical variety. Adriel's twinkling red-gold eyes leave mine, and he looks around the room. I don't take the bait and copy him; I just wait until he gets to whatever it is that he wants.

"This will be your room for the time being. Don't set that pretty head on escaping; you'll have guards on you every second of the day, even when you can't see them." He pauses for a minute, and his eyes land on where Siah is standing in the corner. He stares at him contemplatively for a few seconds before turning back to me. "Come now, pet, let's tour your new kingdom." Adriel holds his hand out to me like he honestly thinks I'm going to take it. I don't move from the bed.

He clicks his tongue at me in a disappointed *tsk'ing* sound and shakes his head. "Now, now, pet. You're new here, so I'll grant some leeway, but when you're commanded to do something, you will do it. Understood?"

We watch each other for a minute, and I debate the best plan of action. I'm hurt and weak, although grudgingly doing a little better since Siah forced that blood into me. As irritating as it feels to *fall in line* like I'm being ordered to do, I need to choose my battles with this mental case very carefully. Is refusing to cooperate now going to gain me anything? I push slowly off the bed. My body protests the movement at first, my muscles stiff and angry, but with each step around the bed toward Adriel, my body feels a little better.

I keep my movements shaky and cringe a couple times for show. According to Siah, Adriel expects me to be down for weeks. I can work with that and play the battered and broken Sentinel to my advantage. All I need to do is find something to cut this fucker's head off, and I'm back in the game, magic or not. Adriel's eyes light up as I make my way sloth-fast over to him. I sneak a quick glance at Siah as I pass, and I try to piece together what his deal is. He brought me here to Adriel and, for all I know, had Sorik attack everyone I left behind, and yet he's trying to get me back into fighting shape as soon as possible and whispers cryptic shit like "*it's not what you think.*"

I rub at my chest and reassure myself that everyone is fine. They're all more than capable of kicking serious ass, and even if they were surprise attacked, it doesn't mean they lost. I would feel it if something happened to them, wouldn't I? I ask myself and immediately decide that I would. We're all connected together through magic, and if that connection was severed somehow, I would know. A reassuring calm washes through me, and I hobble right past the open palm that Adriel is holding out to me. I'll listen to this fucker, but if he thinks I'm going to touch him, he's got another thing coming.

I wait to see if he's going to press the issue of my not taking his offered palm, but he just releases an amused chuckle and falls into step next to me. We exit through the large black doors out into a hallway made of the same stone that the walls of the room were. I look up and gasp at what I find. The ceiling is high, roughly domed and completely made up of crystals. They sparkle from the dim light of the sconces in the hallway, and I run my awed gaze over the various shades of blue and purple. There are small groupings of clear crystals interspersed amongst the other colors, and the whole ceiling looks like a bejeweled image of deep space.

"Magnificent, isn't it?" Adriel asks me.

He looks so satisfied by my appreciative reaction to the ceiling, you'd think he'd hand made it himself.

"There are many breathtaking places in our home. Just wait until you see the dining room or the pools," he tells me and then leads me through the hallway.

I'm certain that we're underground now, but I'm less hopeful that we might be located under the ruins that Siah stopped the car at. I suppose it's possible that the ruins had lower levels that might have connected to these cave systems, or maybe that's just my wishful thinking. I didn't ask Siah how long I was incoherent from the pain the collar caused me, so it's possible they had enough time to move me somewhere else.

My eyes roam over everything we pass, and grudgingly, I have to admit it's a good hiding spot. Whenever I pictured Adriel and where he might be, I figured he had a building or home that was hidden just like Solace. But a fucked up sparkly bat cave is a smart move and not something I would think others are likely to search for.

I'm herded down a hallway and into what looks like a massive lounge room that has different spaces that lamia are congregated around. There's a corner with some pool tables, different sitting areas facing TVs, a grouping of high tables and stools that laptop-using lamia are perched on, and chairs bookending chess boards scattered around the room. Everyone is stunning and appears to be around my age. The place looks like a rad dorm common room or a community center for the super-hot. I look around, and it's not hard to forget that each of these individuals is a supernatural predator and part of the nest that hunts my kind.

I spot female lamia for the first time ever, and I try not to stare at them. I've only ever seen males, and even though Siah said there were females, it didn't register as real until now. I don't really know what I expected, but they possess the same impossible beauty as their male counterparts, and I would guess the same speed and strength too.

A tall male walks into the room. He's holding a leash that's attached to a black leather collar that's been secured around the throat of a female who's walking behind him. He plops down on a lush black leather sofa and pulls on the leash roughly until the female is forced into his lap. It's obvious she doesn't want to be there, and my hackles rise as I watch him forcefully position her the way that he wants.

Adriel is boastfully telling me something, but I can't even be bothered to pretend I'm listening to him as I watch the grimace on the female's face when the lamia brushes her hair over her shoulder and drops his lips to her skin. The lamia says something to the woman in his lap, and she pales ever so slightly. It doesn't take a genius to guess what whispered words would have her on the verge of tears, but the picture grows even clearer when he fondles her breasts, and she shudders and squeezes her eyes tightly shut.

I run my gaze around the room, calculating if I can reach them before any of the indifferent lamia in this room would think to stop me. If I sprint, the couple are maybe twelve paces away. Could I get to them? A cheer goes up around the pool table closest to the black sectional couch, and it pulls my attention away from the couple. Adriel says something to Siah, and before I consciously make the decision to do so, my bare feet are slapping against the stone floor as I sprint toward the noisy pool table.

I'm surprised that my body responds to my pressing demands as quickly as it does with how weak I was feeling, but I don't focus on that as I close in on the rowdy group of pool playing lamia. I drive my foot into the back of a male's knee and rip the pool cue out of his hands as he yelps in surprise and falls forward into another lamia. I turn like a cheetah cutting prey from the herd, and leap over the back of the couch to land next to the couple. I'm shocked that I've gotten this far in a room full of beings that I know first-hand have supernatural speed and strength. Maybe I just shocked the hell out of them with the stunt I'm pulling, or maybe they're more comfortable and complacent at home than they are out in the world.

Shock registers on the face of the lamia on the couch, and he moves to shove the female off his lap. Before he can even shift his weight to stand, I've sunk the pool stick into his neck. He grabs at the wound and a blood-filled gasp escapes his stunned mouth. I move my makeshift weapon from side to side widening the hole I just put in his neck, but I know I don't have enough time to try and rip his head off as roars of indignation fill the room. I give up on my goal of decapitation by pool cue and pull it out of the lamia's neck with a sickening squelching noise. Lamia can die if their magic stores get too low, and Siah said magic is found in the blood. So maybe this asshole will bleed to death.

I wipe the blood off the wood on his shirt so it's not too slippery and turn, my weapon in hand, and step in front of the woman. I'm about ninety percent sure she's human. I know that Talon mentioned something about Beth being a blood slave, and that's exactly what this set up between the lamia and the girl looked like. She's still on the ground, looking up at me in terror, and the rest of the room is very obviously pissed about what just happened. No one has taken one step in my direction, but I'm sure once the shock wears off, that will change. A rage-filled cry echoes around the room, but I don't look for the source as I focus on Adriel and ready myself for an attack.

Surprisingly, he doesn't look even half as outraged as the others in the room clearly are. He seems more put out by what I've done than anything else. A breeze caresses my skin to the left, and a lamia tries to move in closer to me. I twirl the pool cue in that direction, and I smash him in the jaw. He falls to the ground, cupping his mouth, and glares at me but doesn't pop up like I expect him to.

I'm perplexed by the lamia's submission, and it dawns on me that maybe he doesn't know how to fight. Every lamia I've ever run into seemed battle ready, but maybe the whole collective of this nest isn't. Adriel raises his hand, and the shouts and growls echoing around the stone walls grow quiet. He takes a step toward me, and I tighten my grip around the cue, which is thankfully still whole.

"Put it down now, and I'll chalk this up to a misunderstanding. You've yet to be told the rules of my house and therefore couldn't know how serious we take slaves shedding blood. Or what we do to anyone who interferes with an elite and their feeder," Adriel's words move powerfully around the room, and I can tell they're meant for the lamia and their rising anger more than they're meant for me.

I feel the female behind me shakily stand up and press in closer to my back. Adriel takes another step toward me. "I will not ask you again. You will stop this temper tantrum right now, or I will kill the human you're stupidly risking yourself to protect. I will disarm you, beat you, and then force you to watch me rip her apart piece by piece."

The female at my back flinches and then quietly whispers, "They'll torture me anyway."

Her voice is the slightest puff of air as it hits the back of my neck, and I can almost feel the bitterness in it dripping down my spine. Laughter titters through the surrounding lamia, and I glare at the threat that hangs in the air.

"Would you rather die?" I ask, my eyes locked on Adriel, and he chuckles as an amused glint enters his eyes.

"You'll need much more than a pool cue if you want to come for me, Sentinel," Adriel mocks, but I don't miss the *yes* that caresses my shoulder.

I drop the pool stick, and satisfaction lights up Adriel's face. That is, until I pivot behind the female, reach up and snap her neck. She goes limp in my arms, and I carefully lower her to the cold ground. Adriel roars out, "*NO*," but I'm unfazed by his outrage. I brush strawberry blonde locks out of the young woman's face and wonder how the fuck she ended up here? What kind of hell was she living in that would make her rather die than face what might happen next?

I find the buckle on the back of her collar and remove it. There's so much noise and action all around me, but it feels like a dull roar to my ears as I tune it out and add this woman, whoever she was, to the list in my mind who will be avenged when Adriel is ash. I look up to find Adriel stomping toward me. He back hands me so hard that my entire face and neck explode in pain, and I'm slammed to the ground. My ears ring as I try to push off the ground, and I feel a booted foot kick me in the stomach. I try to roll away from more kicks, but someone grabs me by the hair and pulls me up from the ground.

I grab the wrist of whoever's fist is wrapped around my ponytail and try to pull up on it in an effort to distribute my weight and keep chunks of hair from being ripped out of my scalp. I dangle painfully until the face of the lamia I tried to kill on the couch is in my face.

Well, fuck!

I'll have to make the hole in his neck bigger next time.

20

I skid across the rough dirt of the cell I've just been thrown into. I grunt in pain from the impact and cough as the dust my body just kicked up tries to settle in my lungs. The door is closed behind me, and I relax against the ground and breathe through the pain. Blood trickles from my nose and my lip, and it mixes with the hard packed dirt beneath me. The sight and smell of it remind me of the room in the barn that I discovered Siah in, and I internally curse at the fucked up full circle moment.

I wipe at the blood slowly dripping from my face and wince at the pain that throbs in my cheek and jaw. I put up a decent fight against the beating Adriel sanctioned. I got in several good hits those fuckers didn't see coming, but in the end, there was only so much I could do with no magic against the speed and strength of a group of lamia. Lucky for me and my bones, Adriel called it after one of them tried to bite me, and my shields popped up to stop it. The instinctual trigger of my magic sent me to the ground, writhing in pain, and when it happened again, Adriel decided the punishment wasn't worth the risk of losing me.

I grab for my collar and methodically inspect it, looking

for any indication of how it's held together around my neck. The metal is cold against my heated skin, but no matter how slowly I search, I can't find a seam or anything else that indicates any kind of release. The metal collar is smooth against my neck and somewhat rough and porous on the other side. I sit up slowly and press a palm against my right side.

My ribs are tender as fuck, and they're either bruised to hell or they're broken. I debate ripping my sweater up and trying to bind my injured side, but the idea of only being in a bra the next time Adriel pulls me out to play feels like a bad fucking idea.

I look around the barely lit cell I've been abandoned in for the moment to see if there might be something else in here I could use. I'm not sure what I'm expecting to find. I'm pretty sure they didn't throw a first aid kit in here with me, but my eyes roam around, delusionally hopeful all the same. I freeze when I spot a pair of thin legs sticking out from the furthest dark corner. I'm shocked to realize that I'm not in here alone, and I instantly debate whether I'm in here with someone who could possibly help me or hurt me even more.

I haven't been this bad off since I left Beth's house, and as curious as I am about whoever is in the corner, I should maybe give myself as much time as I can to recover before I face the owner of the emaciated legs. I've no sooner decided that when the door to the cell slams open again. A canteen is thrown into the room, and it bounces against the wall, making a deafening racket. The cell door quickly closes again, but the skinny legs have been pulled into the darkness of the corner, and it's clear whoever is over there is now awake.

Neither of us move to retrieve the canteen, even though I'm dying of thirst. We both sit in our unlit corners, waiting and watching.

"Pretty sure that's for you," a dry and obviously unused voice rumbles out from the darkness.

"How do you know?" I question after a couple minutes of awkward silence. I wince as I speak the words, the cut in my lip painfully protesting the movement.

"They've never thrown shit like that in here for me," the disembodied voice offers, and I stare at the canteen like somehow the mystery of its appearance will reveal itself if I can just not blink long enough.

"Well, you probably need whatever's in there more than I do," I tell him, and the cell grows silent again.

I get itchy from the feel of this person's eyes on the dark corner I'm shrouded by. I'm pretty sure I'm as hidden from him as he is from me, but this back and forth is weird. He's obviously in this cell for a reason, and I think it's safe to say it's not because he's a friend of Adriel or his nest. What's that saying…the enemy of my enemy is my friend? I crawl out of my dark corner and over to the metal canteen. I pick it up and slowly shuffle toward the stranger.

"No harm in sharing," I announce when I get within reaching distance of him, and I stretch my arm out, offering the canteen, and push my hair out of my face.

The stranger gasps and leans forward, and the dim beams of light illuminate the planes of a gaunt face that's simultaneously foreign and yet familiar. I lean back in shock, trying to process what I'm seeing.

"Is it you?" the familiar stranger asks me, and I'm too stunned to form coherent words. "How?" he asks again, and this time his Sahara-kissed voice cracks with emotion.

I run my eyes all over his face, looking for some kind of proof. "Dad?" I ask quietly, the question spilling out of me like water, surprise and hope saturating every drop.

He shudders, and his face fills with pain. I watch him physically fight off the blow that apparently my question is to him, and understanding and horror slam into me like a tidal wave. I drop the canteen on the ground and slam a hand over my mouth, forcing the horrified gasp back down my throat.

"Holy fucking shit, Lachlan," I whimper, "what the hell did they do to you?"

I run my stunned gaze all over him, trying to comprehend how this could happen to a person in just over a month. He looks like he's been starving for years. His cheeks are hollow, and his eyes are sunken and swimming with pain. His golden, light-tan skin is sallow, and he's so emaciated and fragile looking, I'm terrified he's going to break if he even tries to move. Lachlan sags against the wall of the cell, proving that just when I think he can't look worse, he does.

I snatch the canteen from the ground, ignoring my protesting injuries, and hastily screw the top off. I offer him the canteen and then press it closer to his mouth when he makes no effort to take it.

"You said they don't ever give you anything like this, and you clearly need to get hydrated way worse than I do," I encourage.

Lachlan's emerald-green gaze settles on mine, and he watches me for a minute before leaning in. I press the mouth of the canteen to his chapped lips and tilt it up slowly. Lachlan swallows a gulp down and then coughs and chokes on his second attempted mouthful. I lean forward and cradle his head as his lungs fight against the liquid he just aspirated. And I'm worried his brittle ribs are going to snap with each violent cough that wracks his body.

"What the hell is that?" he croaks, and then he stares at the canteen like it just betrayed him somehow.

I bring the canteen up to my nose and sniff, prepared to inhale something disgusting, judging by the grossed out look on Lachlan's face. There's definitely a hint of something deep and masculine, which rules out water, but I have no idea how to place the distinct scent that sends tendrils of recognition through me. I take a sip of the canteen's contents, and a rich, somewhat sweet flavor explodes on my tongue, immediately cluing me in to what this is.

"It's blood," I tell Lachlan, offering him more, and his face goes from disgusted to horrified.

"Why the hell would you offer that to me? Better yet, how the hell do you know what blood tastes like?" his question whips out like the accusation it is, and I flinch back.

Well, it looks like they didn't starve the judgmental asshole out of him. Yay for me.

"I was given some blood after they brought me here. It helped me heal, and from the looks of things, you could go for a shit ton of that right now," I observe, not admitting that I didn't willingly take the blood I was first offered either.

The corner of Lachlan's mouth turns up in an unmistakable sneer, and I huff out a tired sigh. "Whether you like it or not, you need all the help you can get. I don't know what they did to you, but you look like death."

Lachlan turns away from me, and his eyes fix on a spot on the wall. It's clear he's back to shutting me out, and I fight back the flash of anger it evokes in me. I debate for a second about pinning Lachlan's head down and forcing him to drink like Siah did to me. He's definitely weak enough. I could probably get away with it, but a piece of me feels like there's no point fighting for someone who won't fight for themselves. I shake my head at him.

"This could very well save your life. Are you seriously telling me that you choose your fucked up stubborn pride over living?" I ask, exasperated. He doesn't answer, just continues to stare blankly at the wall.

I scoot away from him until my bruised back is flush

with my corner of the cell. I raise the canteen to him and toast. "Here's to the stubborn-to-the-point-of-stupidity gene dying with you." I bring the canteen to my lips and drain every last drop of blood. My body sings as it hits my system, and I immediately feel better. I take a deep breath testing my hurt ribs, and I'm relieved when the pain is duller than it was before. I pat at my bloody nose and lip, and my hand comes away blood free, my face not nearly as tender as it was. The fact that I'm not revolted, but actually enjoy the taste of what's in the canteen, is probably proving to Lachlan that I'm some kind of baby demon. The kind of baby demon that's solely responsible for the death of his brother, but I just don't give a fuck anymore.

That thought triggers something in me, and my head snaps to Lachlan. "Have you seen Vaughn? Do you know for sure what happened to him?" I ask, and for some reason, my eyes bounce around the barely lit cell like maybe Vaughn is hidden in a different dark corner I just haven't noticed yet. "Where's Keegan?" I fire off as well, adding to the pile of unanswered questions when my frantic searching clues me in that he's missing from this room too.

Lachlan inhales a pained gasp and clutches at his chest. The sound is so full of torment that I'm instantly alarmed. I move toward him and then stop myself. *This is Lachlan, he's not going to want to be comforted by me.* I sit there awkwardly, not sure what to do or how I feel about second guessing my initial instinct to offer support. In the end, I sit back down and watch him cautiously. Lachlan shakes his head, and his green eyes grow haunted.

"Vaughn's gone. He's been gone for a..." Lachlan pauses and his breath stutters. "He's been gone for a while. I...I should have known, but I just kept hoping."

Lachlan's voice breaks, and he covers his gaunt face in an effort to hide the emotion that's pouring out of him.

My chest feels heavy, and surprisingly, my eyes start to sting. I press my thumb and my forefinger against my closed lids and breathe through the sadness that's crashing into me. I told myself that Vaughn was probably gone. The likelihood that he would still be alive after all this time wasn't high, and yet hearing Lachlan profess it, fucking hurts. I'm stunned by exactly how much it hurts.

From the minute I found out that Grier and Vaughn were my real parents, I've tried not to think about them too much. I didn't see the point in breaking down over people I will never meet, or focusing too much on what my life could have been if I had been raised by them instead of Beth. It would be easy to romanticize how much they would have loved me and how beautiful everything would have been, but there's no way of knowing what might have been different. Things are the way they are, and that's that. Or so I thought.

A sob sits at the back of my throat, and in this moment, I realize just how much I was still hoping that my family situation could be different. Grier is gone, Laiken is gone, Talon is gone, and apparently a piece of me I was refusing to look at was desperately hoping that, against the odds, Vaughn was still alive. That somehow he was out there in the world, wanting and hoping for...me.

I watch Lachlan cry into his skeletal hands, and I realize just how badly I wanted a dad. Tears stream silently down my face, and I breathe through the loss I feel about the unknown. The possibility and hope are gone now, and I ache from the brutal finality of it all.

"They took Keegan over a week ago. I don't know if he's in another cell or if he's..." Lachlan trails off, and he leans back into the darkness of the corner, hiding his grief from me.

"I was told Keegan was still alive," I reassure Lachlan.

Siah could have been completely full of shit, but I hope against hope that he was telling me the truth. I debate for a second about addressing my next thought but decide what have I got to lose?

"I read that when you're Bound to another caster, you feel it when they pass?" I tell Lachlan quietly. "You would know if something happened to him."

Shadows hide Lachlan's features, and I have no idea if my attempt at reassurance garners any reaction from him. Silence fills the stone and dirt room, and I get lost in thought.

"How did you know that he and I..." Lachlan finally inquires, and I wonder how much it's killing him to have to ask me.

"I suspected in the library after you choked me. The way Keegan was comforting you was more intimate than it was with the others. He was always defending you, following your lead, and neither of you ever talked about females," I explain. "At first I thought maybe you two were hiding it from the whole coven, but then I realized that you just didn't trust me to know."

Stifling quiet envelops the last of my words, and I wait to see if Lachlan will say anything. I don't know why a flash of frustration sparks through me when he stays silent. I should fucking know better than to think he's going to open up to me.

"Whatever it is that you think about me, you're fucking wrong," I angrily declare to Lachlan. "I didn't even exist when Vaughn was taken from you. I'm not the one who put him with my mother, and I was born *after* they tried to escape. I am not responsible for what happened."

He doesn't say anything.

"I didn't ask for any of this," I remind him once again,

and I'm surprised when he mumbles something. "What?" I snap.

"I don't blame you for what happened. Well, not anymore anyway," he confesses, and I'm rendered speechless by the fact that he even said anything, let alone *that*. "I work hard. I'm single-minded in my focus to be the best," he admits. "Keegan teases that I'm overcompensating, and as much as I hate to admit it, he's right. Keegan and I are private about our relationship, not because we necessarily have to be, it's just the way we are. The community doesn't look down on us, but I've always felt the drive to prove my worth regardless. I do that by being the best paladin I can possibly be and serving the community that way."

Lachlan grows quiet, and I'm not sure what to say. I'm floored by this peek into who he is, but I'm not sure why he's giving it to me.

"When Vaughn went missing, a part of me went missing too. We all looked. We did everything we could possibly do to find him, but I failed. I failed him. I failed the other families that lost loved ones. I failed the community because I was the best and yet I couldn't piece together what happened. And every birthday and Bonding Anniversary, every good day I had without my brother made me break more and more."

Lachlan leans forward out of the shadows of his corner, and the hollowness I see in his gaze is haunting. He takes a few breaths before he continues, and he looks so shattered as he does. I realize as I watch him that there is no gluing his pieces back together, and it makes me so fucking sad for him.

"You have his eyes," he whispers at me, and he spends a moment blinking away the emotion that confession calls out in him. "One minute you were just there, fighting like you were born for it, blinking up at me with *his* eyes, and I just didn't know how to deal with it, with you. I don't know how to be happy that you exist when I'm just so sad that he doesn't anymore." Lachlan starts crying, and I wipe away at my own tears as I watch my uncle show me his *broken*.

"I'm glad you have the boys and their coven. They're good males, and they will be there for you. They will take care of you. And I know it's wrong, I know it's not fair, but that will have to be enough. Because you will never find what you're looking for here," he tells me, and he slams a fragile, shaky fist against his chest. "I just don't have it in me to give you what you deserve. You need to know that I'm just too fractured, and that's on me, not on you."

Lachlan's emerald eyes turn hard, and I witness as he sluffs off the vulnerability he was just showing. He leans back, letting the darkness of the corner wrap him in its embrace, and I stare after him, once again at a loss for words. I want to tell him that maybe if he would just try, he'd realize that he's not as broken as he thinks. That I've seen moments in his countenance that point to hope. That I'm worth the risk, worth the effort. But I'm once again reminded not to fight for something when the other person isn't willing to fight for it too.

I rest my head back so I can hide in my own shadows. He's right. It's not fair, and it is wrong, but ultimately, it's just sad. He's given up, and there's not a fucking thing I can do about it. There's not enough magic in the world to make someone see, not when they refuse to open their eyes or even believe that they can.

21

A gray haze encases me, and I try to blink it away from my eyes. It feels wet or maybe the coolness of the mist just gives that illusion. I ache, like my body is fighting off a fever, and a painful shiver runs up my spine.

"Squeaks?"

Ryker's voice moves through me, and I try to grab for it, but it buzzes around my head, illusive and just out of reach.

"Squeaks, can you hear me?" he tries again, and I whimper at the longing that coats his smooth tone. *"Focus, Vinna,"* he instructs me. I try to answer him, but this dream hurts so fucking bad.

"What hurts, Vinna?" he asks, like he just plucked the thought from my foggy brain.

"Everything," I confess.

"Thank fuck! There you are," he announces, and it's as if I can snatch the relief in his words out of the air and wrap it warmly around me. *"Are you okay? We've been trying to reach you."*

"My dad is dead. Siah betrayed us, and I've been collared," I tell him on a slur.

"What does that mean, Squeaks?" Ryker presses, his words frantic.

A stinging sensation starts in my limbs, and I try to shake them out. *"I killed a girl, Ryker. She wanted to die. I couldn't fight for her. I killed her. I'm so fucking mad I went for the wrong threat; I chased Siah when I should have been killing Adriel. Stupid. So fucking stupid!"*

"Hey now, no one talks about my girl that way. Just slow down, you're not making any sense. Why can't you fight?" he asks, his tone gentle and reassuring, but I feel the bite of panic in his question.

"He put a collar on me like a fucking dog. I can't use magic. It makes it hurt," I explain, and as I do, some of the gray haze around me lifts. *"I don't think I'm dreaming,"* I announce, and as more of the fog recedes, I become less and less anesthetized. My bones feel like they're on fire, and my heart starts to race as I begin to pant through the pain.

"Fuck, Squeaks. We know where you are, and we're coming, just hold on, okay?"

"Not yet," I tell him, and he growls with frustration. *"I have to find Keegan first."*

With that, a loud bang has me jolting all the way awake, and I'm instantly aware of the bone-deep ache radiating throughout my body. My head has only me in it again, and I feel the loss of Ryker worse than the physical pain I'm currently experiencing. Lachlan is being carried out by two goonish looking lamia. Alarmed, I stand up and move to intercept them, but I'm yanked out of the way from behind.

My back slams into something so hard that it knocks the wind out of me. I tell my brain over and over again not to panic, and *will* my lungs to inflate. Arms wrap around me from behind, and I can't fight their hold while I'm fighting to breathe. I gasp painfully as my lungs finally rebound, and I cough on the air that rushes in too fast.

"Drink this quickly," a familiar voice whispers in my ear.

Another canteen is shoved in my hands, and my feet are being pulled out from underneath me as I'm carried out of the cell. I don't look up at Siah's face as I unscrew the cap to the canteen and down the contents in less than thirty seconds. When the canteen is empty, Siah snatches it from my grasp, and then suddenly it's gone. I have no idea if he dropped it discreetly somewhere or performed some disappearing magic trick. Fuck, he could have shoved it up his ass for all I know, but it's gone in some freakishly impressive sleight of hand, and I have no idea where it went.

The blood works its magic, and my body and mind immediately come alive. Siah carries me up the stairs, and we trail about ten feet behind the goons carrying Lachlan.

"He likes to talk. The more you can keep him talking, the longer everything will drag out. Trust me, that's a good thing. And no matter what happens, Vinna, don't let him feed from you. Adriel can pull memories and magic from blood. Do you understand what would happen to all of us if he knew what was planned?"

Siah's words are spoken quietly and vehemently in my ear. I pull away to stare at his face and try to get an idea of what the fuck is going on. Why is he acting like we're still working together, like we still have the same goal? He betrayed me...didn't he? I think back to everything he's said and done since the moment we stopped at the ruins. He more or less said this was a setup, all part of some contrived plan with Adriel, but he keeps trying to heal me. He just warned me about Adriel and what he can do. And when I first woke up, didn't he tell me it's not what I think?

I take in his hard features and his cold demeanor. I look for the answers in Siah's eyes, in the tic of his jaw, and the way he holds me tightly to his chest, but I just don't fucking know. It's impossible to gauge where his loyalties lie in all of this. And as much as I wish I could find the answer in his glacial eyes, I can't tell if I'm the one getting played or if Adriel is?

Tall black doors slam open, and I follow Lachlan into a long room that's polished, black stone from floor to ceiling. The room feels ominous and uninviting, and a shiver runs through me as I'm carried deeper into the room. I notice other tall black doors spread throughout the room, but my attention is pulled away from them when Lachlan is dropped at Adriel's feet. He's perched haughtily in what can only be described as a fucking throne, and Lachlan lets out a pained *oomph* as a thud echoes around the cavernous space.

I push to get out of Siah's arms, and he hastily drops me to my feet, where I take up position in front of Lachlan. Adriel runs his gaze over me quickly, and I get the distinct impression he's not happy with the fact that I can even stand. He watched the beating his little minions gave me, and he clearly expected me to be crumpled on the floor like my uncle currently is. I mentally add another tally to Adriel's side of who's getting played and know that Siah's blood offerings are, without a doubt, on the down low.

Adriel drums his fingers on the arm of his throne and leans back in contemplation. A hint of amusement flashes in his face as he stares at me and then at Lachlan on the floor.

"I wonder, if the roles were reversed, if he would stand guard over you. Hmmm, pet? Do you think he would face off against me on your behalf?"

"I'd guess, based on his current starved and battered state, he's already been doing that," I tell Adriel casually, not playing into whatever divisive bullshit he's trying to pull.

A sly smile takes over his face. "You know he would trade you for his brother if he could," he announces, and even though his cadence is cavalier, his eyes shrewdly watch for my reaction.

"Tell me something I don't know," I shrug and do my best to adopt an *I'm fucking bored* visage.

The banging of doors bounces around the shiny, black stone of the room, but I don't look to see if that means someone just came in or if someone just left. I took my focus off Adriel before when I was chasing my anger and Siah around the ruins, and look where that got me. No, my eyes, while in the presence of this monster, are only for him. Lachlan moves from where he's lying on his side on the ground, and he sits up. It looks like it takes every ounce of his energy to do it, and it breaks my fucking heart.

I stand where I am, but I drop my hand to my side and offer it to Lachlan so he can help lift himself up. I'm proud as fuck that I'm able to support his weight and mine as Lachlan has to practically crawl up my body in order to stand.

"Is there something you wanted, or can we go back to the dungeons?"

"Careful, Sentinel," he warns. "I rule here. Not you."

"Take this collar off, and we'll see how long it stays that way," I challenge, and Adriel narrows his eyes at me.

"Bring the other one," he commands, and it's followed by hurried footsteps, shutting doors, and Lachlan tensing behind me.

"I've waited a very long time for you, Vinna. I've patiently removed the obstacles in my way one by one, and finally here you are. We both know that I won't kill you, but what you may not know is there are things that I can do to you that are worse than death. So be careful, little one, this can be as sweet or as bitter as you make it."

I fucking hate that this arrogant piece of shit has stripped me of my magic. I hate that I can't walk right up to him in that gaudy, ugly ass chair and rip his power-hungry head off. But what I love right now in this moment is that I know I'm more than just my magic. I'm capable and smart, and I will find a way to kill this asshole regardless of this collar. I just have to figure out how. "*He likes to talk,*" Siah's voice echoes in my mind, and I decide to start there.

"Why am I here?" I ask, as if no one has ever explained anything to me.

Adriel smiles at me and leans forward. "You're here to learn that you and I were meant to rule the world," he tells me with a singsong voice, and I try very fucking hard not to scoff.

"Oookayyy then, and why would I want to rule the world? Better yet, why do you want to? In my experience, there's really no way to make *everyone* happy, and as ruler of the world, you'd be constantly dealing with people and their expectations. That seems like a lot of fucking work," I babble like a young dumb kid, and I can practically see frustration-tinged steam seeping out of his ears.

"It's our rightful place," Adriel growls out at me.

I tilt my head and let my gaze go vacant. "But who decided that?"

"I did," he challenges.

"Why?" I ask doing my best impersonation of a curious three-year-old with never-ending questions.

"Because he shouldn't have been Chosen; it should have been me!" Adriel's features go from frustrated to manic, and I press to keep him talking.

"Who shouldn't have been Chosen?" I ask and try to keep the interest in my tone hidden under confusion.

"Sauriel, my brother," he supplies, and he leans back in the chair, his features turning hard.

Doors open somewhere behind me, and Adriel's focus moves from me to whoever is entering the room. I take a minute to file away what I just learned. His brother was Chosen by a Sentinel, and this fucker is jealous. Is that really the foundation of every fucked up thing Adriel has done? All of this shit traces back to jealousy and some bullshit sibling rivalry?

"Where is your brother?" I ask, but before I can get an answer, a body is thrown to the ground on my right, and Lachlan gasps and lunges for it.

Adriel does nothing to stop Lachlan from wrapping his arms around Keegan. Keegan looks stunned and confused. Lachlan kneels down next to him and pulls him into a hug, and Keegan seems to suddenly recognize who he is and immediately wraps his arms around Lachlan too. Tears stream down both of their faces, and they whisper reassurances to each other as they wipe the sadness away from each other's cheeks.

Their reunion is beautiful and intimate, and it feels wrong to be some uninvited bystander peeking in at their love, at their bond. My throat grows tight, and I try to blink my vision clear of the emotion that wells up in my eyes. Keegan is in a similar state as Lachlan, skinny, malnourished, suffering, and I'm once again completely baffled by how they're this bad off in such a short amount of time.

"Awww," Adriel coos loudly. "Isn't it just lovely to witness? The love, the devotion. Did you know, pet, that they both chose to be tortured so the other wouldn't have to be? Now *that's* true devotion, don't you think? We drained them time and time again, and they still wouldn't turn on one another. It was truly admirable. Dumb, really, in the end, because look at them. Neither escaped interrogation, but they just refused to be the cause of the other's pain."

I feel sick at Adriel's declaration, and Lachlan and Keegan hold on to each other tighter.

"Would you have made the same choice, pet? Would you

do *everything* that you can to keep someone you care about from getting hurt?"

My stomach drops as I realize that Adriel is going to fucking torture them to force my hand. Panic rises inside of me, and I frantically try to think of a way to get all of us out of this.

"Come here, Vinna," Adriel commands.

I glare at him with all the hate and loathing I feel right now, because I can't think of a fucking thing I can do to stop whatever he's about to do. Either I give him what he wants and everyone suffers under the wrath of a psycho with too much power, or I watch as he tortures Lachlan and Keegan.

"Come here, or I will kill one of them right now," he bellows like a spoiled little brat, and I move toward him, even though every instinct I have rebels against it.

I approach him and mentally roundhouse the smirk he's wearing right off his fucking face. Normally, pulverizing someone in my head helps me, but right now it just makes me feel fucking helpless because I can't do shit. I reach his side, and he smiles up at me. I debate if I were to punch him right now whether or not it will connect, but I know who he'll punish if I even try it. I clench my teeth and stare at him, promises of pain radiating from my gaze, but he just looks amused by it.

Adriel rises from his throne and casually moves to stand behind me. It makes my skin crawl to have him at my back, and when I turn to keep him in my line of sight he *tsks* at me.

"Face your family, Vinna. I want you to have a clear view of who you'll be hurting if you refuse me." I breathe faster as adrenaline starts to surge inside of me and fear trickles up my spine. I turn to look at Keegan and Lachlan, and Adriel steps closer to me until his chest is skimming my back. I quickly scan the rest of the room to find a couple sets of guards and Siah standing off to the side at attention. His eyes are fixed on a wall, but the tic in his jaw is prevalent.

Adriel sweeps my tangled mess of hair from my right shoulder to my left, and I go rigid from his unwelcome touch. I close my eyes for a moment and try to calm myself down. I try to convince my body that we can't fight or flee and to breathe through his too close proximity and the alarms caused by his breath on the back of my shoulder. I open my eyes to find Lachlan's enraged gaze and tears dripping down Keegan's face.

"I'm going to feed from you now, Vinna. There's no point in fighting me. If you do, they will get hurt. If I have to pin you down to taste your secrets, I will, but if you force me to do that, I'll let my elite have some fun with you while you watch your family suffer. Understood?"

I don't answer him; I just keep my eyes trained on Lachlan and Keegan and fight the scream that's building in my chest.

"Vinna, don't," Lachlan shouts out, but I close my eyes and will myself not to move as his protest echoes around the room.

I can feel Adriel waiting to strike at my shoulder, and I know the sick fucker is reveling in the fear and anticipation. He moves in closer, and just when I expect to feel fangs piercing my skin, a blue shield explodes out of the runes on my shoulder, and it sends Adriel flying back. Pain ricochets inside of me from the unexpected flare of magic, and I swallow a pained groan and try to stay on my feet.

Adriel's furious roar fills the black, polished stone room, and his guards spread out like they're preparing for a battle. I turn just in time to see Adriel flash up from the ground and blur toward me. He roughly jerks my head to the side and viciously tries to bite my shoulder, but my shield activates again and hits Adriel with such force that he smashes into the wall behind us. The pain the collar causes me is worse this time, and it brings me to my knees. An agonized grunt escapes me, and I place my palms on the cool polished stone floor and wait for the pain to recede.

I look up, and Lachlan takes a step in front of Keegan, his eyes fixed on what has to be Adriel's enraged face. I can tell by his stance and the look in his eyes that he's prepared to die, and surprisingly he looks okay with that. I expect Adriel to come charging from behind me any second now to face off with Lachlan, but in the time it takes me to blink, I realize just how fucking wrong I was.

A guard flashes behind Keegan in less than a second, and before I can even open my mouth to warn Lachlan, the lamia grabs Keegan and tears his throat out. My eyes go wide with horror, and my scream of rage fills the room. Lachlan turns too late and bellows out an anguished cry when he sees what's happened. The lamia pushes Keegan's body away from his own, and Lachlan catches him. They sink to the ground together. I crawl over to them, and my heart shatters as I watch Lachlan hold his dying mate.

Keegan's eyes are wide with shock, and he's choking on the blood that's pouring out of his mouth and throat.

"I love you, I'm so sorry," Lachlan tells him over and over, and Keegan grabs on to Lachlan's arm, his grip panicked and shaky as he slowly drowns on his own blood. I put my hands on the wound in Keegan's neck and call on my Healing magic. Agony rips through me, and I can't help but scream, but I keep pushing as much as I can into Keegan. I close my eyes and try to focus on the teal color of my magic and not on the searing pain that I'm experiencing because of this fucking collar.

I'm sobbing, it hurts so bad, but I clench my teeth and keen out my torture and push more magic into Keegan. I open my eyes, and my heart falls when the injury starts to knit together, but it's too slow, and I know it won't be enough. Lachlan leans down and kisses Keegan and whispers words from his soul against Keegan's lips as he takes his last shuddering breaths. The light in Keegan's blue eyes disappears, and his body grows slack in Lachlan's embrace. An animalistic cry tears out of Lachlan as he cradles Keegan's lifeless body, and I look around the room for the target of the rage that's boiling inside of me.

22

Adriel is standing next to his throne with a smug smile on his face, and I growl at the amusement I see in his eyes as he takes pleasure in Lachlan's agony. My blood sings for retribution, and the familiar bloodlust and demand for action fills me, dulling the pain that's reverberating through me. Adriel turns to focus on me, and his amusement grows at the fury flowing out of me. I call on a throwing knife, and I'm surprised when the pain I feel from this use of magic is less than what I was feeling when I was trying to heal Keegan.

Maybe I'm building a tolerance, or maybe the use of different magic brings different levels of pain. I shove the observation to the back of my mind and focus through the burning sensation I'm feeling and take aim. Adriel's amusement quickly turns into shock as his view of my anger turns into a view of my dagger flying directly at him. He flashes away with a surprised shout, but my blade still nicks his arm. Satisfaction trickles through me, and I pant through the torment as I call on another dagger and take aim.

In a blink, a guard flashes in front of Adriel, and my dagger sinks into his chest instead. Guards rush to get between Adriel and me as I stalk forward, determined to get to him. I call on a short sword and have to take a second to shake the wooziness from my head as the burning in my blood gets worse. I pant, not able to breathe any deeper with the torment wracking my body. A lamia moves in front of me, his smile self-assured and confident as he watches me struggle. Before he knows what hit him, I slash at his throat and watch as his head slides off, and his body collapses to the ground.

I step over it, just as the guard's body turns to ash, and I slowly move toward the next guard that stands in my way. This one isn't as stupid, and I thank fuck for muscle memory as my body works to avoid his hits and land my own. I dodge and strike without giving it any thought, and I give a triumphant shout when his head leaves his body and his blood spatters across Adriel's fucking throne. Unfortunately, I can feel the toll the fight and effort to hold my magic is taking on me, but I don't care if I have to granny-sloth work my way through these guards, I'm going to end this once and for all.

"*Stop*! Or I will kill him," Adriel's voice rings out.

I turn expecting Adriel to be threatening me with Lachlan, and I drop my hold on my short sword and call on another dagger. I know Lachlan would rather I kill this fucker than save him. Lachlan is screaming like a feral animal and trying to get out of the grip of the two lamia who are holding him, but I sweep my gaze right past him in search of the fucker I need to kill. I find him and his smug fucking smile, but when I take in whose throat he has his hand around, I freeze.

Becket stares at me wide-eyed and afraid, and his sudden appearance throws me completely off.

"Fuck!" I scream out, frustrated and enraged and once again completely fucking impotent. I release my hold on the small dagger and feel too much of my energy drain away with my magic.

"Whooooo!" Adriel shouts out excitedly, and his eyes fill with fire. "I knew you would be the one, pet. All that power just waiting for the right vessel to wield it. Did you see her?" he asks no one in particular. "None of the others could ever work through the pain to do what she just did," he announces to the room, and I swear if he didn't have to keep a threatening hold on Becket's throat, I wouldn't be surprised to find him jumping up and down and clapping like a kid at Disneyland.

"What the fuck are you doing here?" I ask Becket, my voice filled with gravel and my limbs growing heavier by the second.

"I was taken," Becket croaks out before Adriel squeezes tighter and his ability to talk is silenced.

"You really should be more careful with your Shields, Vinna. When you let them wander off alone like this one was, you're just begging to have them taken," Adriel teases, and I once again wish I had the energy and ability to rip his fucking head off right now. A small amount of relief fills me at knowing Becket didn't show up here because he was working with Adriel after all, but it's quickly squashed under the reality that Adriel just put another obstacle in my path to turning him into ash.

My legs buckle, unable to hold me up anymore, and my knees slam to the ground as fatigue fights to shut me down. "Shield?" I manage to ask, not able to help my confusion from slipping out as I replay Adriel's words in my mind. He looks a little shocked by my question, and he tilts his head and studies me for a beat.

"You don't know what he is to you?" he clarifies.

"This shit didn't come with an instruction manual," I snark, and I try to fight my vision as it starts to tunnel.

"I have one, pet," he states casually. "Would you like to read it?"

I stare at Adriel's red-gold eyes, and just when I think I can't find anything more to hate about him, he shows me something new. I stay quiet, mostly because I'm pretty sure I'm going to black out at any moment, and I'm trying to conserve my energy.

"Shields can be called as guards or protectors. You bond with them in a unique way, bestowing on them the markings of your choosing, and they live to protect you. If I recall correctly, there's about a page of information on them in the book I have. I'll let you read it, pet, if you're good," Adriel chuckles at his taunt, but I'm no longer paying attention to him.

My brain is slow, and it's like I'm wading through jello as I try to think back to the night Enoch and the others showed up to my house with runes. I work to recall which runes Becket said he had. I think it was my maces, but I'm not one hundred percent sure.

"So I can create bodyguards by marking them with a *weapon*?" I ask Adriel like I'm confused by the concept, but my eyes are locked on Becket's.

I hope he's catching what I'm trying to throw his way, but I realize even if he does, I'm not sure if he'll be able to do anything about it. He hasn't been training with us. He probably has no idea how to tap into whatever I did to him. I blink, the movement slow, and I tilt to the side, not able to keep my exhaustion at bay a minute longer. My body shuts down against my will, but I swear the last thing I see is Becket shoving the tip of an arrow through Adriel's neck before my head slams against the black, shiny stone floor.

* * *

"*Vinna...*" a distant voice calls me, and I groan against the intrusion into my peaceful sleep.

"*Vinna, can you hear me?*" Valen asks again, and I turn toward the sound of it. I grunt in disappointment when I roll over and he's not right there to cuddle with.

"*I miss you,*" I tell him sleepily, and I hear him release a relieved sigh.

"*We miss you! Tell me you're ready for us to come get you,*" he pleads, and I groan against the ache I'm starting to feel in my body as I drift further away from dreams and sleep and move closer to consciousness.

"*Adriel killed Keegan,*" I confess to Valen, and I can sense the shock and subsequent sorrow that flashes through Valen, even though he doesn't immediately say anything.

"*How's Lachlan?*" he asks, a hitch in his voice and worry bleeding out of every syllable.

"*Shattered,*" I tell him resolutely. My chest aches with sadness, and I try to bat away images of Keegan bleeding to death in Lachlan's arms as they rise to the surface of my mind.

"*Fuck,*" Valen laments, and I realize I just accidentally shared the image with him. "*Shit! Valen I think Siah is still with us—,*" I start, but he interrupts me.

"*We're coming, Vinna. Enough is enough.*"

"*I don't even know where I am, Valen. We're underground somewhere, but I couldn't tell you where.*"

"*When you wake all the way up, activate your runes on your ring finger, the ones that signal us. We'll compare it to the tracker we had on the car, and then we'll get into position around that area. The next time you're with Adriel, activate those runes again, and we'll pinpoint where you and he are more specifically and attack. Do you think you can do that?*"

"Yeah, if I don't keep those runes activated for too long, I should be able to manage the pain."

"Okay, we're going to start heading your way now, so just hang in there. This will all be over soon."

"I couldn't stop him," I confess, and sorrow bleeds out of me with the admission. *"You guys were right. We should have never split up. I thought I could do it alone..."* A sob cuts me off.

"I love you, Vinna. We love you. We're coming for you, and then we'll end him together."

Relief floods me and helps drown out the throbbing ache that's hammering my insides. I start to become more aware of my surroundings, and Valen's voice gets further away.

"I'm waking up," I warn him, and a soft echo of, *"We love you, we'll be there soon,"* wraps around me before it disappears.

I open my eyes slowly and look around. I'm in a cell, but I can immediately tell it's not the same one I was in with Lachlan. That cell had stone walls that were darker, but the stone in this cell is tanner and more porous. I test my muscles by trying to sit up, but it hurts and takes too much effort, so I drop back to the cool rock floor.

"Your leech friend told me to give you this as soon as you woke up," a voice sounds behind me. The distinct pang of metal on rock rings out to my right, and with way too much effort, I turn my head to find a metal canteen. I know what's in there, and I'm painfully aware of how badly I need it, but fuck I hurt. I stare at the silver container and realize, even if I can manage to grab it, which is doubtful since I'm pretty sure I just spent all the energy I have turning my head, I definitely don't have the strength to lift it to my mouth.

I close my eyes and breathe through the feeling of helplessness that rises inside of me. I'm getting really fucking tired of feeling this way. I grab onto Valen's promise that they'll be here soon and lick my dry lips.

"I need help," I tell Becket, who's sitting somewhere behind where I'm lying. He doesn't say anything or move toward me. "I wouldn't ask you if I didn't have to, but I can barely move my finger, let alone drink that," I grudgingly admit. I wait in the silence that overtakes the cell, and just when I think he's going to leave me here to struggle on my own, Becket's hand reaches out and picks up the canteen from the ground.

He scoots closer to me, and the next thing I know, his hands are under my arms, and he's pulling me into a somewhat upright position. Becket's legs are sprawled out on either side of my body, and my back is supported by his stomach and chest. He unscrews the top of the canteen and brings it to my lips. I empty the contents quickly, greedily swallowing every last drop of blood, and wait for it to heal all the damage I did in my failed attempt at killing Adriel.

The blood immediately starts to work, and I'm able to tilt my head to the side and look up at Becket. I'm shocked when a very bruised and battered face stares down at me, and I suddenly feel like a selfish bitch for drinking the whole canteen without even offering a sip. "Sorry, I should have saved some for you from the look of it," I tell him, nodding my head at the canteen that he's set on the ground.

"I'd have to be hurt a hell of a lot worse than this before you'd catch me chugging down blood like it was the best thing I'd ever tasted," he tells me, the disgust and judgement in his tone clear.

"Noted," I tell him as I push off his chest and move away from him as fast as my tired muscles can take me. The blood continues to move through me, repairing and fortifying my body, and I stretch out and take stock of any injuries. "So I take it, by the state of your face, that I didn't simply imagine you stabbing Adriel through the throat with an arrow?"

Becket releases a humorless snort, and the corner of his mouth lifts in a smile that doesn't reach the one eye that's not swollen shut. "Some good it did. He didn't die, and his guards were on me before I could do anything else. I got to watch that piece of shit get thrown across the room over and over again when he kept trying to bite you so he could heal. It took some of the sting out of the beating I was receiving," Becket chuckles and then winces when the movement pulls at his split upper lip.

I mentally high-five my magic for continuing to protect me even though I was unconscious. I smile at the thought of Adriel getting thrown into a wall over and over again. "Bet that pissed him off."

"Oh yeah, he finally gave up when he realized he wasn't going to get so much as a hint of a fang in your pinky finger and then turned on me." I tense at his revelation and start searching his exposed skin for bite marks. "But guess which runes you marked me with?" he asks, and his brown eyes light up with amusement.

"You have fucking shields," I recall with a chuckle, and he nods his head yes.

"I got to throw him into the wall five more times before he was carried out of the room, raging and covered in blood. Too bad it's so fucking hard for them to bleed to death," he grumbles, and I grunt in agreement.

"Learned that shit the hard way my first night here," I confess. I lean against the wall and start to work the tangles out of my hair with my fingers.

Silence seeps back into the cell, and it's like Becket just remembered that he hates me and shouldn't be laughing about getting the best of Adriel.

"I didn't know if you would be able to use your runes," I

admit, fully expecting him to ignore the statement now that he's once again classified me as the enemy.

"Elder Cleary practically forced me to start trying to use them. I'm shit with the bow and arrows, and the mace seems a bit useless. You need to update your arsenal. Bring those magical weapons into this century. No one uses a mace anymore," he grumps, and I chuckle.

"I just killed a bear shifter with one," I tell him, and he rolls his eyes.

"Of course you did," he deadpans.

"It's a good option when you need to do damage and work out some aggression at the same time," I offer, and he just shrugs and shakes his head.

"Would you like me to try and heal you?" I ask, gesturing with my hand at the eye that's black and swollen shut.

"I thought you couldn't with that thing around your neck?"

"It doesn't stop me from using magic; it just makes it fucking excruciating."

"You could barely move five minutes ago, and now you want to hurt yourself even more to heal a couple bruises?"

"A couple bruises?" I challenge. "Bruh, you look like one big fucking bruise."

He smiles like he can't help himself and then works to put his scowl back in place.

"You'd be doing me a favor really," I throw out casually. "I need to learn to push through the pain and still function, because who the fuck knows when this collar is coming off. Plus I've had my daily dose of *delicious* blood today, so I'm good to go," I snark. "No pressure or anything, though. We only have a psychotic lamia we have to kill and his nest we have to battle, but if you can do your shit impression of Robin Hood with one eye and all the other injuries you have, be my guest."

Becket rolls his eye at me again but doesn't say anything. The silence grows awkward, and it presses in against me, demanding I say something, but what the fuck can I say? *Hey, can we just move past that whole* I killed your father *thing?* Or maybe I should go with a more casual *so you're talking to Elder Cleary; does that mean you believe your dad kidnapped and was going to rape me?* I don't want to pretend like nothing happened and that we don't have some fucked up history between us, but given the alternative, it's probably the best plan of action while we're in this cell.

I braid my hair quickly in hopes that it will help keep it from ratting up again, and I rip off an already tattered piece of the red sweater I'm wearing, which will need to be burned if I ever get out of this place. I don't look too closely at the darker stains that mar the once soft fabric, as I don't need a trip down the memory lane of horror that this place has now stamped in my mind. I tie off the braid and lean back against the tan stone wall, Becket watching me the whole time.

"Fine," he finally relents. I simply nod my head and move to kneel near him. "This doesn't change anything between us," he warns as I push up his shirt and take in the deep purple and black bruises on his side and stomach.

"Fair enough," I concede and place my hands over his darkest bruises. I pull my gaze from his ribs and look into his deep brown eyes. "Apologies in advance for the screaming," I tell him, and with that, I call on my Healing magic and shove as much as I can into Becket before I pass out again.

23

Chips of stone explode from the wall, and I turn my face to protect my eyes from the projectiles.

"Perfect hit," I cheer, and Becket swings his arm back and then forward to land another one.

The spikes of the mace dig into the stone wall, and Becket yanks hard with a grunt to dislodge them.

"When that happens, instead of spending time trying to free the spikes from whatever they're imbedded in, just release the magic. The mace will automatically disappear, and you can call on it again. It will flash back to you, and you'll have the upper hand again," I instruct.

Becket lets go of the handle of the mace that's still stuck in the wall and does exactly what I just told him to do. The handle of a new mace pops into place in his palm, and Becket stares down at it with a smile that calls to my own.

"Not such a shitty outdated weapon after all?" I tease, and Becket shakes his head.

"Outdated for sure, but there is a certain level of *kickass warrior* you can't help but feel when you use it," Becket admits, and this time I do crack a grin.

"It does have a certain *je ne sais quoi*, doesn't it?" I admit as I push myself up from the ground and stand up. I steady myself on the wall and wait for the dizziness to subside before stepping toward the middle of the cell. "My turn," I announce.

"You just woke up an hour ago. I think you should sit this one out," he advises, his eyes filled with concern as I move slowly into a defensive position in front of him.

"No holding back this time," I warn him. "No one else out there is going to pull their punches, so I can't afford for you to do it either."

"You've passed out three times already. I could fucking blow on you too hard at this point and you'd probably fall over. I'm not pulling punches so much as refusing to beat on a defenseless, stubborn idiot. Seriously, sit down. You can help me with my form some more; my shots are still drifting just slightly to the right."

"Stop babying me," I growl, and Becket laughs.

"First of all, you sound like a grumpy kitten when you do that, and second of all, we've been doing this for hours. You need a break. What if Adriel comes to get us right now? How are you going to hold your own if you get any weaker?"

"I'll show you grumpy kitten...scratch your fucking eyes out, and then we'll see what's what," I mumble as I move to sit back down.

Metal clangs outside of the cell, and it's as if Becket just spoke our retrieval into existence. Footsteps sound on the other side of our door, and it's unlocked and pushed open. Becket and I tense while the hinges of the heavy metal door squeal in protest. Siah steps into the cell, and his eyebrows immediately furrow with confusion as he takes in the state of the space. Nicks and gouges decorate the wall from where Becket's been working on his mace skills. Slivers of rock litter the floor, and Becket and I are both covered in a thin layer of dust.

Siah runs his gaze over me and lets out an exasperated huff. "Why do you look like you're on the verge of passing out?" he queries.

Becket snorts. "Because she is."

Siah looks around the room for the canteen, and his gaze narrows when he finds it in the corner. We used it as target practice, and it's been beat to shit by Becket's arrows and is now sporting several holes.

"Did you not drink it?" Siah asks, his ice-blue eyes moving from the swiss cheese looking canteen to mine.

"I drank it. I've just been doing some training," I offer with a shrug that takes entirely too much effort for me to complete.

Siah runs his hands through his hair. "Shit, I didn't bring anymore. I didn't think she'd need it," he speaks to someone behind him.

I catch a flash of golden hair before Siah moves further into the cell to make way for Sorik. Relief swims through me when he walks into the room, but I quickly dowse it in wariness and mistrust.

"Did you attack my Chosen?" I accuse, and Sorik looks offended by the question.

"Of course not, that's just where we told Adriel I would be to cover what I was really doing," he tells me matter-of-factly as he takes me in. "We're not going to get very far with her like this. You'll have to feed her directly," Sorik tells Siah, and his features are apologetic.

Siah hesitates for a second and then rolls up the sleeve of his navy blue sweater. He walks over to me and crouches down in front of where I've wedged myself in the corner. His pale blue eyes soften when they meet mine, and then a red sheen takes over his irises, and his left hand elongates with claws. His right arm is stretched out to me, and he moves to slash at his wrist.

"Wait," I call out confused. "What the fuck are you doing?"

"Feeding you," he states casually, and then he opens his wrist with a claw-tipped finger.

Blood pools at the cut, and I stare at it as nerves wake up in my stomach, and everything inside of me feels fluttery.

"I'm just going to drink straight from you?" I ask like a dense idiot. I try to ignore the fact that I can smell his blood as it drips down the side of his wrist, and it's making my mouth fucking water. *I have serious issues.*

"I don't have time to go get another canteen, and since you *played* with that one, this is the only option."

I lick my lips as more blood spills out of him, and before I know what I'm doing, I grab his arm and bring it closer. "I just suck on it?" I ask, and Becket snorts. I lean to the side of Siah to glare at him. "I'm not a lamia, asshole, I've never done this before," I defend.

"Could have fooled me. You *downed* that canteen, and you're looking at his wrist like it's fucking chocolate cake. If it quacks like a lamia..." he trails off.

I shimmy into a better position, push up the sleeves of my ratty sweater, and bring Siah's bleeding wrist to my mouth. I look up at him, unsure. The red is gone from his eyes, and he stares intensely back at me. He gives me an encouraging nod, and I seal my mouth over the bleeding cut. Siah's blood coats my tongue, and I'm so fucking grateful that his big body is blocking me from view, because I close my eyes and quietly moan at the taste. I swallow a mouthful of blood and suck on the wound for more. He tastes so fucking good, and my grip tightens on his muscular arm as I suck harder on his wrist.

A deep groan rumbles in the cell, and I open my eyes, worried that I'm hurting him. My concerned gaze meets blazing blue eyes, and as soon as our eyes connect, it's like I can feel the heat in his stare seeping into me. My nipples harden and warmth pools between my thighs. I take another deep pull of his wrist, and his eyes flash with need. He leans into me, his lips slightly parted, and I can just make out a hint of fangs. I want them inside of me, drinking from me like I'm drinking from him. That thought startles me, and yet I'm not at all turned off or terrified by it.

I can feel the cut closing and the flow of blood slowly tapering off. I pull my lips from his wrist when the cut finally seals, and with my eyes still fixed on his, I twist his wrist slightly and lick at the trail of blood there. Siah closes his eyes as my tongue snakes out and connects with his skin, and I like the effect I'm having on him. Purple magic flashes on both of my arms, and I flinch back and let out a surprised squeak at its sudden appearance. I drop Siah's arm and push back in the corner, internally yelling at my magic to calm the fuck down.

Siah watches the flashes move up and down my exposed skin from wrist to elbow, and he reaches out a finger and strokes a streak of purple magic. It jumps from me to him, and another deep growl I can feel in my clit rumbles out of him. I scramble to get up and break the trance we both seem to be locked in. My eyes land on Sorik, and he's beaming at me. I give him an awkward half smile, and then my view of him is blocked when Siah, the hulking lamia, also stands up.

Siah steps toward me, the look on his face primal, and I try not to think about his hard body as it presses into mine. I put my hands on his chest and take a deep fortifying breath. Sabin was right; he's definitely Chosen. I look up into his light blue eyes and pull forward the fading tendrils of unease that taint this knowledge.

"Why the show when you brought me here?" I ask, needing his words to cement my suspicions.

"I'll explain everything in detail when we have more time, but from the second that Adriel had your uncle, he knew it would only be a matter of time before he could lure you out. He was hunting you harder than ever, and Sorik and I knew if we didn't get to you first and get you away, you wouldn't have a chance against him. Adriel instructed that any lamia taken ask to only speak to you, and if they were given the chance, to convince you that they could help you free your uncle. So when I saw the paladin watching a group of hunters, I knew he was my best chance at getting to you before any other lamia could." Siah shakes his head and his gaze becomes beseeching.

"I wasn't going to take you to him," he tells me, his tone haunted with a hint of pleading. "But I tasted your magic, and all I could think about was how you could finally end this for us," Siah explains, and he gestures toward Sorik and then to the door, his words and actions seeming to encompass the lamia he mentioned that didn't want to live under Adriel's reign anymore. "Your protectors had a plan that I thought would work, and I meant it when I said I would help from the inside, but I couldn't tell you about everything with Adriel and risk that he'd see when he drank from you. Your shock and betrayal had to read authentic, or Adriel would see the rest of the plan coming."

I take in the desperation pouring out of Siah's gaze and countenance. I'm not sure if he's desperate for me to understand and believe him or for all of this with Adriel to just be over. Maybe it's all of it. A streak of purple magic flashes on my forearm and then blinks away. I stare at the ghost of my magic and let its presence mingle with Siah's explanation.

"I didn't know..." he trails off and gestures between us.

"Okay," I tell him as I fix my eyes back on his. "Okay," I repeat, the word filled with acceptance and pardon.

"Vinna, you and I—" he starts, but I cut him off.

"I know," I confess. "But not here, okay? Just wait until this is over, and we'll figure it out," I beg, knowing that this is not the time or place to dive into that discussion.

Siah's hungry eyes bounce back and forth between mine, and then he steps back with a nod. I move past him, ignoring how my body lights up as it skims his, and roll my eyes when Sorik moves to hug Siah. His smile lights up his whole face, and he pats Siah's back hard and tells him something I can't hear. Becket gives me a questioning look, and I shrug, not wanting to have to explain that Siah is mate number seven. I'm not nearly as freaked out by this fact as I was when I accidentally marked the first five or realized what Torrez was to me. Maybe it's because the guys already saw it coming and seemed to be fine with it. Or maybe Knox is just rubbing off on me, and I'm getting better at rolling with the punches. Whatever the reason, I welcome the sense of peace that runs through me.

"Okay, well now that we've recharged the Sentinel's batteries, can I ask what the plan is?" Becket inquires, and Sorik turns to us.

"Yes, the plan is to get the both of you out of here. Adriel is *almost* finished—"

"*Finished* healing," a voice announces, and all of our heads snap in the direction of the door. The lamia that I stabbed through the neck with a pool cue takes a step into the dim light of the cell, and I can just make out more lamia behind him. "Our Sire is ready to speak with his pet again. I'm sure he'll be very interested to hear more about what you two traitors are doing down here."

I debate for a second if we fight to get out of this but quickly decide against it. We're cornered and outnumbered. Even if we can ash every lamia standing behind this fucker, there's no guarantee we could make it out of the nest or get to Adriel to kill him. Better to go quietly, call on my runes when they take us to Adriel, and wait for backup. I can feel the tension radiating off everyone in the cell, and behind my back, I send a hand signal to wait that I hope they catch.

"Lead the way, then," I tell the lamia I tried to kill, and he sneers at me.

Fast as lightning, he grabs me by the collar and yanks me toward him. I also grab at the collar for purchase and try to get my feet under me as I'm dragged out of the cell and down the hallway. Lachlan is once again being carried in front of me, but he looks even worse. I don't know if they're still torturing him or if this is the physical manifestation of his grief over losing his mate, but he looks like he's going to die at any minute. I can't turn to see if Becket, Siah, and Sorik are right behind me, but there's an occasional grunt as one of them gets hit and told to move faster.

The tall black doors I wish I would never see again are opened, and I'm once again brought into the polished, black stone room. It's like deja vu from fucking hell because Adriel is once again perched on his throne as Lachlan and I are thrown at his feet. Becket stumbles forward after clearly being pushed, and when he gets his feet under him, he reaches down and helps me up. I activate the runes on my ring finger and try not to wince from the pain. Lachlan is staring dead-eyed at nothing, so I just leave him to whatever world he's found in his head that keeps him far away from what's happening here.

"What's going on?" Adriel demands when Sorik and Siah are pushed forward to join Becket and me.

"We found these two discussing how they need to get *them* out of here while you're still recovering." The guard gestures to me on the word *them*, and Adriel's features grow dark.

He narrows his eyes at Sorik, and his fists tighten around the armrests of his throne. "Explain," he demands, and he leans forward like he's ready to pounce. I have no fucking clue what Adriel will actually do to Sorik and Siah, but I doubt it will be an enjoyable experience. I look at Sorik, hoping he has some kind of story that will get them out of this, but his features are stone-like, and there's an air of resignation to both of them.

I learned my lesson about how Adriel operates, and I whisper to Becket to guard their backs. He moves behind Siah and faces off with Adriel's guards as I step wordlessly in front of Sorik.

Adriel shoots up out of his throne, and we all tense at the sudden movement. "So the baby Sentinel thinks she can protect traitors in my nest?" he jeers, but he doesn't take a step closer.

"If you ever hope to get what you want from me, then yes, I can most definitely protect them," I counter.

Adriel raises an eyebrow at that and motions for me to *go on*.

"You want to be marked, and I can mark you. You can't force me; I have to do it of my own free will, although I'm sure you've figured that much out by now," I challenge. "So give me a reason to want to mark you. Torturing and murdering the ones I care about will just have me tapping into my stubborn as fuck side until I look like him." I gesture to Lachlan who's still lying on the ground, staring off at nothing. "You want to force my hand, but have you ever tried simply earning what it is that you want?"

Adriel's features tighten ever so slightly, and it's clear he doesn't like what I'm saying. No surprise there, as he's a jealous, entitled prick who thinks we should all just bow to his every whim.

"You can keep trying all the same tactics that you tried on the others, and when I die or escape, how long will you have to wait for your next chance? How many female

Sentinels are still out there in the world? I mean, maybe you'll get lucky and only have to wait another twenty-two years, but will she be as powerful as me?"

I decide to shut the fuck up and stop trying to sound so enticing. I want to convince him that if he lets Sorik, Siah, and Becket go, that I'll mark him, even though I never would. I want him to convince me that he's going to do exactly that, even though I know he's calculating right now how to use each of them against me. Really all I *need* to do is keep this asshole talking so my Chosen, Aydin, Evrin, and hopefully a pack of wolf shifters can make their way inside of this place and decimate anyone who thinks like Adriel thinks.

Adriel tilts his head to the side, and his eyes become unfocused. At first, I think he's simply contemplating my offer, but after another second, I realize he's listening to something. His lips purse minutely, and then he turns his attention back to me.

"You make an appealing case, pet, but the one thing you fail to realize is what you have is already mine. You wouldn't exist if I hadn't made it so. I own you and have even before your conception."

I glare at him and open my mouth to tell him as eloquently as I can to fuck off, but he cuts me off.

"You don't believe me?" He laughs, and the sound of it makes every hair on my body rise with alarm. "Ask him yourself, then."

Doors open behind me, but I don't immediately turn to see what Adriel is talking about. He looks entirely too triumphant, and I'm terrified that when I turn around, he'll have one of my Chosen—or worse, all of them.

24

I breathe through the wave of fear that permeates me and finally turn when I hear Sorik gasp in shock. Every thought in my mind stutters to a stop. I stare open-mouthed at the dark haired, seafoam green eyed male who stares past Adriel like he's not even there. I run my unbelieving eyes over the runes on his finger and trace his familiar features until the neurons in my brain fire up so I can process what I'm seeing.

I look from Vaughn to Lachlan, who's still on the ground practically catatonic. I ache for what he must be going through, having just lost Keegan, but Lachlan has spent almost half his life looking for his twin, and he's standing right there in front of us. I crouch down to get in Lachlan's line of sight. "Vaughn is alive," I tell him, and my voice is both filled with awe and shaky from nerves. I force Lachlan to sit up, and he doesn't fight me, which I take that as a good sign. I direct his blank gaze toward his brother. "He's right there," I state the obvious, and I watch as Lachlan's eyes run over his twin. They don't light up with hope the way I expect them to, and I'm confused as fuck when Lachlan drops his gaze and looks away.

"Vaughn is dead," Lachlan announces, his voice monotone and devoid of all emotion, and his eyes drop to the floor.

"What the hell are you talking about? He's right fucking there," I snap at him, and I look up to make sure I'm not fucking imagining things. Vaughn stands tall, a healthy version of what Lachlan looked like before he was caught by Adriel.

"Ask that *monster* what he did to him!" Lachlan shouts, his tone equally as furious as mine.

I stare at Lachlan, horrified for a moment as I realize what's going on. "You knew," I accuse, and Lachlan puts his head in his hands and says nothing. "You told me he was dead, you...fucking asshole. You let me believe that when you knew it wasn't true!" I push him away from me and move to get as far away from him as I can. "You knew this whole time that Adriel had him, and you let me think he was gone? Why?"

"Because he *is* fucking gone! Look at him!" Lachlan bellows.

I turn to Vaughn, trying to understand what the fuck Lachlan is talking about. He looks healthy, and he's right there standing in front of me, staring off past Adriel like he's waiting for a command. That thought sends a spark of warning throughout me, and I take a step closer to Vaughn, my eyes searching, my soul uneasy.

"Vau—" I stop, and suddenly I have to swallow the lump that rises in my throat. "Dad?" I ask instead, my voice smaller and frailer than I've ever heard it. He doesn't respond in any way that would make me think he heard me. No stiffening of his shoulders or clenching of his jaw. His eyes don't flicker to mine for the briefest of seconds. He just stands there stoic and frozen.

Adriel walks over slowly, enjoying the pain and confusion. "What a beautiful family reunion," he coos, and it sends my heart racing even faster. "I always knew I'd get the family back together, didn't I, Vaughn?" he asks as he wraps an arm around his shoulders and pats him hard on the chest, like they're good buddies that go way back. Vaughn doesn't respond in any way to Adriel's touch or question, and my heart drops even more.

"What did you do to him?" I ask, my voice broken, my heart hurting. My dad is standing right here, but Lachlan is right, it's like there's nothing inside of him anymore.

"Do you know how lamia are made, pet?" Adriel asks me, his eyes drinking up my pain like it's water in the desert.

I think back to what Siah told me in the car. *"When they make another lamia, they need to pull all the magic from the being they're draining, but not overload themselves so that it will kill them. They then need to force their magic into the drained, but not deplete their stores so much that it results in death too."* I look from Adriel to Vaughn and try to put together what the question has to do with anything. Then, suddenly it hits me. I turn to Adriel, horrified, and he laughs.

"The draining part went accordingly. I've never felt so full of power and ability, but when it came to forcing my power into him..." He shrugs nonchalantly.

I picture the source of my magic and how it feels to me. I've always pictured it to be this endless cavern I could always pull from. I don't know if other Sentinels experience the same thing, but as I look at Vaughn and the empty look in his eyes, I can see where Adriel went wrong.

"You weren't powerful enough," I blurt, my voice hollow. Adriel glares at me, but fuck him, he tried to turn my father. He didn't have enough fucking magic, and this is the result.

"Or maybe Sentinels just can't be turned." Adriel shrugs.

"Now, where were we?" he asks absentmindedly. "That's right, your beautiful daughter was needing proof that she belonged to me," he declares with a chuckle and pats Vaughn's cheek.

And I completely fucking lose it.

Maybe it's the fact that my comatose father was just paraded out in front of me like it's no big deal, or the betrayal of Lachlan by not telling me the truth. Maybe it's Adriel's arm around Vaughn's shoulders and knowing how many years he's been tortured by this sick piece of shit, but I go right past pissed and straight into feral, psychotic bitch mode.

I scream through the pain as I call on my Sentinel speed and flash as fast as any lamia. I spin at Vaughn's back and bring a short sword down on Adriel's shoulder. My blade sinks about half way through before Adriel flashes away from me with a pained bellow. I scream again as he escapes and fall to my knees, where I breathe through the searing pain and demand that my body stays alert and doesn't give into everything that's hurting inside of me right now.

Chaos breaks out across the room. Sets of the huge black doors that surround the room break open, and lamia, mid-battle with a shit ton of wolf shifters, all pour in. In a matter of seconds, the massive, shiny black room is teaming with bodies. I force myself to my feet, and pain-filled screams and battle cries assault my senses. The smell of blood and ash fills my nose, and I'm bumped and jostled around. I search frantically for Adriel, panic rising inside of me at the thought that he might escape.

A screech filled with promises of pain sounds to my right, and I turn just in time to see a female lamia charging at me. Her eyes glow red, and her claws are fully extended, poised and ready to do as much damage as she can. I gauge her speed and our differences in size in a split second, and I ready myself to take her on. She's three strides away from me when she leaps at me, and then mid-air, a giant gray wolf slams into her, his jaws closing soundly around her neck and shoulders. The female lamia is in pieces before Torrez's wolf paws so much as touch the ground. He lands gracefully and pivots around to face me.

I tackle-hug him, throwing my arms around his big wolf neck and bury my face in his fur. I've never experienced the kind of relief I'm feeling right now, having him here in my arms, and I'm suddenly desperate to wrap myself around each and every one of my Chosen. I'm tempted to look around the chaos in hopes I can spot them, but I can't lose the focus of why I'm here. I won't let what happened to Lachlan, my father, my mother, or any of the others be in vain because I let my emotions get the better of me.

Torrez makes a chuffing sound like he just heard everything that flew through my head and is in complete agreement, and I rub my face against his neck for one more second before I pull away. I keep a hand buried in Torrez's fur, and I methodically start to scan past the fighting, looking for Adriel's distinct red-brown hair. I don't spot him anywhere among the madness, but I do catch glimpses of a group of his guards. They're fighting shoulder to shoulder, their backs encircling something I can't see. Each of them is holding a katana-like sword, and I watch as one guard stabs a wolf in the shoulder and then pulls the blade out, all in the blink of an eye.

Blood splatters the wolf's coat as well as the lamia wielding the katana. The shifter yelps in pain and is quickly shoved out of the way by another wolf, who immediately begins to snap and lunge at the guard. I can't see who they have in the middle, but my gut is telling me it's Adriel. The guards take another step closer to a set of doors before more attacking shifters cut off their path, and I know if they make it out of this room, the hunt for Adriel will start all over again.

I begin to shoulder my way in the direction of the group of guards, body checking wolves and lamia out of my way indiscriminately. Torrez's big ass body helps with my efforts, and I'm only ten feet away from my target when lamia start attacking Torrez and me in force. Torrez's jaws snap around the head of a charging male, and he shakes the lamia like a rag doll until the body turns to ash. I dodge blows and avoid claws as much as possible, knowing if I try to use any magic now, I will be wiped by the time I reach Adriel and have nothing in me to fight him with. I shove a lamia back into the jaws of another shifter, but I don't turn in time to avoid another set of claws coming right for my neck.

It's like I can see it in slow motion, the arc of his claws as they move closer to shred the skin and muscle not protected by this fucking collar that's rendered me useless. I don't close my eyes. I stare death in the motherfucking face and let it know exactly what I fucking think of it. It stings when the lamia's sharp-tipped fingers start to slash through the skin of my right shoulder, but just when I'm expecting to feel hot blood pouring out of a wound in my neck and chest, the lamia is yanked back in a flash like it's been harpooned.

A blue sword explodes out of the lamia's chest, and it turns to ash immediately. Dust and ash drift slowly to the ground, and the sword wielding figure steps through the mess and bellows out a challenge. My heart leaps at the sight of Valen. His hazel eyes are filled with fire and fury, and I know that look well. I wear it anytime I'm fucking pissed that something or someone tried to mess with what's mine. Bastien materializes next to his twin, and I'm in awe of their presence. They're covered in ash and move like they're extensions of the same body.

Lamia charge them, and they both twist and turn around each other, taking out attackers. Their swords arc and slice through lamia almost in perfect synchronicity, and I'm so stunned by how beautiful and magnificent it is that I almost miss a lamia coming at me from the side. I ball up my fists and ready myself to knock the fucker out when Knox steps in front of me and, with a swipe of his short sword, removes the lamia's head.

"I was wondering if you were going to stop drooling long enough to realize we're in the middle of a battle here, Killer," he teases, and then he grabs the back of my head and slams his mouth to mine.

The kiss is hard and fast, and when he pulls away, his eyes sparkle in that naughty way that's entirely Knox. He turns around and starts hacking away at anything that's threatening us, and I smile at his back and then shove a lamia that's running at me into the jaws of a waiting Torrez. He rips him apart, and we all press even closer toward the group of guards. I spot Aydin's giant body holding off any more lamia from getting into the room through a set of doors, and I'm surprised to see Silva and Evrin doing the same thing at a different entrance.

A silver blade slices out at me, and I just barely jump back and avoid getting stabbed. The guard arcs his katana back up toward me, but a blue-bladed short sword comes down on his arm, severing the lamia's limb from his body. Ryker follows through with the blade in his other hand, and the guard screams as his body crumbles into nothing.

"You good, Squeaks?" Ryker asks, his sky-blue eyes jumping from me to the battle around us, on guard.

"I am now," I tell him, and we exchange smiles before Ryker spins and ashes a lamia sneaking up behind him.

I quickly snatch up the katana from the ground and brush the ash off from the handle. I spend a couple seconds getting a feel for the weapon, and I'm stoked when it has good balance and feels like a natural extension of my hand. It's lighter than my short swords, but after a clean swipe through the neck of a lamia that's trying to join a three on one fight against Sabin, I decide this katana is the shit.

Sword in hand, I start doing my part to cut our way to Adriel. I hoot with excitement after a few fancy twirls get me a clean two-for-one beheading, and I'm reveling in the fact that I'm not as useless in this fight as I feared I would be. I hear the words *show off* being shouted at me, and I look over to see a smiling Enoch. I cringe and then chuckle when a wolf shifter accidentally slams into him, almost taking Enoch to the ground before the wolf scrambles to get his footing. The shifter turns around and gives Enoch a slobbery lick and bounds away to join another fight.

Red-gold eyes peek out at me between a row of guards, and when my eyes fix on Adriel's, all the lightness and levity I was feeling at once again being with my Chosen and dominating in a fight, bleeds out of me. I see fucking red, and all I can focus on is getting to him. I want him to hurt, feel a fraction of the pain his actions have caused others. I want to wipe that fucking smirk he's always wearing right off his fucking face when I remove his head. And I want this fucking collar off.

I fix my gaze on Adriel's exact location and move straight for him. I veer to the left to avoid claws and bring my katana up to block a guard's sword aimed at my chest. I get separated from Torrez and the others as each of us battle our own sets of guards. I focus on the three katana wielding guards all doing their best to separate my head from my shoulders. It seems that Adriel is no longer interested in trying to keep me alive. He's apparently abandoned all hopes of being marked and just wants to get the fuck out of his throne room alive.

All the doors are covered by supes here to kill him, and he's managed to get himself boxed into a corner at some point during the fighting. I want to scream at the lamia still locked in battle not to lay down their lives for this asshole—it's not like he would do the same for them—but there's no point. They all seem hellbent on protecting the psycho at all costs. One of the guards attacking me turns to ash as I slice through his neck, and I press the two guards still left fighting, closer to Adriel.

I grunt with the exertion it's taking me to fight off their blows. The metal of all of our swords clang and screech as they meet each other and slide apart. I lean back as far as I can go to avoid a team effort by the guards to scissor their blades at me, and I take the opportunity to cut the backs of one of the guard's knees. He cries out in pain and collapses, and I attack the last guard ruthlessly. His blade sneaks out and kisses mine ever so softly, and quick as lightning, it moves, searching for skin to sink into instead of metal to be denied by. There was a time where I would have appreciated this guard's skill, his technique and finesse, but as I spin and dodge and strike, I don't care how good he is, I need him to die and get the fuck out of my way.

I'm lucky that the fighting has compressed everyone together, because it forces the lamia to move somewhat slower than I've experienced in previous fights. There's not enough space to be flashing around, and it's something that's absolutely saving my ass as I go head-to-head with the last of the guards standing in my way. I aim low, but my slash is blocked. I twist and cut up with my blade and just manage to nick under the guard's arm as he raises his katana to slash down at me. The feel of my blade meeting its mark energizes me, and I start driving even harder against him, raining blows down and focusing them on the side I just injured.

A wolf trying to gain the upper hand in a different fight skids into us. The guard moves to slash at the shifter, clearly not realizing that he just made a fatal mistake taking his focus off of me. I have his head off three seconds later and a clear path to Adriel.

25

My name rings out behind me, but it's not panicked, and there's no hint of warning in it. I don't know who it is, but they can wait. I refuse to let Adriel out of my sight again. He has a sword in his hands, and he lashes out against a wolf who is attacking another one of his guards. The wolf yelps in pain, but it's quickly silenced when Adriel delivers a killing blow.

I step toward him, when suddenly pain flashes down my back. A stinging sensation starts in my shoulder and angles in toward my spine. I hiss and spin, my sword ready to deal with the claw-happy motherfucker behind me, but I'm instantly confused by what I find. Lachlan has his back to me. He's facing off with the guard that I slashed behind the knees, and he has the tip of the guard's blade sticking out of the middle of his back. Lachlan looks like he's holding onto the sword as the guard tries to pull the blade free. I quickly pivot around Lachlan, and with one strike, the guard's head tumbles off and his body collapses to the ground where it breaks down into a gray cloud.

I stare at Lachlan for a moment and try to make sense of what just happened. He looks down at the twelve inches of blade and handle that are sticking out of his chest, and then his emerald-green eyes meet mine. A look of relief washes over his face, and I struggle to catch him as he falls forward and his legs give out on him.

"I tried to stop him," Lachlan tells me as we both fall to our knees. "My magic...it's...weak, but I had to stop him." His words float around my head as we kneel knee to knee in front of each other. Lachlan's bleeding badly, and I'm not sure where to touch him that won't hurt. I trace the source of the blood, and shock fills me when I realize that he wasn't stabbed through the chest like I was thinking. He has a wound that starts at the top of his shoulder and slices down to where the sword is sticking out from now.

Holy fuck, did Lachlan just save my life?

Lachlan reaches up and pulls on the handle of the sword. It makes a weird sucking noise, and it snaps me out of my surprised stupor and into action. I drop my katana and rip at the bottom of my tattered sweater. I ball up as much of it as I can and press it into Lachlan's shoulder. He tries to pull more of the sword out of him, and I slap his hand away.

"Stop doing that; don't pull it out until I can get someone here who can heal it." Flashes of me trying to heal Keegan hammer through my thoughts, and I scream out for Ryker. He was near me before, but I have no idea where he is now. Blood soaks through my sweater, and Lachlan's breathing starts to change. *Shit, shit, shit, shit!* I scream for Ryker again, and Lachlan sags harder against me. He pulls at the sword handle, and I panic even more.

"Stop fucking doing that!" I yell at him, fear making my voice shaky and my heart race. "I can't fucking heal you with this shit on." I pull at the collar on my neck and scream out my frustration. Ryker isn't anywhere to be seen. I start to call for Nash, but my hair-raising cry for help is swallowed up by the noisy fighting that's going on all around us, so I try to get Lachlan as secure against me as I can.

Lachlan whimpers as I pull him closer, and frustration burns my throat and my eyes. "Fuck, I'm sorry. Just hang on, okay?" I reassure him and then look around frantically. I scream for Nash again, but I can't see shit, kneeling on the ground with wolves and lamia doing their best to kill each other all around me. I've been saving my energy as much as possible and not tapping into my magic so that I can go head-to-head with Adriel, but Lachlan is bleeding out in my arms, and help is not fucking coming.

I close my eyes and tap into my Healing magic, and pain flashes through me. A cold wet hand touches my face, and I open my eyes, shocked by the sensation. Lachlan's hand cups my cheek, and his gaze is determined and focused.

"No," he grunts out, and a hint of blood stains the inside of his lips. "Let me go. I want to go." My eyes flit back and forth between his, and I'm not sure what the fuck to do. He must see the debate in my stare, and he offers me a blood-tinged, reassuring smile. "Let me go," he says, nodding as slow tears spill out onto his cheeks.

My breaths start to stutter. Lachlan drops his hand from where it's cupping my cheek, and it falls limply at his side. I stare at him for a moment, his eyes pleading, my eyes uncertain and sad. Slowly, I reach down and pull the sword from his chest. He gasps as the blade leaves his body, but it's not pained, it sounds almost hopeful. I lay him on his back and push his dark hair out of his face.

"Okay," I tell him, and he gives me a look of pure serenity. "Say hi to Keegan for me," I whisper, and his lips tilt up in the smallest of smiles.

"I will," he murmurs up to me, and then just like that, he's gone.

Lachlan's body relaxes as *who he is* fades from his eyes. I stare at his peaceful face for a moment and take a second to absorb what just happened. I'm not sure how to feel about him or what happened between us. I don't know if I'll ever understand the kind of broken he claimed to be, but as I close his eyes, I hope he finds peace wherever he is now. I grab the katana on the floor next to my knees, and in the other hand, I arm myself with the sword I pulled from Lachlan's chest. The blade is still stamped with Lachlan's blood, and I stare at it numbly.

I take a deep breath and stand up and once again push my way through to the last place I saw Adriel. Lamia all around me are either surrendering or turning into ash. The chaos in the room feels like it's starting to settle, and I can almost touch the end of the battle with my fingertips. It's clear our plan has worked, and we're on the winning side of the carnage and ash that's coating everything in this shiny, black room. I spot Torrez's wolf as he and Sabin work together to finish off a handful of lamia. I pass them and notice Enoch, his coven, the twins, and Knox, fighting the last of Adriel's guards.

An injured lamia charges me, but I stop him with one blade and remove his head with the other, not even breaking my stride. I'm in the zone, numb, bloodthirsty, and ready for this shit to be over. I sidestep the last of the small skirmishes surrounding Adriel and find him standing in the corner, waiting. He's leaning against his sword, like he hasn't a care in the world, watching the last of his guards die, with no hint of emotion or concern. He perks up as I step into view, and the smug smile he's always armed with stretches even wider across his face.

I stare at him, the feel of this moment surprisingly anticlimactic. Adriel, the big bad lamia, the reason I exist, the shadow that's been hunting me my whole life, the murderer. I run my gaze all over him and decide he doesn't quite live up to his reputation. He's a petty, jealous psycho who amassed too much power, and now he's going to die. I watch him carefully, not trusting his casual demeanor. I ready my weapons and move my weight to the balls of my feet. I bend my knees slightly and then I wait.

"If you kill me, you'll never get that collar off," Adriel taunts. He takes a step toward me and twirls his katana like it's an umbrella and he's about to pull a Tom Holland and bust out some Rihanna. He's going for cool, calm, and collected, but his movements just announced that he's skilled with the sword, and he's struggling to move his left hand. It looks like he's not recovered from my attempt to cut off his arm, or maybe he just wants me to think that so I underestimate him. Looks like I'm about to find out.

"You know, it didn't have to be this way, Vinna. We could have done great things together," he tells me, like he's truly sad things have come to this.

Adriel brings the blade of his katana up slowly and taps lightly against one of my swords. I recognize the move well; Talon used to do it to me in the ring. Touch his pads to mine to test my resolve or see how tightly I was wound. I wonder offhandedly if Adriel taught the move to Talon or if Talon taught Adriel. I shake off the question and hold firm, not taking Adriel's bait.

"Nothing to say, pet?" he presses, and I watch him shift his weight ever so slightly.

I say nothing. He'll get no monologues from me. No final declarations about how he has this coming and only has himself to blame. He knows what the fuck I'm here to do. I can see it in his eyes, and he can see in mine that I'm not going to be fucking played with. Adriel spins tornado fast, and I get both my blades up in time to absorb the brutal blow. The power that he hits with vibrates from the swords into my hands and up my arms. I clench my teeth against the jarring sensation, and a shriek of metal on metal fills my ears as we both take a swipe at each other and meet the other's blocks.

He mistakes my silence for capitulation. He thinks I'm going to let him lead this dance to death, but I'm not that bitch. So when he skips away from me, thinking he can regroup and come at me from another angle, I charge him. I hammer the fucker with my own raw power and show him, collar or not, he doesn't have shit on me.

"Stop!" rings out around me, but it's not merely a word. It's a command. One that slithers out of Adriel's mouth and wraps around my limbs, my mind, my will, and seizes control. I freeze mid-strike, and Adriel's smirk becomes a self-satisfied grin. "Lower your weapons, pet," Adriel commands, and that same force flows out of his lips and cloaks itself around me, pushing my swords to the ground.

My mind screams with impotent rage, and my heart is pumping with adrenaline and trying to beat out of my chest. I know that this is wrong and that somehow he's taken control of my body, but I have no fucking clue how he's doing it. Is it this fucking collar? Does it make my magic painful *and* force me to comply? Horror spreads through me like a wild fire, and I'm suddenly certain why Adriel wears a perpetual fucking smirk. Because he always knew he could stop me with just a word.

"Look at me!" Adriel demands, and the siren song he's somehow released in his tone forces my terrified eyes to his. The sounds of the battle around me shut off somehow, and all I can do is focus on Adriel and anything coming out of his mouth. He steps into me and runs the tip of his blade lightly against my cheek. I scream in my mind, but my lips are no longer mine, and until I'm commanded otherwise, they stay shut and I stay silent.

"That's a good pet," Adriel coos at me, and he presses

into me to run the tip of his nose up the side of my face. I can't even shudder away from the feel of him. "You didn't think I'd actually let you win, did you, pet?" he asks me, the blade of his katana trailing down my chest. "I heard your friends coming before they killed the first of the guards outside," he whispers into my ear. "And now, I'm going to make you kill them one by one."

26

Panic surges through me, and I know this is about as bad as it fucking gets. I don't know if he can use this ability on more than one person, but I suspect he can. I initially thought this was because of the collar, but if I really think back to everything that I've been told about Adriel, I should have seen this coming. The way Siah, Sorik and Talon said they would feel after listening to Adriel talk, like they were gods and could do anything and *would* do anything he told them to. When my mother escaped, it was because another nest attacked Adriel. Talon told me that the invading nest was winning the battle, but somehow Adriel defeated them in the end. *This* must have been how.

The night that I met him, I had a similar cloying sensation that crawled all over my skin, but I didn't think much of it at the time. But now, as this infinitely more powerful compulsion crawls through my veins, I realize that I've missed all the fucking clues. I want to cry as all my darkest fears are volleying images at me of what Adriel could force me to do, but I push back against the dread and try to think through the fog of his compulsion.

I'm certain he tried to use it on me *before* he collared me that first night, and I try to think back to what was going on in the exact moment that I first felt it. I had just activated my Chosen runes to warn the guys, and then Adriel walked out of the crumbling stone ruin. An idea forms in my mind and I immediately call on my magic. Elation erupts inside of me when I realize, that despite the compulsion, I still can. Agony quickly drowns out my excitement, and I try to hold onto the magic for as long as I can. The pain is searing in its intensity, but I can feel it burning away at the toxic vapors.

A cold hand on my face rips me from my internal focus, and I slam back into the here and now to discover that Adriel is inches away from my face. The desire to headbutt the fucker flashes through my mind, and I'm shocked as fuck when my body responds to my command and does it. Talon always used to tell me that headbutting an opponent was a commitment to pain and should only be used as a last resort. My forehead smashes against Adriel's nose, and I'm reminded why Talon's words were accurate as fuck, because even though Adriel scrambles back with a pained shout, I also let out a cry because, fuck, that hurt.

I ready my swords and stride toward Adriel, when he compels my body to once again "Stop!" I immediately call on my magic and let it burn away Adriel's control, and by the time he steps toward me, his katana ready to run me through, I have a blade up to block him and another slashing down at his throat. He skips out of the way and tries to force me to listen to him again. It fucking hurts, but I wrap my magic in a strangle hold, and its brutal presence in my body keeps Adriel's power from sinking into me and claiming anything that doesn't belong to him.

My two blades sing through the air, clashing with his sword, rebounding and coming at him again and again. I'm relentless in my attack, and the more hits I make in spite of Adriel screaming out his attempts to control me, the more furious he gets. His features morph with rage when it's clear that his power isn't working on me, and his temper flares. His eyes lose their gold and flash all red. He throws his sword in a fit of anger, and one claw-tipped hand reaches out and grabs my wrist as I bring my sword in a downward arc toward him.

I stab him through the stomach with my other katana, but he pushes in toward me like the blade in his gut is nothing.

"You are mine!" he bellows at me, and he presses even closer. He pulls his other clawed hand back, and it's clear he's going to try and gouge me into pieces. I immediately let go of the handle of the sword in his abdomen and call a short sword into my palm.

I scream out in pain as even more fire fills my limbs, but I shove through it. I stab up, and the blue of my blade disappears into Adriel's throat. Claws rake down my left side, but Adriel releases my wrist and clutches at the magic forged blade in his neck. I release my hold on the magic and the blade disappears. I pivot and complete the downward arc of the katana still in my left hand, and Adriel's neck and head separate from the rest of his body.

I stand there, panting through the pain, and watch as Adriel's body disintegrates into dust. The collar around my neck suddenly crumbles, and I tip my head back and exhale a deep, relieved breath. I was fully prepared that this metal choker was going to be a part of my look until we could figure out how the fuck to get it off. Each of the guys are still fighting, and I look around at Adriel's almost unrecognizable throne room. I send a pulse of Sentinel magic out, and all the lamia in a twenty-foot radius instantly turn to ash.

It feels so fucking good to use my magic again without feeling like I'm melting from the inside out. It's been awful being cut off from the power that's always been a part of me.

It's like there's been a wall keeping me from being whole, and I just took a mace and shattered that fucker.

"Awwww, Killer, what'd you do that for? I was two moves away from ashing mine," Knox whines, and a laugh bursts out of my throat. I drop my katana, and it clangs to the ground. I crack up, and I can't tell if I'm laughing or crying. I think it's both, which seems like a solid indicator that I've just officially lost my fucking mind. Tears stream down my cheeks, and I bend over, my hands on my knees, to try and rein in the hysterical laughter pouring out of me.

"By the moon, Knox, what did I tell you about breaking the Sentinel?" Aydin chides, and it makes me lose it even more.

Tears drip off my chin and fall to mix with the inches of ash covering the floor. I shake my head, my tears speckling the ground, and I try to get a grip on everything that's just happened. My mother, Talon, Lachlan, Keegan, the twin's parents, the blood slave, they've all been avenged. And yet, I stand here oddly empty with no idea where to go from here. I look up, and everyone is sort of just looking around with the same *what happens now* stamped on their face.

Sabin snaps out of the shock first. In five quick strides, he wraps his arms around me and lifts me off the ground. He shoves his face in my matted, dirty hair, and it takes me a minute to hear what he's whispering over and over against my neck.

"We did it," he celebrates quietly, squeezing me to him.

His repeated words against my skin break through the numbness I'm feeling, and I'm flooded with relief. I look around, and I can't help but feel so proud of the guys and in awe of the skill I just witnessed. All of the training and their hard work made this possible, and I'm so fucking grateful that they're marked and mine. I hug Sabin tightly, and I look up at the faces of my guys as they all move closer, needing their own hugs and reassurances.

"Where's Ryker…and Siah…and Sorik?" I question when I don't spot their faces around me or anywhere in the room at all. Worry constricts around me like a python, and I push away from Sabin's hold.

"It's okay, Bruiser, Ryker and Nash are helping the injured. Sorik was hurt protecting Vaughn, but they're both okay. Siah took him to feed so he can heal. Ryker and Nash took your dad and some injured wolves to a different part of the caves," Bastien tells me. He pulls me in for a hug, and I wrap my arms around his torso and squeeze him hard.

"Silva?" I mumble against Bastien's chest, and I turn to Aydin.

"Stomach wound," Aydin tells us. "Evrin did what he could to patch it, but he's taking him to get some extra help from Nash or Ryker. It was pretty bad," he admits, and Bastien tenses in my arms. "Lachlan?" Aydin asks, his voice just above a whisper.

I look toward my uncle's body, a dusting of ash now coating it. "He's with Keegan," I offer simply, and Aydin's eyes well up with tears. Bastien wipes at his face, and I hug him harder, wishing I could do more to ease the hurt and loss I know he and the others are wading through.

"I'm going to find Sorik and Alpha Volkov, get some patrols and guards sorted out so nothing else kicks off tonight," Aydin declares, his voice heavy with the sorrow that he's trying hard to tamp down.

Something about seeing the ginger giant fight the desolation he's so obviously feeling shoves the shock and uncertainty I've been floating in away. My throat grows tight with emotion, and my eyes sting as I watch Aydin try to blink away his heartache. "I'm so sorry, Aydin," I offer lamely, hoping it conveys some of the anguish I feel for his loss.

Aydin shakes his head slowly, and then his tear-filled eyes settle on mine. "No, Little Badass, I'm so sorry," he chokes out, and I push away from Bastien and rush to give Aydin a hug. He squeezes me so tightly he's probably going to break something, but I don't say a word, and he surrounds me with his despair and apology. "I'm sorry you'll never know him like we did and that he wasn't what you deserved. I'm sorry I chose him over you in the beginning. Fuck...I'm just so sorry, Vinna," Aydin whispers in my hair as he crushes me to him, and his words breach my walls and coax out my tears.

I pull back and place my palms on Aydin's cheeks. His beard tickles my hands, and I watch as Aydin's pain drips down his face and darkens the red hair. My eyes bounce back and forth between his for a beat. "He saved me. In the end, he took the sword aimed for me," I reassure him. A sob escapes Aydin's lips, and he shakes his head furiously as tears pour down his face.

"Good," he tells me, his voice laced with mourning. "Then he died the person I've known and loved."

I nod my head in agreement, and Aydin pulls me in for one last bear hug before stepping away and doing his best to shake away his hurt. "I'm just going to go and get everything settled and safe," he declares.

Bastien pulls me back into him, and I cling to him like a lifeline as Aydin makes his way over, bends down, and pulls Lachlan into his arms. He lifts him up and drifts out of the room, and we all hover in the sadness left behind.

"Sharing is caring," Valen announces, his cheeks wet and his eyes filled with grief. He steals me away from his twin, and my mind flashes to Lachlan and Vaughn for a moment. My dad is alive, but I have no idea how to process what he is. He feels neither here nor there, and I don't know what that means for me or for him. I exhale a deep shuddering breath and then push the ache and disquiet away. I'll let all of that sucker punch me in the face. Tomorrow. I squirm in Valen's hold until my arms are around his neck, and I'm suddenly driven hard by the need to touch all of my Chosen and feel that they're all okay. I practically tackle Knox next, and he laughs as he catches me.

"I'd kiss you, but you seem to have a little lamia on your face," he teases, the levity not quite reaching his eyes, and then he proceeds to motion to my entire face.

I move to wipe my face on my arm and quickly realize I'm covered in ash and blood. We all are. Torrez shakes out his fur, and then in a blink, he's shifted back into a man, a very naked, very sexy, battle dirty man. Groans of objection escape out of all the guys. I laugh as he pulls me in for a hug, loving the feel of his warm skin.

"Dude, go wolf until we can find you some pants. No one needs to see your hard-on," Knox grumbles as he dramatically covers his eyes and then tries to cover mine. I swat his hand away and then look my fill with a salacious, teasing smile on my face.

Torrez's laughter rumbles against my cheek, and I pinch his nice naked ass.

"Patience, Witch," he teases with a wink before shifting back into his wolf and rubbing up against my side. I groan and push him away from me as he does his best to make me even more disgusting than I already am.

Enoch, Kallan, and Becket stand awkwardly off to the side, and I open my arms in invitation and wait. Kallan hugs me first, and I'm grateful when none of the guys make any sounds of protest. He gives me a couple hard back slaps, and I try not to wince from the pain it causes. I laugh as he releases me and steps back. Enoch steps into me softly, his embrace hesitant and timid. I squeeze him as hard as I can, and when the guys continue to stay quiet, he relaxes.

"I'm so glad you're okay, Vinna. We were all worried for a bit there, and it's good to hold you and know you're fine."

I smile up at Enoch as we separate, and I hear the faintest hint of a growl behind me. I ignore it and give Enoch a reassuring squeeze on his shoulder. I look over at Becket, and I have no idea where things stand between us. We reached some kind of weird truce when we were in that cell together, but I don't know if that falls under the age-old clause of what happens in the dungeon stays in the dungeon. Becket extends his fist, and I awkwardly bump knuckles with him.

"I'd hug you, but I know for a fact that you haven't showered in days, and you're bleeding and shit." He gives me a cheeky smile, and a small weight lifts off my shoulders.

"I can take all of you somewhere to get cleaned up," a voice announces from a doorway across the room, and I look over to find Siah leaning against the frame. His ice-blue gaze runs over me and lands on the blood still slowly seeping out of the claw marks on my left side. Some of the worry that's settled in my chest—and will sit there until I see Ryker and all the others—recedes ever so slightly now that I can see Siah's safe and sound and standing fifteen feet away.

Siah waits for a response, and as much as I want to get as far away from Adriel's lair and all the shitty memories entombed here, between dealing with injuries and figuring out what the fuck to do next, there's no chance I can leave this place in the rearview mirror tonight.

"Lead the way," I tell him and then move to follow him out of the room.

I walk through the tall black double doors and try to find some comfort in knowing I will never have to walk back through them again. I wish that fact made me feel better, but in truth, I'm pretty sure this place will haunt my nightmares for a long time. So much death and pain, blood and terror. It's like I can feel the echo of it in the walls of this place. Adriel is dead, and his reign of terror ends with him, but I don't know if we will ever be the same after what he's done to all of us. We've lost parents and loved ones. Had our trust broken and our sanctuaries violated by his influence. Each of us has been marked and broken by his brand of pain.

A shiver runs through me at that thought, and Valen puts his arm over my shoulders and tucks me into his side. His warmth chases away some of the cold from my ruminations, and I bask in its comfort.

"It's over," he reassures me on a soft whisper, and I stare in his hazel eyes and feel the truth in his words.

"It's over," I agree, and in that moment, I don't see the scars. I see the good. Like my mate holding me as we walk down a hallway, triumph behind us and possibility leading the way.

27

I follow Siah through another tall set of black doors, and tingles of recognition wave through me. This is where Adriel said I would be staying before I got myself thrown in a cell. The gray bedding is rumpled, and the look of the room isn't nearly as kept and clean as the last time I was in this space. Someone's been staying in here, which is weird since wasn't I supposed to be the one staying in here? Well, before I tried to kill a lamia with a pool cue, that is. That same comforting scent touches the air in the room. And I look at Siah, questions clear in my gaze.

He rakes his hands through his brown hair and steps back from me. "Um, this is my room," he tells me, and my eyebrows shoot up to my hairline in shock. "I was surprised when he announced this is where you'd be staying. I don't know if he was doing it because he thought you'd be more unsettled having to stay with someone you thought had betrayed you or if he suspected our connection even then," he explains.

I think about what it could have meant for a beat and then decide I don't care. Adriel's dead now, and I don't need to spend time trying to unravel his fucked up mind. I step further into the room. Bastien, Knox, Valen, Sabin and Torrez all pile in behind me, and I look around the space, even more curious now that I know who it belongs to. I don't know Siah well; he's kind of a hot ball of mystery at this point, and I don't spot anything around the room that further clues me in to the different facets of his personality.

I look back at my guys, glad that it's just us for now. I'm antsy with the need to see Ryker and ensure with my own eyes that he's okay. Enoch and Becket are down the hall in Sorik's room, and Kallan headed off to find Ryker and send him our way when he saw how many of us were in need of healing.

Knox and Bastien both whip off their shirts and wipe at various wounds on their chests and torsos with towels that Siah hands out. I try to do the same, but I wince with pain as I try to pull my shirt higher than the bottom of my ribs. Valen comes to my rescue and helps me take off what's left of my ratty, stained sweater. I smile at him, and he gives me a peck as he pulls his shirt over his head. He turns to toss it on the ground, and I see a massive cut down his back that's bleeding. I hiss at the sight of it.

"You look a hell of a lot worse than me, Vinna, so don't go getting any ideas to shove me at Ryker first when he walks through the door," Valen warns.

I would probably argue if I couldn't feel warm blood dripping down my front *and* back right now. I place my hands on Valen's back and shove Healing magic into him. He gasps as my teal magic surges through him, and I can feel all of his injuries as they quickly heal. The cut in his back knits together, and when I can't sense so much as a bruise anymore, I release my hold on my magic. A wave of dizziness hits me, but I mask it.

"Ryker can heal us, Vinna. Save your energy," Valen scolds.

"You were bleeding, and you're welcome," I snark, and he rolls his eyes at me.

"Thank you," he tells me with a cheeky smile and then flicks my nose.

Sabin chuckles at our exchange and then calls dibs on the shower. He sprints through the doorway Siah motions to before Knox or Bastien can rob him of it. Torrez blinks into a man, and Knox groans his dissatisfaction.

"Abracafuckyourself, sparkle wand, I'm a shifter. This"—Torrez smiles and motions down his body—"is part and parcel. Just don't look at my dick if it intimidates you."

I crack up and immediately regret it. Now that adrenaline isn't flooding my system, I can feel every bruise and scratch. "Sparkle wand," I repeat on a giggle, and Knox glares at me playfully.

"You let Ryker call me Squeaks," I challenge, and he cracks up.

"Yeah, but Squeaks is so cute and accurate."

"Sparkle Wand is cute too," I argue, loving how his face cringes at the name.

"But it's not accurate. Do you need me to pull out my *wand* and remind you, Killer?" Knox wags his eyebrows at me, and my stomach gets all fluttery. Torrez's nostrils flare, and I narrow my eyes at him.

"Keep it to yourself, Wolf," I order as I reach out and place my palm on Knox's huge pec. I drown my thirsty libido in Healing magic and press the power into Knox. His injuries take less time than Valen's, but when I pull my hand away, the room around me fades.

"Shit, Killer, you okay?" Knox asks as he reaches out to steady me.

I try to shake away the floaty feeling I'm experiencing, but I can't rid myself of it.

"She's lost a lot of blood. Where the fuck is Ryker?" Bastien demands, his voice soaked in worry.

Siah flashes behind me, and Knox jumps in shock. "By the fucking stars, warn a dude before you do that, will ya?" Knox puts his palm over his heart like the movement will somehow convince the organ to calm down.

Siah pulls me against his body and leans my head back against his chest. He brings a wrist up in front of my face, and I know exactly how he's going to solve the problem. Excitement sparks through me as he slices his wrist open and brings it to my mouth.

The guys all swear and take a threatening step toward us. "What the fuck are you doing?" Knox demands, but when Siah's blood hits my tongue, I can't help the moan that escapes me, and I take a deep pull.

His blood tasted incredible to me before, but I swear, every time I have it now, it gets fucking better. Siah holds me tightly to him, and I feel his cock hardening at my back as I suck on his wrist until my mouth is full and then swallow. He rubs his nose against the skin of my neck, and I feel the faintest hint of fangs scraping the sensitive skin that's no longer hidden underneath the collar Adriel put on me. I press my ass back into him, not at all bothered by the fact that the guys are watching the two of us together.

They look intrigued and unsure of what to think about this new blood drinking development. As soon as violet magic flashes across my chest and connects with Siah's forearm, the concern in their eyes starts to leak out. Siah moans against my neck, and Knox reaches down and adjusts his growing hard-on.

"Fuck, I'm not sure if I'm freaked out by this or really fucking turned on," Knox confesses, and the others nod.

I take one more hard pull that has Siah grinding into me from behind. I close my eyes and take another moment to get lost in the feel of him. His blood is rich, masculine, slightly sweet, and complex, and I take one last sip before I pull away. I feel a million times better, but I have to work to slow my breathing and actively fight the need to fuck Siah right now regardless of who's watching. Torrez's pupils are completely blown, and he lets out a distinct canine whine as he sniffs the air and all the need now saturating it. Purple magic moves down my arms and torso, and I start to pant against the heat that's surging through me.

Ryker walks in, and all of our heads snap to him. He looks confused for a second, but it morphs into relief when our eyes meet. He steps further into the room, and I tackle-hug him hard. He lets out an *oomph* as I slam into him, and I can't help the pained groan that slips out of my throat as he wraps his arms around me. Ryker puts his palms on my back, and Healing magic rushes into me.

My cuts and gouges start to knit together as I bury my hands in his blond hair and tell him how glad I am that he's okay. I fight the urge to grind against him, even though the need is riding me hard. I roughly remind myself that he's been helping the injured as well as fighting today, and my need to pounce can wait, but when Ryker moves his palm to my chest to heal the wounds there and on my shoulder, I almost lose it. I let out an involuntary noise of frustration, and Ryker looks at me and then the others.

"What's going on?" he finally presses, and Bastien chuckles.

"Vinna's magic is pushing her to mark Siah," he explains like it's a normal everyday occurrence. "He got her riled up, she got the rest of us riled up, and then you walked in."

Ryker nods and moves his hands to my arms where he starts to heal the nicks and cuts all over them. "So are you ready to be marked?" Ryker asks, his questioning gaze locked on Siah.

Siah looks shocked by the question, and his eyes bounce from me to Ryker. He looks at each of the other guys in turn and then lands back on me again. "Just like that?" he asks, his features perplexed.

Sabin walks out of the bathroom, a towel tied low around his hips. He dries his hair with another towel and stops in his tracks to take in the intense looks on everyone's faces. I run my greedy gaze all over his sculpted chest and abs, the sleeve of tattoos on his left arm are dark and delicious against the creamy skin of his abdomen. Water droplets fall from his hair down his chest, and I whine from the self-control it's taking me not to move toward him and start licking the trails of water up.

"What'd I miss?" he queries.

"Vinna's magic needs to mark Siah," Ryker fills him in.

Sabin nods, and I'm once again thrown by how cool they all seem to be about this. "How do you feel about it, Vinna?" Sabin asks, but I'm so busy studying the V of his lower abdomen like there's going to be a pop quiz on it at any moment, that it takes me a minute to process that he just asked me a question.

"Well, judging by the way she just gulped down his blood, I'd say she's on board," Valen announces with a smirk.

"That's new," Ryker observes as he wipes at blood on my hip. "Anywhere else hurting, Squeaks?"

I unbutton my dirty as fuck jeans and push them down my hips. I peel them off and reveal a nasty black bruise on my thigh from where a piece of the cell wall nailed me when Becket was practicing with his mace. My knees are cut up and badly bruised too, and Ryker crouches down in front of me and places his palms on my thigh.

"How long have you two been exchanging blood?" Sabin asks, his tone clinical, and I turn to stare at him, confused.

"I've only fed from her the one time in the barn. She's had my blood maybe five times now, but this was only the second time she's fed directly from me," Siah explains, and Sabin nods like all that information is important to know and not simply a case of TMI.

"What does his blood taste like to you?" Sabin turns to me and asks.

Ryker trails his hands from my thigh down to my knee, and I close my eyes and bite my lip against a moan. Knox snickers at my obvious struggle to keep it together. I ignore him and focus on Sabin's question and the feel of Ryker's hands on my legs.

"Um, I don't really know how to explain it," I admit.

"Do you like it, or does it just taste like blood, and you choke it down because it helps you to feel better?" he clarifies.

"Oh, um...I definitely like it," I tell him, but the response comes out a little squeaky, and I feel like a fucking psycho admitting that I like drinking blood. *Like* is really an understatement in this case because I fucking love the taste of his blood. It's the best thing I've ever tasted, and I'd like to pack it into little Capri Sun pouches and sip on that shit all day, every day. Or better yet, sip on him when he's fucking me hard and then beg him to return the favor by sinking those sharp little teeth in my neck. I shake away that sudden and deliciously graphic train of thought and refocus on Sabin.

He's staring at me like he's asked me another question and he's waiting for the answer. "Um, what?" I ask. I have no clue what he might have just said to me.

"I asked if you'd read any of the books in Lachlan's library about lamia," Sabin repeats to me.

"No, I only stole the ones about the different branches of magic," I admit.

"A lamia knows his mate when he starts to crave the

magic in their blood. It changes the flavor of the blood itself and holds a different quality to them, they develop a need for it. The same can also be said for their mate. The fact that you like his blood, or rather the taste of his magic which is in his blood, since really that's where the flavor comes from, is a big deal."

"Meaning?" I ask, not exactly sure where he's going with this.

"Meaning you two are mates."

"So it was a written in the stars thing, and not my Sentinel magic teaming up with my greedy vagina to be an asshole again? I ask, a little too much excitement in my voice.

"Yeah, that's probable," Sabin tells me.

Guilt drops away from me as I realize that this wasn't another case of my magic just taking what it wanted with zero fucks about who was impacted by it.

"You get to blame fate for all of it," Ryker agrees. "Well, that *and* your greedy vagina." He stands up with a laugh and brushes matted hair off my shoulder. I shoot him an indignant glare, but it's ruined by the chuckle that escapes me at the same time. "Good as new, Squeaks, or you will be after you shower," he teases.

The sound of a lava hot shower sounds amazing, but I know I'm not going to be getting one until this whole new mate shit gets sorted.

"You didn't answer my question," Ryker tells Siah, and all eyes are once again trained on him.

"I knew she was my mate after we got here and I started craving her," he tells them, and his words cause more heat to pool between my thighs. "Lamia are very territorial and protective of their partners. We're not like casters. We're not sharers." Siah shakes his head, and he gives me a pained look. His words and the struggle in them tug at me. I try to think of how fucking hard it would be for me if I had found my mate, and they were already mated to someone else.

When the guys told me about caster culture and the whole multiple mate thing, I was on board. Who wouldn't be though when you're being told that multiple hot men are going to more or less worship you for the rest of your days? It was like a dream come true to me and my thirsty vagina. But what if it had been the other way around? How easily would I have been on board to becoming one of many for my mate?

"I never saw this as being for me," Torrez admits and gestures toward the guys. "Wolves mate for life, and it's very rare that a female would have more than one mate. It shocked the fuck out of me when my wolf marked her the first time I met her. Yeah, she was a supe, and we were technically compatible, but she wasn't a shifter, and I found out quickly she was already coven claimed."

"Wait..." I interrupt. "You marked me the first time we met?" I ask, confused.

"Yep, my wolf sunk his teeth into that very same spot," he tells me, pointing to my left shoulder.

"Okay, you did bite me, but then you tried to rip my head off. That doesn't exactly scream *you complete me, be mine.*"

"Technically, I was going for your throat," Torrez corrects. "Not to rip it out, but to force you to submit. That's very typical for shifters. If you had been a wolf, your animal would have accepted the bond and submitted."

Bastien snorts and pats Torrez on the back. "How'd that whole submission thing go for you?" he teases, and all the guys, except Siah, laugh.

Torrez shakes his head, and an amused smile takes over his face. "She broke my jaw," he fills Siah in. "Anyway, my point is that I fought it, just like you are fighting it now," he tells Siah. "I spent weeks convincing myself that somehow it was a mistake. That there was no way that I was mated to a caster female. Especially not one who already had *five* intended mates," Torrez adds, putting a dramatic emphasis on the number five as he shoots me a cheeky grin.

"She's greedy, our mate," Knox teases, and I can't help but grin.

"But you're here," Siah points out, and a beaming smile takes over Torrez's face.

"I'm here," he agrees. "The little vixen showed up at a pack function, and I was a goner. I followed her around like some lovesick pup the whole night, and there was just no denying it after that. I'm new to all of this. Before, I couldn't even begin to process how it will all work, but they feel like pack to me. More than that really, because I don't feel territorial or competitive with them. I don't know if the magic in our bond helps with that or if my soul just recognizes that this is where I was always meant to be, and that helps me to be at peace with whatever happens. I can't say for sure, but are you feeling protective over her now?"

Siah's brow furrows at Torrez's question.

"Your mate's in a room with other males, one of which just had his hands all over her. Did you need to rip his throat out?" Torrez presses.

"No," Siah admits, and I can hear the surprise in his voice.

"Listen," I say and take a step toward him. "There's no pressure." My magic chooses that exact moment to send a purple flash across my forearm. "Ignore that," I prompt. "It has a mind of its own and no fucking tact. So I happen to like your blood, and you happen to like mine. Clearly, my magic is drawn to you, but that doesn't mean you have to force yourself into a situation that you're not comfortable with. We're all new to this mate thing. We're all getting to know each other more and more every day. And we all know this is going to take a lot of work. It's not for everyone, and if it's not for you, that's cool, no hard feelings. Okay?"

I give Siah a reassuring smile and then do this awkward snap clap thing with my hands before I turn to the rest of the guys. "I'm going to go shower. I make no promises about there being any hot water when I'm done," I announce and then sprint to the bathroom and slam the door behind me.

Yells of protest fill the room on the other side of the door, and I can't help but laugh. I feel flushed all over from all of this mate talk. I also feel confused as fuck and overwhelmed by everything in general. I don't know what will happen if Siah decides this isn't for him. I don't know if I'll feel like there's a missing piece or if my magic will just tag the next eligible bachelor, but even as I think that, the notion doesn't sit well with me. I rub my dirty hands over my dirty face and make my way over to the large glass enclosed shower.

I thought at first that maybe my magic just tagged strong options for me, Chosen who were magically a good fit. But now I don't think that's actually how it works. Each of the guys feels like they've been handpicked just for me. The way I fit with each of them is unique. Our personalities mesh and complement one another, and there's an ease with them that doesn't exist just anywhere. It's like I've known them forever, even though I haven't. I've never believed much in destiny and fate, and yet when Torrez said that *maybe his soul recognized that this is where he was always meant to be*, I felt that. Felt the truth of it resonate in the deepest part of who I am.

Siah's fangs on my neck, Ryker's hands on my body, and Sabin in just a towel flash through my mind, and I stare at the temperature dial in the shower. Fuck, maybe I'd be better off taking an ice bath at this point. *Stupid-ass hormones and hot mates*. A strike of purple magic blinks up my torso, and I roll my eyes at it. *You mind your own damn business, magic, and just so we're clear, hoarding is not an attractive trait.* Violet magic sparks up on my arm and moves across the back of my hand and blinks out at the tip of my middle finger. I stare at my hand, open-mouthed, not sure if I should laugh or be offended by the fact that I'm pretty sure my magic just told me to fuck off.

I laugh. *Cheeky fucking magic!*

28

I look in the mirror and take in the disaster that is everything about me right now. I haven't showered in way too long, and after this battle, I'm covered in a layer of ash and blood. Tear tracks mark my face, and on one cheek, the streaks reveal what looks like blood under the ash. I wipe at it, and the ash disappears to show a bloody handprint on my cheek. I stare at the mark Lachlan left on my face and make a mental note to call the sisters. None of us have had much of a chance to discuss what just happened to Lachlan or Keegan. I feel sad about what happened, how it happened. I can't imagine how the twins feel or the rest of the guys who grew up around a happy and loving Lachlan and Keegan.

It feels surreal to know I'll never see them again, but when I focus on that, I just feel hollow about it. Like I can feel their absence, but I don't know how it will really affect me. I guess time will tell. I strip out of my underwear and bra and throw them into the garbage. I turn the shower on, and the spray comes out warm, probably from Sabin having just been in here. I step underneath the spray and adjust the dial until the water is scalding. A river of black and red flows off my body and disappears down the drain, and I stand under the downpour from the showerhead until the water at my feet runs clear.

I wash my hair and try not to get too lost in the masculine smell of the shampoo. I rinse and scrub my hair twice to make sure it's clean, and I squeak in delight when I find conditioner in the shower too. It smells citrusy and not nearly as good as the shampoo, but it's a fucking miracle. I fill my palm with it and start working it through my very knotted and tangled hair. I'm methodically finger combing the mixture through every snarl when the door to the bathroom opens and shuts.

My vagina instantly clenches in anticipation, and I tell it to calm the fuck down. Someone could just be in here to pee. No one announces themselves, and I wait awkwardly in the quiet bathroom, wondering what the hell is going on. I wipe at the foggy condensation on the glass wall of the shower, and I'm startled when Siah suddenly appears on the other side of it.

"Hey," I greet him awkwardly, my eyes fixed on his icy blue gaze.

He runs his palm over the back of his head and drops his gaze for a minute before bringing it back up, his stare more determined. "They were...um...doing rock, paper, scissors to see who got to come in here with you, but when I stepped in to participate, they said it should be me."

I chuckle and shake my head at the guys and their fucking rock, paper, scissors shenanigans.

"Is...is that okay?" Siah asks, his gaze more unsure with every word.

"Yeah," I tell him matter-of-factly. "If you've decided this is what's right for you, then I'm glad you're here."

I high-five myself for playing it cool, but inside I'm relieved, and I'm leading a fucking marching band in celebration from my heart right down to my vagina. Excitement zings through me and pools at my core, and I step away from the steamy glass and rinse the conditioner out of my hair. Siah watches me through the foggy barrier for a minute as I grab the body wash and quickly clean my body. Heat and anticipation simmer inside of me, and I gasp quietly when Siah pulls his shirt off and moves to drop his pants. I quickly run my magic from head to toe and magic away any unwanted body hair. My nipples pebble as I watch a blurry Siah undress.

I can't make out many details, but my imagination is not left to its own devices for long. The glass door to the shower opens, and in steps Siah in all his naked glory. I'm not shy or reserved in my perusal of him, and he chuckles at my brazen visual exploration. His skin is silky and perfect. He's soft and smooth over muscles that are a hint too big to be called lean. He has a trail of brown hair that starts just below his belly button, moves down past his Adonis belt, and disappears into more hair around his thick hard cock.

Siah reaches down and strokes himself as he returns my perusal. His light blue eyes rake down my body and caress slowly and appreciatively back up. I wait for him under the stream of hot water, liking how it flows down my hard nipples, past my stomach, and through the dark curls that crest my thighs. I dip my head back so water can stream down my back, and I squeak in surprise when Siah flashes in front of me pressing his chest into mine and wrapping his arms around my waist.

He pulls me into him, and his mouth is on mine in a blink. He sucks on each of my lips in turn and coaxes me to open up for him. One of his palms traces down to squeeze my ass, and the other is pressed up between my shoulder blades, both of our hard nipples pressed firmly against each other's chest. He kneads my ass and groans into my mouth, and I grind against him. He feels foreign to me as I trace the planes of his arms and shoulders and lose myself in our kiss. And yet there's that pull, that strange foundation of comfort that I've had with all of my Chosen.

I've never run my hands all over his wet hard body like I am now, but he still feels like he's mine as I explore him with my fingertips. His hard cock is pushed up and trapped between our stomachs, and I stick my ass out to create room and press it down between my thighs. I stroke him a couple times, liking his growl that fills my mouth and the feel of him in my palm. I grind against his hard shaft as his tongue leads mine, and we kiss until we're both panting.

"Are you sure?" I ask him as magic comes to life all over my arms, and he moans as he absorbs it.

"Yes," he pants and claims my mouth again.

I shove Sentinel magic into him, pulling away and sucking on his bottom lip as I fill him with my power and will it to mark him. I've never marked any of my Chosen and then immediately after had sex with them, and I'm not sure if Siah will just get Chosen runes or all of them when this is done. He squeezes my ass even harder and guides my hips up his length, and I love the sensation, but I need more. I open my mouth to demand it, when Siah kisses down my throat and laps at my sensitive, hard nipple. He picks me up with his other hand and leans me back against the wet, cool stone of the shower wall.

He teases my nipple, each flick of his tongue like lightning straight to my clit, and then he sucks on it hard and thrusts into me. I moan and grind down against him, and he pauses inside of me for a minute before pulling out shallowly and then pumping back in. His pace starts out slow, languid and disciplined. He circles his hips against my clit with each deep push inside of me, and he moves up to kiss me. He explores my mouth and my body, learning what elicits a moan or a pant or encouragement. He fucks me slowly against the wall until he knows my body better, and then he moves down and sucks hard on my nipples and picks up his pace.

The sound of his hips slamming against mine fills the shower, mixing with our moans. Siah's attention moves from my breasts back up my body, and I feel the tips of his fangs teasing my skin as he sucks on my neck and then my shoulder. Magic and need surge inside of me, and I press his head more firmly against my neck. He groans and moves in and out of me faster. I nip at his earlobe.

"Siah, I need you to fuck me harder and sink those fangs in my neck," I demand, but instead of immediately listening, he brings a claw up to his neck and nicks his right side.

He doesn't even have tell me what he wants me to do, because as soon as he moves his hand away, I lock my lips around the cut and suck at his neck. His blood fills my mouth, and he tastes and feels so fucking good. I hold on to him tighter, moaning against his skin as his blood and cock fill me up and light up all of the nerve endings in my body.

He bites into me right where my neck meets my shoulder, and as soon as his fangs are in me, it takes everything to a whole other level. It's like every inch of me becomes a million times more sensitive. I can feel everything so much more intensely, and it immediately sends me into a mind-blowing orgasm. I suck on his neck hard and then have to pull away to moan and mewl through my release.

Siah feeds on and fucks me hard right into another orgasm, and my entire body starts to tingle from the overload of pleasure. He buries himself deep inside of me and licks at my neck, and just when he comes, he bites me again, and I shatter around him for a third time. I spasm around his cock over and over again, and he grinds against me, riding out his release. Blood trickles down his chest, and I lean forward and lap it up. He moans, and a thought pops into my head. I lick at the cut on his neck and then bite down a little on it and suck hard. Siah shouts out and tries to move even deeper inside of me, and I know I just made him come again.

After a minute, he relaxes against me, and I nuzzle his shoulder for a beat before I bite him again. I laugh as I do it, and he tenses and groans and dives right into another orgasm. I choke on my evil giggles when Siah gives me a payback bite, and the orgasm that slams into me is so intense I almost black the fuck out. I scream and hold him tightly, begging him to have mercy on me, and then I sag against his shoulders and feel him chuckle against me. We lean against each other, panting, and I'm not even sure if I have the energy to separate myself from him.

"Sneaky mate," he mumbles into my shoulder, and I vibrate with lazy laughter and realize I have the muscle power of a wet noodle.

"Well, it's official, you're stuck with me now," I tell him, my tone deliciously sated and way more chirpy than usual, but I guess multiple back-to-back orgasms will do that to a girl.

I can feel Siah's smile against my shoulder. He kisses each of the bites on my neck and shoulder and then pulls out of me. I slide down the wall like a lethargic jellyfish and thank the fucking stars that I don't crumble to the ground when I get my feet underneath me.

"Jokes on you," Siah teases. "I'm a cover hog, I leave piles of dirty clothes around my room all the time, and I dog ear pages in books."

I gasp in mock horror at the last one. "Not the books," I plead.

Siah shakes his head shamefully. "I know, I know. I buy bookmarks in bulk, but do you think I can find the sneaky fuckers when I need one? Nope, like socks in the dryer, they just disappear," he tells me and then looks off into the distance longingly.

"I'm pretty sure they go to the same place all my hair ties disappear to," I sigh.

"I just hope they're happy, wherever they are," he whispers dramatically, and I crack up and hop under the still warm spray to clean up.

"So if I bite you right now, will you come again?" I ask, half teasing and half curious.

Siah takes a step away from me, and I chuckle.

"I honestly don't know how long that particular side effect lasts," he admits and grabs the shampoo.

Siah lathers up his hair, and that yummy man smell fills the shower again. I step out of the warm spray and lean against the wall and breathe deeply until my head is swimming with the deep scent.

"I wonder how many orgasms I could have consecutively before I imploded?" I ask offhandedly, and Siah laughs as he rinses his hair out.

"I don't think I could handle more than four before I shriveled up into nothing. Pretty sure males aren't meant for multiple back-to-back releases."

"Yeah, that is a lot of magical ball butter to lose in one go," I agree, and Siah barks out a laugh.

"What the hell did you just say?" he questions on a guffaw, and his laughter is contagious.

"I read it somewhere, and it cracked me the fuck up. I've always wanted to use it in the right context, and here we are." I motion to his dick and then the shower. "Look at you, owning this mate shit already and making my dreams come true," I razz and raise my hand for a high five. He gives me one and laughs even harder. "For real though, don't shrivel up and die; I really like your blood, so as a good mate, I vow to not force you to have more than four orgasms consecutively," I tell him.

Siah snickers and shakes his head at me. "Fine, as a good mate, I vow to make sure that you *do* have at least four orgasms consecutively."

I laugh, and we shake hands to seal the deal. Siah pulls me back under the warm water and runs his gaze over my face before dipping down to kiss me slowly. I run my fingers through his wet hair and get lost in the feel of his lips on mine.

"Mmmm," he mumbles against my lips. "Look at you, owning this mate shit already and making my dreams come true," he parrots on a whisper, his lips skimming mine. I smile, and we both study each other for a moment.

"I think I like you, Siah," I tease, and he hums his approval.

"Good 'cause you're stuck with me," he counters.

"What made you finally decide?" I ask, curious.

"Your mate Sabin told me to trust the magic. He explained that there was a time when he had doubts and worries and didn't know how things were going to work out. But he said when all else fails, he's learned to trust magic because it's pure, makes us who we are, and always leads us exactly where we need to be."

My throat gets tight, and my eyes sting with emotion. He told me the same thing once, and I never really thought much about how true it is. "Fuck, I have some good mates," I announce and wipe a stray tear away.

"Looks like you do," Siah agrees.

"We should probably get you dry and somewhere comfortable before your runes show up and you question whether being my mate is all it's cracked up to be," I joke and push the shower door open and reach for a towel.

"Sorik told me once about what it felt like to get his

Chosen runes. I know what I'm in for, Vinna, and there won't be a moment, no matter how agonizing it is, where I'm not completely honored and grateful for what I'm being given."

I hand him a towel and swallow past emotion that's making my throat tight. "Thank you, Siah. That means a lot." I give him a small smile and step out of the shower to dry off.

I use my magic to dry my hair until it's straight and shiny. Siah watches me, fascinated, as he towels off and steps into a pair of sweatpants. A knock sounds on the door. I open it to find Knox standing there squeaky clean with a smile on his face. He extends his arms and offers me clothes that I recognize.

"I grabbed these for you when I went to get stuff for everyone." I stare at a pair of black leggings and a gray slouchy t-shirt that belong to me, and my heart warms with gratitude. I didn't even give much thought to the fact that I just threw away my bra, underwear and other destroyed clothes and didn't have anything to replace them with. I take my pile of clean clothes, and Siah walks past me out the door. He smacks my ass as he leaves, and I let out a surprised squeak. Knox gives him an approving nod, and Siah smiles at me.

"That Squeaks nickname makes a lot more sense now."

I roll my eyes and shut the door on both of their smiling faces. I search my pile of clothes for underwear and quickly realize there isn't any.

"Knox?" I ask as I open the door again, and all my Chosen turn to look at me. Each of them is clean and showered and look like they're ready for bed.

"How did this happen?" I ask, gesturing to their ash and blood free selves and the new mattresses that are spread out on the floor.

"Siah told us the two rooms over belonged to Adriel's guards. They're not going to be needing them anymore, so we went and showered in there and rehomed their mattresses."

"Oh," I say nonchalantly, but inside I'm calling dibs on Siah's mattress. At least I know who's been sleeping in that one. I turn to Knox, suddenly feeling more tired by the second. It's like just hearing Adriel's name has reminded my body of everything it's been through in the past twenty-four hours. "Um, I don't have any underwear," I tell him and then look around the room for my suitcase. It's not there.

"Oh…uh…I must have forgotten to grab you some," he tells me, but something in his tone is off. I look over to Torrez and raise an eyebrow.

"Total bullshit," he confirms, and Knox throws a pillow at him, but Torrez catches it and fluffs it a couple times and lays it under his head.

Knox looks at me and tries to adopt an even more innocent mien, and I narrow my eyes at him playfully. I walk out of the bathroom toward Knox, and when I'm about five feet away from him, I drop my towel. There's a collective intake of breath in the room.

"Oh, okay. I guess I'll just have to go without," I say to Knox, and then I bend over to pull my foot through my leggings. I put my other foot in and then do an exaggerated shimmy to pull them up my thighs and over my hips. I grab my heather-gray shirt and pull it on, and my hard nipples are very prevalent through the knit jersey fabric. I run my hands down my front in an oversexualized smoothing motion and then look up to heated stares. A couple of them adjust themselves, and I shoot Knox a wink and then run and belly flop on Siah's bed.

Knox gives me a hungry growl and rubs his face with an exasperated huff.

"Serves you right for making me go commando."

"Fuck, Killer, don't say commando right now. I'm too tired to punish you properly."

I laugh at Knox's words, and Ryker gets up from the mattress on the ground and crawls into the bed next to me. He lays his head in my lap, and I bend over to kiss his temple. He looks exhausted. We all do. I run my hands through his hair, and he relaxes into me.

"Can someone set an alarm for four hours? I need to go relieve Nash so he can sleep," Ryker asks, and then the next thing I know, he's breathing heavy in my lap, down for the count. I lean back against the headboard of the big bed and quickly follow Ryker's lead and leap into oblivion.

29

Pain demands my attention, and I'm pulled from sleep by the flash of fire in my body. The first thing that runs through my mind is that I'm still in the cell. *Do not fucking tell me that all of that was some kind of messed up dream.* Panicked, I claw at my throat. I will rip this fucking collar off of me if it's the last thing I do. A sob stutters out of my chest. Hands grab mine, and I whimper in frustration.

"Squeaks. It's okay. You're okay. You're safe with us in the room."

I go still as Ryker's words permeate the pain and fear, and I try to breathe through the panic and agony coursing through my system. I open my eyes and relief mixes with the burning inside of me as I see that I am, in fact, in Siah's room. I look for him and find him writhing in pain on the mattress on the ground. I move to go to him, but a new wave of agony seizes me, and Ryker pulls me into his lap and pushes my sweaty hair out of my face. "It's okay, Vinna, we've got him," Valen reassures me, and I slam my eyes shut and groan-screech through whatever new runes are showing up on my body.

"It's okay, Squeaks. You've been there and done that more than any of us, and you know it will stop hurting soon. Just breathe through it. I've got you. I've always got you," Ryker comforts, and I fist my hand in his shirt and press my forehead against his chest.

I really should be used to this by now, but maybe no one ever really *gets used to* pain. Adapt, maybe. Work through it, if I'm lucky, but I don't think getting used to it will ever be in the cards for me. Bastien announces that Siah's runes are starting to appear, and I force myself to look and see what's showing up. It's not just his Chosen marks. My Sentinel runes rise slowly to the surface on his arms and chest, and I'm glad at least that we're now all connected. It feels right in a way I don't have words for, and I feel a pure sense of peace sink deep inside of me and settle there.

There's always been this underlying drive in me that was searching for something. Home, my place, purpose, I could never quite put my finger on what I felt was missing. But as the pain flairs one last time and then starts to recede, I realize I have all of those things with me right here and now. My runes light up, and everyone else gasps when theirs take on the same ethereal glow. Bastien and Valen both hiss in pain, and I turn my attention to them, worried.

"Just...getting...new...runes," Valen bites out, and I look around at the rest of my Chosen and see that the same thing is happening to them too.

It's all over in less than a handful of minutes, and everyone slowly powers down like our batteries finally wore out. "Everyone okay?" I ask, running my gaze over Siah and the others. Everyone nods absently as they stare at the new runes on their hands. Siah's rune is lined up and just as bold as all my other Chosen runes, but the new rune on everyone's palm is the one garnering the most attention. Six thin black diamonds, evenly spaced from each other and forming a circle, now fill up the entire palm of all of our hands.

"You've got a new one there too," Sabin tells me, and he points to just right of my neck.

My eyes flash over to Siah, and he cranes his neck to see what Sabin is pointing at. I just know this new rune has something to do with Siah's abilities as a lamia, just like the new runes I got from being with Torrez were about his abilities as a shifter. I don't even try to deduce what this new rune could be for.

"Fuck, you think it's going to give me fangs?" I ask, not sure how I feel about that, and the guys all shrug. "I mean, I already have the speed and like to drink blood—"

"My blood," Siah interjects.

"Does that distinction matter?" I ask.

"Yes," he answers simply.

"Okay, correction, I like to drink your blood. What else can you do?"

"Well, aside from speed and strength, we can heal relatively quickly, we can feed off of others' magic. Some lamia can use different aspects of magic after they feed, but it doesn't last long, and it's pretty rare. We all possess the ability on some level to compel. There is the whole fangs and claws thing." Siah looks up like he's going through a mental checklist. "Yeah, that's pretty much it."

"The compulsion thing could come in handy," Knox admits. He runs his hand over Bastien's face and makes his eyes huge. "It's my night with Vinna; you feel the need to make cupcakes and do my laundry," he monotones and waves his hand as if he's attempting to hypnotize Bastien. I chuckle and immediately start jonesing for a cupcake.

"Should we test the new runes out?" I ask no one in particular, but sudden pounding on the door demands everyone's attention. Torrez jogs over to save the door from the assault it's under, and Kallan, Enoch and Becket come pouring into the room, their various magical weapons ready.

"You okay?" Enoch demands, his eyes roaming over the room and everyone in it.

"Yeah, what's wrong?" I demand, worry rising inside of me at their intensity and obvious concern.

"We all lit up like fucking glow worms; did that not happen to you, too?" Kallan asks, his throwing knives disappearing from his grasp.

"Shit, sorry, I figured it would just be my Chosen that lit up like a Christmas tree. Did you guys get new runes, too?" I ask, as I raise up my palm and display the circle of six diamonds.

Enoch and the others quickly look at their own hands and then back up to me. "No, nothing new that we know of."

"Oh you'd know it," Valen tells them. "There's no mistaking when a new rune shows up."

Everyone in the room gives a simultaneous shudder, and for some reason, it makes me smile. "I guess the Shields lucked out in the pain department on this one," I tease.

Everyone except for Becket gives me a confused look.

"Fuck, I can't believe I forgot to tell you guys about this," I apologize, and I move off the bed and over to Enoch and the others.

"Adriel told me what your runes are. Apparently, Sentinels can mark what Adriel called Shields. He said that they're like guards, and that's why each of you has weapons and is connected to me through my magic. Shit, that reminds me too, we need to search this place. He said he had a book about Sentinels. That it had a bunch of information in it about all of this," I say and gesture to Kallan and the others. "He knew a hell of a lot more than the fucking readers knew, and they supposedly have a whole archive on Sentinels," I add.

"Hold on, wait, so he said they're some kind of bodyguard runes, and you're just taking his word for it?" Enoch questions and takes a step toward me. "Why would you believe anything he said?"

I pause for a minute, a little taken aback. It's a valid question, and I think back to the exchange and to why I didn't doubt at all what he told me. "He thought I already knew when he brought it up. He seemed shocked that I didn't know," I tell Enoch, and I look to Becket for backup. "He was a psycho, so I get why you wouldn't want to accept anything he said at face value, but he didn't have any reason to lie," I explain.

"That you know of," Enoch counters.

"Enoch, what he said made sense. There's the fact that you have only a couple of weapons, your runes are different, and I told you from the beginning that you didn't feel like Chosen to me." My eyes soften, and I try to be easy in how I say all of this to him, but it's obvious Enoch doesn't want to hear any of it.

"Or he was manipulating you, and our connection is incomplete just like Torrez's was and now isn't," Enoch argues, and I release an exasperated huff.

"She's telling you that's not how it is, and you're not listening," Valen asserts, and Enoch gets even more irritated.

"No, she's telling me what some serial killer lamia told her, and nothing about that is definitive."

"Enoch, just stop," Kallan interjects, and everyone goes quiet. "We'll look for the book Vinna is talking about and see what it says. I'm tired of all this fucking fighting. What purpose does it serve? Guards or Shields or whatever we are, it's fine. If Vinna wanted us that way, she'd be with us in that way," Kallan tells him and then gestures to Siah. "She doesn't hold back when she wants something," he adds, and the air in the room grows heavy with what Kallan isn't saying out loud.

Enoch runs his gaze over the Sentinel runes that Siah is now sporting, and I see the flash of hurt in his eyes. I fucking hate that he and Kallan look so fucking crushed, and I wish there was something I could do to make it better, but I stay quiet. They won't want my pity or to feel like consolation prizes. They're not Chosen, but they're still marked and important to me. I hope someday sooner rather than later they'll see the truth in that and realize that I was never the one for them. We're meant to be connected the way that we are; I don't know why, but like Sabin said, I trust the magic.

A phone in the room chirps with a reminder, and Knox moves to grab it and turn it off. "Ryker, you've got about ten minutes before you need to go relieve Nash," he calls out, and the phone in Knox's hands reminds me of something I made a mental note to do.

"Do you think Aydin or anyone has called the sisters?" I ask. "Do you think they know..." I trail off, and Ryker gives my shoulder a squeeze.

"I don't know," he admits, and no one else says anything.

I reach out my palm toward Knox, and he gives me a sad smile and places the phone in my palm. I take a deep breath and click on Birdie's contact and then put the phone on speaker. The line rings a couple of times, and then I'm greeted by a voice that makes my heart squeeze and longing swell up inside of me.

"Vinna, my love, you have the most perfect timing," Birdie announces, and I can't help but laugh. The sisters say they're nulls and don't have more than a thimbleful of magic, but I don't know how accurate that really is when they always seem to just know things, like it's me calling from Knox's phone and not him.

"We just got done dropping off the Fight Master and Body Opponent, and everything went smoothly! Cyn—"

Panicked, I cut Birdie off. "Oh hey Birdie, I've got you on speaker phone," I announce, and I work hard to maintain my composure and not give anything away. I don't even dare look at Sabin and risk that he might somehow put those out of context clues together.

"Oh hello, everyone, you're just going to *love* the new equipment that came in for the home gym; it's pink!" Birdie says with a squeal. I internally send her long-distance, high five vibes for that smooth as fuck cover up and then make a mental note to buy actual pink gym equipment so no one ever figures out what we're really up to, and by no one, I mean O Captain, my Captain himself, Sabin.

"So who all is with you, my love?" Birdie inquires, and I quickly name off everyone in the room. Birdie must have put us on speaker on her side too, because Adelaide and Lila greet everyone right alongside Birdie. There's a pregnant pause that fills the room after everyone's hellos have been exchanged, and I'm not sure how to tell them what I need to tell them next.

"Oh, my love. Who is it?" Birdie asks me, her voice immediately sad and knowing.

"Keegan," I tell her, and my eyes well up with the empathy I feel as the sisters gasp. I can hear their stifled whimpers, and I can just picture them huddled together, hands over their mouths and tears streaming down their faces.

"And Lachlan," I add, and I drop to my knees as I hear three of my favorite women in the world break.

Sniffles sound off in the room, and I know the loss is thoroughly sinking into the boys too, their grief churning to the surface as they hear the sisters lament the men they loved like their own children.

"Lachlan was with Keegan when he passed," I tell them, feeling like they need those comforting details. "I was with Lachlan. He said he was ready to go and that he'd say hello to Keegan when he saw him again."

Siah sits down next to me and pulls me into his lap as tears drip off my chin and wet my shirt. Bastien, Valen, Knox, Ryker and Sabin are huddled together, hugging and supporting each other as they wade through their mourning. I watch them for a moment, so grateful that they have each other. They all grew up with Lachlan and Keegan in their lives, and I know they'll help each other remember the good times and the love in ways that I'll never be able to.

Siah wipes at my cheeks, and I'm reminded that there's more to tell them. "Sisters?" I pause and take a breath to try and control the emotion in my voice. "Fuck, I love you, and I'm so sorry, but there's more."

"Oh no," Lila begs, and I instantly realize what I just said.

"No, shit, I'm sorry, I didn't mean it like that; everyone else is fine. It's just that...Vaughn is here."

Adelaide gives a surprised shout, and then there's a bunch of noise on the phone like maybe it was dropped. After another second of fumbling, Birdie's voice comes back crystal clear and determined.

"We're on our way," she announces, and I stare at the phone, surprised. "We should have come in the first place, but we thought we'd be in the way, and...but if we'd just gone then, we'd be there right now to hold each of you..." Emotion overtakes Birdie's ability to speak, and Lila takes over.

"We're on our way; we'll let you know when. We love you all, and we'll be there as soon as we can, okay?"

"Okay," I agree. "We love you, and we'll see you soon," I confirm, and the guys all say the same thing before the sisters hang up so they can start making plans to get here. I stare at the phone for a couple beats and feel the small circles that Siah rubs at the small of my back. I feel drained. Witnessing the sisters' pain and loss felt worse than experiencing it myself.

I look up and notice Becket wiping at his face discreetly, and I'm reminded that, despite his efforts to stay strong while we were in the cell and dealing with Adriel, he has a shit ton of hurt he's dealing with too. We never talked about what he learned when he stayed back in Solace, and I wonder if he's been able to talk to anyone about what happened with his dad. I make a mental note to ask him, even if I'm the last person in the world who he'd probably want to talk to.

30

A knock at the door calls everyone's attention, and everyone takes deep breaths or wipes at their cheeks. I watch the guys tuck away their sadness as Becket moves toward the door and pulls it open. Nash is standing on the other side, looking exhausted. His eyes get wide with confusion when he spots his coven inside, and he steps into the room.

"I was going to grab Ryker and update him on Silva and the others before I pass out," he announces, looking at Enoch and the others like one of them is going to give him a look that fills him in on what's going on.

"We can step out," Ryker motions toward the door, and Nash looks from Ryker back to Enoch.

"I'll come with you," I tell Ryker, and I give Siah a quick peck before he helps me up from his lap. "I wanted to go check on Sorik and Vaughn," I explain, and Ryker gives me a sweet smile and puts his hand out to me. He intertwines our fingers, and we both move for the door.

"We're going to come check on Silva," Valen and Bastien announce, coming with us.

"I'm going to come and check on the pack," Torrez decides.

"We're coming too," Knox shouts out, and he, Sabin and Siah all rush to join us as we head out the door.

I smile and don't blame them for wanting to leave behind the heaviness that permeates the air in this room right now. Everything that just happened was intense, and it seems like everyone could use a break. I realize in this moment that I want all of them as close as I can have them from here on out. No more solo missions to save anything or splitting up because it's the *only way*. It's us against whatever comes at us now, exactly as it should be.

As we make our way to where the injured are, I notice that, aside from Siah, I don't spot any other lamia. We need to talk with Siah and Sorik soon about what happens now with what's left of this nest. I have no idea how many lamia were killed in the fighting or exactly what's going to happen now for any of the survivors. I don't want to be responsible for their well-being, but I don't want to leave them to the wolves, literally or figuratively, either. Siah said there were good lamia here that didn't agree with Adriel and what he did, and they deserve to build a life somewhere they feel safe and protected now that he's gone. And we need to figure out how to make that happen.

We walk into a long room where mattresses have been arranged neatly on the floor. Most of them are empty, but a few have sleeping shifters in them. Ryker kisses my hand, and then he veers off to go talk to Aydin and Evrin who are in chairs next to the bed Silva is in. I give Aydin and Evrin a wave, and they return it before turning to Ryker and listening to whatever it is he's saying.

"I'm going to go speak with Alpha Volkov," Torrez tells me, but I grab his hand when he moves to walk away.

"I'll come with you," I tell him. "I want to say thank you.

We would have been screwed if they hadn't agreed to fight with us."

Torrez gives me a smile and then pulls me into his side. We spot Fedor standing in the middle of a group of shifters as he assigns tasks. It sounds like he's making arrangements for patrols and the pack members who are almost done healing. Slowly shifters break away to go about doing what they've been told, and Fedor's gaze lands on us.

"Torrez!" he greets boisterously, his face lit up with excitement. He stomps over to us and pulls Torrez in for a bone crushing hug and administers several back breaking man slaps. "How's mated life treating you?" he asks and gives me a wide smile and a friendly nod.

"Couldn't be better," Torrez tells him as he straightens up, and I swear I hear every one of his vertebrae snapping back into place.

"I'll say," Fedor agrees. "I mean, what better honeymoon can there be than to battle side by side and then fuck all night while wearing the blood and ash of your enemies?" Fedor declares, and I try not to scrunch my face up at that very vivid and disturbing visual. I probably shouldn't be shocked; this *is* the dude that thinks Brun would make a better mate than me. He's obviously got a fuck ton of screws loose.

"Alpha, thank you for your help. We couldn't have done it without you," I tell him, and his smile grows impossibly wider. "If you or your pack ever need anything, I hope we'll be the first call you make," I offer.

"You know, now that you mention it, I would like to set up some breeding exchanges with the Silas pack. Now, I know you're not a current member," he tells Torrez, "but you left in good standing, and if you'd make the introductions between me and Alpha Silas, I would be very grateful. I have a number of unmated females, and the packs nearby aren't producing the same quality of shifter that clearly the Silas pack is," he adds.

I fight the smile that wants to creep across my face and work hard not to laugh. I picture a whole van full of Brun look-alikes chasing the Silas pack wolves around, and I can't wait to do everything in my power to make that happen. "Absolutely," I assure Alpha Volkov. "As soon as we get back to Solace, we'll speak with Alpha Silas and get things rolling."

He pulls Torrez into another rough hug, and I don't miss the look of irritation that Torrez sends me over his shoulder. I chuckle and then spot a familiar blond head of hair. I thank Fedor again and ask him to pass it along to Manya, and then I excuse myself from Fedor's description of all of his eligible bachelorettes, to slowly make my way to where Sorik is sitting in a chair next to Vaughn. Seeing my dad again makes my whole chest ache, and I take some deep breaths as I approach them.

"Hey," I greet Sorik when I get closer, and he pauses whatever he was saying and looks over at me with a smile.

"Hey there. How are you feeling?" he asks me, and I return his smile.

"I'm good, I should be asking you the same thing. Siah said you were hurt."

Sorik waves away my concern. "It was nothing a little magic couldn't fix," he teases with a wink, and he turns to watch Siah make his way towards us. Sorik's smile turns beaming as he takes in the runes all over Siah's arms and hands, and he turns to me, radiating pure happiness.

"It looks like congratulations are in order," he tells us, and I chuckle at the bashful smile that sneaks across Siah's face.

He clears his throat. "Thank you," Siah finally tells him, and he reaches over and takes my hand.

"Chosen, and by Grier's daughter." Sorik shakes his head in happy disbelief, but I see a hint of sadness in his eyes. "I'm overjoyed for you, friend, and I'm grateful to see some good come from all the bad." Sorik looks away for a moment, and I can practically feel the loss and loneliness that covers him like a cloak.

I feel like I'm intruding on his pain uninvited, so I pull my gaze away and let Sorik be alone with his emotions for a minute. I focus my attention on Vaughn and work to ignore the stab of sadness in my chest when I take in his vacant look. I'm not sure what to do, so I just stare at him as he stares at nothing.

"He follows commands, oddly enough," Sorik announces, and I look over to find him watching Vaughn. "If you tell him to eat, he will. If you tell him to walk, he will. But he doesn't respond or show any indication that he can hear me or knows who I am. I activated the runes behind my ear to talk in his head, but he doesn't talk back. When I share how I feel with the runes on my chest, he stays exactly as he is now."

Listening to Sorik talk about Vaughn as his compeer, someone he's connected to through runes and magic and love, hits me deeply. I picture any of my Chosen in this position, one of them lost while the others try to find him, and it breaks my fucking heart. It makes Vaughn as a person so much more real to me and not just this figment in my head with Lachlan's face and my eyes.

I look at him and know he's my dad, but that's just an empty title to me at this point. I don't really know what it is to have a dad, and so there's no emotion other than maybe loss that I can really associate with the lost man in the chair in front of me. I know he's Lachlan's twin, but I don't know what his personality was like. Would he have resented my existence like Lachlan did? Would he have looked at me and felt the absence of his mate? Or would he have seen me, his daughter?

There's so much I don't know and don't really have the capability to process when it comes to Vaughn, and I'm just not sure how to see or understand who he is to me. But as I watch Sorik interact with him, I can see who Vaughn was to Sorik, and I can understand and relate to *that* because of how my Chosen are with each other.

"What do you think we should do, Sorik?" I ask, my voice quiet and my eyes trained on the details of Vaughn's face. "Do you think he can come back from whatever Adriel did to him?"

Sorik watches Vaughn for a moment and then looks at me. "I don't know. All I do know is I'm not ready to give up yet."

I nod and give him a small reassuring smile. Sorik knew Vaughn better than any of us did, and it makes sense to defer to him about what he thinks we should do.

"Maybe the others will know," Sorik says offhandedly, his eyes searching Vaughn's face for something.

"Others?" I query, not sure what he's talking about.

Sorik stares at me expectantly for a second, and then realization dawns in his eyes. "I never got to tell you." He slaps a palm to his forehead. "I could have sworn I said something in the cell, but I just realized that I didn't. Do you remember when Siah and I first tracked you down to warn you?" I nod. "I told you that I was working on something to help keep you safe."

I nod again. "Yeah, but you didn't say what."

"Grier used to tell us stories about what it was like where she grew up. She never told us specifics as far as the location, just that there was a city of Sentinels and they kept themselves hidden for reasons that are obvious," he explains.

A strange feeling starts buzzing through me, and it's an odd combination of adrenaline, anticipation, and shock.

"I never thought much about it until I saw you in the club that night. And when Faron took you, I knew then that you would only be safe in that city. So I started hunting for it. I took what I knew from Grier and combined that with what Adriel shared from when his brother became Chosen. I mapped things out and went searching." Sorik pauses for a minute, and it's all I can do not to shake him and make him keep going.

"I found it," he tells me, and his tone and gaze are filled with the same shock and awe that mine are. "I didn't know if I ever would, but I did. As soon as I saw the barrier, I knew what it protected, and I immediately turned around to go get you. I came here to let Siah know, but you were already here. That was when we came up with the plan to break you out. I was going to take you home."

Home.

The word moves through me like a warm breeze, and I try to reach out and touch it, but it flutters just out of reach. *I'm not the last*, I tell myself, and the words feel hopeful on my tongue, but my chest is heavy with uncertainty and nervous hesitation. I lean into Siah and he wraps an arm around me as I bringing my shocked gaze back to Sorik's.

"Holy shit," I finally squeak out, and an understanding smile breaks out over his face.

"You, of course, don't have to go now that Adriel isn't a threat to you, but if you want to, I'd be honored to show you the way."

I activate the runes on my ring finger, and Siah jerks a little from the jolt it gives him. I shoot him an apologetic smile and realize we need to start working with him right away on his runes. In less than a minute, I'm surrounded by the rest of my Chosen. They loom over us, looking at me and my still shocked face, and wait patiently to be filled in on whatever is going on. I clear my throat and look up at each of them.

"If everyone is cool with it, I'd like to leave first thing tomorrow and follow Sorik to the city of Sentinels that he found."

Their faces light up with surprise and they look from me to Sorik and back. There's a moment of pause, and then emotion makes my chest tight as they swallow down the millions of questions I see in their eyes and each of them voice a resounding, "We'll follow you anywhere."

The End of Book 3

THANK YOU SO FUCKING MUCH FOR READING!!!

I wouldn't be shit without you reading, reviewing, and recommending. Thank you so much for all you do, and for all I get to do because of you!!!

You can stalk me on Instagram, my Facebook Reader Group, BookBub, my Facebook page, or my website for updates on this series and more.

ALSO BY IVY ASHER

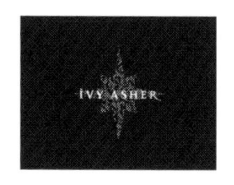

The Sentinel World

THE LOST SENTINEL

The Lost and the Chosen

Awakened and Betrayed

The Marked and the Broken

Found and Forged

SHADOWED WINGS

The Hidden

The Avowed

The Reclamation

MORE IN THE SENTINEL WORLD COMING SOON.

Paranormal Romance

THE OSSEOUS CHRONICLES

The Bone Witch

Book 2 coming soon

HELLGATE GUARDIAN SERIES

Grave Mistakes

Grave Consequences

Grave Decisions

Grave Signs

Shifter Romantic Comedy Standalone

Conveniently Convicted

Dystopian Romantic Comedy Standalone

April's Fools

ABOUT THE AUTHOR

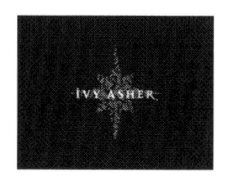

Ivy Asher is addicted to chai, swearing, and laughing a lot—but not in a creepy, laughing alone kind of way. She loves the snow, books, and her family of two humans, and three fur-babies. She has worlds and characters just floating around in her head, and she's lucky enough to be surrounded by amazing people who support that kind of crazy.

Join Ivy Asher's Reader Group and follow her on Instagram and BookBub for updates on your favorite series and upcoming releases!!!

- facebook.com/IvyAsherBooks
- instagram.com/ivy.asher
- bookbub.com/profile/ivy-asher
- amazon.com/author/ivyasher